WITH INTENT TO

Also by Frances Ferguson

Missing Person
No Fixed Abode
Identity Unknown

WITH INTENT TO KILL

Frances Ferguson

HEADLINE

First published in 1996
by HEADLINE BOOK PUBLISHING

10 9 8 7 6 5 4 3 2 1

British Library Cataloguing in Publication Data

Ferguson, Frances
    With intent to kill
    1. English fiction – 20th century
    I. Title
    823.9'14[F]

ISBN 0747213887

Typeset at The Spartan Press Ltd,
Lymington, Hants

Printed and bound in Great Britain by
Mackays of Chatham PLC, Chatham, Kent

HEADLINE BOOK PUBLISHING
A division of Hodder Headline PLC
338 Euston Road
LONDON NW1 3BH

To Rosemarie, Roma and Linda,
for their invaluable help

Prologue

He had thought he wouldn't kill again. That it was a period of his life which was over. The whispering in his head, the deep inner rage, had gone away, dissipated into the past, so that it was somehow easy to forget another person had ever dwelt inside him as a terrifying but familiar companion. An alter ego *with an enticing voice which talked of revenge, power, the exhilaration of risk, the sheer pleasure of killing.*

Only in dreams did the memories occasionally come; dreams which brought him awake soaked in sweat and shaking. Then his eyes would find some vestige of light, some familiar outline, and the pounding of his heart would gradually calm. This was here, now. The other was unreal. And gone.

And besides, for a long time now the voice had left him alone. As if satisfied.

He wasn't sure when it came to him that he would have to compass one more death. The thought was simply there suddenly. It was absolutely reasonable, this time: not an experiment, not a random slaying out of a choice of victims, just the disposal of somebody who was a nuisance. Possibly even a danger. It was, quite clearly, the obvious thing to do.

Just the once. But oh, the absorption of it! The choice of method. The web of complexity to be woven. Everything considered, as possibilities unrolled themselves inside his head. He hadn't used his brain like this in—

A long time, said the voice.

The soft, clear whisper almost stopped him in his tracks. Then he accepted it. It was just an echo inside his skull ... and he could control it. After all, things were different now; he was different.

One death. Just one.

And since the PC Plods who would have to investigate the body were undoubtedly as stupid as the others had been, there would be no danger that they would find him. It would simply be amusing to set them running round in circles, and following their noses into dead ends.

Chapter 1

'What I'm saying is, this would be a good time for us to get married. And,' Adrian added, tacking it on as if it were no more than a natural concomitant, 'start a family.'

'We get married, we get pregnant, like in a Victorian novel?'

'I'm just being logical. You've reached the rank of inspector but you're not dotty about your present job. OK, so that could make it the moment to take a couple of years off. When you go back you can look for an area which will interest you more. If that's what you find you want to do. Then, the practice,' he went on quickly before Jane had the chance to do more than open her mouth. 'As soon as the merger's gone through we'll be part of a larger veterinary cooperative instead of a two-person band, just Fliss and me. That means more security, and, hopefully, less rush with no loss of income. So it's a good time all round to make plans, isn't it?'

Jane gazed at him. He was propped on one elbow, looking down at her. His face was calm, his voice reasonable; only the tousled dark hair suggested what their joint occupation had just been. Various answers were trying to frame themselves in her mind, ranging from something as lightly flippant as her first response, to a very dry, 'Are you telling me, or asking me?' She settled for a languid stretch and a smile.

'The sheer romance of your proposal has rendered me

3

bereft of speech ... Seriously, Adrian! Radical life changes usually get discussed, not just flung down in casual conversation!'

'I wasn't being casual.'

'I know.' She did; and that he must have been brewing this behind a quiet face. She wondered briefly how much it would startle him if she simply smiled with post-coital mellowness and gave him the answer, 'Fine, I agree, good idea!' For a moment the temptation was there, surprisingly strong. Then it was swallowed up in other factors. She cast him a look of deliberately amused exasperation. 'You really have picked your moment. You're due to catch a train in, what, less than an hour? And you choose now to put this nicely laid-out plan to me?'

'You can't say we've never talked about it.'

'Sure – theoretically – some time in the future!' She began to scramble out of bed. It was time they moved in any case: he had an evening train to catch to London, and then across London for the night express to Edinburgh where he was due to attend a veterinary conference for five days. 'Come on, we really do have to move. You said you wanted something to eat before you leave. And at this rate you won't—'

'All right, I'm coming.'

'Look ... I'm not just brushing it aside, OK? But now really isn't the moment to start making decisions like this!'

'I'm not expecting an immediate decision. Only to think about it?' He touched her lightly as he came past on his way to the shower. There was, thankfully, no sign on his face that he was about to drop into a sulk. In fact, when she looked, his eyes were ruefully amused. 'I'm used to your reactions by now, aren't I? So ... if you think about it while I'm away, you might have worn out some of your million panic-stricken objections to being tied down before I come back. And be able to talk about it rationally?'

4

The bedroom door closed on his grin, and just before the pillow she had seized up and hurled landed with a thump against the wood. 'Manipulative sod!' she called out after him.

Sometimes he could read her far too well. Though sometimes not. 'Panic-stricken' wasn't an adjective she would have chosen.

She went downstairs to find him some food. There was only time for him to snatch a quick snack, glancing at his watch, and then he had to go. She offered to drive him to the station, since it was a cold and buffeting February night with the sharp threat of snow in the air, but he refused, reminding her it was only a short walk. He had no more than a soft leather grip to sling over his shoulder. Then he was gone, with a quick, 'See you Saturday!'

Thought seeped back with his absence. Marriage was part of their long-term plans . . . probably. At least, they had certainly touched on the idea. After all, they were living together, and had been for fourteen months.

But this marriage-and-a-baby package . . .

It was all very well for him to say, reasonably, that she was discontented with her job so that now would be a good time for her to take a couple of years off. It was true, however hard she tried to hide it, that her current post still seemed to her no more than a shadow of real police work. After a year in the job she was used to introducing herself as 'Inspector Perry, Community Liaison', but there were moments still when she chafed against the fact that she hadn't stuck it out to try and work her way up in CID. But to follow that with the conclusion that now would be the ideal time for her to take a break to have a child . . . That left out a large part of the equation. And there was another point, too: she had been hard put not to ask accusingly, 'Has this got anything to do with the fact that Elizabeth Hollings is pregnant?'

Because she was damned if she was going to have a baby just because her ex-CID boss's wife had just announced she was having one. Even supposing it was as easy as that.

Jane let out a sharp sigh, aware of confusion, exasperation, a tinge of resentment. She felt a strong urge to reach for the phone and ring Matty. Matty was someone to whom she could grumble – or even wail, if necessary, – 'I love him, but. We get on fine, but. Whatever commitment I give him, he wants more. And he wants it now, when I don't know if I want it *yet*!'

Before she could succumb to the temptation to use her friend as agony aunt, the phone took on a life of its own and let out a virulent warble. Jane moved to lift the receiver off its bracket on the wall and recited the number. A female voice, almost unrecognisable in its huskiness, greeted her.

'Jane? Hallo, it's Felicity. Is Adrian still there?'

'No, he's gone, you've just missed him.'

'Damn,' his partner said faintly. 'Oh. Oh well, I'll just have to go, I suppose. I'd hoped he might not be leaving until later. Or perhaps I can get the locum to do it tomorrow when he comes in, but they really did want the medicine tonight—'

'Adrian wouldn't have had time to go out on a call *and* catch his train, anyway,' Jane pointed out, trying to sound polite about it. She added the silent thought that it was just as well the practice merger would soon be through, since, good vet though she was supposed to be, Felicity never seemed to stop having crises.

'No, I suppose not. If Harry were here I'd get him to deliver the stuff, but he's away doing research for a book. It's just that I've started this putrid throat, and I really don't want to make it worse.'

'It's no use me offering to do anything, since I don't know enough about animals to—'

'It's only delivering a repeat prescription of antibiotics to a dog-breeder. Could you really? She doesn't need advice, just the medicine. She's had it before and she was going to come in and fetch it this afternoon but then she couldn't because one of the bitches started whelping. She does need it urgently so as not to break the continuity and I promised I'd get it to her, only then my throat got so much worse.' It did sound painful, Jane had to admit. 'Could you really take it, Jane? It's so nice of you to offer, and it really would be a load off my mind. I don't want to wake up in the morning and find I've got thoroughly ill, with Adrian away!'

Charity battled with truth and won. Jane forbore to say that, actually, she hadn't offered, she had said she wasn't offering. 'OK, I'll go,' she said with resignation. 'As long as it's just a delivery. Where has the stuff got to be taken to?'

'A place called Mellows End in Lyminge Forest. The directions are a bit complicated but I'll write them down for you, and you should be able to find it even in the dark. I'm sorry, I really would have asked Harry if he'd been here.' Harry Morpeth, her live-in man, was someone Jane privately found a pain because he was far too consciously charming, but he seemed to keep Felicity happy. 'If you'll come round I'll give you the package, and I'll ring Mrs Easington to say you're on your way . . .'

Lyminge Forest of all places. No doubt one of those isolated smallholdings up a remote track barely visible amongst trees, and even less visible on a cloudy and blustery night. Deciding drily that at least she was being given good cause for feeling martyred, Jane went to put on a padded jacket, then picked up the keys of Adrian's four-wheel drive. It was just as well he had remembered to leave them rather than going off with them in his pocket.

An hour later she was congratulating herself on finding her destination with less trouble than she'd expected. Felicity's

7

directions had been a model of clarity, with accurate rights and lefts along the mainly unsignposted lanes which now and again took vertiginous swoops down and then up, presumably crossing some hidden stream among the crowding trunks and massed foliage lurking just outside the arc of the headlights. It was intensely dark beyond their beam: no urban march of streetlamps to guide the traveller out here, just the occasional white flash of a cottage standing back from the road and snatched into view by the wash of light, or the clumped glow of curtained windows where three lanes met. Mellows End, however, was as unmissable as Jane had been assured it would be as long as she had taken all the correct turnings; it was set on a small hill with an unexpected piece of open field around it, and Mrs Easington had left a bright outside light burning as promised.

The lamp spotlit the pale sprawl of an ugly modern bungalow, and if Jane had been in any doubt, the cacophony of barks audible immediately she opened her car door would have reassured her that she had reached the right place. She gave a sharp rap to the front door and after a moment a teenage girl opened it, took the packet of antibiotics Jane handed over, managed a 'Mum says thanks' across a renewed high-pitched yapping from beyond the entrance lobby, and shut the door again quickly just as something small, black and fluffy managed to scrabble its way through with the obvious intention of escaping.

Jane huddled into her collar as she hurried back to her car. Out here the wind seemed even more bitter, with a sting in the air like ice-cold razor blades. Sure enough she had barely restarted the engine when sleet began to whip against the windscreen, coming and going in spatters on the wind. She was halfway down the steep hill when the light behind her abruptly went out, leaving her suddenly disorientated. Had there been another turning at the bottom of the hill, or just the one she came in by . . . ? It would be idiotic to get lost going back when she had found the place so satisfactorily!

Idiotic, but not, apparently, impossible. She could have sworn she had been reversing the rights and lefts of her outward route correctly, but the crossroads she was expecting which would lead her back to the Elham road failed to appear. Instead her headlights abruptly lit a straight stretch between what was recognisably a stand of pine trees. That had definitely not been part of her outward course. Damn . . . It was a surprisingly good piece of road, however, and must lead somewhere. In fact, her memory of the map suggested it might take her out on the other side, on to the Minnis. That would give her a reasonably easy way home, since the ancient common with a village scattered around it would lead her to Stone Street, the old Roman road which still lay ruler-straight through the countryside as a direct line between the city and the coast.

She had slowed, irritably weighing up the choice of assuming she was right and going on, or finding somewhere to turn and plunging back into the twisting lanes through the forest in the hope of finding something she would recognise. Suddenly it was just as well she had reduced her speed so thoroughly. Just ahead, apparently from a right-angled track leading into the trees, a vehicle shot out, its headlights springing into life as it came, to dazzle her eyes while it swung directly across and then past her, and sped off the way she had just come.

Of all the stupid manoeuvres . . .

Jane eased her foot off the brake on which she had instinctively stamped, even though she had been travelling at a mere crawl. Perhaps it had been an illicitly courting couple – and maybe her slowing lights on the empty road had thrown as much of a scare into them as they had into her by appearing! Or a poacher setting traps, always supposing one would bother in such bad weather, and if there was something worth trapping in a piece of what looked like Forestry Commission pine wood. Either way, whoever it was ought to be done for careless driving... Ruminating sourly that she wasn't in the traffic police, and was supposed to be off duty besides, Jane knew that her annoyance was doubled because what she could actually have done with was someone who would stop and tell her where she was.

It seemed a better option to go on rather than turn back, however, and she sighed, glanced exasperatedly at the dashboard clock which was now showing eleven p.m., and set off again. This road must lead somewhere, and at least it didn't look as if it promised to lead her in circles. She hoped.

A sharp turn at the end of the straight stretch gave her a moment's doubt, but then, triumphantly, she found a crossroads with a signpost. Stelling Minnis, only half a mile ahead. She *had* been right. The common began to open itself out around her, grass and low scrub instead of confining forest. It was dark and empty, with no houses to be seen yet, but she was definitely on her way back to civilisation.

Not so empty after all. Half a dozen running figures were suddenly visible up ahead, shadowy as they dashed away from the road to vanish into the scrub. Jane wound down her window to peer after them, mystified – one at least had seemed to be in long robes, a touch which seemed singularly out of place – and wound it up again quickly as a handful of sleet flung itself down her collar. It was unimaginable that anyone should be out for pleasure on a night like this. Or even for exercise. So what were those fleeing figures actually doing? Or had she just imagined them?

Apparently not, as another smaller group was abruptly caught in her headlights, making as if to cross the road, then veering urgently away. A quick, somehow exotic impression

10

of dark faces washed pale by the white beam of her lights; of loose clothing in material thin enough to be moulded against bodies by the wind. And at least one of them was a small child.

Something, definitely, was going on here.

Jane reached instinctively for her two-way radio, before she remembered belatedly that she was driving Adrian's car, not her own.

Chapter 2

A cracking yawn caught her unawares, and Jane smothered it with her hand, then grinned up at Detective Sergeant Doug Phelps as he stood beside her table at the canteen. 'Sorry – like I said, it ended up as a heavy night. That's why I'm starting the day with a lot of very black coffee! I didn't get to bed until the small hours.'

'SEPST had had an anonymous tip-off, you say?' Doug asked, using the shortening for South-East Ports Surveillance Team, the mobile arm of the immigration service.

'Two, in fact. The first one said there was a container lorry with illegals hidden inside it on its way up the M20, still this side of the Newington turn-off, but the anonymous caller rang off without giving any other details. Then when they'd set up a roadblock and were stopping everything a second call came in – same disguised whisper, they think – to say the lorry had gone a different way and was now sitting parked on the road across the Minnis. So they got a team across there fast, and by the time I drove into the middle of things, they'd just arrived and found the illegals had been let out and were running all over the place.' Jane paused, her mind going back to the frightened faces in the cold and dark, the general chaos of trying to make sure everyone had been rounded up; to a hastily commandeered village hall and the borrowing of blankets and hot drinks while SEPST waited for wagons to be sent by the Dover police. If the figures she had seen fleeing had succeeded in hiding themselves on the common, they would have been in greater danger of dying from hypothermia in their thin clothes than they were from capture. 'I stayed to help,' she said, 'and I think we must have got them all. The poor souls were too cold to run far, let alone not having an earthly as to where they were! There was a disguised hatch on top of the container, and apparently the driver opened it up and then scarpered. He seems to have intended his cargo to get out, but they must have spent some time arguing about it amongst themselves, because when SEPST arrived they were still climbing out.'

'Do they have any idea who the anonymous caller was?' Doug asked.

'No. They had a couple of people from Kent Ports Police with them in the hope of arresting the driver, but there was no sign of him. Nobody in Stelling Minnis village seemed to have any idea the lorry was there – you know how scattered the village is, and the lorry was on the emptier end of the common.' Jane took another gulp of her coffee, thankful that the canteen made a stronger cup than the watery offerings from the machines. 'It could even have been the driver himself who made the calls, though it's a bit of a mystery why. Unless it was a sudden fit of conscience. The vehicle didn't seem to have broken down.'

'Maybe he hadn't been paid enough. Or else he *had* been paid so decided not to bother with the rest of the journey,' Doug said drily. 'How many illegals were there in this batch?'

'Thirty. About half of them women and children. I wouldn't have liked to travel the way they did,' Jane commented, with feeling. 'The floor of the container was padded with old mattresses, but otherwise ... It looked as if they must have been in there for several days.' It had smelled like it, as well. 'Barely a word of English between them, so presumably somebody was planning to meet them at whatever the intended final destination was.'

'Southall, at a guess. Or Bradford. Somewhere where they'd blend in. Leastways, from your description of them I suppose it was another load of Pakis,' DS Phelps said with a cynical look.

'Hard to tell where they were from when they had no papers on them. The SEPST officer I was talking to thought they might be Kurds.' Jane answered him neutrally. She could have pulled him up for sounding racist, but there seemed little point during an otherwise friendly conversation. 'The container lorry was Dutch, so I guess Immigration will try to send them back there. Or France, since they were brought through the tunnel. I don't suppose either will want them. They'll play the "not our responsibility" card, and so it will go on!'

'Well, at least we don't have to sort it out,' Doug said cheerfully. 'That's Immigration's baby, and they liaise with Dover, not us. With SB to do any arresting that comes up – if they can catch up with whoever was facilitating the illegal entry!' Kent Ports Police were officially part of Special Branch, though working under their own regulations. 'I'd better get into the office and see what our own villains have been doing during the weekend. Ma'am!'

He sketched her a friendly salute and left her. He was right, Jane thought, and it was no more her job than his, now, to ponder on the doings on the Minnis overnight. SB would have the job of trying to track down the missing driver, and Immigration would be searching for the ends of the chain. The illegal immigrants would go on coming, she supposed, for as long as somebody could make a heavy profit out of the trade. But she had become involved merely involuntarily, and had stayed to help only because her offer to do so had been gratefully welcomed once her identity was established.

She had helped in the attempt to question some of the pathetic group, too, while they waited for the wagons, since her own liaison job gave her a variety of European languages to try, and she also had a smattering of Arabic remembered from her childhood. It was only in the latter, mixed with mime and the odd word of German, that she had elicited anything at all. One old man had broken out of sullenness to communicate despite the hushing of his family sitting blanket-wrapped around him. He had been beside the ladder below the hatch when it was opened. He saw the face of the person who opened it, who beckoned to them to get out. It was 'a demon'. At first Jane took him to mean a betrayer, a breaker of promises, since he was shaking with anger. However, he repeated the words several times, as if trying to make her understand. Finally he spat on the floor at Jane's feet as if in disgust, and lapsed back into silence.

It was always possible Jane had mistranslated his words, particularly considering his accent and his lack of teeth, but she had passed it on anyway to the Kent Ports SB inspector who had also been trying to question the illegals. She had done so with a lift of her eyebrow, and he had grinned back at her with a shrug. The transport wagons had arrived then to take the pathetic group to detention – where they would at least be warm and fed while somebody tried to find out where to send them back to.

Jane pulled a face, consigned the brief adventure to the back of her memory, and pulled herself up from the canteen table with a quick shake of her head. She was awake enough now to concentrate on the various meetings she had to set up and attend – so as Doug had said, she might as well forget it.

The nuts and bolts of her community liaison job took her out and about until late afternoon. Then she ran into DC Kenny Barnes, getting out of his car in the station yard just

16

as she was emerging from hers. He greeted her with a smile, but added a wry grumble.

'Whatever happened to global warming, ma'am? This wind's coming straight off the steppes of Russia without hitting anything on the way, from the feel of it!' He tapped out the number to let them in at the back of the station and went on talking as they scuttled inside to the relative warmth. 'It's brass monkeys out on the Minnis, I can tell you!'

'Oh? Have Immigration asked for local help after all, on whether anybody saw anything last night?' Jane asked, her ears pricking at the reference.

'Sergeant Phelps did mention you'd said something about being out there half the night getting mixed up with some illegals,' he said, giving her a grin. Being Kenny, and having worked for her in the past, he managed to put the suggestion into it that she would find herself in the middle of trouble if there was any going. 'No, we haven't been asked for any help. This was a question of somebody finding a body under a bush on the common. No visible marks on him, looks as if he just lay down and died.'

'Oh hell, don't say we missed one? And he died of exposure as a result? Foreign clothes, Arab or Middle Eastern looks—?'

'No, nothing like that,' Kenny told her in swift reassurance to her appalled reaction. 'A local man. Well, local to the city, not the village – the paramedics looked in his pockets for identification – and that's why they called us rather than Dover. Nothing they could do for him by that time: they thought he might have had a heart attack and lain there for several hours. They called us out to take a look before they moved him, just in case. And since then,' he said stoically, 'I've been going round to check if anybody saw him walking about earlier, but nobody did, so it was a waste of time.'

'When was he found?' Jane asked sympathetically.

'Just before midday. It's not exactly the weather for a casual stroll, so it's a bit of a puzzle to know what he was doing on the unpopulated part of the common. He hadn't gone out to walk a dog – unless of course it's run away – and as he doesn't live thereabouts we've been looking for his car, but there doesn't seem to be a stray one around.'

'Maybe some tearaway spotted it and took it joyriding,' Jane suggested. 'If he was driving through, and stopped to walk away from the road to take a leak in private, and then had the bad luck to have a coronary . . . You've got an ID for him anyway, you said.'

'Yes, credit cards and driver's licence in his pockets, and a wallet with money and photos in it. Name of Lionel Hughes, with a home address at the north end of the city. Well—'

'Wait a minute, I know him!' Jane exclaimed as Kenny was about to walk away. 'At least, I've met him – if it's the same man, and Lionel's an unusual enough name to suppose it is! I was introduced to him by – well, that doesn't matter.' It had been Felicity's Harry who made the introduction. 'If it is the same one, he's a journalist. Well, more of an ex-journalist by now, I think, though he takes care to mention he used to have a regular byline on one of the nationals . . . But that might be an explanation as to why he was out on the Minnis this morning: maybe he still works as a freelance from time to time.' She gave Kenny a brief explanation about the dumping of the illegal immigrants, in case Doug hadn't passed on the details, and finished, 'He might have heard of it through a contact and thought it would make a saleable story. I suppose it is the same man – not very tall, running to fat, reddish-grey hair, bad-tempered face?'

'That fits the description. Not that he was looking bad-tempered when I saw him. Just dead. Anything else I can pass on to the guv while you're being so helpful, ma'am?'

'I seem to remember there's a wife, much younger than

18

him, I think, and relatively recent. That's all I can give you. I may as well come along and tell the DI myself, since I'm passing.'

The CID room was familiar territory, faces looking up at her which had been there when it was her stamping ground. DI Hollings was absent, however, and since, according to one of the DCs, he had gone to see the deceased's widow, he would by now know everything Jane could have told him. She left a message pointing out the possible connection with last night's events, but since it looked as if this one could be wrapped up, merely a death by natural causes, it was not surprising she had heard nothing from Chris Hollings by the time she went home. It was unlikely he would want any further input from her.

She had her own job to do . . .

Discontent was the worst possible reason to have a child, though. Whatever Adrian might say. Thrown back into the memory of his parting suggestion as she moved round the empty house, Jane was annoyingly aware of the tug-of-war of her thoughts. She could get as broody as the next person, for goodness' sake. Good sex did that to you. She was also all too conscious that she had just had her thirtieth birthday, even though he hadn't used that as an argument . . . yet. Anyway, that was one which wouldn't work; she'd only counter it by telling him she had another ten years before time started to run out. It was all very well for him to suggest it would be easy for her to take a break and then go back into an area which might interest her more – if he really thought that, he hadn't listened to a word she said about the innate chauvinism of the police force! Sure, she might claw her way up the administrative ladder as a married officer with children. It had been done, if with difficulty. But anything else – anything carrying risk, or long and irregular hours, or the ability to command in the field – no, it would immediately be assumed that she wouldn't be single-minded enough. That she would have too many other priorities. She might still have a career, but its options would be cut in half!

She could say all that to Adrian. The trouble was, love him as she did (and she did, didn't she?), open-minded as he might pretend to be on the surface, she had the suspicion that if you scratched through that surface hard enough . . . She really didn't want to know about that. Or not until she could decide what she was prepared to settle for. What she really wanted . . .

She went to bed discontented, made even more irritable by the awareness of missing him. Simply, his warmth beside her in bed, the companionship of someone else there. Even more, she decided in the morning, his habit of getting up first so that the heating was properly on when she came downstairs. By the time she had banged irritably round the small kitchen and sworn at the fact that she had run out of milk, she had convinced herself that she had only woken up cross because she was cold, and maybe suffering from SAD because the mornings were still lightlessly grey with the end of winter. That, surely, was enough of an excuse!

She had been in her office for half an hour and was still dealing with the post when Chris Hollings buzzed through.

'Jane? Are you busy right now, or can I pick your brains?'

'Pick away and welcome!'

'This Lionel Hughes character – our body on the Minnis? I got your message, and Kenny says you know him.'

'Slightly, yes. You've got a problem?'

'You don't know his wife as well, do you? His widow, as she now is?'

'I've never met her. I've only met him, oh, twice – he's a friend of Harry Morpeth's, the guy who lives with Adrian's partner. They've got interests in common, since Harry's a writer as well. All I know about his wife, though, is that

20

she's his second, and quite a bit younger – Angela? Andrea?'

'Angelica. There's a baby daughter as well. Damn, I hoped you might be able to give me the low-down on her. Whether she's the imaginative type even when not distraught with grief.' Chris sounded singularly unsympathetic. 'I spent two hours with her last night, after she'd formally identified the body, with her raving at me that Lionel *could not* have died of a heart attack, that he may have been in his fifties but he was perfectly healthy, and he must have been murdered. She also said that he hadn't been at home for several days and was supposed to be in France visiting his ex-wife. He was probably kidnapped and killed on his way back, she says. By sinister establishment figures afraid of appearing in his memoirs. Did I mention she's Italian?'

'And excitable with it? She'll get cause of death from the autopsy eventually, won't she? Or do you feel that even if nothing comes up except the expected coronary, she'll claim a cover-up, or at the very least death under duress?'

'All of that, I'd say. It's a pity you don't know her. I was hoping you might, then I could ask you to go and use your soothing skills. I've been on to Matty Ingle and asked her to give this autopsy priority ... I warned her that anything they find is likely to get queried, too, unless Mrs Hughes calms down. I'd hoped she might by this morning,' he added, sounding sorely tried, 'but she's already phoned in asking to speak to someone senior, got herself put through to Superintendent Annerley, and demanded to know what's being done about her husband's "murder".' He paused, then went on, 'It's a pity we haven't found his car. Angelica says he was driving. Also that he always took the same route when he went to France, there and back via Folkestone and the tunnel. And if he was coming back from France I'd have expected him to have his passport on him. They still do

21

check them ... In fact, the French have been particularly insistent on passport controls through the tunnel ...'

He sounded as if he was thinking aloud. 'Cause for doubt, then?' Jane asked, her interest quickening.

'I shouldn't think so for a moment. The passport's most likely in his car, which is probably either looking thoroughly innocent in some public place we haven't spotted yet, or it's been nicked, TDA.' He was clearly thinking along the same lines Jane had suggested to Kenny: Taking and Driving Away was common enough at the best of times. 'He may even have left the keys in it,' Chris added with resignation. 'They certainly weren't in his pockets. Still, at least Mrs Hughes was able to give us its registration, so that may help.' He went on, 'Oh, the other thing – your suggestion that there might be a connection between Hughes and those immigrants?'

'It occurred to me that he might have gone out there in search of a story about them, that's all. Perhaps he knew somebody who lives in the village and they tipped him off. We did have to wake up quite a few people when the round-up was going on. Still, if he was on his way back from France ... Wait a minute, though. Immigration said the container lorry came through the tunnel on the trucker shuttle; the manifest told them so. I wonder ... I suppose there isn't any possibility that Hughes died on Sunday night rather than Monday morning?'

'I suppose he could have, unless the autopsy tells us otherwise. I think I can see the connection you're making – Hughes could have found out something the other end, if he was coming from France and so was the container lorry. And both by the same route ... They load cars and lorries on different trains, but I suppose he could have taken an earlier shuttle and then waited to tail it this end. Yes, an interesting thought!'

22

'Even more interesting when you add in that somebody tipped Immigration off that the lorry had come through.' Jane gave him a quick run-down about the phone calls to SEPST. 'An additional part of the story, from Hughes' point of view? He wanted to be there when the shit hit the fan. And there's another thing: seeing a car on his tail might have been what made the driver panic and change to minor roads, then abandon the whole thing! He could even have—'

'Yes, I take your point,' Chris said, before she could finish. 'Only one objection to that: we can't say the driver decided to dispose of his tail in a final manner, because whatever Angelica wants us to believe, Hughes *was* found without a mark on him. Still, it's certainly something to bear in mind. Thanks – useful that you were in the thick of things! I think I'd better get on to Immigration straight away and see if they've discovered anything which might be relevant.'

'Let me know what happens,' Jane began, but he had already gone, leaving a blank line.

That was the way it went nowadays; she might be in on the start of an investigation but after that it wasn't her job.

Jane let out a sigh. Oh well . . . At least she had been able to offer Chris a theory as to why Lionel's body should be on the Minnis. If the lorry driver had killed him, to silence him . . . No, but why not drive on? Remove both yourself and the evidence of motive? There had been nothing wrong with the lorry; Dover police had finally driven it away.

And besides, as Chris had said, Lionel appeared not to have died violently. All right, then; suppose the driver had panicked, stopped, opened the container, run off – and Lionel had stumbled off into the dark for some reason after seeing all that, and died of a heart attack while waiting for Immigration to arrive?

And then, in the dark and chaos, his body had been overlooked. And during the subsequent hours while it was

23

still unfound, the car, with its keys conveniently left in it, had been seen as easy pickings. That would certainly cover some of the queries.

It was little use her trying to fit the puzzle together. However, for her own satisfaction, at least she could find out what the autopsy results on Lionel Hughes were. It was more than useful to have a close friend who was assistant forensic pathologist for the area. Chris had said urgency had been asked for, so by this evening the autopsy ought to have been done. She would give Matty a ring tonight and see if there actually was anything interesting about Lionel Hughes' death.

In fact it was Matty who initiated the phone call, coming on the line just after Jane got in from work. She accepted Jane's 'Hi, I was planning to ring you!' with a chuckle which came clearly down the line.

'Now, I wonder why I guessed you would, or am I just being cynical? Before we get on to that, though, I'll deal with the first reason for my call. You remember we were making a tentative arrangement to get together on Easter Sunday, you and me and Adrian and Shakti?' Shakti was her current man, an Indian doctor from the hospital – described by Matty in her standard, somewhat hard-hearted fashion, as 'temporary but pleasant'. 'I know it's over a month ahead and you probably haven't thought any more about it yet,' Matty went on, 'but I'm going to have to cry off. My mamma's come up with the equivalent of a royal summons, and you know how she is: if I don't cooperate on the rare occasion she asks for my help, I'll never hear the last of it!'

Matty's mother, temperamentally regal and diplomatic-ally important, swooped in on her only daughter very sporadically but always in a manner difficult to ignore. Jane made a sound of amused sympathy.

'What is it this time? Is she flying in for some special ambassadorial bash and demanding that you should be present?'

'Not quite. She wants me to look after an American opera singer who's coming over for a charity gala in Sussex. It's on the Saturday night but it'll go on very late so I'll have to stay over, and there's something on the Sunday too, I think. Anyway, Mamma has absolutely promised him that her daughter will be there to hear him sing and accompany him to the party afterwards. He's a brilliant Afro-American baritone and she's dying for me to meet him, et cetera, et cetera . . . She also mentioned, as an afterthought, that he's unmarried.' Matty's voice was dry, and she added with a drawl, 'I doubt if the poor man wants to meet me any more than I do him, and I'm half inclined to say no. Still, I've no doubt she's prepared for that and is waiting to bombard me with telegrams. So I've decided to say yes, and go, and pretend to be tone deaf.'

'You might find you like him.'

'It's far more probable that we'll hate each other on sight.' Unlikely, Jane thought, on the visiting baritone's side: her friend's striking African beauty was apt to attract males like wasps to honey-water. It was equally true, however, that – like the wasps – they were as often left to drown. 'I really can do without my relations suddenly deciding to introduce me to someone "suitable",' Matty went on with asperity, 'and why an opera singer who spends his time travelling all over the world should be suitable for a busy working doctor, don't ask me! However . . .' She audibly relaxed, with humour coming back into her voice. 'Oh well, these things are sent to try us! How's Adrian, by the way?'

'Away at a vets' conference, so I'm as free as air if you want to meet one evening. Instead of lunch? Think about it. That wasn't actually why I was going to ring you. I wanted to ask you—'

'If I know yet what your dead body died of, because you heard on the grapevine that your CID wants to know as a matter of urgency? Go on – you can ask me straight out, if Adrian's not there to complain that you're taking an interest in murders again!'

Jane accepted the teasing note in her friend's voice, but almost without noticing it as her mind seized on the last few words. 'It wasn't a coronary, then?'

'Well, he certainly suffered a cardiac arrest. The question is, what happened to him on the way there.' Matty's voice offered that smoothly, but then she relented. 'No, all right. Just bear in mind that I'm not supposed to pass our findings around. Dr Kremer's got a thing about confidentiality and reports only going to their correct destination. And as he's my boss, and I don't want the sack, you don't know anything until you're officially told, OK?'

'It's all right, you can trust me to look blank, I won't give anything away! Go on – what did you find?'

'We gave him our usual thorough dissection,' Matty began, her voice showing a typical pathologist's lack of emotion, 'and cause of death was all too clear. Nothing so simply as a coronary. I can't give you all the details, mind, only an outline—'

'But what?' Jane demanded, cutting through what promised to be pathology flannel. 'What did you find?'

'Poison,' Matty said succinctly.

Chapter 3

'*Poison?*'

'That's what I said. And that's what killed him. But it's no use asking me for a time of death. You must know by now how difficult it is to tell!'

'An estimate?' Jane appealed.

'All right. Backtracking from when he was brought to us, anything between eighteen hours and, say, a minimum of four since death. I can't be more accurate than that. We've got hypostasis to tell us he'd been lying where he was found for some hours; we've got the beginnings of rigor, but since he was out in the cold, its onset could have been delayed. He didn't simply walk across the common and lie down, anyway. It looks very much as if he was dead when he was put there. And that's about all—'

'What poison?' Jane asked quickly.

'Sorry, can't tell you. We've got some ideas, but since we were warned that this was one where questions were likely to be asked, Kremer's being doubly careful and we've sent the organs off for a second analysis. I suppose I can give you the fact that it was ingested – no puncture wounds anywhere on the body; he took whatever it was by mouth. In fact,' Matty went on, 'I'll go as far as to say he'd had a couple of sandwiches not long before he died, and at some point he'd drunk some milky coffee, and a slug of alcohol. Death will have happened about half an hour after that,

27

unconsciousness sooner. You could postulate suicide—'

'Except that somebody else must have been there to put him where he was found.'

'Quite, I was just going to add that. What else can I remember, off the cuff? Oh yes, there was no sign he was suffering from any life-threatening illness; he did have a pretty cirrhosed liver, but that looked like long-term alcohol abuse and wasn't due to be fatal for a good few years yet. I suppose he could have taken poison by mistake, but again we've got this other person who dumped the body.'

'Which indicates it was deliberate, and therefore murder.'

'That's for your CID to sort out. All we do is provide the facts, ma'am, nothing but the facts. But look,' Matty added, dropping her nasal imitation of an antique American cop show, 'this really is off the record, and you don't know any of it unless or until someone lets you read the preliminary report we've sent over. We wouldn't have provided that yet if we hadn't been hassled for it, so Kremer's not in the best of moods as it is.'

'I've said, haven't I? And thanks,' Jane added. 'I just wanted to know—'

'As always, as curious as the elephant's child. I don't know why you ever let yourself get moved out of CID. Yeah, all right, I do. But knowing the way you come to life when there's a puzzle to solve, was the promotion actually worth it? Sorry, pointless question, or tactless anyway. Are you going to tell me to shut up?'

'Not when I owe you,' Jane answered lightly. 'I took it anyway, didn't I? The promotion. And the European liaison side of things is OK. How about you – don't you ever get a twinge of regret for changing over to pathology?'

'Once or twice, when I'm doing yet another early morning shift in the morgue and I catch myself wondering why I spend so much of my life underground with dead people.'

Matty's answer was prompt, but if the words were rueful she also sounded tranquilly amused. 'And I have the faint wistful memory that live patients do occasionally say hallo! But then I remember lack of sleep and long hours in theatre, so there's something to be said for being in a job that's peaceful!'

'Sounds as if— Oh hell, someone's pealing on my door-bell. Can you hold?'

'I won't, because I'm off to a dinner party and I've got to get ready yet. If you want to meet up this week give me a buzz – when's Adrian coming back?'

'Saturday.'

'OK, we'll try and make something. 'Bye!'

The person on Jane's doorstep was a teenage boy with an identity card and a pack of household goods he wanted to sell. He might have done better without a sullen expression which made it easy to resist buying a packet of overpriced tea towels she didn't need. Even so, as she shut the door on him Jane wondered with exasperation why she had to feel faintly guilty for not buying anything. Because he was at least trying to make a living? And she had a secure job? Though she might not have even that to go back to if she ever left it. Particularly not if short-term contracts came in. Damn, her mood was plummeting again; this really would not do!

The information Matty had given her could act as a distraction. Why had somebody chosen to poison Lionel Hughes? There was something hurried about the way he had been dumped – no attempt to bury him – yet poison surely had to be planned. That seemed to rule out any theory about the container lorry's driver. Yet it still seemed too heavily coincidental that Lionel, an ex-newspaperman, should have been found dead in the same area where a story was break-ing. Wasn't it reasonable to suppose there was a connection?

Angelica Hughes had been right after all to scream that her husband had been murdered. What was it Chris had said she'd been suggesting – sinister establishment figures, afraid of appearing in his memoirs?

Poison could certainly be a political weapon: there had been that case years ago of the Bulgarian and the poisoned umbrella ... Matty had said quite definitely, however, that there were no wounds or puncture marks. Lionel had taken something by mouth. Was it the type of poison which could be concealed in a sandwich filling? Or in the things he had drunk?

There was nothing to be gained from speculation. Matty had been firm on not divulging what they thought the poison was, which was understandable when pathologists never liked to give out facts until they were sure ... Lionel Hughes definitely appeared to have been murdered, though. Some time between four and eighteen hours before he was found; which meant between six on Sunday evening and eight on Monday morning.

Next day, she was unsurprised to hear that a contingent of uniforms had been bussed out to the Minnis to go over the ground again, along with a belated scene-of-crimes team. They must be on a minute search for anything which might lead to the identity of the person who had dumped the body. For the moment, however, the details were being kept under wraps, since the word still seemed to be that they were looking into a natural death. As Jane was not supposed to know anything she kept her thoughts to herself and tried to avoid her own desire to theorise. However, in mid-afternoon she received a summons from Chris Hollings to the CID room, and as soon as she was through the door of the DI's small office, he handed her an already well-thumbed copy of the preliminary autopsy report.

'Have a read of that, and then we'll talk about it.'

Jane ran her eye quickly down the typed pages, taking care to stop here and there and look surprised. One thing did give her a genuine if brief pause because it was something Matty hadn't mentioned; though it was a seemingly irrelevant detail. 'A diamond drawn in blue biro on his wrist?' she asked with a lift of her eyebrows. 'Sounds more like something a schoolkid might do in a boring lesson.'

'Mmm. You know how it is, they always take care to mention everything. But cast your eye over cause of death. The widow was all too bloody right about murder, wasn't she? We've been keeping it low-key so far, but Geoff Madox is setting up an incident room for us now. And you're co-opted into the team, by the way – has the Super been on to you about that?'

'No—'

'Presumably he will. Developments suggest we're likely to be landed with some foreign liaison, and that brings you in. This would have to happen when the DCI's on leave. I've got enough on my plate,' he added irritably, but went on before Jane could do more than reflect drily that as far as she was concerned, her old enemy DCI Morland was no loss. Particularly when he would have made a point of showing he felt Jane's involvement in the murder team was entirely unnecessary. 'It seems the investigation's going to run across a lot of borders,' Chris went on, 'since Lionel Hughes was last seen alive in France, and in addition, his car's turned up in Calais.'

'In *Calais*?'

'Yes, sitting innocently in a parking space in one of the town squares. In fact it had been spotted for overdue parking and was about to be towed away. When I talked to Immigration we discussed the possible connection you'd come up with, then they put me on to SB, and I passed the car registration on because they thought there was a possibility the lorry driver might have taken it. They came back to me first thing this morning.' Chris paused to marshal his facts, then continued. 'I'd better tell you what Immigration and SB between them gave me on the container lorry. It was apparently pre-booked on the truckers' shuttle which arrives at our end of the tunnel at around ten p.m., and there's film from one of the overhead cameras showing its arrival at the Calais terminal. Dutch registration, a manifest showing it was supposed to be carrying large electrical goods. It may have been X-rayed, since they do that randomly, but it had been given a rather cleverly patterned lead lining.'

'A professional job,' Jane put in as he paused.

'Yes. It went through the usual surface searches but was cleared and loaded. I don't know if you know the system they use . . .'

'Only vaguely.'

'The drivers steer their vehicles on to the train, then they're taken by coach along the platform to the club car at the front. So SB are trying to track down other drivers on that shuttle to see if anybody remembers this one. It doesn't seem very likely, they say, with the amount of freight going through.' Chris paused again to draw breath. 'Anyway, SB were very interested in the idea that the mysterious driver may have been followed by a journalist, and suggested a couple of theories of their own.'

'They know about the poison, presumably?'

'Yes, but let's leave that for the moment since something else has come up on it since. First theory: maybe Hughes left his car in Calais because he wasn't just following the lorry, the driver had given him the information for his story and had even agreed to take him along in the cab. Perhaps he was aiming for a headline saying something like: "Your intrepid reporter reveals how to get illegal aliens smuggled into the country". The second theory's the one I've already mentioned: that Hughes *was* following, in his own car, and the driver spotted him, disposed of him, then used the car to make his escape back to Calais.'

'But—'

'Bear with me, I can see the objections. Such as, is poison something you usually carry with you in case of emergencies? A cosh would be more logical. However,' Chris went on quickly, 'now I've given you the background, I can tell you what's come up since then. An interesting one. And it might fit quite neatly with the idea that Hughes was travelling in the cab. Mrs Hughes – Angelica – has been in to see the Super with an allegation. No, not the "sinister establishment figures afraid of appearing in his memoirs": this time she's come up with something more rational!'

'She has?'

'Yes indeed. As soon as the Super broke it to her that the autopsy suggested poison, she said she'd already guessed it might be that, and that's why she'd come to see him. To point us in the direction of the one person who had every reason to want Lionel dead, and who would be perfectly capable of using that means to kill him. His ex-wife, Rowena.'

'Wait a minute, wasn't that who he was visiting in France?'

'Yes. And according to Angelica, the ex-Mrs Hughes has a strong motive.' Chris drew a breath and consulted some notes on the desk in front of him. 'I'll summarise. Although Rowena and Lionel have been divorced for four years, they still own a house jointly, here in the city. It's been the subject of a dispute between them for some time, because Lionel wants it but Rowena won't give it up. Six months ago she promised to make it over to him. She'd already put one of her sons – from an earlier marriage – in as a tenant, along with his student friends, in order to stop Lionel taking it over; now, in spite of her promise, she was refusing to sign the property transfer after all. It's an ongoing quarrel, and the reason Lionel has been making frequent visits to Rowena in France is to persuade her to give the house up. With me so far?'

'Yes. Is Rowena French?'

'No, English; but she bought a farmhouse in Normandy after the divorce and did it up to run as a fitness centre. She lives there full time. Anyway, this time, according to Angelica, Lionel went over armed with threats to take her to court if she wouldn't back down, on the grounds that he needs the house and she doesn't, and it was his money which bought the property in the first place.' Chris went on drily, 'As far as I can judge there's a certain amount of sexual jealousy between the wives as well. Angelica claims that Rowena is unwilling to let him go, that she doesn't like the fact that Angelica is his wife now, that she's jealous of the new baby... He didn't have any kids with Rowena. Angelica, in fact, refers to Rowena as "a witch and a vampire".'

'And maybe Rowena holds the same opinion of her?'

'Who knows, she may! But what Angelica is telling us – and most emphatically – is that Rowena has a financial motive for wanting her ex-husband dead. To stop him taking her to court, and to gain full possession of this large and theoretically valuable house.'

'Where is she supposed to have done the poisoning? Not in Normandy, surely: isn't death supposed to have been fairly rapid? At least, I thought I gathered that...' Jane made a quick point of consulting the papers in front of her, hoping it wasn't simply something she had got from Matty. 'Unless she's suggesting Rowena killed him and then brought him all the way here to throw us off the scent!'

'No, what she says is that Rowena was in the habit of

giving Lionel a thermos for his journeys home. And if that's true . . .'

'The drink in it was designed to kill him some time during the journey?' Milky coffee, Jane remembered Matty saying; that might well be offered in a thermos. 'So she's suggesting both motive and means! Do you buy it?'

'It would certainly make life a whole lot easier if it turns out to be domestic after all,' Chris said drily. 'Besides, you see what it gives us? Suppose Lionel set off from his ex-wife's house carrying a poisoned drink with him. Perhaps he was supposed to drink it during the journey – while driving – and crash, with a good chance of destroying the evidence. However, let's suppose he was also, unbeknownst to Rowena, following up a story about illegal immigrants. He's in the cab, as we said before. After they've arrived this side of the Channel, he takes a drink from the thermos. He dies, the driver panics and decides to dump the whole shebang. It does have a certain logic to it, and gives us an answer to some of the difficult questions.'

It did. 'Are we hamstrung from following it up until we know what the poison was?' Jane asked thoughtfully.

'I don't know; I'd have thought we had enough to make a start, but it's down to the Super. When I left him, he was busy trying to convince Angelica tactfully that we couldn't arrest her predecessor purely on an unsubstantiated accusation.' Chris pulled a face. 'I can tell you one thing, *I'm* certainly not going to be the one to get a flea in my ear for asking Dr Kremer how long the extra tests are going to take. You know what he's like.'

'Yes, you'd get the spiel about pathology being an exact science which can't be hurried for mere police underlings,' said Jane, grinning.

'In spades. We've got a fairly clear idea of Hughes' movements now, anyway . . .' He proceeded to fill her in.

Lionel had apparently set off for France on Thursday morning, by car. He had rung Angelica from Rowena's house to
say he had arrived. He had intended to be back home on
Sunday night, or possibly Monday morning if anything delayed him. He hadn't said what might: that was a point Jane
immediately picked up on, wondering if it pointed to a pre-
knowledge on Lionel's part that there was a story to follow.
Angelica had been asked about that but had merely said with
a shrug that he might have decided to follow a story if one
came up but she didn't know. Lionel, it seemed, ran his own
small-circulation magazine from home nowadays – but was
short enough of cash to try to freelance if necessary.

'I've rung Immigration again to ask them as a matter of
urgency to let us know if there was a thermos in the lorry cab,'
Chris said. 'They're supposed to be getting back to me.
But even if not, I'd imagine the driver might have taken it
away with him to dispose of, thinking he might be held
responsible.'

'If SB could just find him, it would give us a few clear
answers!'

'Yes, well, they're looking for him urgently from their own
point of view, in the hope of being able to prosecute. And find
out who was behind him. They've promised to pass over the
fingerprint check their forensics have been doing on the cab,
and anything else they come up with. They're fingerprinting
Hughes' car as well. Right, that's everything so far, so shall
we go and see how Geoff's getting on with the incident room?'

'Are you in overall charge of the case?' Jane asked as they
got up. 'Or—'

'The Super, but me day-to-day. I could have done without a
murder case just now,' the DI added wryly, 'let alone one
with these complications, when I've got the usual pile of
other things, and meetings to go to on the DCI's behalf on top
of that. Oh well!'

Jane gave him a grin, and forbore to comment that she herself found the prospect a great deal more cheerful than a diet of public relations exercises. It seemed clear that at some point, and possibly soon, somebody would have to go to France to interview Rowena Hughes. And she was the obvious candidate . . . Her mind was already flying over her contacts, since formality would require a request to the French police.

As they made their way to the incident room, Chris asked, 'How well did you say you knew Lionel Hughes? Is there anything else we ought to know about him?'

'As I said before, I've only met him twice. And only casually. The only time I remember hearing him talk was when we were all at the same pub one night and Harry was asking him questions, trying to pump him for some background for the thrillers he writes.' Harry Morpeth's books were, to Jane's mind, exceptionally violent, and although she had tried one to be civil she didn't intend to repeat the experience. 'All I really gathered was that Lionel had worked on overseas stories rather than domestic ones, and that it was all way back. I wasn't listening very hard, I'm afraid.' She glanced at Chris and added quizzically, 'If we have to go back to the memoirs theory again, in spite of the latest developments, I'm afraid I can't be much help!'

'Let's leave that one out, it would offer far too many complications – even more than we've got already! And Angelica seems to have dropped it very thoroughly by now, thank goodness, in favour of something more down to earth!'

They found Sergeant Madox organising things with his usual efficiency, undiminished as always by the fact that he was wheelchair-bound. He had gained himself a reputation for unflappable capability in the year since his appointment as collator, so no detail was likely to be missed. Relevant maps and photographs were already in place on the wall. Everything was being confined to one corner of the large office rather than taking up the whole room, but that made sense, Jane thought: this might be a murder enquiry which spread itself over more than one country, but in some ways that meant less space required here, in the main a collating point for reports gathered from external sources. From here, a second run of house-to-house enquiries was under way round Stelling Minnis village, she gathered, in case anyone had heard, seen or noticed anything on that Sunday night which had not already come to light. The brief excitement the illegal aliens had brought had caused at least some of the village to be roused from behind closed doors, so there was always a chance.

Chris hadn't mentioned that anything had come out of this morning's comb of the ground, and Geoff Madox confirmed that. Although there had been no time for a complete analysis yet, there appeared to be nothing which could be classed as hard information. One fact was clear: Lionel's body could not have been lying where it was found longer than eighteen hours, since someone had walked a dog through that part of the common at around six the previous evening. That fitted with the outer timespan Matty had given Jane. Geoff Madox was just pointing out on the large-scale map where the body had been left when his eyes slid past Jane and he produced a formal 'Sir!'

Jane turned to see that the Super had arrived, looking his usual smoothly efficient self. He nodded and murmured, 'Sergeant' in response, glancing round approvingly at the progress. Then he gave Jane an acknowledging smile.

'DI Hollings has told you we want you as part of the team? Good.' His glance brought Chris Hollings in on the statement. 'I'm hoping we won't have to allocate too much manpower to this for too long,' he added, to Chris. 'Have you had any further thoughts on what you'll need?'

'Just a small team once we've finished the house-to-house, sir. And that should be through by the end of this afternoon. I can't see anything to be gained on this one from throwing numbers at it.'

'I agree. If anything new comes up I want to know about it tonight, please. And Jane, see that you know whatever facts we've got so far, also tonight. I'd like a full case meeting tomorrow at ten a.m., please, in here.'

'Yes, sir.'

'Right, carry on.'

The door shut behind him. Chris moved up beside Jane, looking rueful.

'Damn, tomorrow morning I'm supposed to be going to an admin meeting at Area. Oh well, another phone call!' He sighed. 'Like I said, this is happening at just the wrong time. And it's sod's law that I should be extra busy just now, to coincide with Elizabeth's still having such lousy morning sickness that it goes on all day! And we'd reached the point where it was supposed to be over . . .'

'Poor her. It's one thing to be over the moon about the baby, but another to have to cope with the symptoms.'

'Oh, we haven't stopped being over the moon – and we'd planned it for this year so we can only be delighted it's actually happened. She keeps trying not to look pale and wan, that's all, and tells me to take no notice because this stage will pass, and at least we get a baby at the end of it.' He gave Jane a grin and added, 'She's more worried about whether the dog will be jealous – well, you know how dotty she is about our lollopy hound – so tell Adrian not to be surprised if she rings him up to ask if he's got any tips!'

The amiable friendship between the four of them, stretching to the occasional sociable dinner party, had developed probably more out of Adrian's position as vet to the

Hollings' labrador than on the circumstance of Jane and Chris working in the same building. It was, however, an established thing. 'I'll tell him,' Jane said pleasantly. 'He may well have some ideas to offer. Look, is there anything else I've got to mug up before tomorrow morning?'

'I think I've given you most of it, but check with Geoff, he's in the process of getting everything entered. I'd better go and see about delegating the other CID cases, and rejig my tomorrow morning's diary, so I'll leave you to it.'

His face had shown no sign of finding her switch back to work abrupt, Jane thought. Neither did hers show – she hoped – that she really didn't want to talk about babies just now. Not anybody's, but (perhaps unfairly) certainly not Chris's, which she still suspected had given Adrian ideas, and which brought up an involuntary feeling inside her that *it was all very well for men*. Fatherhood asked for nothing except celebration. It was bad enough that last night's television had seemed abnormally full of devoted mothers applying disposable nappies to small pink bottoms, looking extremely happy to have nothing better to do, and leading Jane to switch the set off in exasperation, feeling as if she was being haunted.

She walked firmly across to Geoff Madox in the interests of concentrating on the job in hand – murder.

Chapter 4

The case meeting brought together a relatively small number of people to be briefed on the facts available so far. Kenny Barnes was there to report on the various searches of the Minnis, together with a uniformed sergeant who had been in charge of the combing of the ground and, later, organising additional manpower for the house-to-house enquiries. WDC Rachel Welsh was also seconded to the case, since she had gone with the DI to see Angelica Hughes in the first place; but both CID sergeants, along with the rest of the DCs, had been left to run the general work of the department. There were a couple of constables to work to Sergeant Madox on communications and collating, but that, for the moment, was the sum total.

Superintendent Annerley looked round at the attentive faces. 'As you all know, we've got a probable homicide. It has some confusing features and we're short of the full facts, but I want you as a team – and including Inspector Perry as our European Liaison Officer – to have all the information at your fingertips so that if anything new comes up, you're in a position to switch back to the case from whatever else you're doing in the meantime. Now – a comprehensive account of what we do know.'

He ran through it quickly, finishing, 'As I've said, we're waiting for a full forensic report, including further information from Immigration and the Kent Ports Police. The

41

assumption we're making so far is that the body was left some time during the night – rather than the morning – *here*.' He indicated the map. 'That's some four hundred metres from the road where the container lorry was parked. It seems likely – and I can only say likely at this stage – that it was dumped from the container lorry. Yes, Sergeant Callow, you've got something to add?'

'Neither we nor the SOCO team found any drag marks. If he was dumped from the container lorry it does look as if he was carried.' The uniformed sergeant added, 'He wasn't a big man, but no lightweight either, so whoever carried him must have some muscle on him. It's probably manageable in a fireman's lift, but it'd still need a certain amount of strength.'

'Thank you. We also know there were no tyre marks visible near the position of the body. At the moment we're acting on the presumption that Hughes was in the lorry cab. That seems likely from the fact that his car was found in Calais.' The Super continued his swift run-down of the facts. 'What we really need is that fingerprint check from the lorry cab – could you check with Immigration, politely, if Dover forensics has completed it yet?' he asked, looking towards the DI.

'Yes, sir. And I'm still waiting to hear from them about thermos flasks, cups, anything like that, too.'

'Yes. Now, does anyone have any points for discussion?'

'Sir – you said a "probable homicide". Isn't it definite?'

'I'm covering all the bases,' the Superintendent replied. 'We know we have a dead body. We know he died by poisoning. We don't know, for sure, that the poison was deliberately administered. It seems a fair assumption, but we have no hard proof. We need the missing driver – as do Kent Ports SB, who are actively hunting him.'

'We've put the word out that we're interested in any hitch-hikers anyone may have picked up in the early hours of Monday, or anyone trying to hitch,' Sergeant Callow put in.

'Yes. It's more than a pity that the house-to-house enquiries didn't give us anyone who'd seen anything.'

'Everyone was indoors – and considering it was late, dark, and half snowing, that's not surprising,' Kenny Barnes offered. 'We tried again for the time after some of them had been woken up to get shelter and hot drinks for the illegals, but by then they were asking people not to come out more than necessary, anyway, so as not to add to the confusion.' He glanced at Jane, knowing that this was in confirmation of her own account, then looked back at the Super. 'Sir? About those tip-off phone calls to Immigration? Are we supposing Hughes got the driver to stop for some reason and nipped out to make the first one? Because the problem is, if we go with the theory that Hughes was in the cab, and died there, and that's why the driver stopped, then he couldn't have made that second call, could he? Because that one said the lorry was parked on the Minnis, as I understand it, which would mean Hughes was already dead.'

Jane heard a sharp 'Damn!' from Chris and knew that he, like the rest of them, had totally omitted to consider that one. The Super's eyes narrowed as he thought about it. Then he said, 'A very good point... Inspector Hollings? Are we going to assume Hughes made the first call, the driver the second?'

'We'd have to, and that one disguised whisper could sound much like another,' Chris agreed, the expression on his face showing he was reworking his ideas fast. 'I'm not entirely happy about the first call either, now the subject's been raised. Would the driver have stopped? But ... if Hughes was using a mobile phone, then he'd have to have called from the cab and in the driver's presence. That is possible. The man had let him travel in the cab, so maybe there *was* collusion. Yes, actually, that makes quite a lot of sense – freedom from prosecution in exchange for shopping the whole trip!'

43

'Lionel Hughes did have a mobile phone, Angelica said so, but he had to be careful not to use it much because they couldn't afford the expense.' That was Rachel Welsh, who seemed to have elicited unexpectedly useful information during her visit to the widow. She received a querying look, flushed a little, and said, 'It came up when she was going on about the memoirs, that first time – she started to moan that Lionel ought to have called for help if he was in danger, and seemed to put the fact that he hadn't down to worrying about the bill.'

'Thank you, Constable Welsh.' The Super gave the WDC a brief smile. 'We've rather forgotten the phone calls, haven't we, since they seemed to be more of a subject for SB's investigations than ours.' He paused for thought. 'Yes, I think we'll have to go with the idea of collusion; as Inspector Hollings pointed out, it does make some sense. So, we'll assume it was the driver making the second call – from Hughes' mobile phone, or from the village callbox. And then he did a very rapid vanishing act – took off into the woods, possibly, since that would give him good cover.'

He would have had to surface somewhere, at some time, but a fit man, on foot, and in the dark, could probably get quite a distance. The Super looked round.

'Has anyone else anything further to raise? No? Then let's sum up. We have a dearth of positive information at the moment, in spite of all our efforts. We don't know yet exactly what the poison was, so we can't establish its source. We do have an unsubstantiated accusation by Mrs Hughes against the previous Mrs Hughes, and we'll be following that up as best we can. But all I can ask all of you to do – for now – is collect up any facts which may come to hand, any scrap which might be important, and make sure everything goes to the collators. We may have no more than theories to go on at the moment, but everyone here should keep the case in the back of their minds, and keep up to date with the collated information. So if there are no more questions—'

'Is Mrs Angelica Hughes in the clear, sir?' Rachel Welsh asked, suddenly finding her voice again.

'I think we'd have to say she is. Do you have a doubt on that?'

'No, sir – only that she raised the subject of murder before anyone else had thought of it.'

'Yes, I see what you mean. The DI looked into her movements, though – yes? – and she's merely been at home leading her normal life. She had a friend to stay with her for the weekend. The neighbours saw her out and about with the baby in a pushchair. She doesn't have a second car. It seems very unlikely that she could have picked her husband up from a ferry or from the shuttle terminal, poisoned him, then taken him back as far as the Minnis. And considering he'd been away for several days, I don't think she could have poisoned him from a distance. I'd be inclined to say we could rule her out as a suspect.'

His tone of voice made it clear that he viewed the question as a reasonable one, however. Murder within the family, Jane thought cynically, was the most common kind. But here, the ex-wife seemed more clearly in the frame than the wife. Unsubstantiated accusation or no, Rowena Hughes' home was the last place Lionel was apparently known to be, alive and well. His return journey from there was, so far, a matter for guesswork.

Jane glanced up at the map of France on the wall, where Rowena Hughes' address had been marked. A farmhouse near Compainville, not far from Neufchâtel-en-Bray. Compainville was forty or so kilometres from Dieppe, say a hundred and sixty from Calais. Roughly a three-hour drive for Lionel Hughes on that Sunday, if he'd taken a direct route. A drive on which he had unknowingly carried his death with him?

The Super was dismissing the meeting now, but beckoned to Jane to stay.

'You've arranged with Chief Inspector Lowell to free yourself from other duties at the moment? Good. We need an interview with Rowena Hughes, don't we? Even if, at the moment, all we can reasonably ask her is whether her ex-husband did come to visit her, how long he stayed, and when he left on his return journey.'

'How soon do you want that done, sir?' Jane asked.

'I think we should try to fix it up at once,' he said. 'It would be helpful if we saw her before she's likely to have heard of the death from other sources. She has a son living here in the city, but we've managed to avoid any press coverage on the case so far . . . Can you get in touch with your contacts in France straight away and see if you can go tomorrow?'

So he had decided to send her. 'Right, sir,' Jane told him.

'Come back to me when you've organised it and we'll talk further.'

Jane went away to make her phone calls. An hour later she returned to him with the news that the local French police wanted her to leave it for another twenty-four hours. Tomorrow was a public holiday, but on Saturday an Inspector Hilaire Russe of the Police Judiciaire would be available to accompany her.

She had expected that they would insist on one of their own officers going with her. It would have been the same in this country. Superintendent Annerley considered thoughtfully, then nodded.

'Saturday – yes, very well. We can't expect them to let us rush in with less than a day's warning, I suppose, when we aren't suggesting an urgent arrest. Now, how to handle it . . .'

He went on to discuss what questions Jane would need to ask, and how much of the situation Rowena Hughes needed to be told. 'But I'll leave that to your judgement on the ground,' he finished. 'If you feel you need to stay overnight so as to pursue things further next day, report back. I suggest you explain the case in full to your French counterpart, in case we need their help later. Have we covered everything?'

'Yes, sir, I think so.'

'Your impressions of the ex-Mrs Hughes will be valuable in any case. And if we're lucky, some of the information we're waiting for might come in during the next twenty-four hours, so that you'll have more to go on.'

It would be unlikely to include a lab report on the poison, Jane thought that would take several days at least, or even weeks if the labs were busy. Or if the substance in question offered problems of identification. Still, she might as well not look on the gloomy side of things – particularly not when she did at least have a trip to France in prospect. And it was always possible that they might be very lucky indeed, and a thermos flask might have turned up containing the dregs of what had been used to kill Lionel Hughes.

A couple of hours later she had to acknowledge that that had been asking too much. She had been given a message from the DI on her return to the incident room asking her if she would handle the reminders to Immigration, and she had duly put in a call. She had been told somebody would phone her back, but when the return call came in it was from the Kent Ports Police HQ at Cheriton – in fact, from Dave Leacock, the Special Branch inspector she had met on Sunday night.

'Your enquiries were passed over to us,' he said easily, 'since we seem to be handling the nitty-gritty, so to speak. Right, what was in the lorry cab. No flask, I'm afraid – no cup either, cardboard or otherwise. No food or drink of any kind, in fact. We've got a team going over the vehicle inch by inch and sifting through everything they can find; some people would be surprised to know what they leave behind without realising it! Prints – yes, we've got those, and a copy's already on its way to your forensics.'

'Were there many?' Jane asked.

'Some, though we've also got a lot of smudges which suggest one at least of the people most recently in the cab was wearing gloves. Also that an attempt had been made to give the interior a wipe – not a very good one, though, in fact no more than half-hearted, I'd say.' He sounded cheerful about it. 'Our people managed to lift several partials, and a few whole ones. Should be enough to see if you've got a match with your body. What else – oh yes, a few hairs, but as they're fair-to-blond they won't belong to your man. There were a couple of brown ones too, but there's no saying how long any of them had been there. Oh, one other thing – and this explains that description you passed on to me. There was a fright-mask stuffed under the driver's seat.'

'Oh hell, I should have thought of something like that. *That* was the old man's "demon"!'

'Must have been, mustn't it? A disguise so that none of the immigrants could identify him if – or when – we do catch up with him! It's one of those Halloween-type things covering the whole face, and with an aureole of scarlet hair – definitely something you could mistake for a demon! Forensics are giving it a good going-over in the hope there's something on the inside to offer a DNA profile. Which of course will only be useful if we get something to compare it with, but . . .'

'But could be thoroughly useful if you do.'

'Yeah. OK, that's the cab. Now, the car at Calais. No thermos flask or cup in that either, I'm afraid. It's a fairly tidy car altogether, the owner didn't seem to go in for filling it with rubbish. There was a small grip on the back seat containing a couple of dirty shirts, underwear, and a razor. And some letters from a lawyer; I'll get those sent to you since they don't seem relevant to anything we're doing. The car's been dusted for prints as well. I wish you luck if you're going to try and track them all down, though, since the word I've had on that is that they were innumerable, old and recent, the kind you'd find from general use.'

'I don't suppose his passport turned up, in the glove compartment or somewhere?'

'No, nothing in there but logbooks, credit card receipts for petrol, the usual bumph. We've had the car brought over, but since it doesn't seem as if there's anything in it which relates to our side of the investigation, we should be able to release it to you pretty soon. By the way,' he added, 'the SEPST officer who made the guess was right, this particular bunch of illegals were Kurds. All the way from northern Iraq.'

'Some journey . . .'

'Yes. They're not the first batch from there, and we'd dearly like to know who's set up the business of bringing them in. If your corpse knew something,' he went on drily, 'it's a pity he's a corpse, and even more of a pity he didn't contact us with whatever he'd got! A bit sooner than making anonymous phone calls during the journey, too!'

'We're beginning to conclude he may have persuaded the driver into helping to blow the operation,' Jane offered, giving information in exchange for that given. 'We've got another theory on the death, too – though it is only a theory as yet – that there's more of a domestic connection and it only got mixed up with your end of things by chance. Our DI passed it on to you that the autopsy came up with poison, didn't he? Well, we're looking into the idea that Hughes may have been given it in a flask by – let's say a disenchanted relative! It does seems to explain why the driver vanished. Because – we think – his passenger suddenly died on him. But we're still assuming he must have dumped the body, so we do want to talk to him if you find him.'

'Hm, an interesting one. As for wanting to talk to him, don't we all!' He hesitated, then added, 'I suppose there's no harm in telling you we think we've identified him. He's Dutch, like the lorry. We've got a line on his girlfriend. If he turns up back with her, we'll know – but I have to say, if we do catch up with him what we want most is to let him run so that we can find his employers.'

'Understandable,' Jane assured him. 'I'd want the same in your shoes. But if we *can* get to him to put some questions ... Well, you know! If we come across anything which might be a help to your end of things we'll pass it on at once, of course. Oh, by the way, those letters you mentioned, in Hughes' suitcase. You couldn't possibly get them sent over to me by tomorrow, could you?'

'I'll give it my best try. Would a faxed copy do?'

'Yes, that'd be fine, thanks.'

'I'll see to it, then. Anything else, while we're on?'

'I don't think so. Thanks for your help.'

'That's OK. Nice talking to you!'

An amiable contact as well as an informative one, Jane thought, as she set herself to make a thorough note of all he had told her for the case records. She should have guessed about the fright-mask: it seemed obvious now it had been found.

The driver had been careful, even in what must have been a state of panic over Lionel Hughes' sudden and unexpected death.

If that was how it had happened.

Jane paused, frowning, trying to pick her way through the circumstances which seemed almost designed to confuse.

Why had the driver not dumped the dead man and then driven on? Panic did make people do irrational things. The alternative – that it was, after all, the driver who had poisoned Lionel – would lead to an entirely different set of conclusions. For instance, that the body had been deliberately left to be found as a warning. A kind of 'thus perish those who might go public'. Which would, then – surely – mean the driver had been acting on instructions from those who employed him. Or perhaps he wasn't an employee at all but one of the organisers of this particular immigrant-smuggling business . . .

The whole thing was far too fraught with ifs and buts. Once all the forensic reports were in, perhaps a clearer thread would emerge. Meanwhile, an investigation of Rowena Hughes did seem the most sensible thing. It would be more than interesting to see what impression Jane could get of the ex-Mrs Hughes.

It was only when she got home that evening that Jane remembered Adrian was due back on Saturday lunchtime. By that time she would already be in France.

Oh well, she would just have to leave him a note.

Chapter 5

Friday brought the information that there was no match on fingerprints between Lionel Hughes and those found in the lorry cab.

'Damn!' the DI said, ruffling his hair in frustration. 'Still . . . Hughes was wearing leather driving gloves when he was found, wasn't he? Yes, I thought I remembered that detail: it was one of the reasons why we assumed his car must be somewhere about. So we *could* reason that he kept his gloves on all the time he was in the cab – either because he was cold, or was too canny to take them off while he was travelling with the illegal load. That would fit in with the smudge marks. I see they've found a definite match for the driver, though, and think they know who he is.'

'Yes, my contact last night said as much.'

'They've even given us a name now. Claus Armfeldt, Dutch national. Small beer, apparently, with a minor record for petty theft.' The DI was reading from a fax which showed the prints which had been identified. 'They found a match with these in Claus Armfeldt's girlfriend's flat. They're luckier than we are if they can go in and do that kind of comprehensive search on no more than a suspicion! Right, what we need now is a thorough and detailed look at the entire mess of fingerprints taken from Hughes' car – just in case one of Armfeldt's turns up amongst them. It's an outside chance, but it's always possible Armfeldt got into the car to discuss things before agreeing to take Hughes along. We need that connection.'

'Is there a photograph of Armfeldt? To circulate in this hunt for a hitch-hiker?'

'No, unfortunately. There's a description – twenty-five, medium height, fair hair, blue eyes. A bit too general to be much help, but worth noting.'

There was nothing further on the poison analysis. For that, they could only wait.

Setting off for France early on Saturday morning, Jane took a file with her giving the general details of the case. She had thought about translating the whole thing into French so she could leave it with her opposite number, then decided that was too long a job; she would simply have to give the information verbally. Inspector Hilaire Russe, she had been instructed, would meet her at the Commissariat de Police in Dieppe. Making Dieppe her arrival point in France would have meant a drive to Newhaven and then a four-hour ferry crossing, however, so she had opted for the easier and quicker route, through the tunnel and then a two-hour drive at the French end. As she started out, she was glad the late spit of winter had loosened its grip at last. March had brought an abrupt change of weather, the wind swinging round to the south; though it had come in with its usual blowiness and an open sky showed narrow streaks of cloud high up. However, a weak sunlight was brightening the early morning, and the prospect of a drive into Normandy seemed inviting.

Once through the tunnel – a wait to load, with a glance at the freight shuttle on a nearby platform; then the short, rapid train journey with nothing to do but sit in the car – there was the mass of one-way systems and flyovers to negotiate, then the endless concrete was behind her. Even the Pas de Calais had its domesticated countryside, spreading itself on either side of the road as she turned westwards. Spring had started to arrive here; trees were greening, hedgerows bursting into life. Signs offered her Amiens at first but it was more direct to go via Hesdun and Abbeville, and she made good time to the latter, where she threaded her way through dignified and typically French architecture; then there was a kilometre or two of industrial estate before farming country took over again. Before long, she began to see the black-and-white beaming which was typical of the farms and barns of Normandy, its ground lush and fertile, herds of brown-and-white cows scattering themselves across bright grass, a tractor ploughing its way across a field set at an angle above the road.

The turn-off for Dieppe and the coast came up. Jane took it, and soon the small but busy seaport was drawing her into its narrow streets crowded with Saturday-morning shoppers. She caught a glimpse of a castle set high on a green hill. Helpful directions had been given her for finding the Commissariat de Police which, apparently, lay in the Rue Napoleon, running off the Place de Victoire. All she need do was follow the town's one-way system, avoiding signs to the long sweep of the seafront. Her informant at head office in Rouen seemed to find it a matter for regret that she would discover the Commissariat to be a modern building rather than the heavily triumphal tyle of architecture common for French public offices. She would, however, find that its more recent construction gave it the advantage of ample car-parking space.

It came into view, a glass and concrete building with a tricolor flying from a flagpole above the door, and sure enough she could drive into its courtyard and park. Inspector Russe must have chosen to hang about in the foyer for her, because she had barely walked in when he stepped forward to greet her in formal but good English. He could be

55

her own age but looked younger, and Jane's first impression was that he was almost unfairly handsome. He was tall for a Frenchman, his height evenly proportioned inside a dark suit, and had a lock of brown hair which flopped artistically over his brow, a film-star profile, and a moody mouth. Her second impression, following rapidly on the first, suggested that the good looks were somewhat spoiled by a lack of animation; and she found herself with the immediate suspicion that the moodiness of his mouth owed as much to his having been delegated to look after her as it did to its natural curve.

An older man he had been talking to who was plainly a colleague cast her a much more appreciative look as he moved quickly over to join them, and murmured audibly to Inspector Russe the French equivalent of 'That's her? Jammy bastard!'

Both men had the grace to look disconcerted when Jane responded to the Inspector's greeting in her fast and idiomatic French. Trust a small-town French cop to assume— Jane stamped down on that thought quickly; she was here to cement good relations, not to indulge in stereotyping. She went on speaking instead, still in French, with a pleasant smile but in a crisply efficient tone.

'It's very good of you to give up your time to help us. I've brought a file with me on the investigation we're pursuing. Perhaps we could—'

'If we'd known you spoke such good French any one of us could have gone with you,' the older detective said, butting in to give her a look which could have been classed as a cheerful leer. 'How about it, Hilaire? If you want your free weekend after all I'll happily stand in for you. I'm sure I can square it with the boss.'

'We'll leave the arrangements as they are.' The words were delivered stiffly. Inspector Russe also switched back to English – deliberately, Jane thought – as he turned back to her. 'I suggest we set off for Compainville straight away. I shall drive. My car is in the car park at the back, so if you would care to come this way?'

'Yes, fine, if that's the way you want it. As I was saying, though, I'd like to go through the case file with you.'

'We can discuss that on our way.'

He seemed determined to hustle her off – and without even the offer of a cup of coffee after her drive, Jane thought wistfully. She could definitely have done with one. Still, if it should really have been his free weekend, no doubt he wanted to get his escort duties over as fast as possible. The older detective bowed over her hand by way of farewell with a further appreciative leer and a mocking glance in his colleague's direction.

As Jane was escorted round to the Commissariat's rear car park, she broke a silence to ask, in French, 'My car will be all right left where it is?'

'Certainly.'

She had half expected to drive on in her car with him as passenger, but since his manner suggested that would have been against formality she didn't raise the point. Even his driving bespoke extreme propriety as they threaded their way through the busy town centre, which seemed cheerfully full of strollers and cars stopping abruptly or pulling out without warning. It seemed inappropriate to make conversation until they reached a throughway out of the town where the traffic, though busy, was more orderly. Then she said politely, and still in French, 'I passed Neufchâtel-en-Bray on my way here, and I believe Compainville is not far from there?'

'Fifteen kilometres or so, but the house you want is a little way from the village.' He responded in his own language, but sounded as stiff as ever, though he went on politely, 'Do you know France well?'

'I've visited quite a few times. I've never lived here.'

'Too many English people have bought houses in France in the last few years,' he said with clear disapproval. 'As if we were a – a cheap source of holiday houses in the country.' He overtook a car in a sudden irritable surge, then braked to his previous decorous pace. For a moment it was on the tip of Jane's tongue to ask him if he disliked the English in general, or was it her in particular? She resisted the impulse, and was about to suggest instead – in an attempt to soften him up – that anyone might fall in love with Normandy when it was such a beautiful area, but he was already speaking again. 'Your French is very good. Good enough to suppose you might have lived here, or even had French relatives, in fact.'

'I went to a couple of international schools when I was young, where French was the first language. Your English sounded very good too,' she responded politely. She glanced at him, and decided to see if sympathy would take the edge off his woodenness. 'And that's why you've lost your weekend off to look after me, I suppose – I'm very sorry!'

She was half expecting a formally polite disclaimer – but all at once he relaxed, looking even younger and oddly vulnerable. 'It's just that my fiancée isn't pleased about it,' he confided, casting her a wry look. 'It's very difficult to explain to people who are not in the force that one's career . . . It's not the same for you, perhaps, but—'

'Oh, it is!' Jane gave him that in such heartfelt tones that he raised an eyebrow.

'You also have a fiancé who makes difficulties?'

'Something like that. I'm not likely to be popular when I get back either, for working unexpectedly this weekend.' And particularly not when Adrian was quite capable of deciding she had done it deliberately, as a gesture of independence. 'I'll tell you what you'd better do,' she said,

58

giving her companion a grin, 'don't tell your fiancée I could speak any French, make it absolutely clear I wouldn't have managed at all if you hadn't been there to get me from place to place. I don't mind if you make me sound like an idiot, in the interests of peace!'

He cast her a sidelong look of surprise, but then pulled a rueful face, accompanied by a Gallic shrug. 'Unfortunately, as she has a cousin who works as a secretary at the Commissariat – and as Michel, Sergeant Brocat whom you met, likes to tease – she's likely to hear all about you. So while it's a kind suggestion, I don't think it's practicable!'

So Sergeant Brocat teased him, did he? About his good looks, among other things, Jane guessed. 'All right then,' she suggested, 'you can be absolutely truthful and say that since I'm going to be conducting an interview in English, and we may need your help in future, it's important that you've heard the questions and answers at first hand. She can't argue with that, can she?' He was still looking slightly surprised by her friendly interest, but at least he was becoming more human by the minute. 'I do need to go through the case outline with you before we get there,' Jane went on, reverting to efficiency but smiling at him. 'I could read it out to you while you're driving, but—'

'It would be better if we stop at Neufchâtel. There's a café there which is usually quiet. I – I'm sorry, I should probably have offered you some refreshment after your drive.'

'Well, I could certainly do with a cup of coffee.' And a loo for that matter, but she wouldn't embarrass him by pointing that out. He asked, then, if she would mind if they talked in English because he would like the practice, and she agreed. The fact that Dieppe was a port with its share of foreign visitors had, he told her, been one of the reasons why he was given promotion and appointed to work there; nevertheless he would like to improve his vocabulary and his accent.

By the time they reached Neufchâtel, at the head of a striking river valley, they had compared notes on the different methods by which the French and English police would approach a case, and she had learned besides that he had a widowed mother, a younger sister, and an uncle who was a Commissioner of Police in a different region. The last made her wonder drily about nepotism, but it seemed merely to be the source of an earnest desire to fulfil family expectations by rising eventually to the same rank. In the café she settled down to go through her case notes with him, in the reviving aroma of strong French coffee. She found he asked intelligent questions with an unexpectedly sharp interest. That made her suddenly and guiltily aware that she had been making assumptions about him based on his almost excessive good looks. And that perhaps that kind of underestimation often happened to him. She gave him a quick smile.

'So you see, it's a less than simple case, in fact more of a muddle.'

'Unless Madame Hughes – this Madame Hughes – gives away something to show she's guilty.'

'Quite. But all I can do at the moment is ask her about her ex-husband's visit, and see what her reactions are.'

'Then let us go and do that. She might even confess – though not, I think, if she's aware that things are so confused that you've got no proof,' he added as they got up. 'But then she won't know that, will she? Since it would be difficult to suppose she could also be involved in this smuggling of immigrants ...'

'But on the other hand, I can't pretend we've got proof when we haven't. The copies of the lawyer's letters might rattle her, I suppose. Oh, look!'

It was a notice taped onto a shop window which had caught her eye. It was curling at the edges, as if it had been there some time, and announced, in large letters, 'Les Exercices

Aerobics', with a list of times, an address, and a telephone number for enquiries. And the address was the one they were about to visit – Les Beaux Vents, La Pellonnerie, Compainville.

'Hmm. So she advertises her classes all over the area,' Inspector Russe commented, reverting to his own language and sounding disapproving again. 'I can't think why it should need an incomer to teach exercises when there must be a perfectly good French gymnasium somewhere nearby.'

'It looks as if she's quite successful. Two of the classes have been marked off as being full.' Jane dropped back into French too, then glanced at him and decided they were on good enough terms by now for her to risk a light tease. 'A while ago you were objecting to the English buying holiday houses here; now it seems you don't like them working here either. Does that include me?'

'No, of course not. I—' As he caught her grin, he broke off, flushed, and switched abruptly back to English. '*You* are here for a specific purpose. And besides, when I say "incomers" I also mean people from other areas of France, who buy weekend cottages here and then make a great fuss when they're broken into while empty and cause us, the police, a great deal of trouble!'

'And push the price of houses up as well, I expect,' Jane said, allowing him to get out of it. 'We have the same trouble in parts of the UK. In Wales they don't like weekenders owning houses either; in fact from time to time they burn them down. Let's go and see what we make of Mrs Hughes, shall we?'

Compainville itself was a fair-sized village. La Pellonnerie, on the other hand, was one of those tiny gatherings of houses almost too small to be called a hamlet; three or four dwellings huddled together in a zigzag pattern, with a modern bungalow standing at its edge on a piece of fenced land clearly carved out of a farm field. The bungalow was heavily curtained and looked untenanted, and directly after that the road ended altogether in a closed gate bearing the carved legend, 'Les Beaux Vents'. They had reached their destination.

Little could be seen beyond the gate but the tops of trees, suggesting that the ground fell away; though the shape of a large brick barn showed itself inside the gate to the right. Next to the left-hand gatepost a notice pinned to a board read, 'Centre pour s'entrainer a la bonne forme' in neat printing, with the translation 'Fitness Centre' in brackets below, and the words 'Aerobics – Dance Exercise' below that. Added apparently recently in large handwritten black letters at the bottom was 'Chambres – B&B'.

Jane opened the car door. Presumably it was possible to release the gate from its fastening and drive in . . . Yes, it was. A short piece of rutted roadway led downhill, then opened into a surprisingly wide area which already held two cars, a motor-scooter, a battered-looking van and a couple of bicycles. Beyond that, flanked by trees, stood the house: two-storey, solidly beamed with a patterned brick infill, with deep windows and a tiled roof.

It looked attractive, and had obviously been well modernised. A couple of new skylights showed up on the roof, and a second open-fronted barn tacked on to one end of the house held another parked car, but in general the place had been kept in character. Now that she was out of the car Jane could hear the regular thump of music coming from the direction of the nearer barn. She ducked back to speak to Hilaire – they had reached first-name terms during their discussion of the case – and indicated with her hand.

'The house is down below. We may as well drive in rather than blocking the exit – visitors are obviously expected to, and you should find space to park. It sounds as if Mrs

Hughes may be holding a class. Still, we can knock at the front door and see if anyone answers. I'll shut the gate behind you.'

No attempt had been made to plant a garden. The property was bordered on each side by tall wild hedges, and aside from the area in front of the house which had been flattened and paved, there was nothing more than rough turf. The front door was of solid wood but had been decorated with a dolphin knocker. Its use brought a surprisingly prompt answer, as if someone must have been passing at the moment they knocked.

It was a young man who stood blinking at them in the open doorway – very young, Jane thought, probably no more than late teens. He was tall, but with the willowy look of youth. He began, 'Oh, er, bonjour—' but with such an obvious groping for the right word that Jane cut in to address him in English.

'Is it possible to speak to Mrs Rowena Hughes?'

'Are you bed and breakfast people?' he asked, his face clearing. 'Look, you'd better come in – my mother's taking an aerobics group at the moment but she won't be more than five minutes. If you'd like to come through to the living room . . . It's that door in front of you there. I'm sorry, this hall's a bit dark. I'm sure we do have a room free because it's, um, early in the season yet . . .'

He really was trying quite hard, Jane thought drily, but he shouldn't smoke pot in the morning when people might call. She caught a faint but characteristic whiff on his clothes, and the glassy, dreamy look in his eyes spoke volumes. A girl who looked up from a window seat in the wide room they were ushered into obviously realised what he'd been up to, because the boy had barely begun, 'Bed and breakfast people, Chantal—' before she jumped to her feet and was making a barely concealed attempt to shoo him away.

'Yes, of course – why don't you go upstairs, Josh, and see that everything's tidy? Please come in, Mr and Mrs ... I'm Chantal, I work for Mrs Hughes as her assistant. Josh, do go along and – and check the bedrooms? And then after that you could go outside and help Malcolm with that tree he's digging up.'

She clearly wasn't his sister, since she was plainly French, the light touch of accent in her voice showing it. Also, though she had dark hair just one shade browner than his, she was small, round-faced and olive-skinned against his thin lankiness and northern pallor. There was something very protective in the way she looked at him, however. As he moved out of the room she hissed after him, 'Don't wake the baby when you go up!'

To pre-empt the further query about their names which Chantal might be about to make, Jane moved as if drawn to the sight beyond the windows which lit this wide central combination of kitchen and sitting room.

'What a magnificent view! I hadn't realised from the front, but on this side you can see for miles!'

'Yes, the house is built against the slope so it has an extra storey this side. When it was a farm they stabled some of the animals at the bottom, but now there are extra rooms downstairs. The bedrooms this side have the same view. And they're very comfortable.' Chantal seemed determined to offer a sales pitch, and stepped forward to point out of the window to the spread of meadows and trees which dropped away into a valley below, then rose gently to a horizon several kilometres distant. 'You can almost see Forges-des-Eaux in that direction, if it were not for the woods, and this is a very good centre for touring! Will you excuse me? I'll go and see if Mrs Hughes has finished. She really won't be long.'

It was a relief that she had decided to go, since that

avoided a continuation of the unplanned deception. Once they were alone Jane glanced at Hilaire and raised an eyebrow.

'You might be surprised that someone wants another house when they have this one,' she said softly, in French in case Josh should suddenly reappear. She had gained the distinct impression that he was no linguist. 'This place must be worth something, and has obviously had money spent on it, too.'

He answered her in the same language, sounding thoughtful rather than disapproving this time and offering a considered judgement. 'But not recently – the morticing on the front windows is cracked and needs redoing, and I saw a corner of the roof which wants repair.' An electric saw started up somewhere outside, and he stepped forward to peer out of the window, but whoever was using it was out of view. He looked round at the room they were in, with its attractively displayed beams, its scrubbed table, a kitchen area at one end, a wood-burning stove surrounded by chairs and a sofa at the other. 'In here, too – it's some time since these walls were repainted, and the chair covers are shabby. More than on purpose. I'd say there *was* money, but it's run out.'

'It sounds as if she's got more of a household to support than just one person, too— Hush.'

The warning was unnecessary since he must have heard just as well as she did the voice which came clearly from the hall outside. It spoke in English, and was female, with a pleasant timbre. 'Fine, Chantal, thank you, dear. Yes, I'm sure you did!'

A figure, obviously Rowena Hughes, came through the door on a rush of energy and with a smile of welcome. She was very trim, in leotard and leggings, with a pink towel slung casually round her neck, and she looked remarkably young, Jane thought, to be the mother of the tall Josh. Blonde hair was piled up on her head in loose curls restrained by a band, with a few tendrils escaping. If there were any grey hairs they were concealed by her fairness, and she had the kind of clear skin which needed no make-up. Tiny lines fanning out around sparkling hazel eyes were the only indication that she must be in her forties. She was undeniably attractive, in both looks and manner – and was certainly a good advertisement for her own fitness programme.

'I'm terribly sorry to have kept you waiting,' she said, bounding over with her hand held out. 'Bed and breakfast, yes? Did you find us through my advertisement in the tourist office? I didn't expect to get a result so soon!'

'I'm afraid your son must have misunderstood us,' Jane said with polite apology, claiming her hand back. 'We're police officers – I'm Inspector Jane Perry and this is Inspector Hilaire Russe of the PJ. And you're Mrs Rowena Hughes?'

She had kept her eyes attentively on the other woman's face, and there was no mistaking a sudden freeze into stillness, though it lasted for the barest fraction of a second. And when the smile flashed out again – possibly wider than before – there was for a moment something fixed about it, despite a deliberate wrinkling of the brow in polite enquiry as she looked from Jane to Hilaire and back again.

The word 'police' had shaken her. No, it was more than that: for that brief instant of frozen immobility, what Jane had seen in her eyes had looked almost like panic.

It was gone now, replaced by a questioning air and an attitude of puzzled helpfulness; but she had not been actress enough to hide it.

Chapter 6

Rowena Hughes had barely glanced at the identification
Jane held out to her. Now, however, as she began, 'But
you're English—' something seemed to occur to her and she
seized the warrant card out of Jane's hand, stared at it wide-
eyed, then spoke on a caught breath and with a different and
quite unconcealed panic. 'And you're from— Oh no. No!
You haven't come to tell me something's happened to Sam?'

'Sam?'

'My son Sam – Sam Connolly! He lives— Oh, no, forgive
me, I'm sorry, you obviously don't know who I'm talking
about, and if it was that you would!' She put a hand to her
brow and managed a laugh, with a great deal of relief in it. 'I
thought for a moment... He's a student at the University
of Kent, you see. Isn't it awful about motherhood? Even
when they're grown up you can't help worrying that they
might fall under a bus like a toddler!' She laughed again and
gave Jane one of her appealing smiles. 'Please don't worry,
that was just a piece of maternal fright! You haven't even
heard of my dear reliable Sam, have you? So...' She
glanced again from Jane to Hilaire. 'Do sit down and tell me
what I can do for you. It can't be my permission to work in
France, surely? I'm absolutely sure my *carte de séjour* is in
order and hasn't run out.'

The question sounded no more than bright and friendly,
but she had turned away to offer them a chair each beside

the table and take one herself. Once they had settled and she could observe Rowena's face again, Jane launched smoothly into speech. 'I gather your ex-husband Lionel Hughes came to visit you last weekend. On business?'

'Yes, he did,' Rowena agreed, then added lightly with a lift of her eyebrows, 'though I don't know why you should say "on business" like that. He comes to visit us quite often! Oh, but . . .' A sudden frown came into her eyes. 'Good heavens, you can't mean . . . No, that would be the outside of enough! Lionel's sent *police* to see me about that bloody house?' Abruptly a sound seemed to attract her attention and she turned her head quickly. 'Chantal? Is that you? I'm talking to some police people, they weren't candidates for our bed and breakfast after all!' The girl appeared in the doorway and stood there hesitantly; why did Rowena seem to find the sight of her unexpected, when she had called out her name? 'It seems to be about Lionel,' Mrs Hughes went on, then swung back to Jane, to continue with an air of trenchant outrage. 'Really, he does have a nerve, we haven't even been to court yet! Or have you come to deliver a subpoena? It's quite unnecessary, because I certainly intend to appear whether I'm instructed to or not! And I *don't* think any court will back him up, when I've told him I'll give up title to the damned property at the end of the summer! All I'm asking for is the use of it until then, so that I can move out of here for the summer months and let this as a gîte, to recoup . . . Well, as you can imagine, a place like this needs a lot of maintenance.'

Her words fulfilled Hilaire's comments, even if a high colour suggested she would have preferred not to talk about money. Chantal was still in the doorway, half in and half out as if waiting for instructions. Rowena seemed to decide abruptly to give her some.

'While I'm talking to the police perhaps you'd go and ask Malcolm if he'd go to the supermarket for some shopping.'

'I'll tell him.'

'*You* needn't go too.' The girl vanished silently and
Rowena turned back to Jane. 'Now, Inspector ... Perry? If
you have got a subpoena, let me have it, but as I've said, it's
more than unnecessary.'

Who was to accompany Malcolm on the shopping trip
instead of the carefully stressed 'you'? Josh, Jane could
guess, to get him out of the house in case the French police
inspector should choose to notice his use of cannabis. It
scarcely seemed important. It was time to correct Rowena's
apparent misapprehension, either a clever ruse or a genuine
lack of knowledge that her ex-husband was dead. 'I haven't
been sent with a subpoena,' Jane said politely, 'though we
had heard of a disagreement between you and Mr Hughes
about some property. What I'm here to do is try and trace
his movements. I'd be grateful if you could tell me when he
arrived, how long he stayed, what time he left.'

'Why? Is he in some kind of trouble? Oh God, don't say
he's disappeared on a drinking binge!' Rowena gave a look
which was somewhere between exasperation and concern.
'He came here on Thursday night and left on Sunday afternoon. Just as he always does; he's a creature of habit these
days. As far as I know he was planning to go straight home.
He was in an awful mood when he left, though. If he's doing
that again – oh, stupid, stupid man! I divorced him because
he drank so much, you know. But I thought he'd pulled
himself together, what with Angelica and the baby. Mind
you, I'm sure it's Angelica who's been getting at him about
the house, because he's only started being unreasonable
about it lately. It's jealousy, I suppose; not that she has any
need.'

She sounded more maternal than critical, and certainly
kinder about the present Mrs Hughes than Angelica was
about her. But then Rowena as a rival was probably quite a

formidable prospect, Jane thought; she had charm, warmth, looks and obvious energy. Had she, as Angelica claimed, resented Lionel's choice of someone younger? And was there a ruthlessness enough to kill behind the apparently genuine manner? Jane was opening her mouth to ask again for the details of Lionel's departure, but there was a further interruption as yet another member of the household appeared in the doorway.

This one was older than Josh – somewhere in his thirties, Jane thought – and had one of those pudgy faces which you could see in any English city and which always seemed to be combined, as his was, with mousy hair and glasses. He came in rubbing his hands absently down the sides of a grubby pair of jeans, glancing incuriously at the two police officers before he addressed Rowena in a voice which was educated but colourless.

'Chantal said you wanted me to leave the tree and shop?' he said. 'Is there a list?'

'You don't need one, it's just the usual stuff. Go to – to Gournay rather than Gaillefontaine. I know it'll take longer but they've got more things. You can get a whole lot of stores with two of you to load them into the van. Thanks, Malcolm.' Then, turning to Jane and Hilaire, 'This is Malcolm Jackson, he's my very helpful general factotum. These are police officers, Malcolm, wanting to know when Lionel left here last Sunday. He seems to have gone missing.'

'I wouldn't know when he left. I wasn't here, if you remember, I went off on Saturday morning on that weekend job. Maybe he crashed his car on the way home. I'll get going, then—'

'Don't say that. My poor Li, I know he's been shouting at me lately but I'm still fond of him! Oh, Malcolm, money!'

'Don't worry, I got paid for the tiling.'

He was gone again. 'He helps out by taking on building jobs for people doing house improvements,' Rowena said, looking after him with an air of distraction. Jane thought drily that she was probably wondering whether Malcolm had grasped the nub of her instructions – take Josh out and keep him out. Perhaps protectiveness was part of her character. She certainly seemed almost exaggeratedly determined to shield her son from a possible rap over the knuckles for his smoking habits. She was much jumpier over Josh than she was over Lionel. To test that out Jane gave her a limpid look and asked:

'How many people actually live here? We met your son, I believe?'

'Yes, Joshua – he's Sam's twin, they're both twenty, though they actually don't look very alike. Josh came to live with me, oh, a year ago, because he'd been quite ill with glandular fever and he still isn't all that well. It recurs.' Yes, she was jumpy about him; it showed by the speed with which she went on, 'Then there's Chantal and her baby. Her parents threw her out when she got into trouble – I really don't know how people can do that! Then there's Malcolm, who helps out, as I told you. That's all of us. If you need to know exactly when Lionel left, it must have been about two o'clock on Sunday.' She frowned, then gave Jane a wide-eyed look. 'The same as always. I don't *think* there was any change. The Gachets up the hill probably saw him go past – not the bungalow, that belongs to a Parisian couple and they haven't been down yet this year – but he usually gives the Gachets at the end house a wave as he goes by, or stops for a word with Pierre about fishing. Though perhaps he wouldn't have done this time, considering he left in such a bad temper! Oh dear. Did he really not get home?'

'No.'

'And I suppose you've checked hospitals, and ... oh damn, any town with a bar *en route*! If he's let temper send him back into old ways, he's as likely as not in some motel sleeping things off, and without the least memory of how he got there!'

She sounded exasperated, but also grieved. Jane gave a thoughtful look at the woman in front of her, then picked her words with care.

'I didn't say Mr Hughes was missing. As a matter of fact we do know where he is. He was found dead.'

Rowena stared at her with the colour draining out of her face. The look in her eyes had to be shock, or a remarkable representation of it. She opened her mouth, then shut it again. Then, unexpectedly and abruptly, she got to her feet. She walked across to the kitchen end, opened a cupboard, pulled something out and stood hugging it. A thermos flask. After a second she turned her head and spoke in a shaken voice.

'I'm – I'm sorry. I expect it sounds quite mad ... I didn't even make him up some herbal tea to take with him, because we'd been quarrelling. I usually do, to give him something to drink so that he isn't tempted to stop at a bar. I know I said I thought he'd changed, but it was a kind of – I don't know, habit, insurance! And this time I didn't, and it may sound like a stupid small thing but it's – it's the sort of thing which suddenly seems unbearable!'

If she was acting, it was a brilliant performance. Tears had started to roll down her face, and there were sudden lines round her mouth which aged her ten years.

Abruptly she pulled herself together. She put the thermos down gently, reached for a piece of paper towel to wipe her wet cheeks, drew a breath and spoke in a husky but steadier voice.

'I'm sorry. I know we were divorced but I was still fond of

him. As – as a friend. You have a history with someone . . . What happened? Was it a heart attack? Or a stroke? Did it happen on his way home from here? If – if he wasn't found at once, poor Li, I'm surprised Angelica didn't ring me!'

'He was found on Monday. On Stelling Minnis common, in Kent.'

'Yes, I know it, we used to live not far from there. He almost got home then . . .'

'It would help if we could trace his journey, because we can't be sure exactly where he was when. For instance, did anyone go with him?' A definite shake of the head. 'Was he planning to meet anyone that you know of? Had he mentioned a news story he might be following up?'

'No. No, he was just thoroughly cross all the time he was here. Particularly when— No, that's not important, it's just that I wasn't in a mood to listen to him properly. I *wish* I didn't have to remember that!' Rowena wrapped her arms round herself in an instinctive gesture of comfort, then sighed, shook herself, and made an obvious effort. 'I'm sorry – no, he certainly didn't say anything about a news story. Is it important? Because you've got some missing time between when he left here and when he was found? He probably wouldn't have told me anyway since it was all house, house, house.'

Before Jane could answer her questions Rowena moved across to the door and called, 'Chantal?' A door banged somewhere above, then there was the sound of footsteps on stairs and the girl appeared, looking slightly sulky and with a round-eyed baby of about eighteen months balanced on her hip.

'Yes? The others have gone out—'

'Have they? Good. Chantal, last weekend did you hear Lionel say anything about a news story? Or someone he had to meet?'

73

'No, but then we were all—' She broke off abruptly, swallowed, and went on quickly, 'We were all together all the time, so if he said anything you'd – you'd have heard it too. But I don't remember that he did.'

'And when would you say he left?'

'Two o'clock, quarter past? It must have been, because I'd just finished giving Shoshi his lunch.'

'Lionel's dead,' Rowena said forlornly, and accepted the hug the girl rapidly moved to give her. 'It's so *sad*. After everything he . . . After all those years we were married. We *were* happy once, even if it didn't seem like it later.'

'Josh will—'

'I'll tell Josh.' The words were almost a snap. 'I'll have to ring Sam, too, and Isobel. He was their stepfather for almost ten years, after all.' Abruptly she seemed to remember the two police officers sitting silently at the table and turned to them with a kind of mechanical politeness. 'I'm sorry, I should have offered you something – not coffee, because I don't have it in the house, it's thoroughly bad for the system, but herb tea? And I'm sorry if I haven't been much help. Is there anything else you need to ask me?'

'I wonder if you know whether Mr Hughes was at all knowledgeable about poisons?'

'Not that I— Why?' Rowena's stare suddenly sharpened. 'Oh my God. You didn't say how he died when I asked you. You just said he was *found*. You can't be suggesting suicide? No, you're quite wrong! He wouldn't. Wait a minute, you asked if I knew whether he was meeting anyone. It wouldn't have been suicide, Lionel's much too fond of himself for that, and besides, he's got a baby daughter now and he's terribly proud of her! If you're saying he took poison, then somebody else must have given it to him!'

It didn't seem to occur to her that the person under suspicion might be herself. Might have been – because in spite of the gesture with the thermos flask, which ought to have seemed a deliberate ploy, Jane's gut feeling was telling her strongly that none of Rowena's reactions had been an act. And before anybody could say any more, Rowena's agitated face abruptly drained of the small amount of colour which had come back into it, and her eyes turned upwards in their sockets. With a small moan, she sank to the ground in a dead faint.

Chapter 7

Hilaire unexpectedly came into his own. He was on his feet almost before Rowena hit the floor, and moving rapidly to her. He knelt down, felt for her pulse, then lifted her in an easy movement on to the settee and set a cushion under her feet while he snapped something in rapid French to Chantal. The instruction sent the girl flying for the kitchen, dumping the baby unceremoniously on Jane as she passed. The infant seemed to accept the transfer with more equanimity than Jane did, gazing at her round-eyed for a moment, then giving her a gummy beam as if he liked the look of her, and as if being dumped on strangers was a normal facet of life.

Thus hampered from going to help, Jane could only watch as Chantal came back and passed a bottle into Hilaire's outstretched hand. A moment later the strongly acrid smell of ammonia came drifting across. The means might be basic but the result was rapid. Rowena gave a choking cough as the bottle stopped wafting under her nose, and her eyes fluttered open.

'Oh . . .'

'Please don't try to sit up, Mrs Hughes. You fainted momentarily.' He snapped, 'De l'eau, pour boire!' and Chantal rushed back to fetch a glass of water. Rowena's eyelids seemed to be fluttering with embarrassment now as she took a carefully guided sip under the young inspector's restraining hand. It occurred to Jane involuntarily and with a flash of humour that it might well be disconcerting to revive to find a young man with Hilaire's film-star looks bending solicitously over you. She quelled that thought quickly and began to get up awkwardly, balancing the baby's solid warmth against her. As she did so Rowena was beginning to reassert herself.

'I think – I think I'd like to sit up and put my head between my knees, if you don't mind. Thank you ...' She folded herself in half for a long moment, then came up slowly and glanced up at the hovering Hilaire. 'Yes, I would like a bit more water ... I'm so sorry! I haven't done that for years!'

'It's understandable, madame, under the pressure of shock.'

Chantal reclaimed her child; or rather was forced to, as Jane deliberately held him out. The infant seemed to take just as amiably to being dangled in mid-air. As Rowena saw Jane coming to join the tableau at the settee, she lifted her head from the water glass and attempted a smile.

'Please forgive me, that was so stupid! It was ...' She gave a brief shiver. 'Chantal, dear, could you get my cardigan? It was just like being taken back into the past suddenly. You see, Lionel—'

'Please don't talk until you are sure you feel better, madame.'

'I'm fine now. Really. I need to tell you, because you won't know. Lionel used to be an investigative reporter years ago. And there was a time when he fell foul of a kind of network of multinational companies, over an arms-dealing story. I'd swear they tried to get rid of him, more than once. He had several unexplained accidents. It was very frightening at the time. I'm talking about ten or twelve years ago. This suddenly brought it back. The story got spiked under a D notice and it all died down. But if Lionel started stirring *them* up again, don't you see? He's always muttering about getting down to his memoirs. If he's been poisoned, that could be why!'

The memoirs theory again. And offered with a sincere urgency. It would have to be noted, since Rowena obviously believed in it. She was the person who had known Lionel in his palmier days, too. 'Can you give us any details?' Jane asked. 'If you can I'll take a note of them . . .'

'I can't remember any names. I'm sorry, I may have been told some of them at the time, but it was all very hush-hush and safer not to know. Angelica should have his papers, if he kept anything from those days, or if he's been trying to write it up again.' Rowena broke off, looking distracted. 'He got on the wrong side of the Triads once too, so I suppose it could be them. Please do believe me, it *won't* be suicide.'

'We do have things which lead us to believe it wasn't. I'm truly sorry to have given you so much distress, Mrs Hughes. But I'm sure you understand that we did have to come and ask you for your ex-husband's movements.'

'I'm just grateful that somebody told me at all.' Despite the cardigan which Chantal had returned to drape round her shoulders, Rowena shivered again. 'I think if you don't mind – I think I'd like to go and lie down on my bed. I'm sorry, it's ridiculously weak of me! Do you have any more you want to ask me? Lionel was here for three days, c-cross but normal . . .' She was obviously trying to control the tremor which had come into her voice. 'And when he drove away on Sunday he was perfectly all right. He'd eaten a good meal . . . I've told you, Pierre Gachet may have seen him go by. He was aiming to go back through the tunnel, he always has since it opened. I don't think there's anything else I can tell you.'

'Yes, please do go and lie down if you need to. I've

covered what I needed to ask for now, and we can always come back another time if any further questions crop up.'

'Of course . . . Chantal?'

'Let me.' Rather than have the baby thrust at her again Jane moved to help Hilaire steady Rowena as she stood up, and added pleasantly, 'I'll help you upstairs as well, shall I? Would you like both of us . . .?'

'No, please, I'm not really crumbling!' She took Jane's proffered arm, however, and gave Hilaire a tentative and distracted smile too as she was led away. Chantal followed. Narrow wooden stairs led up out of the dark hall, though above, pale wood and white lath-and-plaster made everything much lighter. An open door at the end of the corridor showed a modern bathroom. Rowena's room held a double bed puffed with duvet and pillows, photographs tucked round the frame of the dressing-table mirror, a friendly clutter of personal possessions. She crawled quickly under the duvet as if cold was chilling her bones, and Jane asked with concern, 'Shall I get you another glass of water? Or perhaps Chantal should make you a hot drink?'

'Just water, if you wouldn't mind. There should be a glass in the bathroom . . .'

Coming back with it, Jane's rubber soles were quiet on the polished board floor. She caught the soft mutter of Chantal's voice, and the name 'Josh'; then a snap from Rowena.

'Do you think I don't know? Oh, do go downstairs, Chantal, and give Shoshi something to eat before he chews off all his fingers!'

She sounded distinctly sharp. Jane paused, then came on and met Chantal as they both arrived at the doorway. Rowena was lying as she had left her, a face in the depths of a pillow. She managed a smile as Jane put the glass down on the bedside table.

'Thank you for being so kind. I really am sorry to be so ... so spineless! But you will go back and make them understand that it couldn't possibly be suicide, won't you? That somebody must have poisoned him? And that it could be an assassin from the past, if he's been— Oh, why couldn't he have taken warning from what happened last time?'

'I'll pass on everything you've said. And I do apologise again for the distress I've caused you. Have you a doctor you can call if you need one?'

'Yes, but I won't. Please don't feel you have to stay. I suppose,' she said on a sigh, 'even though she hasn't been with him for as long as I was, it's really worse for Angelica. How is she taking it – do you know?'

'She's very upset, naturally. And she's equally sure that somebody else must have given her husband poison.' Jane hesitated briefly, then added, 'Just in case we need to ask you any more questions, would you be kind enough to let us, or the Police Judiciaire in Dieppe, know if you intend to leave for any reason?'

'Yes, of course—' The words were only half out when she saw a sudden flash in Rowena's eyes. 'Oh no,' she said helplessly, and turned her head wearily away on the pillow. 'Angelica? Yes, I suppose it's the first thing she *would* think of! Oh, the silly girl ...'

She didn't appear to want to say more. Nor did Jane feel it necessary to confirm that Angelica had voiced the accusations which Rowena had now plainly guessed. She waited for a moment longer, but seeing the older woman's eyes were closed, she turned to leave the room. Rowena's voice, suddenly stronger, called her back.

'Inspector?' She had lifted her head from the pillow and was regarding Jane with sudden resolution, a touch of defiance in it. 'I may as well tell you now – though I'll let you know exactly when, of course – that I do intend not to be here for long. I'll just get this place tidied up for letting, and then I'll be in England. In the disputed house, and you can make of that what you like! I was going to wait until after Easter, but if Angelica's – well, let's say I'm not going to risk *her* trying to get the students evicted so she can get her hands on it. Now I'd like you to leave me alone, please, and would you close the door on your way out?'

Jane left the room quietly. She really had had to ask Rowena to let them know if she was going anywhere. It was a pity to have been left feeling she had handled the tail end of the interview badly. However, and despite the bitter words just spoken, she knew that when she gave the Super her impressions of this Mrs Hughes, it would be a clear Not Guilty. Unless, of course, some incontrovertible piece of evidence came up to prove her wrong.

Hilaire was waiting where she had left him, holding a conversation with Chantal which sounded slightly wary on her side, but appeared to be no more than polite enquiries about the baby on his. Since she had a saucepan in her hand and the infant trying to pull himself up to a standing position against her legs they assured her they could show themselves out. The front courtyard was now empty of all the other cars and bicycles, though their car was still parked in the adjoining barn. As they reached Hilaire's Citroën he spoke.

'Do you want to stop and ask these neighbours, the Gachets, if they saw what time Mr Hughes passed?'

Jane considered for a second, then shook her head. 'No, I don't think we need bother them. We've had two statements as to his departure time. I'll walk up and – oh, the gate's open. We can drive straight out then.'

She glanced at the small huddle of La Pellonnerie as they passed through it; stone houses with deep windows, a small tidy garden where the zigzag of the road allowed a space. A man in a beret was busy digging it and stared at them curiously as they drove by. What did her near neighbours make of Rowena Hughes? Jane wondered. She glanced across at Hilaire and broke the silence.

'I think we've got Rowena in the clear. I assume you followed everything? Could you see her as a murderess?'

'Not unless she's a very clever actress, and I didn't have that impression.'

'Nor me. It's a pity, when it would have been the simplest solution. And Lionel clearly didn't mention anything about the immigrant story to her, so we're no further on with that either.'

'I noticed you didn't raise the subject with Madame Hughes, except to ask in general terms if he planned to meet someone to follow up a news story?'

'No, my superintendent felt it would only throw in a complication, unless Rowena already seemed to have heard of it. I must write everything down as soon as possible while it's in my head, and while I've got you to remind me if there's anything I leave out. Can we stop somewhere – maybe for lunch?' Her watch was showing that it was after two, but presumably they could find somewhere which was still serving. 'On me,' she added quickly, 'since I'm on expenses!'

'Thank you,' he said, after a brief hesitation during which it looked as if he was feeling he ought to object. 'I was just about to suggest— What sort of food would you like?' He added drily, 'If your expenses are anything like ours ... I do know a place which isn't elegant, but the food's good.'

'Sounds fine by me. What did you make of the boy Josh?'

'Drugs, plainly. Certainly *le chauvre indien* – cannabis, you say? I'd like to check up on him, since it would be a good idea to find his supplier. Unless you wish it left alone?' he asked, with a quick querying glance at her.

'No, check away. Rowena was thoroughly determined to

get him out of the house, wasn't she? You seem very practised with fainting females,' she added, making it a light but faintly amused compliment.

'Well, women do faint, don't they? So one becomes used to it. What?' He cast her a faintly puzzled look at the sound she had made. 'Did I say that so that it means something different?'

'No, not at all. I was only feeling inclined to challenge you and say "Don't men faint too?"'

'Of course, but less often. I'm not sure what you . . .'

'Don't worry about it,' she said, giving a grin at his puzzled expression. It scarcely seemed the moment to accuse him of a chauvinist comment, and she sobered back into consideration of the case. 'I'm convinced that Rowena had no idea I was going to tell her Lionel was dead, and still less that we believe it was murder. In fact she was desperate to persuade me that it must have been. So the other Mrs Hughes has sent us barking up the wrong tree. I wish I could have recorded the interview, but that would have looked a lot too formal.'

'We always have to put everything on paper. Paper, paper and more paper, with everything detailed and accurate enough for the Juge d'Instruction, unless we want trouble,' Hilaire commented wryly as they negotiated the lanes he had turned into instead of taking the road back into Neufchâtel. He went on, 'We had a case round here not long ago. That's how I know all the short cuts which will take us to Les Hayons, and that we can find something to eat there.' They reached a better road, climbed briefly, then dropped again. Jane had no idea where they were, save that it was pretty. 'This Malcolm Jackson,' he continued after a moment, 'would you say he's Madame Hughes' lover?'

'Not unless she's got unexpectedly poor taste! He looked far too characterless for someone like her. Why, did you think so?'

84

'No, like you I'd find it surprising, on balance. But she's a very attractive lady, and he's younger, so who knows?' He sounded rational about it, and very French. 'She seems to collect – what word would you use, strays?'

'Yes, she's definitely the maternal type.' Almost overwhelmingly so, Jane thought, and it was an attitude which stretched to cover her ex-husband too. She had even managed to sound protective about her successor, until that last moment of angry bitterness. Jane contemplated Rowena for a moment, trying to decide whether there was anything she might have left out in her assessment of the other woman's character. 'I think, if you wouldn't mind, it would be helpful if you could make a general check on Mrs Hughes. What opinion people have of her in the area, anything about her since she moved here. Would that be possible? I know we've concluded she can't be the poisoner, but since she does have a relationship to the victim it would be a good idea to know as much as possible about her.'

'Yes, I can do that, no problem.'

'She's coming to England soon, but— Oh, I didn't mention that to you, did I?' Jane told him quickly what had been said upstairs. 'If she's emptying the house to let as a gîte, presumably Josh will be returning to England with her, so if you're going to look for his supplier you might need to get on to that fast. I'm sorry, I should have mentioned that earlier.'

He accepted her apology without speaking, merely giving a nod of agreement, since he had slowed for a tractor turning clumsily off the road into a field. Once the obstruction had cleared he suggested, 'If Madame Hughes' husband visited her regularly, it may be just as well to find out if there have been any strangers about while he was there, people watching the house during his visits. In view of her conviction that he had enemies.'

'Yes, that's a good idea.' After Rowena's reaction and the facts she had given them, 'enemies from the past' was a line they would have to follow up. 'It could be relevant to the immigrant scam as well, I suppose . . . But it could also be that we've been muddling up two things which aren't related at all,' she said with frustration. 'That's the trouble – it's easy enough to produce a theory, particularly when it's one which tidies up various loose ends. But it's all had to be guesswork so far, without a single provable fact!'

'Some detail may come up which makes the whole thing fit together. My uncle used to say that it's often small things which solve a case.'

A notice beside the road announced that they had reached Les Hayons. It was not one of the prettier villages though the upper windows of some of the houses might offer a pleasant view of the woodlands which crowded to one side of it. Hilaire drove into a central square and pulled up, indicating an ugly plate-glass window through which could be seen plain but clean tables.

'You won't mind this? It doesn't look much, but the *patron* cooks well enough, and after we've eaten you can sit and make your notes. The place stays open all day so there'll be no objection. Unless you'd rather—'

'No, it looks fine,' Jane assured him. She almost gave him the cheerful addition that he need not worry because, left to herself, fast food from a takeaway would probably be her usual level of consumption; but then decided not to in case it set him off on another fit of disapproval of the English. She smiled at him instead, saw his face clear, and followed him in through the door which bore the chipped legend, 'Café Merlot'.

Chapter 8

The food had been excellent, even to Jane's untutored taste, redolent with herbs and served on piping-hot plates. A large jug of coffee had been placed on the table afterwards with the promise of a refill if they ran out, and the obvious acceptance that they wanted peace and quiet to sit and work. In fact Hilaire had been recognised on arrival with a cheerfully jokey, 'Oho, so we're being camped on again by the *flics*? Don't tell me another farmer's been found with his head bashed in?' Jane's appearance had been treated with interest and some approval, and she had had to be introduced, hands shaken formally all round, not just with the proprietor but also with some of the customers. 'The cops' had obviously become regular customers at the Café Merlot during their last case.

Popular, too, Jane thought drily, trying to visualise any English workman's café treating a police presence with such friendly welcome – even if it might only be for the pragmatic reason that it was good bill-paying custom. Certainly, when it was she who produced a wad of francs to pay the extremely reasonable *addition*, the proprietor's reaction was to give Hilaire a cheerful wink with the words, 'So she's the one on expenses, eh?'

Her record on the interview with Rowena was as detailed as their joint memories could make it. There seemed no reason to stay overnight; Jane could see nothing to be gained from a second call at Les Beaux Vents. They returned to Dieppe, and as they arrived outside the Commissariat she stretched and gave Hilaire a smile.

'Thank you for all your help. I hope you'll get your Sunday off, even if I've taken up your Saturday!'

'It doesn't matter. It has been very interesting. And I've enjoyed your company,' he said, looking as if he meant it. 'You have to go back today? They have only given you a very short time for a foreign assignment!'

'It's not really so far to come. Where I'm stationed is only just the other side of the Channel. Oh, I must give you my numbers so that you can contact me direct . . .'

'You'll have time to come in, surely, before you go? Come up to the office, and I'll write down the things you want me to be able to tell you, and give you our number here, too.'

'OK,' Jane said amiably. She gave him a sudden grin, thinking how much more companionable he was now than when they started. 'As long as you aren't afraid Sergeant Brocat will tease, and cause you even more trouble with your fiancée.'

'Elise will have to get used to the fact that some detectives I work with are young and attractive, not middle-aged and plain,' he said – quite tartly, and with a suddenly determined jut to his chin. He glanced at Jane sidelong, however, and with a slight flush; but still sounded determined as he added, 'As for Michel – if he's still in he'll probably try to flirt with you, but I can always pull rank and tell him to behave!'

Jane thought of telling him that while she was grateful for his gallantry, she thought she could manage. However he was already out of the car, so she scrabbled to collect up her briefcase and shoulder-bag and satisfied herself with a light 'Merci bien du compliment!' as he opened the door for her. They went into the building by a back entrance and he led the way through various anonymous corridors. It felt, she thought, very much like any police premises anywhere, save for the distinct whiff of Gauloise cigarettes coming from an open door as they passed. The upstairs room he took her to looked like familiar CID territory, too, with its desks and telephones and a ubiquitous Coca-Cola machine against one wall.

They exchanged phone and fax numbers. Jane handed Hilaire the copy case file she had brought with her.

'I'll leave this with you, then, just in case anything else comes up this end. And I'll fax you a copy of the interview with Rowena after I've typed it out . . . Thanks again for all your help, and in advance for those checks you're going to make for me. I really had better set off now!'

A trip to the Ladies; then finally they were downstairs again in the foyer. Hilaire insisted on walking out with her to her car and they exchanged the inevitable formal handshake without which she could not have been allowed to go.

'Perhaps you'll come to England on an inquiry some time,' she told him. 'Anyway we'll be in touch.'

'I'll look forward to it.'

Both pleasant and useful, Jane thought as she drove away, with a glimpse of him in her side mirror watching her departure. Brighter than he looked, too. Today had been satisfying in its way – even if it had brought no answer to the conundrum of Lionel Hughes' murder. Except for a return to the bloody memoirs . . . That line would have to be checked more thoroughly now, with a request to Angelica to go through Lionel's papers for names. *Were* they actually looking at an assassination by persons unknown, to prevent the man from blowing the facts about an old story?

It was late and dark by the time she drove into the city streets which would lead her home. She was aware of being tired, and that it had been a long day since her early-morning start. It was less than welcome, therefore, when she found herself being flagged down as she drove slowly past the veterinary practice, making for the next corner and her own street. She had seen Harry Morpeth strolling towards her along the pavement with a cigarette between his fingers, the streetlight glinting on his fair hair, but she certainly would not have stopped if he had not stepped out virtually under her wheels.

'Hi!' he said cheerfully when his presence had forced her to wind down her window. 'I've just nipped out for a smoke. Trying of Felicity not to like it in the flat, but never mind. You're home, then!'

'Hallo, Harry. Yes, I'm home. Why?'

'Only that we've had Adrian round at our place most of the evening. Feeling fed up because you weren't there, I gathered. Even if the excuse was that he wanted to hear how the practice had been going in his absence.' He gave her a conspiratorial grin, though she was sure what he was actually doing was seeing if he could stir it. He was like that – an apparently tactless word here, a repetition of something he swore had been said there, though with a hasty and rueful 'Oh God, shouldn't I have said that?' 'I'm glad I've caught you, anyway,' he went on now, leaning casually against her car so that she couldn't drive on, 'because I heard the news today about poor old Lionel! Tried to ring him up for something, got Angelica, heard about his death. And murder no less, poor old sod! What's the police angle on it?'

'Not my line these days . . .'

'Oh, come on, that one won't wash, you're bound to know what's going on! It sounds an interesting one, too – poison, a spot of *crime passionnel*—'

'I don't think it's going to be one you can turn into a novel. As far as anything I've heard, which isn't much,' Jane amended quickly. He had tried to pump her before for what he called 'tales from the case files'.

'Have a heart, lovey, you know how I like a nice bit of faction! Dressed up, of course, and with plenty of gore added. Anyway, you know you're not telling me the truth. Adrian says you left a note that you'd gone to France, for work, and the ex lives in France. Which means you're on the case.' He gave her a reproachful look. 'Go on, be a mate, tell me how things are going. The old boy was a friend of mine, after all. And I swear, cross my heart and hope to die, I won't let on in any quarter at all where I got my news from!'

'Sorry, Harry, I'm much too tired to be a mate, and I want to get home.' It never seemed to occur to Harry that his charm wouldn't work on everybody. Jane had to be civil to him because he was Felicity's partner, but she would have been glad not to be obliged to. She said pleasantly, 'Let me go, there's a dear, or you might find yourself falling over as I drive off. Little as I want to be responsible for your tumbling over in the street!'

'Oh dear, you're in your iron knickers mood,' he said lightly, gave her a smile which seemed intended to convey sympathy, and stepped back. 'Off you go to lover-boy then, he's been—'

She missed the rest because she let in the clutch and moved off. How about Harry as Lionel's murderer, killing him to get first-hand knowledge of what it felt like? Felicity had said he was away doing research for a book, after all! Nice idea for a vicious moment, though if there was still the death penalty it would make it even more inviting as a fantasy!

Jane shook her head, aware that she ought to be thoroughly ashamed of herself. Just because she disliked the man . . .

As she let herself into the house she heard Adrian moving about, but when he turned at her entrance he gave her a thoroughly amiable smile, then came across quickly to kiss her. 'Oh good, you're back, I was just wondering if we'd reached the point where it was going to be tomorrow. France, you said in your note?'

'Yes, I had to go over and do an interview,' Jane said, returning his affectionate hug. 'How was Edinburgh?'

'Good. Interesting. I'm glad to be home, though,' he said, and kissed her again. 'Maybe because I missed you. What kind of a week have you had – busy?'

'Everything bar the kitchen sink,' Jane said lightly. 'Oh, and – God, it seems ages ago already! – I had to use your car last Sunday night to run an errand for Felicity, just in case you've already had the chance to wonder why there's a lot less petrol in it! Maybe she's told you, if she's been catching you up on what she and the locum have been doing while you've been swanning off up north. I mean, of course, being thoroughly dedicated and professional!'

'Thank you,' he said, but grinned. 'It *was* a five-star hotel, as it happened! Pity you couldn't have come too and joined the swan. Edinburgh's a beautiful city.'

'Tell me about it. I've absolutely got to have some tea while you do, though – I'm buzzy from too much driving!'

Adrian started telling her what he had seen of Edinburgh in between listening to learned papers. It would be time enough to mention tomorrow that she had to go into the station in the morning, Sunday notwithstanding, to type up her notes on the Rowena Hughes interview. And there was no need to spoil tonight's reunion by anticipating disapproval, either: all she would be doing was letting Harry's little jab get to her, since far from being fed up, Adrian could not have been more amiable and loving.

At the station mid-morning she was aware of feeling scratchily irritable – and for the ridiculous reason that Adrian had looked disappointed rather than disapproving, merely saying, wistfully, 'Damn – today as well? And I told Fliss she could go on managing without me, in the hope we could have a lazy day!' So then she had felt guilty – and without the least need, considering she had told him she would only be a couple of hours. The station was quiet, the incident room not even manned, an indication that there was nothing urgent for it to do. Jane moved a typewriter in there from the CID room and settled down to make a tidy copy of the account she and Hilaire had worked on. She was about halfway through and concentrating when one of the telephones buzzed, causing her to look up and frown. Then she remembered that she had told Communications she would be in here, and reached over to lift the receiver.

'Yes?'

'Inspector Perry, I've got Dr Ingle calling you. I can take a message if you don't want to be disturbed.'

'No, that's OK, put her through ... Matty? Hi – how did you find me?'

'I rang you at home and Adrian told me you'd gone into work. So am I, as it happens – at work – though it's not for your lot on this occasion. I got called out to Faversham for a stabbing.'

'A nice straightforward one I hope? As a matter of interest, how did Adrian sound?'

'Resigned,' Matty told her with a chuckle. 'He did mention that he'd only seen you briefly since he came back, rather as if you'd flitted in and out and it might need a butterfly net to catch you, but—'

'Briefly my eye, I was there all night! And for a late breakfast!'

'I was going to say, but he was as civil as ever. I made sympathetic noises and told him you and I hadn't managed to meet while he was away and that was why I was ringing

93

you. What it is actually is that the second poison test results have come through. They've already been sent on to you and should be there tomorrow, but knowing your interest I thought you might like a spot of advance knowledge.'

'Would I not! And I'm officially on the case now, so you needn't worry about secrecy. What was it?'

'A confirmation of what we thought. KCN – potassium cyanide.'

'Doesn't that cause convulsions?'

'No, just loss of consciousness in approximately one minute, coma, and death between fifteen and forty-five minutes later. On a fairly empty stomach, though, and with his constitution, it would have been nearer the fifteen. It's actually a fairly peaceful death; in coma the person merely appears to be sleeping very heavily. There's a couple of interesting things about KCN . . .'

'Yes, tell?'

'First, your poisoner must have known what he – or she – was doing: if the dose had been too large we would have found burning in the throat, and we didn't. So you can assume a murderer with knowledge of the minimum amount needed to kill. Secondly, after it's mixed – in cold tap water; mineral water won't do because of the acidity – it won't last for more than a few hours before it becomes undrinkable. KCN on its own isn't lethal, but mixed with water it becomes HCN – hydrogen cyanide – which is; but it isn't something you're going to carry around ready-mixed. Or not for long. Helpful?'

'Could well be . . . It has to have been put into water, you say?'

'Yes. Dissolved in water, which would take about five minutes. Then it's clear and tasteless – as long as you haven't used too much. The tests suggest, and please note I only say suggest, that he took it directly after that slug of alcohol I

94

mentioned to you before. Which was whisky, by the way. He could have topped up the whisky with the poisoned water, in fact, as long as he tossed it back straight afterwards. Before any reaction showed up. With me?'

'Yeah. Either a dilution but drunk immediately, or a water chaser. Thanks. How commonly obtainable is potassium cyanide, I wonder?'

'Hard to secure because of its known dangers, unless you work in chemistry or some of the heavy metal industries,' Matty said promptly. 'Has some use in photography too, I think . . . for etching, anyway. But if you've got someone with knowledge, you've probably also got someone who knows how to get hold of the stuff – legally or illegally. It does exist in the leaves of some plants, and you could chew those leaves without any ill-effects as long as you didn't drink any water . . . But we have no sign that your man had been chewing plants, so that's fairly irrelevant! And I'd say you'd need a *lot* of knowledge to be able to extract KCN from its plant form in any sort of exact dose. In fact I wouldn't even be sure it's possible.'

'Right. Where would I be without you to explain it all to me?'

'You'd read it in a book,' Matty said tranquilly. 'No doubt there's one of the standard tomes on poisons on the CID shelves. Anyway, that's the report you'll be getting on the test results, and the lab's done them nice and quickly for you too. I hope you're duly grateful. Where have you been, by the way, so that that poor man of yours has hardly seen you? Surely not stuck in the station all the time poring over the files?'

'No, I went to France. Work, not pleasure – interviewing a suspect who fairly rapidly stopped being one.' There was even more cause now, Jane thought, to conclude Rowena's innocence: from the sound of things the killer must have been *with* Lionel, on the spot to offer him a carefully measured dose of poison. She was suddenly aware that Matty had asked her something, and came rapidly out of her brown study.

'What? Sorry, I was just brewing a few thoughts . . .'

'I said, "And how was France, when you'd finished with your suspect?" Or isn't it any use asking you a question like that when you're deep in a murder?'

'Don't, I'm not that bad! France was fine. Pretty. Good roads. Great coffee. Splendid food – yes, even me!' Jane said with a chuckle, remembering how when the two of them had shared a flat Matty had always accused her despairingly of not noticing what she ate. 'And what's more I had the company of an extremely dishy French detective all day. Ah – it might be just as well not to mention that one if you're talking to Adrian, though. If the subject should come up I shall probably claim I was escorted by somebody middle-aged and with a strong likeness to an orang-utan!'

'Well, well. Sounds to me as if you might be getting restless, girl . . . We really must manage to meet up so you can tell me all about it!'

'Nothing to tell,' Jane retorted, to the mockery in her friend's voice. 'Dishy was just an aesthetic comment. Oh yes it was, so you needn't choke like that! But I have to say, you could almost write the description "tall, dark and hand-some" round him. However, I'll add that he's as dedicated to his career as I am to mine, and he has a jealous fiancée. So there!'

'Sounds as if you got to know a lot about each other. Like I said, we must— Interruptions, I've got to go. See you!'

Dr Kremer, making the unexpected choice to come in on a Sunday, Jane guessed. Or somebody else high enough up in the hierarchy to make Matty put the phone down promptly and look as if she had been doing something official.

Talking to Matty had made her feel a lot lighter of heart, anyway, and the information she had passed on was more than interesting. Hard facts at last, instead of mere speculation.

Superintendent Annerley called a case meeting for the homicide team just after lunch the following day, to discuss the new forensic evidence which had come in in the morning, and for Jane to give a report on her interview with Rowena Hughes. Only one other piece of information – or non-information – had come in over the weekend: the DI had received a call from Kent Ports Police to say they had had no success in tracking down any driver from Sunday night's trucker shuttle who could recognise either the photofit of Claus Armfeldt or the photograph of Lionel Hughes.

'The stewardess who hands out the pre-packed trays of food wasn't any help either, though she thought she "vaguely" remembered somebody who might fit Claus Armfeldt's description,' the DI finished, adding disgustedly, 'she can't remember whether he was sitting alone or with some body else, though! SB said they're still hoping Armfeldt will turn up at his girlfriend's flat, and have got the local police watching it – but there hasn't been a sign of him so far.'

'Since the lab tests and Inspector Perry's report both tell us the ex-wife wasn't the poisoner, we seem to be left with Armfeldt,' somebody said. 'It looks as if he was the only one with the opportunity, doesn't it?'

'We could draw that conclusion,' the Super agreed. 'The difficulty we have is why. Why cooperate, and then kill – and in that particular manner? If Armfeldt's our man and the poisoning was as pre-planned as it looks, we'd have to assume he was acting under instructions, I think. We'll have to look more closely at that now. Mrs Rowena Hughes does seem to feel very strongly that it could be assassination . . .

97

The next thing to do, clearly, is to approach Mrs Angelica Hughes for any papers her husband may have kept and any notes he may have been making for his memoirs.'

'I'll go and see Angelica as soon as we've finished this meeting,' Chris agreed, adding, 'Kenny, Rachel, I'll take you two with me.'

'Good. I see no reason why she should be uncooperative. Disappointed, perhaps,' Superintendent Annerley added drily, 'but I'm sure you'll manage to tell her conclusively, if tactfully, that we can see no possibility of her predecessor's guilt. You'll have to ask her again if she can think of any more recent enemies her husband may have made, and look for any notes on current articles he was working on, in case there's something there. Very well, then—'

One of the telephones gave an abrupt buzz, cut off as a communications clerk picked up the receiver. She looked to the DI.

'It's Dover police for you, sir.'

Chris moved to take the call after a nod from the Super. Quietly murmured comments had begun to be exchanged between the others when a sudden sharpness in his voice brought everyone's full attention.

'He's where? And he's been there how long? No, sorry, of course I'm not saying it's your fault . . . But you're absolutely sure now that it's Armfeldt? Yes . . .'

For a few moments more he was simply listening. Then he said, with a grim note in his voice. 'Thanks. Thanks for letting me know. Yes it is, isn't it? OK – 'bye.'

He drew a sharp breath as he replaced the receiver on its rest. Then he addressed the room in general.

'A body was fished out of Dover Harbour three days ago. No identification on him, and not very recognisable, since it – he – had been in the water some time. During the weekend they got round to doing an autopsy on him and found he'd died of a heroin overdose rather than drowning. Last night, apparently, it occurred to somebody that the age and build of the corpse might just fit with the description SB had been circulating of a man they wanted to interview, so this morning they got round to informing them. From the state of the body the pathologists think he's been dead for at least a week – but they've managed to lift enough of the prints to show it's Claus Armfeldt.'

There was a moment's silence while everyone took it in.

Then a voice was raised from somewhere and spoke for all of them, in dry acknowledgement.

'That's one confession we're never going to get, then, isn't it!'

Chapter 9

There was a further pause. Then Superintendent Annerley spoke, looking at Chris.

'Conclusions?'

'Off the top of my head, sir? One possibility: Armfeldt did as he was told, was paid in heroin, and overused it. Against that we've been given no indication that he had a habit. So secondly: he committed the murder under orders and was disposed of to make sure he didn't talk. Perhaps also because he panicked and didn't complete the run. In either case we've got him reporting back to someone. But' – he frowned – 'there's a third possibility, and I think we ought to start considering it. That is, that we're looking at two separate events. Armfeldt's death and the immigrant run on the one side, the Hughes murder on the other.'

'You feel we should detach the two cases?'

'We could have been relying too much on there being a connection between them. I know it has seemed like it, and I've believed in it myself. But what if we've been making all the wrong links? It's possible that Hughes met somebody else entirely at Calais. Even with the new forensic evidence we still don't know exactly when he was dumped. It could be a matter of sheer bloody chance that he turned up in the same place! From what we've heard of Armfeldt, it's hard to believe in him as a professional killer; the police report I was given on him was that he was small beer. In addition . . . if somebody wanted Hughes dead, why set it up in that complicated way?'

'Yes, I take your point.' The Super spent a moment in contemplation, frowning. 'We may have been letting ourselves be distracted; after all, stranger things have happened than two separate cases showing up on the same ground.' He thought again, then seemed to come to a decision. 'Very well. Investigation into Armfeldt's death isn't down to us anyway, it's a matter for Dover, along with SB and, I suppose, the Dutch. We must follow our own line of enquiry, and I think you're right, we should detach our minds from connecting the two cases unless anything comes up to counter that. We'd already decided on our next move anyway: an examination of Hughes' papers. So we'll go with that.'

Shortly afterwards he called an end to the meeting and the group began to break up. Jane found herself being beckoned over, and went across to see what the Super had to say to her.

'Your liaison with Inspector Russe should prove useful,' he commented. 'If we're following the line of enquiry suggested by Rowena Hughes, we certainly do need to know whether there were any signs of her ex-husband's being watched during his visits to France.'

'Yes, sir. As I said, Inspector Russe promised to see if he could find out anything on that.'

'Good. We need as much background as we can get, and the sooner the better.'

'I could ring him and ask him to speed his enquiries up—'

'No, I suggest you simply add a polite note when you send him the fax of your interview. Rowena Hughes will need to be seen again, in case there's anything more concrete she can remember from the past . . . but if she's coming to

England soon we may be able to do that here. It all depends on what we find among Hughes' notes.' Annerley looked thoughtful, then gave Jane a smile. 'Aside from gathering what you can from the Dieppe police, which will be ongoing, there seems no reason for me to go on taking you away from your own job.'

'I don't mind, sir—'

'No, but I think Chief Inspector Lowell does, and I can't expect you to clear your calendar when there isn't anything specific for you to do. Keep in touch with any developments we may have, but apart from that, and from passing on whatever Inspector Russe can tell you, it seems only fair to let you go.'

He smiled at her again and walked away. Jane had to accept it. There really was nothing for her to do on the case which required her full-time presence– and even if Lionel's papers did show some murky record involving multinational companies and illicit arms dealing, it would probably mean high-level liaison with Scotland Yard rather than any use for her particular talents. It was dispiriting all the same, just when she had got her teeth into something really absorbing for once. Just when she had been able to start thinking and acting like a detective again ...

She sent off her fax to Hilaire, then decided that since the Super had told her to keep in touch with developments, she could at least put off a return to her own department until tomorrow morning. She was still in the incident room, therefore, going through all the notes made about the case so far, when the DI swept in, looking tight-lipped. Kenny and Rachel trailed in his wake.

'Problems?' Jane asked, looking at the expressions on all three faces.

'You could say that,' Chris said between his teeth. 'You could say we should have been quicker on the ball! The

Super's not in here? I'd better go and report to him upstairs, then.'

He swept out of the room again. 'What happened?' Jane asked Kenny.

'Mrs Hughes seems to have had a break-in, ma'am,' he said deadpan. 'She doesn't know when. Says it could have been yesterday because she went out for the day, or it could have been earlier in the week. Or even the weekend before, since she and the friend who was staying weren't in the house all the time, and she hadn't noticed the scratches on the drawers of her husband's desk anyway. Someone's cleared out his files. And his computer disks. There's sweet fanny adams in there now to show us if he was working on anything from the past!'

'Shit! *Everything*'s gone?'

'All the important stories he'd ever worked on going way back,' Rachel confirmed. 'Angelica says he'd transferred a lot of it on to disk for easier storage, but those have gone, and the files he kept rough notes in, and his cuttings file. Some of it was locked up, some of it was in open drawers. The only thing left was a current file on an article he was working up for his magazine. A sort of philosophical–political piece, not news.'

'Signs of how the thief got into the house?'

'Not that we could see. But then she "doesn't always lock the french windows",' Kenny said, giving it scornful quotation marks. 'You could see where a couple of the desk drawers had been forced, and that wouldn't have taken anyone long, the locks were flimsy enough. But the rest must have been an easy walk-in. Oh, and nothing else was taken. No sign that anyone had even been into any of the other rooms in the house. That's why Angelica hadn't noticed anything: she never went into his study, she says, because he didn't like her disturbing anything. And she didn't want to go in there after he was dead ... It would have been too painful. Besides, she knew his will wasn't in there because it's lodged in the bank,' Kenny added drily. 'So, until we asked, she had no idea she'd had this selective burglar!'

'Jesus. It looks as if the memoirs theory's going to hold water after all. What—'

Jane was interrupted by the rapid return of the DI. 'I've asked for a scene-of-crimes team up there straight away,' he said crisply, adding, 'fat chance they'll find anything at this late stage, but still! Rachel, I want you back up there as Victim Support while the SOCO team's there. I know we left that neighbour with her, but I want you there too, if only to stop her getting in everyone's way. Kenny: I'm aware we've already asked the neighbours if any of them saw anyone hanging about, but once the scene-of-crimes lot's finished, go back and join Rachel at the house, and see if that paternal manner of yours can draw anything more accurate from Angelica about when she might have gone out, how often she forgets to lock the french windows, and so on. Then we can ask the neighbours all over again. Oh, and try Angelica again on any place Lionel might have kept copies of his disks.'

'Right, guv.'

'You've heard what we found?' Chris asked Jane, raising an exasperated eyebrow. 'This far-from-random burglary leads us to the conclusion that we should have started from a different angle from the beginning! All these bloody side-lines we've been following – the ex-wife with the money motive, the damned immigrants—'

'We did have a good case for making a connection with the immigrants. No, all right,' Jane added quickly, to counter the impatient look he was giving her, 'I'm just saying it was a set of reasonable assumptions! By the way, there's a detail in the file which might suddenly look relevant after all. I've just come across it again and it made me wonder. You remember the diamond shape drawn in biro on Lionel's wrist?'

'Yes, I suppose so. At least I remember your raising it when we first had the autopsy report. What about it?' He was still looking impatient.

'It occurred to me, that's all,' Jane said, 'that if we're looking at a hitman – or an organisation which might employ a hitman – the mark could mean something. It could be, oh, a signature – a warning – even something Lionel drew himself when he realised he was in danger, to leave a clue.'

'Sounds a bit far-fetched. Still, you can enter it as a suggestion in the file if you want to. And I suppose you could ask Rowena if it means anything to her, when you see her again. Since she did, I gather, mutter about Triads as well as multinational arms dealers!' He sounded thoroughly grumpy. 'I suppose I'm going to have to set somebody on to looking up all the stories the bloody man ever wrote, in whatever newspapers he ever wrote for! And we've scarcely a hope of finding out what was in one which was spiked twelve years ago. As if I hadn't got enough to do ...'

He departed, frustration showing in every line of him. Jane could sympathise. He had possible leads falling like skittles; he was aware that up to now they seemed to have been running the investigation on quite the wrong lines; and like anyone ambitious he hated failure. He had wanted to make his mark while standing in for the DCI at area meetings, too, Jane could guess. In fact, if Morland ever decided to vacate the post Chris would be in for it like a ferret. He had admitted he could do without a murder case just now; more particularly, he could do without one which looked as if it was turning into a mess.

He probably had Elizabeth still being sick at home, Jane remembered abruptly, and she probably should have asked how she was. But no, not just now; in his shoes she wouldn't have wanted that kind of question in the middle of an investigation.

She still wouldn't mind having his job, she admitted with a sudden sharp honesty. Heavy or not. She had wanted it when he got it, and there was certainly a part of her which still did.

She sighed and pushed the thought away. No point. There *had* been a rumour not long ago that DCI Morland might be in for a sideways push which would take him to area headquarters, into a job which would suit his administrative tastes. The rumour might have been wishful thinking anyway, Jane thought drily. The man was scarcely popular, given his passion for cost-cutting and his habit of playing favourites on every possible occasion. However, even if he did go – and even if Chris moved up a rung – there was no guarantee at all that the changes would get Jane back where she wanted to be. Though this time, she might at least be considered for it ...

It was time for her to go back upstairs to her own office and brighten Chief Inspector Lowell's day with the promise that she would return to assist him in community liaison from tomorrow. She duly did so. It was small use to let her mind be nagged with questions, even if they surfaced persistently.

Why had Lionel's body been left in England but his car in France? If he had really been brought over by somebody else, and there was no connection after all with the immigrant scam ... The theft of Lionel's files had happened in England; somebody had been busy. They had considered, once, that the car might have been taken back to France by the lorry driver – but Claus Armfeldt was dead, here. So, had somebody actually met up with Lionel here in Kent after his return, killed him, then taken his car to France to point pursuit away from England? If so, that meant the murderer was here somewhere and had hoped to throw dust in the police's eyes.

The burglary from Lionel's house might make the Super consider it more urgent for a second interview to be conducted with Rowena, to see if she could elaborate on the facts she had offered about her ex-husband's past. So Jane might be in for a second trip to France after all. However, before any decision on that had been made, the idea was pre-empted. Mid-morning the following day, Communications rang her to say there was a call for her from an Inspector Russe. Jane told them to put it through and gave a greeting in French, to hear Hilaire's voice responding with a touch of relief as if, good English speaker or no, he preferred his own language when it came to the telephone.

''Allo, Jane? Good, I've reached you. I thought you would wish to know straight away that we've had a call from Madame Hughes to say she intends to travel to England tomorrow. It appears they're all leaving; she said the house will be empty until she can let it. She seems to have resolved to move quickly, doesn't she?'

'Yes, she does.' Jane imagined Rowena motivated by angry energy, suborning her entire household into clearing Les Beaux Vents to make it ready for early holidaymakers. She had said quite clearly that she intended to take personal possession of the property she and Lionel had been quarrelling over, to prevent the risk of Angelica getting her hands on it, and must have decided that speed was her safest course. 'Thanks for letting me know,' Jane said, and went on, 'we've had a development here which means we're going to want to ask her a few more questions on that stuff she told us about Lionel's past.' She explained quickly about the missing files. 'If Rowena's going to be taking up residence here, at least she'll be easily available. I . . . don't suppose you've had time yet to look into the other things we discussed? No, sorry, of course you haven't, it's much too soon!'

'Some, in fact – I began making enquiries on Sunday. Oh, and thank you for your fax,' he added, 'but even before I had it, I thought you might like answers as quickly as possible.' That was more obliging than she had dared hope. 'It's only general information, and I haven't found anything so far to suggest strangers have been watching the house when Mr Hughes was there. Generally, however— You'd like this?'

'Yes please.'

'OK. Madame Hughes bought Les Beaux Vents four years ago, with a mortgage from a French bank for about half its value once renovated. She did it up with local workmen. In July last year she asked for a second mortgage, saying she needed a lump sum urgently for further maintenance and repairs, and she was granted it; though it appears from enquiries that she hasn't so far done any extra work on the house. She is well thought of locally; in fact, I had the impression that she's generally liked, and considered very hard-working. Also respectable, there's no adverse gossip about her. When she first moved in she had a daughter living with her, her eldest child I believe, and her twin sons would visit from time to time for holidays. The boys were, I think, at school in England so it was only during the vacations. After about a year the daughter returned to the UK where she has since married. You want all this?'

'I may as well, and you seem to have been very thorough.'

'Tradespeople talk quite readily. Let's see what else came up . . . Oh yes, Chantal Mentiment. She's the daughter of a *notaire* from Aumale, and Madame Hughes took her in a year ago, with her baby, officially to help out in the house but in fact it would seem out of friendship for the girl. Chantal has no police record. For your interest,' he added, 'she has started describing herself recently as Joshua's girl-friend. In fact, it's seen as a charming romance ... though whether Mrs Hughes approves, my informant was not quite sure!'

'Befriending's one thing, having your son romantically involved is another? Or maybe she thinks it's Chantal who's introduced him to the wrong people in the local youth culture. Anything to be had on Lionel's visits?'

'Merely local gossip so far. He's known to be Madame Hughes' ex-husband, and it's no secret that he stays regularly. This didn't happen at first, only during the last eight or nine months, and recently he has been arriving with great regularity. Approximately at three-week intervals. It's felt there was still an affection between him and Madame and that he was, so to speak, part of the family. It was he who brought Joshua to live with his mother four months ago – because the boy had been ill, they say.'

'I thought Rowena told us Josh had been there a year ... Never mind, it's beside the point.'

'Four months was certainly what was said to me. Rowena tells people that he was at college, and doing well, before he became ill. He looked it when he arrived, too, they say.' Hilaire paused in his account, then went on, 'I don't know if it's particularly relevant to Mr Hughes, but Malcolm Jackson came to live at Les Beaux Vents at the same time as Joshua. There's an impression that he is ... I don't know, not quite a nurse; a companion for Joshua?'

'A minder?'

'Not quite so definite, perhaps. He also does jobs – casual stuff, as we were told – which take him away from time to time. He hasn't applied for a permit but in the circumstances I'm letting that pass. Nobody knows him very well, he's inclined to be uncommunicative, but locally he's accepted as somebody Madame Hughes has taken into her household. There would seem to be little connection between him and Mr Hughes, apart from being on normal speaking terms. The idea that he was there because of Joshua was just a hint, but I thought I'd pass it on.'

'Thanks.' She would run a PNC check on Joshua Connolly, Jane thought, to see if he had been in any serious trouble over drugs. It sounded as if he might have been: brought suddenly to live with his mother instead of staying on at college; someone who might be an unofficial minder arriving too, perhaps to keep an eye on him? It might merely be local gossip, but there was enough to make it worth checking, if they were about to have Joshua on their doorstep. Hilaire's mind must have been travelling along the same lines, since he said:

'I only include this as Joshua will be on your patch rather than ours from tomorrow. I haven't yet looked into the drugs side, merely put out a few feelers. If his past includes something more serious than cannabis . . .'

'Yes, I'll check up on it. Apart from anything else, it might mean Lionel had been investigating drugs dealers – which would give us another line to follow.'

She told him the news about Claus Armfeldt, and that they were abandoning the connection between Lionel and the immigrant smuggling – at least for now. He promised to go on investigating the possibility that Lionel's visits to Les Beaux Vents had been the subject of outside observation, and they chatted generally for a few more minutes. Before he rang off, he made a point of expressing regret that she would not be returning to France to interview Rowena again. Perhaps there would be some other occasion . . . He sounded more than merely formally polite, and Jane, agreeing that she hoped so, found herself smiling as she put down the receiver.

111

Well, it was nice to be appreciated. And by someone with whom she could share her absorption in the case rather than having to avoid— She shut down on the thought quickly and concentrated on writing up what Hilaire had told her, then went to ask Geoff Madox to run a check on Joshua Connolly.

It came up blank; there was no record that Josh had been charged with any drug offences, either recently or in the past. They were drawing blanks on who might have burgled the Hughes' house, too, she heard. Two days later she also learned – with a touch of annoyance – that the DI had already been to conduct the second interview with Rowena. Lionel's former wife was now ensconced at number nineteen Willowfield Way, a large detached house in one of the better areas of the city. Jane had hoped to be asked to do the follow-up herself, and was in an involuntary brood about it as she reached into her kitchen cupboard that evening for a couple of coffee mugs. She found, abruptly, that Adrian had come up behind her to slide his arms round her waist.

'Talk to me!'

'What? Oh, sorry – I just got distracted, that's all.'

'Yes, I know, you've just done the washing-up without seeing it. How many miles away were you?'

'Not that many. You know Lionel Hughes got murdered? That friend of Harry's? I was just thinking about his ex-wife. She's the one I had to go and interview in France, but she's back in the city now. I'm not surprised they were fighting about ownership of the house,' Jane added. 'It's one of those Willowfield Way ones and it's probably worth a bomb!'

'If you could sell it on today's market. What's it got, six or seven bedrooms?'

'Must have. She told me there were students in it and that she wasn't going to have Angelica – Lionel's widow – evicting them and taking it over. I suppose she must have

112

evicted them herself, though.' Unless she had allowed some of them to stay, packed into the attics. 'Anyway, Chris went to see her today, to see if she could offer any further ideas on who might have killed Lionel. He didn't get anything, apparently. Which is a pity, because—'

'Oh, I see. Work, rather than houses. You aren't really involved in that side of it any more, so why bring it home with you? Have you . . . thought any more about what I said?'

'Move, there's a dear, or I'll spill this coffee.' Jane turned round to hand him a mug as he did so. She looked at him and decided not to pretend not to know what he was talking about. 'Yes, OK, I did think about it. And I decided, let's wait a couple of years. Fair enough?'

'A couple of years? Why?'

'Because I do have a career. And taking a break from it might only look like taking a break to you, but from where I stand it would certainly put the kibosh on—'

'So does Elizabeth have a career. One she's very good at. It doesn't stop her having other priorities.'

'Oh have a heart, Adrian. You can probably be a micro-biologist with a baby in a Moses basket under the desk! Which you *definitely* can't do in the police!' Jane caught at the rags of her temper and strove to keep her voice light and reasonable. So it *was* Elizabeth Hollings' pregnancy which had set him off. 'They've been planning theirs for ages, anyway. Chris said so. And I'm very glad for them – but having children's hardly a competitive matter!'

'*What*? Oh, for heaven's sake, Jane, what an idiotic accusation!'

'All right, I take it back. And I don't want to quarrel. It's just that I think I'm being perfectly reasonable. So why don't you?'

'I would if I didn't think there was an undertone in your voice of "if you don't like it you can lump it!" '

113

'That's unfair...' But they were going to quarrel; she could see it from the set of his mouth. Her temper was one which blew up quickly, his was slower, but when they both hit the same moment the results could be bruising. However, if he wanted a row she might as well put all her cards on the table. 'We don't really know yet if we've got a permanent enough relationship to bring a child into, do we? In the beginning you didn't seem to mind my job; nowadays, if anything to do with crime comes into it, rather than boring conferences, you'll change the subject if I mention it. But it's what I do – what I am! I'm sorry if what you wanted was a straightforward little homemaker, because – because, if it is, that's not me. And I have to wonder, if that was the idea you had in mind, what the hell were you doing choosing me in the first place?'

'You really have been thinking about it, haven't you? I suppose it's no use saying, what about love?'

'Love isn't all of it... Love's a gift, anyway. It isn't about changing people into what you want them to be. It's about... oh, I don't know, sixty-four thousand other things! But one of them, surely, is accepting that the other person has a valid point of view, and an identity, and a life! But if you can't even take it when I want to say, let's wait and see...'

She left the words hanging in the air between them, sinkingly aware that they sounded far too much like an ultimatum. And that, from his expression, he was ready to take it as such.

Chapter 10

'Oh, we're still together. I thought at one point he was going to walk out, but he didn't. We made it up.' Jane looked across the lunch table at Matty and sighed moodily. Her friend was looking extremely smart in a bright orange suit: the sharp colour might have overwhelmed some people, but on Matty it complemented her chocolate skin and scalp-hugging black hair to render her even more striking. 'Well, never mind. I'm sorry to vent it on you, and just when we've managed to meet up at last – but I have, so now let's forget it and go back to what you asked me right at the beginning. No, I can't see any reason why I shouldn't be free to come round the boutiques with you on Saturday and help you look for something suitably formal to wear for this opera-fest. Considering you've known about it for weeks, you're leaving it a bit late, aren't you? Easter Saturday's only a week after that! But if you really think you need a second opinion, I'll come along and give you one.'

Ten days had passed, and investigations into Lionel Hughes' murder seemed to have reached stalemate. Rowena had been able to offer no extra information. The burglary inquiry had still come up with nothing but blanks. By now the whole homicide team had been forced to return to other duties, the murder no more than an open file in the background. Superintendent Annerley had picked up on Jane's suggestion that the blue diamond drawn on Lionel's wrist might mean something, and both Angelica and Rowena had been asked about it, with no result; the Super had therefore decreed, given the lack of any other lead, that a note of the mark should be put in the *Police Gazette*, asking if anyone had come across the same thing or had any idea as to its meaning. Hilaire had rung again from France but only to confirm that he could catch no whisper of any stranger observing Lionel's visits. If there was a professional assassin, it was one who had been careful.

There was certainly no more for Jane to do on a case which was at a standstill. She gave another sigh, stretched, and tried to appear cheerful. Matty, she saw, was giving her a considering look.

'Do you want a second opinion on Adrian?'

'I'm not sure. Do I? Not if you're going to bring up my dishy French detective again!'

'All right, leave him out of it. I was only going to say, in all the time I've known you – God, how many years *is* that by now?'

'More than we care to mention? All right, what are you going to come up with?'

'Just that you have always fallen for conventional men. Oh yes you have, I've got a good memory and I could name a few! Unlike me, who would only look twice at the wild ones,' Matty added with a grin.

'Leaving all the others languishing by the wayside,' Jane retorted. 'Poor pining souls. Go on, then, what's your point? Are you telling me I make my bed so I should lie on it?'

'No, I'm just saying that you pick 'em, then you run slap bang into the fact that they *are* conventional, and for some reason you're surprised! Think about it. Yeah, I know,' Matty added, pulling a face, 'I crash into the walls from time to time, but at least I know I'm doing it! Whereas you – well, if your fancy ever did light on somebody who wasn't straight

116

and suitable, you'd block it off and fall into the arms of a serious type instead. Go on, try telling me *that* isn't true!'

'I could say, fat chance I've got of running wild with a police career to think of. But then according to your character analysis, I'm only ever going to fall for someone who wants me to give it up, aren't I? Oh great, I'm always going to be faced with "either or"!' Jane deliberately kept her voice light. 'Thanks a bunch, Dr Freud, and let's change the subject. Away from my character and on to yours. Since you claim to know yourself so well ... I'll lay you a bet that you want to pick a new dress for the opera gala because you intend to be done up to kill. Despite Shakti—'

'Who's fading fast, actually, but never mind that.'

'All right, then, despite the fact that it's your stated intention to dislike the American baritone on sight!'

'I can hardly go dressed in rags,' Matty pointed out sweetly.

'No, but that's not the point, is it? The point is that you actually intend to wind the poor guy round your finger and then wave him a casual goodbye. Serve you right if you find he's just your type after all, and you're the one to fall!'

Matty accepted the teasing reproof with good grace, merely saying silkily, 'Yes, wouldn't it? Perhaps after all I'd better be good, and go dressed as an Ugly Sister!'

That highly unlikely vision set them both laughing, and allowed a slide into different subjects. When they parted a little later, they had kept satisfactorily off the subject of men for the rest of the conversation. She and Matty, Jane thought, had a shared history which led to ease, small pinpricks about each other's character notwithstanding. Old friendships allowed for that.

And Matty was probably right, she thought ruefully.

Walking into the station brooding gloomily that she was, clearly, as hopeless at self-knowledge as she was at relationships, Jane's mood was not improved by running into DCI

Morland, back from leave for the past two days. She gave him her usual sweet smile in response to his habitual disapproving glare, said 'Good afternoon, sir!' with meticulous politeness, and decided as she walked on that he did at least provide a counter to any desire on her part to be back in CID.

She took that with her as a small consolation as she dutifully went off for her stint on overseeing the Crime Bus, currently parked at one end of the city's main shopping precinct. It was attracting no more than the usual casual interest, and occasional grumble. Jane was just resticking a poster which had blown free in the spring wind when a tall figure caught her eye.

Josh Connolly. He came wandering by, saw her, hesitated, pushed a nervous hand through his dark-brown hair, then gave her a sudden and remarkably sweet smile. He was still pale but not, Jane thought drily, stoned this time. She could also see that he wasn't sure why he knew her face, so she said pleasantly, 'It's Josh, isn't it? I called on your mother in France.'

'Oh, that's where ... Are you part of this?' He waved a hand towards the bus, seeming vaguely surprised that she should be. She was out of uniform, but then she had been last time he met her too.

'Yes, I'm Inspector Perry. Do you want to come in and look round?' she invited.

'No thanks, I'm pretty sure I wouldn't make a cop.' He gave an odd little shiver. Before she could tell him that the bus was intended for information rather than recruiting, he went on, in the voice of one who really wanted to know, 'Have you found out who killed my stepfather yet?'

'I'm afraid not. But it's bound to come to light eventually,' she told him, seeing his troubled face.

'Will it? Mum's very upset about it. We all are. Even me,

and I'm the difficult twin.' He said that with a sudden bitter twist to his mouth. 'But then people do die, don't they? It doesn't have to be a jinx.'

He walked away with an abruptness which left Jane blinking. Strange boy. Maybe, she thought drily, he had taken too much of something and it had frazzled his brain. Surprisingly, however, she was aware that she found him oddly likeable . . .

'Did I glimpse from a distance that you were having scant success with the city's youth?' a voice enquired, and she turned her head to see that Harry Morpeth had stopped beside her. Before she could respond she saw the mocking grin fade from his mouth and the light-blue eyes sharpen. 'Wait a minute, though – wasn't that the Connolly boy? Li's stepson? I'd swear it was, the old boy had a photo of him. I wonder if I can—'

'I wouldn't, Harry,' Jane said. She was glad to find that the steely note in her voice disconcerted him enough to stop him from setting out in pursuit. 'I doubt if Josh particularly wants a chat with a total stranger about his stepfather's death – and didn't I hear you describe yourself the other day as being in Angelica's camp?'

'Oh, did I? I could do with an introduction to Rowena, though, now she's back in this country. If you don't feel it would be the acme of tact to ask the boy, how about you getting me one?' He gave her one of his wheedling smiles, turning to reproach as she shook her head. She moved away from him towards the bus, to give a clear indication that she was too busy for conversation. Annoyingly, he came after her into the empty interior with its display of posters and leaflets. 'Oh come on, Jane,' he coaxed, 'poor old Li's murder is the most interesting thing to happen since I came to live here. Give a poor starving author a break! Li would never tell me what goodies he'd got tucked away from his past – or only the odd hint and a tap on the nose, you know the kind of thing! – and I have to say, I always thought the old boy was just trying to build up his own importance. But now it does look as if there might have been something, what with his papers disappearing like that.'

'And where did you get that from? It's not a fact that's been released to the public.'

'Angie, of course. Now, she *is* informative to sympathetic friends. In between railing on about "that woman" taking over *her* house,' Harry said with a grin. 'So I can't help feeling I'd like to meet the siren in person – out of interest, as well as to see if I can pump a few facts out of her.' He was so unrepentantly thick-skinned that Jane could have slapped him. 'Anyway,' he added, giving her a smug look, 'some of your lot came round to see if Li had lodged any copies of his computer disks with me. I couldn't help, though. Too bad, isn't it?'

'Yes, too bad.' She should have guessed that Angelica might have provided his name as one of Lionel's intimates.

'I could always try just dropping in, I suppose. On Rowena. Offering my sympathy. Maybe I could try . . . oh, suggesting that boy of hers could do some research for me. He must know quite a bit about the drugs scene, after all.' He was watching for her reactions, and must have seen something in her face which made him adopt a look of innocence as he added quickly, 'From the distant past. I wouldn't dream of getting the lad into trouble with your lot *now*! But I do seem to remember Li telling me some story about Joshua getting mixed up with amphetamines in his teens, and one of his friends dying of it, but Joshua and the others got off with a caution rather than being charged – you don't know about that?'

'If he wasn't charged, why would I?' Jane said repressively, to his innocently enquiring expression. Josh's odd, abrupt remark was explained now, perhaps; a ghost from the past. A couple of people got on the bus, giving her the opportunity to switch to her official persona. She said sweetly to Harry, 'Do stay and look through any leaflets you may find interesting!' as she turned away.

Fortunately he appeared not to want to take her up on the offer, and departed with an airy wave. By the time she packed up and went back to the station, she had managed to forget him – save for a brief reflection that at least his liking for gossip had offered her some information on Josh. Maybe the boy's problems *were* all in the past; maybe he really had had glandular fever, and the idea that Malcolm was his minder was nonsense. She found herself hoping so.

She had things to sort out in her office before she went home. However, she had barely reached it before her internal phone buzzed, and she found herself talking to the Super's secretary.

'Inspector Perry? Superintendent Annerley would like to see you in his office straight away, if you can manage that.'

It was an order rather than a question. Jane walked swiftly along the corridor, knocked, and was summoned inside. The Super had somebody with him, she saw; a big man in a baggy suit who lumbered to his feet on Jane's arrival and stood looking at her assessingly. He was in his sixties, with iron-grey hair slicked straight back, a heavily lined face, and small, intelligent, very dark eyes. Jane would also have laid a considerable bet that he was, or had once been, a policeman.

'This is Inspector Perry,' the Super told his visitor. 'Jane, this is Detective Superintendent Rogalleh from the West Midlands.'

Still currently on the force, then. He had stepped forward to offer her his hand, saying humorously, 'You won't know how to spell it, so I may as well start by doing it for you:

121

R – O – G – A – L – L – E – H.   And   if   that   sounds foreign, it's not; I'm Birmingham born and bred!'

She could have guessed that from the heavy Midland accent. She accepted his hand, which was broad and firm, and said, 'How do you do, sir.'

'And you're the one who raised the point of the diamond mark, I'm told,' he commented, his eyes still assessing her. 'I've seen the photo your people took of it, but I'll want to see it on the body as well. Your superintendent's been kind enough to suggest that you look after me while I'm here.'

So the advertisement in the *Police Gazette* had brought a response. A rapid one, too, with the current issue only just out. Jane looked from Rogalleh to Annerley, suddenly aware that the latter's expression was at its most deadpan. And when he looked as blank as that . . . She said, 'Certainly, sir,' and waited to see if she was going to be told any more. Apparently yes, since Superintendent Annerley waved her to a chair. Once she was seated, and Rogalleh had settled heavily back into his place, the Super spoke.

'Inspector Perry has been working on the case, so she knows as much about it as anyone. But before we go any further I'd like to make sure she understands that anything said in this room now is confidential. I don't feel that any of my other officers – or anyone else at all – should be informed of anything at the moment. Jane?'

'Yes, of course, sir; anything I hear is confidential.'

He accepted her assurance with a nod. He was genuinely worried by this one, Jane thought. It showed in his voice, though his face was still inexpressive as he added, 'There's really no point in starting hares until we're sure!'

His words made the detective superintendent from the Midlands give a shrug – though the jut of his lip suggested he was already sure. However, Rogalleh said only, 'Do you want to give her the background, or shall I? She'll need to be properly filled in to my mind if she's going to take me around and understand the questions I'm likely to ask her!'

'I agree. You, I think, please.'

'Well then, Jane.' Rogalleh used the informality of her first name without question, fixing her in a friendly fashion with those intelligent dark eyes. 'Ever read about any crimes committed in the West Midlands six years ago? I don't suppose so, though if you had you might remember. Several murders, and the press was having a field day with them by the end of it.'

'No, sir, not that I recall . . .' She had been in the Met then, and still finding her feet. 'I don't think so,' she said apologetically.

'Well, I've got a file left open, since it's one I never solved. I'm hoping you'll be able to help me close it.' There was a grim look on the heavily lined face, a distaste for something left unfinished. No, more than distaste. 'It began seven years ago, and it was six years ago when it . . . ended. We had a series of murders. Seven of them in all. All men. All of them killed in different ways. Nothing to connect them – or not the first three – but after that the murderer started leaving us a signature. He let us know that he did the first three, too. Started playing his killings like a game; him against the police. And I expect you're with me by now: the signature he used was to mark his victims with a blue diamond. That was never publicised, since we didn't want any copycatting.' He drew a breath, his eyes brooding. 'He was a clever one. And a risk-taker, too; once or twice he let a witness see him leaving the scene. Only a glimpse, but done deliberately. He phoned me to say so. More than one call I had from him. But we never got him. A year it went on. Then it stopped. No more killings, no more messages.' He looked up at Jane, a beetling look under dark brows. 'You know the definition of a serial killer, do you?'

'The standard FBI one? Yes, sir. Murderers who are involved in three or more separate events, with an emotional cooling-off period between each homicide. It's the cooling-off period which distinguishes the serial killer from other varieties, and they usually target a type of victim rather than individuals. And there's usually a desire for publicity,' Jane added, searching her mind for anything she might have left out.

'Yes, you've got it pat. And ours was by the book. Six weeks we had between each murder – almost to the day.' Rogalleh shifted a little, a movement of the heavy shoulders. Then he said grimly, 'They don't usually stop; it's out of character. I always felt he'd be back. I've waited for it. And now – well, even if he's taken a six-*year* cooling-off period this time, if that blue diamond drawn on your corpse doesn't mean what I think it means, I'm a monkey! I don't care what other theories you've been working on. It's the same thing over again: a male corpse, and old enough to be an authority figure; killed and dumped in a public place – and when they weren't public, they were somewhere where they were meant to be found, with no attempt to bury the body or otherwise conceal it; and that signature. He's back. Not on my patch this time. But something's started him off again, and he's back, and up to his old tricks.'

Chapter 11

They had become known as 'the Betty killings', after a journalist had found out that the police had had a muffled telephone call claiming the murders, knowing too many details about them, and offering the identity 'Blue Betty'. The 'Blue' had got dropped, the police all too willing for it to be so when it was connected to the signature they wanted to avoid publicising. The press had made great play with the idea that the killer was a woman, suggesting that it could be a prostitute murdering men in revenge for the Yorkshire Ripper case. Expert psychological profiling, however, had insisted otherwise. The posited killer was definitely male, white, educated, youngish, fit and active; possibly a transvestite, due to the name offered and a witness sighting of someone in a long skirt and a headscarf; not, however, a transsexual, nor a homosexual. He was classified as the Organised Non-Social Type, which meant that he was likely to be intelligent, in work, and a car-owner; he would be methodical, but secretly hostile to society generally, with a desire to get even. Classically, according to one of the psychologists, his state of mind would be called 'malignant narcissism', killing for self-esteem, needing to reassure himself that he was more intelligent and more valuable than those around him.

Jane learned some of this during the next few minutes, more during the hours she spent in Detective Superintendent

Rogalleh's company both that evening and the next day. That evening, he asked her to take him to the morgue. Used as she was to viewing dead bodies, it was still strange to inspect one she had known, however briefly, in private life; to look at Lionel Hughes' still and waxen face with the memory of him talking loudly and with sarcastic animation in a pub. Rogalleh lifted the wrist to study the mark drawn on it. After several moments he returned the arm to its place, signed to the morgue attendant that he had finished, but spoke no word until he and Jane re-emerged into the evening's soft rain.

'That's him.' He glanced at Jane and bent his head absently to let the umbrella she had opened cover him. His face was a shadow-pattern of deep lines. 'The last time I saw that, it was drawn on an ankle. Just above the top of the sock. And the ankle belonged to my DI.' His voice was quiet but grim. 'Yes, the last killing was one of us – one of my team. Jimmy Kenton.'

'I'm – I'm sorry to hear that, sir.'

'I'm not likely to forget it. My responsibility. He was found on a piece of waste ground with a knife between his ribs – straight up into the heart, he'd have had no chance to defend himself. It was late at night, his wife said he had a call offering information on a burglary that was going down. He should have had more sense.' The soft voice with its heavy Midlands accent held no inflexion. 'Next morning I had a note in the post – standard computer type, no prints – saying, "How do you like that, Rogalleh?" No blue diamond on it, he saved that for the bodies, but I knew who it was from all right. It was me he was showing off to by that time: him against me.'

Jane could feel the chill in it; colder even than the air in the morgue, and she had to hold back a shiver. Before she could speak Rogalleh had given his big shoulders a shake

126

and came back out of the past, looking down at her.

'Well, young lady, can you find me a small hotel for the night? I won't take up any more of your time after that. We'll go on with this tomorrow. But I'll get him this time. It's taken a while, nearly up to my retirement, but even if it had taken longer than that . . . No, this time, I'll have him.'

It was personal, and he wanted her to know it, Jane thought. This time, whatever it took . . . She drove him to a suitable hotel; he was without a car, having come down by train. Then she went home, her mind sobered and icy with implications.

She found Adrian asking her with careful and unquarrelsome sympathy what had made her late, so that she responded with equal care that she was sorry she hadn't been able to let him know, there had been no chance, after she had suddenly been asked to act as escort to a visiting senior officer. It was all part of liaison work. Then she remembered that it was tomorrow that the veterinary practice merger would finally go through; no change of premises, but a larger partnership allowing the two previously separate practices to work in concert. That made an easy subject to switch to, to show she was taking an interest, and she took deliberate care not to seem abstracted or unduly quiet. It was ironic that just when Adrian was trying to show that he was sympathetic to her career by trying to draw answers from her about her day, she couldn't talk about it. It was hard to make love, too, with the consciousness of something much darker and colder . . . Was Rogalleh right? He seemed absolutely sure of it. But the can of worms *that* opened up . . .

She arrived at the station in the morning to find that Rogalleh had taken over her office. He was ensconced behind her desk which was covered with papers: everything concerning the Hughes case, Jane could guess, seeing files, handwritten notes, computer printouts. He had been here some time, evidently, from the thin brown cigarette stubs visible in an ashtray, and a fug in the air. As Jane hesitated in the doorway he beckoned her in.

'I'm not aiming to drive you out, it's just that I need to be somewhere more private than your incident room while we're keeping this under wraps. We can both fit in. And there're details I want to ask you about, too ... Something the matter?'

'Nothing, sir. But would you mind if I opened the window?'

'Ah. I'd say "don't tell the wife" except that you're not likely to meet her all these miles away. I'm supposed to have given up, but I can't concentrate sucking pencils! Yes, go on, let some air in.' It was clearly the most she was going to get by way of apology. In fact he added irascibly, 'And don't pretend to cough, either – I've got a secretary who does that if I so much as put my hand in my pocket, *and* she hides the ashtrays! Sit down. Now then.'

He quizzed her on everything she knew about Lionel Hughes, every additional detail, however small, which might not have got into the files. Then he told her more about the offender profiles the West Midlands force had been offered seven years ago. There had been more than one. The force had been grasping for any help they could get, so a second criminal psychologist had been drawn in for another assessment. That one had held the view that Blue Betty really wanted to be caught and stopped – but that was an opinion Rogalleh rejected.

'He's not some namby-pamby wanting Daddy to sort his life out for him,' he said grimly. 'No, he's a bad bastard. He kills for fun, he enjoys it! He's a stalker, he watches his prey, plans everything ... Does that sound to you like someone "transferring self-hate" and all that rubbish? We had all that from the second psychologist. That one had a theory for why the killings stopped, too; said the perpetrator had probably committed suicide since by his conclusions it was "what he had wanted all along". No, I don't go along with that. I don't know why he stopped – unless it was just that once he'd killed Jimmy he knew we'd have a net round the city so tight that he wouldn't get away with *anything* – but suicide? No! I've never believed it, and now I'm proved right!'

'There was nothing sexual in any of the killings?' Jane asked thoughtfully.

'No, that was one you could rule out. The press made a lot of play with it, but one thing both the boffins seemed sure of was that our killer wasn't homosexual. No evidence that any of his victims had inclinations that way either. "Authority figures" – that's what we were given. All the men he killed were forty and upwards, no connection between them, but all of them had some kind of . . . I don't know, one of the early ones was no more than a school caretaker, but I suppose that could count as an authority figure on his own ground! It was always males, that was the only thing you could thoroughly count on.' He gave Jane a broodingly frustrated look. She could guess what he was thinking. That all the profiles in the world had not caught his killer for him. That he might have been over-reliant on outside experts and been led in the wrong direction. However, he pulled himself abruptly out of it and went on with a new briskness, laying one large hand on the papers spread out across the desk. 'We've got all this for technology to cross-check for us now. It'll need to be put in with the rest of the Blue Betty stuff on the HOLMES database. I must talk to your superintendent about that!'

It had always struck Jane that whoever had invented HOLMES as a name – even if it was a genuine acronym for Home Office Large Major Enquiry System – must have had a sense of humour.

Rogalleh was obviously one of those senior officers who had attended the Bramshill course on the management of serious and serial crimes, since he was clearly prepared to use anything modern technology – and modern thinking – could offer him. He gave Jane a considering look, then said, 'All right, you've heard what we think we know about Blue Betty, and you've been working on the case here. It's the officers on the ground who see the evidence, and process it inside their heads as much as any machine does. So what do *you* think about it?'

That was a challenge. Jane frowned. She had to go along with the idea that they were facing the same killer; Rogalleh seemed completely sure, even after all this time. 'You say Blue Betty plans things, sir,' she said slowly. 'So he doesn't do anything randomly . . . Unless he's changed, in the years in between. So if he'd decided Lionel Hughes was the person he was going to kill, would he – would he have used something to lure him with? Like the immigrant smuggling, for instance? We'd abandoned the idea and started treating the two things as quite separate, but—'

'I've been pondering that, though I can think of a couple of objections. In one sense it'd be like him; he used to enjoy working out elaborate scenarios from time to time. There was one I remember which he'd obviously planned in detail . . . I won't go into all of it, but we found the victim in the house of some people who'd gone on holiday, trussed up in the bedroom in such a way that the more he moved his head, the more he strangled himself. And he was surrounded by mirrors. Made to look like a death-by-accident during sexual experimentation; that is, until you saw that there were blue diamonds cut out of sticky paper on every fingernail.' Rogalleh brooded on the past for a second, his eyes distant. Then he came back to the present. 'He *might* have found out there was some immigrant smuggling going

130

on, because he's a clever bastard, as I said. Letting the immigrants loose would amuse him too, to cause maximum confusion and provide a distraction for the police to play with! But on the other hand, he always gave every sign of being a loner. And for this he'd have had to have worked with someone else. The dead lad, Claus Armfeldt. I'm not against the idea that if he'd used him, he'd do him in afterwards – and not mark him necessarily, either, since it would just be on the side. But not work alone? That doesn't fit. Unless he's changed. Is that what that look on your face is trying to say?'

'No, not that. I was just wondering...' Jane frowned. 'Looking at what your second psychologist said, couldn't it be possible that Claus Armfeldt actually *was* Blue Betty?' She went on quickly, 'Suppose he was living in Birmingham seven years ago; he'd have been student age then. Maybe you lost him because he went back home. That would explain the gap – particularly if there've been murders in the Netherlands; that would need checking up on. But then this time after he'd killed he did finally commit suicide? It is always possible that he was rolled for what was in his pockets afterwards and thrown in the water.'

'No,' Rogalleh said flatly, an echo of the denial Jane had already seen in his face. She thought he was almost angry. 'No, I don't go along with that! I said before, Blue Betty's an evil bastard, not a mixed-up one; I've never believed he'd kill himself. Oh, we can prove I'm right by looking into Armfeldt's background – and no doubt we'll have to get that done, waste of time though it'll be – but he's not our man. *He*'s still out there somewhere! And I'll tell you the way I think this one happened. Hughes set out from his ex-wife's home at two, right? So to my mind he caught that train through the tunnel a lot earlier than nine thirty, the time you've said the immigrant lorry was loaded. I think he met somebody this side, in Kent. Somebody who'd watched him, knew his regular movements, knew when he was likely to arrive. You've a note here that his ex-wife said he always left at the same time. I don't know where he and Blue Betty spent the hours in between, but at some point he was killed, then dumped, then his car was taken back to France to throw us off the scent and Blue Betty came back innocently as a foot passenger on a ferry. That's the way I see it.'

'Did he – did you always calculate before that he left his victims on his own ground?'

'I did. There were other theories on it. But to my mind he was there, somewhere, within a radius – because he watched what *we* were doing too. So I don't think he'll have changed out of his pattern.'

It seemed to Jane that he might have, after six years. Rogalleh was the expert, however, as well as being her senior officer by a long way. She wondered again, with a flicker of doubt, whether he was too determined to believe Blue Betty was here, re-found at last, under his hand; whether the case had grown into an obsession. It would be understandable . . . She said, neutrally, 'I wonder why he's waited six years this time to kill again? If there haven't been any cases that you've heard of anywhere else—'

'It's not important – only that something's set him off again. And I can make a guess on what that something might be. Remember those stolen files – the victim was a newspaperman. And the same type as the other victims: an older man, and a bad-tempered and bossy one by all accounts. But it seems to me,' Rogalleh said on a sudden note of satisfaction, 'that he may have made a mistake at last. Before, he was operating in a big city – Birmingham. Plenty of chances to observe people anonymously, study them, follow them around unseen. Here – well, it's a small city, isn't it, with countryside all around. The kind of place where people know each other, look at each other. So it's going to be more of a risk choosing somebody here. Why would he need to take that risk?'

'You said he liked—'

'Forget that, I said *need*. And need to get hold of all the victim's disks and notes and cuttings, too. I think your newspaperman may have written a story about the Betty killings at some time. And it's come up in conversation with someone he's met. Maybe just casually, but enough to be an annoyance. Perhaps, even, enough to give the suspicion that there was something in the notes which led a little too close to home. So what I want to do next—'

The sound of voices outside in the corridor made him break off and look up with a frown. Jane could hear that one of them was Chief Inspector Lowell's, protesting with a touch of querulousness.

'But if you take her away all the time, and without giving me any warning—'

What came next was lost in somebody giving him a softer answer, but then the Super's voice sounded more clearly, obviously very close outside the door, and speaking pacifically.

'I do see, Charles, and I apologise, but I'm afraid for today it's necessary. Bear with me, would you?'

'Oh, very well, but I would like to make the point that my department does have its importance!'

It could be guessed from the receding voice that CI Lowell was walking away in a huff. Almost immediately there was a light knock on the door, which opened to reveal Superintendent Annerley. His brows twitched into a frown, though whether it was the sight of Rogalleh seated at the desk with papers spread out in front of him, or the wafts of cigarette smoke which caused his tight-lipped expression, it was difficult to tell.

'Ah, you're here . . .'

'Been here for hours,' Rogalleh rumbled. 'No point in not starting early! I told them downstairs where I'd be, in fact it was one of your constables who showed me where I'd find Inspector Perry's room, since that was what I asked for. Didn't they pass it on?'

'Perhaps we could have a word?'

The way the Super stood back made it clear that the word was to be private, and in his office. Rogalleh lumbered to his feet, looked wryly at the fresh cigarette he had just lit, and stubbed it out before he moved to accede to the request. Then the two men were gone.

Having observed the way the Super's eyes had lingered on the papers on the desk, Jane made a guess that he had taken the other superintendent away to voice objections – in the politest possible terms – to Rogalleh's raid on the case files, on the grounds that it would cause gossip when confidentiality was the order of the day. However, there was certainly no way she could have told a detective super-intendent that he should have waited, or behaved more tactfully.

It was clear from the words spoken outside her door that for today she was still to act as Rogalleh's escort. While the two men had their private talk, she might as well tidy up in here. She stacked the papers on the desk into neatness, opened both windows wide to try to rid the room of smoke, and wrinkled her nose as she picked up the ashtray. The contents of that could definitely go into the closed bin in the toilet rather than her open waste-paper basket. Even if, she thought with resignation, it was all too likely that Rogalleh would fill the ashtray up again on his return.

The office seemed quiet without his garrulity. He had given her plenty to think about, however. Not least the question which had been haunting her ever since last night.

Rogalleh had talked of Blue Betty being 'up to his old tricks'. And wasn't it characteristic of serial killers . . . Jane sought round in her mind for the details of any articles she might have studied on the subject. Yes, murder was thought to act as a trauma reinforcement, leading to more murder. Trauma started in childhood and led to dissociation, which then led to fantasy; the fantasies became more violent, more concentrated on power over others; that led to acting out, often mild at first but growing more violent in its turn. Then an actual killing, the ultimate demonstration of power. But the satisfaction didn't last, fantasies restarted, the whole sick cycle began again. And yet, Jane remembered, less than two per cent of serial killers had been assessed as being insane. That seemed mad in itself, considering that some authorities claimed a genetic predisposition. Others, however, countered that it was cultural . . .

Either way, did it mean that Blue Betty – if it was really he – would kill again, here, now, as a follow-up to the first murder? Did the break in time make no difference, once he had started again?

This one could be different, though. Surely. If Rogalleh was right and Lionel Hughes' murder had been based not on some inner compulsion, but on self-protection.

It was fervently to be hoped so.

Chapter 12

Rogalleh was back within half an hour, alone. He looked, Jane thought, as if he had won an argument. 'Come on,' he said, 'we're off to interview the wives. Yes, I've got your superintendent's permission, and yes, I'm going to be as tactful as all get out – we won't be asking them anything they don't think they've been asked already! We'll take the widow first, I think, and then the ex. And hope one or other, or both, comes up with something useful!'

He had apparently decided not to try to make an appointment; they were to call on spec. Jane drove him to Angelica's address, which turned out to be a small semi-detached Victorian house in a quiet street – nowhere near as classy as Willowfield Way, Jane noted; no wonder Angelica had had her sights set on the other house. This one had the tiniest of front gardens, somewhat neglected, but a neat front door and heavily lace-curtained windows, and since it was the end house, it was possible to guess that there was a gate into its back garden from the alley which lay just beyond. An easy and private means of reaching the back of the house and the french windows . . . Yes, the crime report on the robbery had mentioned that.

Their knock on the front door was answered by a young woman with a pale face and a cloud of black hair, dressed in cotton trousers and a thick jumper. Rogalleh asked politely, 'Mrs Hughes, is it?'

'Yes. 'Oo are you?'

'Detective Superintendent Rogalleh, and this is Inspector Perry. Could we come in and have a word with you?'

'Oh, more of you?' Angelica said bad-temperedly, after peering at their warrant cards. 'I hope you've got some news this time. I was starting to think my poor 'usband's death was being conveniently forgotten! All right then, come in!'

She had a slightly guttural voice and her accent seemed to veer through the aspirates. Jane, interested in her first sight of the second Mrs Hughes, thought she was a very different type from her predecessor; a lot plainer, for one thing. Though perhaps that was an unfair judgement and Angelica could display more charm when not under so much stress. They followed her through a small passage and into a very pleasant sitting room, small but light and done up in pale colours with a couple of attractive embroidered wall-hangings. Angelica plonked herself into an armchair and gave a wave of her hand to indicate that they could be seated if they chose, then said with no diminution of bad temper, 'Please don't talk loud, my baby is asleep upstairs. So? What 'ave you got to tell me?'

'I'm afraid it's questions rather than answers, Mrs Hughes,' Rogalleh said, giving her a sympathetic look. 'I'm sorry, it must be very trying for you to have to go over things again. And when you've had a bad enough time of it, goodness knows. How old's the baby?' he added in a pleasant and friendly tone.

'Louisa is a year and a half. And now with no father!'

'Yes indeed, that's very sad. I've a grandchild that age,' Rogalleh said, all sympathy. 'I'm sure she's a great comfort to you, if anything could be. It's a bad business when you lose someone. Well, we must do everything we can to find out who's responsible. So if you'll bear with me . . .'

The soft paternal rumble was soothing. It certainly seemed to work on Angelica, softening the aggression with which she had greeted them. It went on working, too, drawing answers to the questions Rogalleh gradually produced. Where had her husband worked in the past? What kind of stories did he write? When, actually, had she realised his papers and disks were missing? As a journalist, he must have been a gregarious man; did he go out and about a lot and make friends? New acquaintances? Did he bring them home to entertain? Those and a lot more, establishing the pattern of Lionel's life, his habits, his days. When she veered resentfully on to Rowena, he listened sympathetically to that, too.

'That woman – she never want to let him go, that's 'er trouble! "Oh Lionel, there's a problem, you've got to help me" – "Oh Lionel, please come out and see me, I need you." And me, I'm not to be told any details, when she snaps her fingers and he comes! "Things to sort out about the family", when we 'ave a little baby of our own by now! And now, *now*, she 'ave my house, which should be for Louisa! Lionel promise this, *she* promise this! Why don't the police turn her out of there? I still say, if anyone kill him it's her!'

'It must be very distressing for you, Mrs Hughes. I'm sure you were very patient with all those visits your husband was making – and it can't have been very nice for you to have everyone know that he was going off to see his ex-wife all the time. Even if it was purely business.'

'All *my* friends know it was business. He said for anyone to hear lately that she's an ungrateful cow after all 'e's done for her,' Angelica retorted, brooding back into aggression. There was a sudden cry from upstairs, the fretful sound of a baby waking, and she lifted her head. 'My little girl . . .'

'We must let you go and see to her. I'm grateful to you for giving us so much of your time.'

As they left, Jane wondered what Rogalleh had got out of it. She glanced at him as they got back into the car. He was frowning. She asked, 'Not a lot of help, sir?'

'I wouldn't say that. I'm getting the feel of the man. He played it close to home – according to this wife – but when he did go out it was on his own, for an occasional evening at the pub meeting friends and acquaintances. Not that he drank much, just the odd sociable one.' He glanced at Jane. 'Not the soak the other wife said he was, or not nowadays, anyway.'

'Rowena did say she thought he'd changed.'

'Sounds a moderate fellow recently, doesn't he? So he wouldn't have been rolling home drunk and easily vulnerable . . . He knew a lot of people, she says, on a casual level, but he didn't bring them home. They didn't entertain because they couldn't afford it, according to her, though it sounded as much to me as if he wouldn't bother. Liked his home, didn't stir from it much except for the evenings out without the wife – and the regular trips to France. Those were the only times he was really out on the loose, so to speak, and moving on a predictable course. Which provides a good reason why one of those trips was the time chosen to kill him.' His voice held a touch of grimness for a moment, but when he continued it was merely thoughtful. 'The stuff he's been publishing lately was all about politics, so there'd be nothing in that – but it's a pity his wife's so sure he only wrote overseas stories in his heyday. Wasn't ever based in the Midlands, either. Still, that's not to say he didn't know other newsmen who might have talked to him . . . and he might have come out with that in company, mightn't he? Right, let's go and see what kind of picture we can get from the other wife!'

He had the determination of a steamroller, Jane thought. She admired his questioning technique, however – all gentleness and understanding, but bringing out the points he wanted without ever appearing to stress them. If you knew what he was looking for you could see the reasoning behind the questions, but Angelica would not have been aware what she was being asked: where had her husband been which might have given him certain information? Who did he meet, and where? Many people? A few? Was he a silent man in company, or a talker? How predictable were his movements?

When, and where, might he have run into his killer?

Willowfield Way was a long, curving road of tall, solid detached houses, each individually designed, some with high gable fronts but others of a squarer aspect, most of them probably built in the nineteen twenties when there was still money to be had for large town houses with room for a servant or two to sleep in the attics. Some of them had been converted into flats, and another showed brass plates to indicate that its large rooms were now in use for the practice of some therapy or other. Number nineteen stood behind a high hedge and looked slightly less all of a piece than its neighbours – a legacy perhaps of its recent student occupation – but still managed to give the respectable appearance of a highly desirable residence for anyone rich enough to afford something that size. A bicycle propped against the porch suggested that somebody, at least, was in.

Jane wondered how many of her French household Rowena had brought with her. As she and Rogalleh came round the hedge she saw that the battered white van she had last seen in France was parked in its lee – with the bonnet up, and half a person visible leaning in to peer at something under it. The sound of their footsteps brought movement and Malcolm Jackson's head appeared, but he merely cast them an incurious glance and then dived back to continue whatever he was doing with the engine. So Josh's possible minder had come with them ... He didn't appear to have recognised Jane or to be at all interested in their presence, so they moved on to the front door without speaking to him. There were broad windows to each side of it, and a large vase of spring flowers could be seen on the windowsill of one of them. Jane looked to Rogalleh for confirmation, then rang the door bell.

It was answered after several seconds by Chantal. So she, too, had joined the move to England. Jane smiled at her.

'Hallo, Chantal – you probably remember me, Inspector Perry? And this is Detective Superintendent Rogalleh. We're terribly sorry to be a bother, but do you think we could see Mrs Hughes, if she's in?'

'Oh, you've answered it, Chantal. Who is it, someone for Ma?'

The speaker, arriving in the wide hallway behind the girl, had to be a son of Rowena's, even without the betraying title. He was an inch or so shorter than Josh, fair-haired, fine-featured; there was likeness enough to see that the two of them might be brothers, though a surprising difference if this was the other twin. He was, however, very like his mother, with a compactly masculine version of her athletic figure, and the same hazel eyes. He said, with the slightest breath of a stammer, 'Hallo, I'm Sam Connolly, can I help you?' and offered a smile whose sweetness suddenly was reminiscent of Josh's.

Jane offered the introductions again and saw him look doubtful, then resigned. 'OK, you'd better come in. Ma's in the back sitting room – well, it's the only sitting room actually, now she's emptied the front one to give exercise classes in! Chantal, I think Shoshi's probably trying to get at the cat-food bowl again, and while I've put it out of his way, I think . . .'

Chantal let out an exclamation and fled towards the back regions of the house. Sam led the way in the same direction, but opened a door to one side of the rear of the hall. Jane heard Rowena's voice beginning, 'Darling, do you think you could—' but the sentence was broken off as the visitors became visible. She looked, Jane thought, rather less than welcoming this time.

'Oh dear. Some more about Lionel? Yes, it must be, mustn't it, though that nice detective inspector did say there wasn't any further news when I— It's Inspector Perry, isn't it?' The charm had returned, if a little forced, to her smile, and she added with light ruefulness, 'I promise I won't faint this time!'

Jane introduced Rogalleh, then stepped back out of the way. This room, looking to the back on to a garden, was crowded with an odd asortment of furniture, set somewhat higgledy-piggledy on a worn carpet which looked as if it had given good service; another rolled-up carpet stood against one wall in the corner. She heard Rogalleh explaining with apology that he had another set of questions for her, that he was sorry to make her go over and over the same facts but any small thing was helpful in a case like this. Rowena managed a smile in response, though there was a touch of apprehension in it, Jane thought. However, she gave a quick sigh, and said with rueful charm:

'I'm afraid you've caught me rather disorganised. Please do sit down, Superintendent – and Inspector. Yes, if you wouldn't mind, just turn that chair round . . .'

'Shall I make some tea, Ma?'

'No – I mean, get Chantal to make some, and then come back here, I'd like you with me.' This son clearly wasn't one she wanted to keep out of the way. She looked tired, suggesting that even her considerable energy was temporarily flagging, and as Sam left the room she looked after him as if his departure removed a prop. The reliable twin, Jane remembered . . . hadn't she said something like that? She was, however, continuing to make conversation, apologising

143

again for the state in which she was having to entertain them.

'Always hard when you're moving into a new place,' Rogalleh rumbled comfortably, planting himself in the chair he had duly turned round, though not until he had waited courteously for both Rowena and Jane to seat themselves. 'And you haven't been here long, I'm told.'

'This time, no, but we lived here before. For about a year before the divorce. We had a cottage in Lower Hardres before that, but we bought this and moved into it as a kind of a— It's odd, isn't it, how you can think a new place will make a difference to a relationship? But then, of course, it doesn't.' Rowena looked sad for a moment, but Sam's return brightened her. He came to sit on the arm of her chair and she smiled briefly up at him. 'Sam's been caretaking it for me lately, anyway, haven't you, darling? My real home's in France nowadays, and – and with luck we'll be off back there in the autumn. And I'll be able to settle down properly instead of trying to get this place into some kind of order, and rest my bones!'

She sounded both exasperated and weary, but the comment made Sam grin down at her. 'It's no use your pretending to feel old, Ma, when you can wear the rest of us out any day of the week!' he told her, and glanced across at the visitors. 'Take no notice, she's only saying that because her last two ewe lambs are going to be twenty-one next week!'

'Oh, *you*. But it is a milestone, isn't it?' Rowena appealed, looking up at him affectionately in response to his teasing.

'Sure is. It means that even if you wouldn't stop worrying about us when we became legal adults at eighteen, now you've got every excuse to!'

The words were light, but held a private point of their own, Jane thought. It seemed that Rowena thought so too, since she became official suddenly and turned her head quickly towards Rogalleh. 'Superintendent, you wanted to ask me

144

some more questions about Lionel? I really do think I've told the police everything I can—'

There was an interruption in the form of Chantal bearing a tin tray with mugs of tea. These were handed round, sugar offered, and conversation had no chance to resume until she had left the room again. Then Rogalleh picked up the thread in his easy manner and began his low, seemingly casual series of questions.

They concentrated on Lionel's past first, since it was what Rowena could be expected primarily to know about. There was a difference in atmosphere, however, from the questioning of Angelica. It was lent mainly by Sam, sitting listening, chipping in occasionally when he felt his mother had forgotten something. There was a moment when Rogalleh had just elicited that Lionel had never – as far as Rowena could remember – worked for any of the Midland papers, when Sam put an oar in.

'He was after a job on the *Birmingham Post* once, wasn't he? When twin and I were at that dire school up there? At least he always claimed that's where he was going, every time you came up to visit!'

'I'm afraid it was only a claim, and he was actually going off to drink as much as he could get down him in the time without it showing,' Rowena said, sounding waspish about her ex-husband for once. 'If you don't remember how unsteady he used to be when he came back, I do!'

'Be kind, he probably got smashed with some other newsmen, and he could have been talking about a job as well, couldn't he?'

'I'll say yes just to keep your illusions intact – though I very much doubt it. I'm sorry, Superintendent, you were asking . . . ?'

'Nothing much, and I think you answered me. What was the school?' Rogalleh asked amiably, looking at Sam. 'I come from up that way, as you can probably hear. Will I have heard of it?'

'I shouldn't think so. It was on the edge of Birmingham and called Hallowby Hall, but I'm pretty sure it closed down not long after we left it. Went bust I'd imagine, and quite rightly too—'

'There's no need to go over that kind of old history,' Rowena interrupted, flushing, and cutting Sam off. Rogalleh, however, gave her one of his smiles.

'No, I'm always interested to hear what the young think of their education,' he rumbled pleasantly. 'So what was the matter with the place? Too strict for boys of – what age would you have been?'

'Thirteen and a half through to fifteen,' Sam answered, adding with a wry grin, 'and it wasn't strict, it was unbelievably free-thinking. And experimental. You didn't have to learn anything if you didn't want to, you could stay out all night if you wanted to, the head was completely bonkers and spent his time giving us commando training, and—'

'Sam, that really is enough!'

'Sorry,' he said, sobering suddenly. The look he gave his mother held a quick apology; then he raised his eyes again to Rogalleh and said, with the breath of a stammer back in his voice, but an attempt at a laugh, 'We went to a quite normal boarding school in Scotland after that, and since Izzy – my sister Isobel – ended up marrying our housemaster from there, you'd have to say it was a good thing!'

'Do stop being distracting and let the Superintendent ask his questions about Lionel,' Rowena reproved him – almost on a snap, though she managed to offer Rogalleh a distracted and apologetic smile. 'I'm so sorry I haven't been able to remember any more about that gun-running story which put Lionel in danger before,' she said with a quiver in her voice, 'but I've racked my brains, as I told the other detective who came to see me. It was all terribly hush-hush even then, you see, and—'

'Please don't upset yourself. If there're something to track down I'm sure we'll manage it in the end,' Rogalleh told her, automatically soothing. 'Difficult trying to rake up the past, isn't it? Maybe we can get at it by trying to think what your ex-husband may have been doing lately . . .'

He went on with his apparently casual probing, though Rowena, Jane thought, was less easy to draw answers from than Angelica had been. After she had given a rather pointed glance at her watch Rogalleh decided to call it a day and began to get ponderously out of his chair.

'Thank you for your time, Mrs Hughes. I know it must seem like the same questions over and over, but I've come in new to the case, you see, and I do like to have all my facts in order. We'll leave you in peace now – and good luck with getting your house straight.'

'Sam, will you show them out?'

'Actually, Ma, I've got to run myself. I've just remembered I ought to go back up to the uni because there're some books I haven't taken back to the library, and I'd better before they close for the vac. I need some others out, too.' Sam, already on his feet, cast his mother a look of apology and added, 'Sorry, I'd forgotten, but I'll be back later – maybe about six – and I'll help with the furniture-moving then, so *don't* try and do it all yourself!'

He bent to plant a swift kiss on her cheek. Then he was ushering Jane and Rogalleh back through the wide hallway. There was no sound to suggest Josh was anywhere in the house, though the quiet murmur of Chantal's voice could be heard from somewhere at the back, its cooing sound making it clear she was talking to baby Shoshi. As they came out through the front door, Jane saw that the white van had gone from its parking place; Malcolm must successfully have completed whatever he was doing to the engine. Once the front door was shut behind them Sam abruptly seemed to lose his hurry. He was half blocking their way so that they would have had to walk round him to leave, and he gave a glance up at the house, then spoke.

'It's not altogether easy for Ma being back here, so if she didn't seem ... I mean ... Well, this house has a lot of fairly bad memories for her, I think, all the quarrels and the divorce and everything.'

'Oh, she was as helpful as she could be, I'm sure,' Rogalleh answered easily. He went on conversationally, 'Bad memories, eh? I'm surprised she didn't want to get shot of the place, then, and let your stepmother have it!'

'My st— ? Oh, Angelica! Sorry, I find it hard to think of her as that, when she's not really related – and besides hates the lot of us!' Sam said that on a wry laugh, but it was replaced by a distinct anger as he added, 'She's bloody stupid too, trying to make out Ma would have poisoned Lionel. Yes, I did hear about it. Ma tried to turn it into a joke, but that's not what I'd call it!'

'I wouldn't worry about it, lad, we're used to people giving us jealous nonsense. You're at the university, I gather? What are you studying?'

'Politics.' Sam said with a slight air of humorous apology. 'Which doesn't actually mean I'm aiming to go into Parliament and overthrow all the institutions—'

'Like the police, you mean?' Rogalleh allowed his large frame to shake with friendly laughter, but his eyes were sharp, Jane thought, and he was waiting – as she was – to see why Sam had wanted to stop them. He said only, 'You must be a bright one, then, to get into university after that bad schooling you were telling us about.'

'I guess we recovered. And actually I'm not the brilliant one in the family, that's my twin. He always has been, no matter what, and he got a Cambridge place while I only made Kent. We used to have a standing joke: I was born first, he waited twenty minutes and got the brains.' Sam said that with a slight jerkiness, a minimal return of his stammer, as if it was a subject for defensiveness. As well it might be, Jane thought; brilliant but unstable? And Josh certainly wasn't studying at Cambridge at the moment. As she pondered on this, Sam abruptly came out with it, looking directly at Rogalleh.

'You think Lionel was killed by someone he knew, don't you?'

'Now what makes you say that?'

'The fact that I was listening,' Sam said drily. 'You may have been wrapping it up, but that's where some of it was leading, anyway. You *don't* think it was some anonymous hitman, the way Ma does, do you? Oh, it's all right, I shan't talk to her about it, she's got enough to upset her already. But that is what you think, isn't it?'

'We've still got a lot to do before we can decide. But if you can think of anything to help us . . .'

'I'll tell you. I can't at the moment – I haven't seen much of Li since he married Angelica. As I said, she doesn't like us. OK, I suppose I might have guessed you wouldn't tell me anything, and I'd better go.'

He jumped on the bike and pedalled off without a further word. The Connolly twins seemed to make a habit of leaving abruptly . . . though this one had given every evidence of a sharp intelligence before he did so. Rogalleh looked thoughtfully after him; then he and Jane were moving towards the car.

'Interesting,' he said ruminatively when they were inside.

'Sam? Or generally?'

'Both, I'd say.' His large frame shook again on a brief chuckle. 'We should try and recruit that one into the force

149

when he's finished his studies: he knows how to listen to questions as well as answers. There's one answer I got out of him that he didn't catch on to, anyway. Lionel Hughes may not have worked in the Midlands, but he was visiting up there during the time Blue Betty was on the rampage. Exactly then. Thirteen and a half to fifteen, and they're just going to be twenty-one now... Hughes was going to see his stepsons in the Birmingham area seven years ago, up till six years ago, and very likely talking to newsmen on the *Birmingham Post* while he was up there. We've got our connection!'

Back at the station, Rogalleh surged off to talk to Superintendent Annerley. As he didn't appear to want Jane, she went off to have lunch in the canteen. Life was going on as normal; the snatches of conversation she caught were about everyday things, burglary, overtime, football... Sitting quietly alone in her corner, Jane found herself reviewing the interview with Rowena. Rogalleh was right, he had found a connection between Lionel Hughes and Birmingham for the relevant time. The Blue Betty time.

That boarding school the Connolly boys had attended had probably been where Josh got into trouble with amphetamines. That must be why Rowena had shown so much discomfort to have Sam talking about it. If Josh had managed to land a place at Cambridge even after that, he must have a genuinely good brain, as his twin claimed... but what had happened to him since, to spoil it?

She got up to leave, and saw Kenny Barnes and DS Doug Phelps both giving her amiable grins from across the room. She smiled back, but took care not to pass their table in case either of them asked her curious questions about the visiting detective superintendent whose presence must be common knowledge by now. Upstairs, she found a note on her desk summoning her to a meeting in

150

Superintendent Annerley's office at three p.m. Further discussion was obviously to take place.

This time, the group had widened to include the DI and the DCI. Both of them had clearly had a preliminary briefing. Morland ignored Jane pointedly as usual, while Chris raised an eyebrow at her with a pursed mouth which spoke half disbelief, half worry. And afterwards – with Rogalleh remaining with the Super – he walked silently along with Jane to her office, speaking only once the door was shut behind them.

'So that's what it's all about . . .'

'Yes. Not funny, is it?'

'Not if it's true. Do you believe it? I'm not sure I don't go along with the Super, that it could simply be chance, a coincidence . . .'

'Rogalleh's sure.'

'Yes, but he would be, wouldn't he? It's what he wants most in life – to catch up with this Blue Betty at last, after failing last time.' Chris gave a gusty sigh and pushed a worried hand through his hair. 'What the hell can we do about it, anyway? We've investigated every last inch of Lionel Hughes' life already, and we can't do anything more on the theft of his files. I'm entirely with the Super on keeping this confidential between the four of us – well, five of us if you count Rogalleh – because there's no point in starting a lot of gossip and a likely panic if the idea gets out. But other than that, what the hell *do* we do?'

'Wait, I guess. Like the Super said.'

Rogalleh hadn't liked it, but that was what had been said. And finally decided upon.

'Yeah, wait. Keep the file open. See if anything else happens. Hope it doesn't – or not in the way that's been suggested, anyway.' Chris gave a grim look; then as abruptly relaxed. 'God, it's all go, isn't it? But I'm not going to live with *that* in my head, day in and day out. It's just going to have to lie fallow! Oh, by the way... Thanks for the flowers Adrian brought round for Elizabeth. He said they were from both of you, but I guess it was your idea, wasn't it? She is feeling a lot better at last, thank goodness: the sickness finally seems to have gone away.'

'Oh – oh good.' What flowers? With Chris giving her a grateful grin, Jane hardly felt able to say that the graceful gesture had been all Adrian. Not that she wouldn't have agreed, if he had consulted her. She gave Chris a smile, and said with a fraction too much heartiness, 'Back to normal, then?'

'Yes, thank goodness. As long as she doesn't eat – what is it? – bananas. Or Marmite.' He grinned again, shook himself, and made a clear and deliberate attempt not to let grimness creep back into his eyes. 'I'm off to catch up on what's on my desk. I'll talk to you again if – if anything comes up. Meanwhile ... well, see you!'

He left. Rogalleh would be returning to the West Midlands this evening; that had been decided too. He would go less than willingly, Jane thought, but he had his own region to run. Even a senior serving officer had to be where he was supposed to be ... though he was taking a copy of the Lionel Hughes file with him, was determined to feed its data in with the rest of the Blue Betty information, would – undoubtedly – be heard from again.

Like the rest of them, he would also wait.

Jane caught herself on a shiver, then decided firmly that Chris was right. No point in living with that in one's head; let it lie fallow. If a vicious serial killer was out there somewhere in the shadows ... No. Leave the idea alone. She had seen cases as bad in the past, or almost. There was certainly nothing to be gained in trying to second-guess this one. They were on a 'wait and see': well, so be it. Nothing might happen, anyway.

Wait.

Chapter 13

There were a few things which could be done. Claus Armfeldt's death was in the hands of Dover and the Kent Ports Police SB, but they could be asked to check his history, via the Netherlands police, to see if he had ever lived in England. Whatever Rogalleh thought, it was clearly a necessary enquiry. It was made, couched in carefully general terms, Jane heard from Chris, and gathered from him later that a negative answer had come back. Mention was made this time that Armfeldt's girlfriend was Turkish – which, Jane thought, probably explained how he had been recruited to drive the Kurds – but it was apparently definite that he had not at any time in the past been resident in Britain. A line could be drawn under that one.

Daily life went back to normality. Rogalleh's visit and his interest in the Hughes file had caused curiosity, but after the first buzz was assumed to have turned out to be a dead end. Only those in the know were in a position to wonder if anything was going to come out of the HOLMES database to confirm Rogalleh's certainty ... but that, too, would take time. In the meantime, if the subject of Lionel Hughes' unsolved murder came up, the hitman theory was the one generally bandied about. Chief Inspector Lowell made a point of complaining to Jane that liaison was one thing, having her snatched away by CID whenever they felt like it was another, but he had allowed his ruffled feathers to be

155

smoothed by the weekend. And on Saturday – with no other duties to take her away – Jane went to help Matty make a tour of the boutiques to find something striking enough to wear for an operatic gala.

'You know damned well you could wear a black dustbin bag and still look incredible,' she offered, a pretence at a jeering grumble as they emerged from the third shop with The Dress stowed in a brightly logo'd bag.

'Hm, a dustbin bag? I wonder, *should* I have chosen the beaded number you said made me look like a Christmas tree instead?' Matty cast her a sidelong grin, but dangled the bag in a satisfied fashion from one finger. As well she might, since their search had finally come up with something long, fluid, deceptively and expensively simple-looking, but in an exotic dark crimson which suited her to perfection. 'Cheer up, honey, I'll lend it to you sometime, it'd look just as good on a blonde! If you and Adrian are ever going to anything where you want to look knock-'em-dead— Wrong subject?'

'No, we're getting on fine. More or less.' It was Jane's fault if there was the occasional less, though she had been trying hard to keep her abstractions to herself and appear cheerful and loving. 'I was almost in trouble for forgetting to tell him we weren't getting together with you on Easter Sunday after all,' she said ruefully, 'which only came up when he'd just turned down an invitation from somebody else!' It was Elizabeth Hollings, in fact, asking them over for Easter Sunday lunch, and that – inevitably – had made her omission worse. Jane had caused a slight silence too for protesting mildly that she was sure Chris would feel he and Jane had seen quite enough of each other at work lately anyway. 'Never mind, it's all water under the bridge, innit? Let's go and find somewhere to have a coffee!'

The city centre was showing every sign of having woken up to spring as they made their way through it. In the small open square which fronted one of the newer shopping precincts a boy in facepaint was juggling, not very expertly, with three coloured balls, mainly ignored by the passers-by. Behind him a small crowd had gathered, looking up; a bunch of people in bright orange hard hats were clustered high up on a flat roof, with one figure leaning back off the edge on the end of a rope, forming an unlikely angle against the sky. A banner tacked to the wall said 'Sponsored Abseil', and Jane saw the familiar face and uniform of one of the station constables standing below to keep things in order. It was too early in the year for the average busker to try his or her luck, save for one man in a top hat and striped trousers who was tootling on a pipe at the same time as dancing a clown puppet up and down; mostly, the street singers were still lurking in the shelter of the underpasses, to send the echoes flying with twanged guitars and bad renditions of Bob Dylan classics. A normal Saturday morning, Jane thought, as she dodged round a charity stall set up on the open pavement. A cart on wheels, presumably with the necessary street licence since it was trading openly, was being trundled up the centre of the street, offering fluffy yellow ducks and Easter bunnies.

It was useless to wonder involuntarily whether there was somebody in the crowds – someone who six years ago would have been described as a youngish white male but definitely a non-social type – with a secret hunger for death and a liking for drawing blue diamond shapes on his victims.

Jane responded to a hopeful request to buy *The Big Issue* which was being loudly touted by a young man with spiky hair, an earring, and tattooed fingers, and followed Matty as she dived into the sidestreet which would take them to Freebody's coffee shop. The blue of the tattoos served to act as an echo to her thoughts, try as she might to resist them. As they sat down and ordered she looked up to find Matty's brown eyes fixed on her consideringly.

'You've gone very quiet. Men? Work?'

'Sorry, have I? No, I said, it's OK with Adrian, we're – well, working things out, anyway. Work's dreary, but there's nothing unusual in that, it has its phases.'

'Nothing new on the you know what?' Matty asked, aware that 'murder' was a word to be avoided in company, even if her voice was a low enough murmur not to reach any of the nearby tables.

'Zilch,' Jane said lightly. She leaned forward suddenly, her eye caught by two figures out in the street. Sam and Josh Connolly, walking slowly along together, deep in conversation. Whatever it was they were talking about, it was absorbing both of them. While she watched, Sam said something which made Josh break into a laugh, his face today less shadowed and happier. 'I know those two,' Jane said, waving an explanatory hand. 'You wouldn't think they were twins, would you?'

'Definitely not monozygotic,' Matty agreed, following her gaze. 'Fraternal, though – same profile? Oh bugger, there's somebody I recognise too, quick, pass the menu and pray he's not coming in here!'

She shielded her face rapidly, then peered round it with relief. 'No, they've walked on. Dr Kremer, didn't you notice him?' she enquired ruefully. 'And I'd guess that must have been Mrs K with him – she looked suitably crushed, anyway. Honestly, as if I don't see enough of the old blankety-blank at work!'

'Well, you know what they say – it's a small city, and if you keep still for five minutes you're bound to see somebody you know!'

It was a pity her flippant answer had to remind Jane of Rogalleh's words. She tore her mind away from that yet again, annoyed by the way she seemed unable to prevent its haunting her. 'For God's sake let's forget work altogether,' she said with unusual force; saw Matty's eyebrows go up; and managed a creditable imitation of a laugh. 'No, seriously, though, let's! Unless of course you actually want to favour me with some of your Kremer stories?'

'No, you're right, I can well do without the old bully, in thought as well as in person! OK ...'

It seemed unlikely that they would meet up again before Easter, so when they parted it was on a light-hearted promise that Matty would report back after her gallivantings. Jane went home, and wished she wasn't aware as she walked into the house that she was glad Adrian was working today, out on a familiarisation with the other half of the enlarged practice. It was unfair of her. On the surface things were perfectly amicable. It was probably only her own defensiveness which kept telling her that the quarrel between them, supposedly over, was still there lurking underground. She put on some music and buried herself in a book, which was distracting enough to take her away from everything.

On Monday she looked at her office calendar and realised it was four weeks since Lionel Hughes' body had been found on the Minnis. If, as they estimated, he had been killed on Sunday night, then next Sunday it would be five weeks since his death, the following Sunday, six. Six weeks. Blue Betty's previous span ...

She clamped down on that. There was no reason for it to be the same. She was letting Rogalleh's certainty hypnotise her – and anyway it had been six *years*, for goodness' sake, since the last known Blue Betty killing. She should – must – put it out of her head. And she did, too, successfully, becoming so cheerfully efficient that by the end of the week Chief Inspector Lowell had even begun to look slightly hunted whenever she appeared round his door with yet another suggested agenda for him to approve.

Easter Saturday dawned bright and clear. Despite the fact that it was April the forecasts were promising sun for the entire Bank Holiday weekend. Adrian was not on call, Felicity the one to deal with any emergencies which might come up. And Jane and Adrian were, after all, to go and be sociable with the Hollings, for tea on Saturday afternoon.

It had come up midweek, Adrian saying a little too casually that when Elizabeth had rung him at the practice with a question about her dog, she had issued an invitation for Saturday tea instead of the original Sunday lunch. And he had told her it sounded fine to him but he would get Jane to ring back to confirm it. She knew it would be ungracious to say no – and she did like Elizabeth, anyway – so she had answered merely, pleasantly, 'OK, as long as she's sure Chris won't mind!'

'Why should he? We had them over last, anyway, even if it's months ago. You'll ring and say yes, then?'

'I'll do it now.'

Elizabeth sounded sunny and welcoming. 'I'm sorry it's not dinner, like we used to do, but I get really sleepy in the evenings,' she said on a rueful laugh. 'And I know it's been our turn for months but I really wasn't eating! Thank you again for the flowers, that was really sweet of you. I warn you, Chris will probably try and set you to weeding if it's fine. He's still trying to organise the garden, even though we've been in this house six months. But if he does we'll let Adrian help him while you and I just sit and watch!'

'Probably just as well if you don't want the wrong things pulled up. I'm not very good on what's a weed and what isn't. Well, I suppose I'm not quite that bad, I can probably manage under instruction! We'll see you, then – what time?'

'Come about half past three. Oh good, we'll look forward to it!'

The house the Hollings had moved into six months ago

was larger than their last, clearly with the intention of having room for the planned baby and with a good-sized garden for it to play in as it grew. Jane had seen the house before, though that had been at night, at a dinner party. This time, they could see how well situated it was for a household with a large dog, since the back garden looked out on to open fields. There was a hedge in between, thick enough at the bottom to stop the dog scrabbling through, and a tall open-work gate which led out to the footpath round the edge of the nearest field.

'We had to replace the original gate with a high one to stop Hector leaping over,' Elizabeth said, pulling the young labrador's ears affectionately. 'He's such a goop, he might have got lost or forgotten which garden to jump back into! And look, we've got a shed – Chris put that up, and it's good and solid – and space to stack the garden rubbish down this end too, all nicely invisible from the house thanks to the apple trees. It's great, isn't it?'

'You've been busy,' Jane told Chris with a grin. He was looking very un-DI-like, in jeans and a grubby shirt.

'Haven't I, though?' he said with satisfaction. 'I've got some slabs to lay for a patio next – if anybody would like to offer any assistance . . .?'

'Oh dear, I did warn you!' Elizabeth said, and cast her husband an amused glance. Pregnancy seemed to be suiting her now that she had stopped being sick; she looked chubbier, but blooming. And very happy. She began to lead the way back up the long garden. The young golden labrador lolloped along ahead of her in a zigzag course, tracking back now and again to check on both his owners and the visitors. 'Aren't we lucky to have found something right on the edge of the city like this?' Elizabeth went on. 'Chris usually takes Hector out into the field first thing in the morning – well, I haven't been at my best then, have I, darling?'

161

'Early morning's nice, with the dew on the grass,' her husband put in easily. 'Gives me a bit of exercise as well as the hound. As long as Lizzie hasn't lost the gate key . . .'

'I didn't, you swine, it was you who mislaid it! He'd dropped it in the grass right by the gate, as it turned out,' Elizabeth said scathingly. 'Honestly, men! And after insisting on putting a decent lock on it too, like a properly careful householder!' She gave Chris a grin, cast Jane a look as if inviting her to join in the reproof, and then turned to Adrian. 'Listen, if you don't want to help him in the garden you don't have to. We honestly didn't ask you to tea just to make use of you!'

'I don't mind a bit. As long as you can persuade Hector to let go of my sleeve!' The dog had now decided his vet was fair game for a bit of tugging, and had taken the corner of Adrian's jacket in his mouth with an air of mischief in his eyes. He was both too well behaved and too soft-mouthed to bite hard but was still young enough to want to play.

He was allowed his game, but transferred to a tug-of-war with a stick. Chris told Adrian he was a soft touch, but he was not alone, since both the Hollings were the same where their pet was concerned. 'We really will have to make an extra fuss of him when the baby comes,' Elizabeth said to Jane, giving the animal a hug after the two men had gone off to discuss patio-laying. 'He may be almost three but he's such a baby himself . . . Listen, if we take a couple of deckchairs down on to that piece of lawn, we can be out of the way of the workers until it's time for tea! Hector, bring your ball – come on, *bring* it, don't stand over it hopefully as if it might throw itself!'

In fact Jane went to help the men after ten minutes or so, claiming that the job needed three and she would be brains to their brawn. It did require three, as it turned out, since there was a regular need for someone to persuade Hector that laying flagstones wasn't another interesting game. It was an idyllic day, warm enough to be outside but with that freshness only April could bring. It was remarkably pleasant to be working and laughing out in the sun, with no cares except to lay the heavy stones properly level and discourage the dog from thrusting his nose just where one was about to be dropped. Jane threw the ball as far away as possible over and over again only to have it joyously brought back to her far too fast. Finally, amongst much mirth, Elizabeth took the animal inside with her when she went to organise tea, and he could be seen with his nose pressed hopefully up against the long glass doors, begging mournfully to be let out again for more fun. Then there was a large tea to be eaten, with satisfaction for work well done. Eventually it was time to go home, and Hector was shut away firmly inside while both the Hollings waved them off from the doorstep.

'Many thanks, sorry if you hadn't expected to be a work gang!' Chris called after them with a half-rueful, half-laughing lift to his eyebrows. 'It would have taken me the whole weekend without you, though!'

'No problem!' Adrian responded, while Jane called back with a grin:

'You can send for us when you decide to put up an Alexandra Palace of a greenhouse, if that's next! Thanks for the tea . . .'

Back home, Jane stretched, mellowly aware of the pull of rarely used muscles. 'That was nice . . . I don't know about you, but I certainly shan't want any more to eat this evening after all that cake!'

'Nor me. Unless we get the munchies later for scrambled egg in front of the telly.' Adrian gave a cheerful grin. 'Elizabeth was looking well, wasn't she? Blooming. If mentioning it won't make you snap my head off.'

'Oh come on, don't—'

'Sorry, sorry, pretend I wasn't stupid enough to say that,' he said rapidly, moving to give her an enveloping hug. 'I didn't, all right? It *was* a nice afternoon, wasn't it? And with Fliss on call until Monday, tomorrow we can have a lazy day.'

'Unless you'd like to get our tiny garden in order?' Jane enquired, allowing the peacemaking gesture, and hugging him back to show she was far too relaxed to let anything spoil the mood of the day. 'Not that we can actually do much to it, though I suppose we could get some pots from a garden centre or something!' She let out a chuckle. 'And with no Hector to dig them up so he can bury bones! He really is a comedian, with that expressive face – but rather gorgeous.'

The evening went on in relaxed mood. Sunday promised to be mellow too, with no need to be anything but idle if they didn't feel like it. In the morning, Adrian went down to make coffee and toast and brought it back upstairs so that they could have breakfast in bed. He had just put the tray down and was climbing back into bed when the telephone downstairs let out its sharp warble. He frowned.

'Oh no. Who the hell wants us at half past eight on Easter Sunday morning? Surely Fliss hasn't run into something she can't handle!'

'I'll get it, shall I, and claim you're too fast asleep to be disturbed?'

'No, I will, you stay there.'

Jane took a sleepy sip of her coffee. Bloody Felicity, even Adrian admitted she came up with too many crises. She heard him coming back upstairs at speed; he was already speaking, urgently, as he came through the door.

'Throw some clothes on, quick, will you? That was Chris, and he wants both of us. You too, he particularly said. God—'

'What's happened?' Jane asked, already out of bed.

'Something to the dog, and Elizabeth's desperate. Chris sounded pretty bad too but I could hear her in the background and she seemed frantic. Come on!'

Jeans and a T-shirt, the nearest things to Jane's hand, were flung on. They made the journey at a speed which would have got them stopped by any passing patrol car, but Jane had no objections. The Hollings' house looked as peaceful from outside as they had left it, bright in the morning sun, its pleasantly spaced neighbours quiet too and several of them still with drawn curtains. Chris pulled the front door open as they reached it.

He had blood on his shirt, and another dark smear of it on his jeans. Jane saw that even before she saw his face, and that he was white to the lips.

'Come in. Jane, come with me, would you? Adrian – Hector's dead so there's nothing you can do for him, could you – could you stay with Elizabeth, just for the moment?'

Elizabeth could be heard sobbing. She was curled up in a corner of the settee as they came into the sitting room, but looked up, all big eyes in a racked face, and there was blood on her too, smears of it all down her front and on the skirts of her pale housecoat. She looked almost too blind with grief to know who was there, but at her husband's return she began in a hoarse scream:

'Get it out, Chris, get it out, you can't leave him like that, you can't . . .'

'He's dead, Lizzie. It won't be hurting him. Adrian, could you— Jane?'

It seemed the wrong way round, but since he clearly meant her to come with him she followed him out at a run through the open patio doors, across the slabs so carefully laid yesterday, down the long garden. They came past the screening apple trees and reached the shed. And Jane stopped, sickly, when she saw what was there.

The young golden labrador was pinned to its side by a crossbow bolt which had passed through his body into the wood. His corpse hung limply, all life gone from the glazed eyes. And there was blood everywhere; on his sides, on the grass. 'His throat's been cut as well,' Chris said hoarsely. 'I – I didn't come out with him this morning. I just let him out on his own for a run in the garden, early. We were having a lie in. Then when we got up Lizzie realised he hadn't come back, so she wandered down the garden to see what he was doing. And found him . . . I heard her scream and when I came down she was trying to pull the bolt out but— Better not touched. Because that's not all. Look.'

Jane had had no eyes for anything but the pathetic golden corpse until then, but now she followed his pointing finger. Above the body, on the wood of the shed, somebody had chalked a sign, about a foot square.

A blue diamond.

'This was stuck in the middle of it,' Chris's voice said. His hand came out offering a dart – and a folded piece of paper. 'Yes, I know, I shouldn't have touched it, but – but I'd pulled it out before I'd even thought, I wasn't thinking straight. I didn't add it up, I was just so angry and I wasn't being . . . and I was trying to cope with Lizzie as well. Here.'

He had opened the paper so that she could read it without touching. There was a smear of blood across it – more than one – but the words, cut out of newsprint capitals and stuck tidily in line, were clear. And offered a chilling message.

They said, ROGALLEH SEE IF YOU CAN CATCH ME NOW.

166

Chapter 14

'Five weeks,' Jane said abruptly. Her voice felt unlike her own. 'It's Sunday today, isn't it? Five weeks instead of six.'

'What?'

'Sorry, I was just— Chris? It was meant to be you! Those letters were done in advance. And you usually take the dog out in the early morning. Christ, it was meant to be you!'

'I don't give a fuck.' The words were both flat and violent. 'The man's obscene. Catching him's personal to Rogalleh; well it's personal to me as well now, and if—'

His voice ceased abruptly as Adrian appeared round the screening apple trees, grim-faced and with a blanket folded over his arm. He took in the sight before him but said nothing, throwing the blanket down on the grass in front of the shed, then kneeling down swiftly. One hand supported the dog's body, the other reached for the bolt. Chris began harshly, 'Don't—' but Adrian turned his head to give him an icy glare.

'No, don't *you*. I promised Elizabeth and you can go to hell before you stop me! What do you think it's like for *her*?' Even as he spoke the scathing words he had given the bolt a sharp twist, drawing it out with a forceful heave. He threw the metal shaft aside in almost the same movement and caught the golden body, laid it on the blanket, flipped the sides over to provide a decent covering. Then he came neatly to his feet and went on with the same iciness, his

167

words apparently addressed to Jane as well as Chris. 'I'll leave him there for now, since I suppose I must. Playing detective's one thing, but how you can let her go on visualising that kind of nightmare ... I'm going back now to tell her it's done, since neither of *you* seem prepared to consider her feelings!'

As he made to come past them, for a moment Jane thought Chris was going to hit him. Shock, bad enough already, must have come back in full force with the release of the dog's body and the unfairly harsh words, robbing him of speech but sending his muscles bunching and his face into a snarl. Jane made a rapid movement to get between them, but Adrian was already walking away and she saw Chris make a phenomenal effort and rein himself in, keeping himself still as the other man went out of sight. She saw that he was shaking. She said swiftly:

'He doesn't mean it, Chris, and he doesn't understand either, but I apologise for him, OK? Listen to me. We need to call the Super; have you got his home number? He's the only person we can ring, and we'll need to do that before we get a team in, so let's pray he's available!'

She made her voice briskly practical, knowing – ache though she might for both the Hollings – that sympathy could break his precarious control. She saw Chris turn his head towards her blindly, then pull himself with another enormous effort into some semblance of normality. He drew in a deep breath.

'Yes, you're right. And I have got his number. I'll – I'll—'

'I'd suggest you let me do it, but I think it should be you.' Giving him something to do might stave off his breaking point; besides, every instinct was telling her to get him back indoors. Blue Betty was probably long gone, but just in case ... 'If you want, I'll stay here to make sure nothing else is touched,' she went on, still firmly practical. 'Or I'll come with you if—'

'No, I – I'd like there to be somebody here. I can get into the house the other way so that Lizzie won't see me. There's a phone upstairs. I'll need to look up ... If I can't get hold of the Super, what do I do?'

He wouldn't normally have asked her. 'Get on to the station and get a team in anyway, since the sooner that's done the better,' Jane said, making the choice for him, 'but we don't need to provide them with any extra details. There's enough without— You don't need to meet that unless it happens, though; try the Super first and then you can leave all the decisions to him.'

She would have added, gently, 'and then you can concentrate on Elizabeth' and nearly did so; but thought it unwise when he was still so dangerously near the edge. He gave a nod and walked stiffly away. He would manage, she hoped. She hoped too that Adrian would be too occupied to hear him moving about in the house and confront him again. With part of herself she wanted to tear Adrian to bits for his abysmal tactlessness, though even as the thought came she acknowledged that he had been suffering from shock too. Her mind, hopelessly scattered, suddenly came up with the memory of Hilaire and her claim to him that shock might make men, as well as women, faint. She had been wrong. What it did to men, most commonly, was strip away the veneer of civilisation and send them into a state of violent aggression. She had seen it happen often enough.

The garden seemed eerily quiet, and the brief sound of a cheerfully raised voice from another garden, a snatch of distant music from a radio, somehow made it all the more unreal. Easter Sunday, families waking up to go about their normal lives. She couldn't help being glad that Hector's body was just a covered shape on the bloodied grass. She made herself look across the hedge at the field. Blue Betty had come from out there somewhere, and had meant to get

Chris . . . That had to be true. Another DI; another 'author-ity figure'. He must have been stalked and watched, the dog a substitute for his owner when Chris didn't come with him for his usual early-morning walk.

Did that mean Chris was still in danger? Rogalleh had never said whether Blue Betty had ever had another try after failing once.

She could only stand and wait, moving as little as possible so as not to muddle any possible traces. Blue Betty had been here – inside the gate, even though it stood innocently closed – to leave his mark and his message. And to cut the dog's throat. How early had it been? Would there really have been nobody to see him leave? He must have been bloodstained himself . . .

Blue Betty had known of Rogalleh's visit. How? Where had he seen him? Or was the note just a throwback to the past, a use of the name of the man who had hunted him before?

It seemed a long time before the Super arrived, though it was probably less than half an hour. After that everything went into rapid motion. A scene-of-crime team arrived, to don overalls and begin their minute inspection. Members of CID appeared. If anyone wondered why all the stops were being pulled out during a public holiday for the death of a dog, nobody asked, the violent circumstances of the killing offering perhaps explanation enough. Chris disappeared; later Jane heard that he had been sent off to the hospital with Elizabeth, whose shattered state was deemed to need more than her own doctor's care. Jane saw Adrian but only in the distance; he was being asked, she guessed, questions about the corpse which a vet would be in the best position to answer. He had gone before she could speak to him, and then she left too, following Superintendent Annerley to the station on his instructions.

She got home at four in the afternoon to find – to her annoyance – Harry Morpeth lurking on the doorstep. She began, 'Not now, Harry, do you mind?' but he gave her a reproachful look.

'I've only come round to collect a book Adrian offered to lend Felicity, but he doesn't seem to be in. Now *you* are, maybe you could find it for me? Some heavyweight novel set around her home area of Lincolnshire, *The Wide Sky* or something like that.' He added, regarding her, 'Been having a day out in the country? You do look a bit as if you've been dragged through a hedge backwards, if you'll pardon my mentioning it. And I hope you two haven't had a fight, to bring you back alone.'

'No. You'd better come in, I think I saw the book on the side yesterday.' Giving him what he wanted was probably the best way to get rid of him. She let him follow her indoors. 'I think this is what you must want – *The Open Sky*? I seem to remember Adrian said he'd finished it and that it was good.'

'Thanks,' he said, accepting the thick paperback she was holding out to him. 'One of those rural epics, I gather – a lot too rural for me to want to read, anyway! Oh, by the way, Angie told me some new senior cop came and asked her all the same questions over again about Lionel – still at a dead end, are you?'

'Seems so,' Jane said shortly.

'I can't say I go for this theory about assassination. I mean, dear old Li, when he wasn't much more than a hack even in his good old days? Still, Rowena's very keen on it ... I did manage to get in to see her, by the way, by introducing myself as a good friend of Li's. Nice lady, isn't she? Rather a stunner, too,' he added appreciatively, 'and I bet she was even more so when she was younger. I'm really quite well in there now!'

171

'Honestly Harry, you're the crassest and most thick-skinned person I've ever met. You ooze your way into people's lives because you think it might be to your advantage—'

'Oh dear, temper temper! I really can't help it if I know how to make myself popular. What's set you off – a touch of PMT?' He had the nerve to pull a sympathetic face at her. 'Or is it because Rowena's work to you, and today's a holiday? Now it's funny if it's that, because Felicity told me that Adrian's apt to complain you never think about anything *except* work . . . All right, all right, I'm going!'

He did – fortunately for him. It appeared to make no difference that for once Jane had told him what she thought of him, either, since he flashed her a wide smile as he left. She found she was shaking with anger – though it was, she knew, much more a reaction to the day. But Harry, on top of it, was too much.

She had had a bath and washed her hair by the time she heard Adrian come in from wherever it was he had been. It was possible they had asked him to do some kind of official post-mortem on Hector . . . She kept her back to him as he came into the bedroom. She heard him clear his throat, then he said:

'Sorry about what I said to Chris. I was – Elizabeth was—'

'It's all right, I know.' She glanced at him over her shoulder. 'We *weren't* just playing detectives—'

'I've said, haven't I? And I, as much as anyone, hope you catch the vicious moron who did it!' There was loathing and disgust in his voice. He came further into the room. 'She really loved that dog. I guess Chris did too. But she was in such a state . . .'

'I think they're going to keep her in hospital for a few days. I heard that, anyway. Adrian—'

He must have caught the wobble she couldn't keep out of her voice because he moved to her quickly and they held each other tightly. There were things she knew and he didn't, that she couldn't share; there was still, for now, an incredibly close wrap being kept on information. However, human warmth was a comfort, and the sense of shared pain for friends. She could even switch her mind off, for a moment or two, from the grimly urgent discussions which had started today, and would go on for the days ahead.

It was no use supposing that nobody would connect the chalked blue diamond above Hector's body with the blue diamond on Lionel Hughes' wrist, when that had particularly been raised and advertised. The Super, therefore, called a conference for the original Hughes homicide team, all of CID – though with the DI absent – and the heads of the uniformed departments, on the Monday, Bank Holiday or no Bank Holiday. He offered a succinct explanation that they were assuming a connection between the two cases, though without mentioning Blue Betty. On that, he merely said gravely, to the silent, listening faces:

'Some of you already know there was also a note referring to Detective Superintendent Rogalleh who was here ten days ago. He came because a similar blue diamond mark turned up on a case in his area some time ago. We have to consider the likelihood that there's a connection there too, and I'll give you more information on that later in the week. As regards the killing of DI Hollings' dog, we're taking that either as a warning . . .' He paused for a second, and then went on, 'or, in view of the fact that he was usually in the habit of taking the dog out in the mornings, we may have to assume that DI Hollings was originally intended to be the target, and that it was only chance which prevented it.' There was a sharply indrawn breath from somewhere, and Superintendent Annerley glanced across. 'Yes, I'm afraid it is a possibility we have to consider. He's been asked, therefore, to stay in a safe place for the time being. He's

173

somewhat unwilling to do so, but has agreed for now. Now, publicity.

'It's vitally important that nothing, and I mean nothing, about the blue diamond mark is mentioned outside the station. You all know why. If it gets into the press we'll have a rash of similar marks to distract us from the proper investigation. I'm stressing this and I want it properly understood by all departments. Yes?'

A murmured 'Yes, sir' ran through the room. He glanced round again, then went on.

'We can't hope to keep the fact out of the papers that the dog was killed. Probably some reporter may get on to the means of killing too, since we'll be asking a lot of people a lot of questions. As far as the general public's concerned, therefore, I want it stressed that we're looking into a piece of mindless cruelty to an animal, which we consider very important but not a matter of danger to the general population. I shall put out a press release to that effect if it seems to be necessary. We want to know the usual things: whether anybody saw anyone in the field early on Sunday morning. Whether anyone's ever been seen watching the house or the back gate into the garden. Whether anyone has recently sold a crossbow which takes bolts like this—' He held up the steel bolt for everyone to see. 'And whether anyone has cut this key recently.' He showed them a plain key of standard shape. 'Unfortunately, Inspector Hollings left his own key in the lock one morning when he went out – he now thinks – and it was found later in the long grass beside the gate. This key, found in the same grass yesterday, is a copy.

'Forensics will give us everything they can on the site of the killing. We can only hope they'll come up with something useful. I've said everything I have to say for the moment – unless anyone has any relevant questions?'

174

Some faces looked as if they would like to come out with one, then minds were changed and nobody asked anything. It was a sober group which broke up and moved to go about its business. It would be an even soberer one, Jane thought, when more of the facts came out – as they inevitably would – when Rogalleh came back. Because he would come back; that was a sure bet.

They might, of course, have caught the perpetrator in the meantime. Surely Blue Betty had taken one too many risks this time. The city was, as Rogalleh had said, so much smaller than Birmingham. Somebody must have seen something . . . to give them leads to follow, evidence to find. Forensics were probably more advanced than they had been six years ago; DNA testing certainly was. If he had left just one sign . . .

Two days later she came in from work feeling shattered. She knew that everything which could be done was being done, everyone available drawn into it, so far with very little result but one could always hope. She knew, too, because the Super had told her this afternoon, that Rogalleh would be arriving at the end of the week to take charge of the investigation. A senior officer with the relevant experience often was appointed to take over a case with the ramifications of this one. Usually it would be an assistant chief constable – but this time Jane could guess that Rogalleh had moved heaven and earth to argue that he was the right person for the job, in spite of his previous failure. She came in to a dark house – but when she switched the light on Adrian was there, sitting in one of the armchairs, raising a hand to shield his eyes from the sudden bright light.

'Hi. Why were you sitting in the dark?'

'I just hadn't got round to putting the light on,' he said flatly, and then, 'Matty rang you earlier.'

'Yeah? I'll ring her back sometime.' She hesitated, then, 'I don't know if you've heard, but—'

Frances Ferguson

'If it's something about your bloody job, I don't want to know. I'll tell *you* something. Elizabeth's lost the baby. She miscarried late last night.'

'Yes, I – I know.' It was what she had been about to say. She had just been to the hospital, in fact; that was why she was late. She was opening her mouth to say so, but he looked up at her with angry eyes.

'Oh, how? Did you go in to ask her questions, and then find it wasn't exactly the moment? Or did you go on and question her anyway?'

'No, actually.' She had asked the Super to send somebody else to ask Elizabeth a series of careful and gentle questions, on Monday evening, when she had been reported as being calm enough to receive them. It seemed to Jane that she might find it easier with an impersonal stranger, one who had not known and played with her beloved dog. Tonight's visit, made awkwardly with flowers and a loss to know what to say, had been personal, and because Jane had heard the tragic news earlier in the day. She had not stayed long, but she had wanted to show ... Adrian was speaking again, with a stare which was definitely accusing.

'You're not going to pretend you care, I see. Well, you wouldn't, would you? With your fixed opinions on the career versus babies argument!'

'You sound as if you've had several drinks. If you hadn't you wouldn't be so—'

'Truthful?'

'Look, I'm trying to be calm and not get into a fight. Of course it's sad, of course I feel for her—'

'Oh, do you? Well I am surprised. Considering you preferred to stay out in the garden looking for clues instead of coming back and trying to help her when she was in such a desperate state on Sunday, I rather know what to make of your idea of sympathy, don't I?'

176

'Oh, for Christ's sake, Adrian! I'll put what you're saying down to the fact that you're upset and in shock, and—'

'Don't you patronise me!'

'I'm not.' Anger was flicking inside her, hard though she tried to crush it. 'Elizabeth is my friend. What the hell makes you think you've got a monopoly on feelings? I feel for her, and I feel for Chris, and you can stop sounding as if she wouldn't have miscarried if I'd come in and held her hand on Sunday, too!'

'Yeah, well, neither of you did, did you? I know you wouldn't care, but I should have thought Chris—'

'Oh, shut up! Shut up and go to hell! You don't understand one thing, and – oh, I've had enough!'

She turned on her heel and swept out again. Going who knew where ... It was her home, and she would have to come back to it sometime; but not before he had had the chance to sober up. And she had had the chance to calm down. It had been bad enough ...

Bad enough seeing Elizabeth, pale and listless, trying very hard to smile rather than cry. Bad enough not knowing what to say to offer comfort. Awkwardly aware that there really was no comfort for her double loss, and that Jane's presence must only remind her of the first one. She certainly couldn't offer, 'It might have been Chris, you know' and frighten her as well.

As it was, when Elizabeth suddenly gulped, reached for her hand, and said, 'You were so sweet with Hector!' all she could find to say was an earnest 'We will get the person who did it!'

'Yes, Chris seems to think that matters too. I'm – I'm not so sure it makes any difference.'

Somebody else came visiting then, another friend, so Jane could leave. Should she have said encouragingly, 'You can have another dog – and another baby?' It would have seemed the acme of tactlessness to do so.

All she *could* do was throw herself into finding the man who had killed Elizabeth's beloved pet, and might have killed her husband instead if the circumstances had gone a different way.

That knowledge still gave Jane a shiver.

And a further one, to fear that they could have more from Blue Betty yet.

Chapter 15

She thought of going to see Matty, but went to the pictures instead, disinclined for any personal company. It was better to sit alone in the dark and try to be distracted by a piece of extremely noisy science fiction whose plot she totally failed to follow. When she went home it was late, and she found Adrian had gone go bed. One bedside lamp was on, dimly lighting the hump under the bedclothes, but he seemed to be genuinely asleep. She hesitated for a moment, then collected her things very quietly and went to sleep in the spare room. When she got up in the morning it was to find he had already left. As a situation, it was all deeply unpromising, she thought with a touch of bitterness – but she wasn't prepared to spend time thinking about it.

Too much else to do.

House-to-house enquiries had found a neighbour of the Hollings who had seen, from an upstairs window, the figure of a woman crossing the field early on Easter Sunday morning. Merely a glimpse from behind; a tall woman in a headscarf and wearing a cloak, memorable because a cloak had seemed slightly unusual ... A suitable way, however, to hide a crossbow. The figure had been moving away from the houses, some time around seven thirty a.m. – though the witness could not swear to an accurate time – and there had been no view of a face.

Nobody had been noticed hanging around in the field

179

at any other time or showing particular interest in the Hollings' gate. But then a variety of people used the footpath round that field, ramblers and walkers, children playing; no particular note would be taken of a stranger, as long as that stranger behaved in an ordinary way.

No sports shop so far remembered selling a crossbow. It was not something commonly held in stock. The one gun shop in the city – which did sell them, under security, since a crossbow was definitely an offensive weapon – could demonstrate the type of bow which must have been used, but had not made any recent sales. Nor had there been any robberies reported where a crossbow had been stolen. Bolts could be purchased separately but none of those appeared to have been sold anywhere locally either ... Enquiries had gone out further afield and they were also looking into the type of magazine which might offer postal purchases. Sports and archery clubs were also being checked. Particularly since it would appear that a crossbow needed both strength and a certain expertise to fire it accurately.

Forensics was still going meticulously through every minuscule item found at the site. Much had to be slowly eliminated – marks left by Elizabeth, by Chris, by Jane and Adrian, fibres from Elizabeth's housecoat ... The bolt had no prints on it aside from Elizabeth's and Adrian's – his had been taken on the day, Jane had heard, Elizabeth's later – and on the dart and the note there were no prints apart from Chris's; while the blood on the note was canine and had clearly been left when Chris handled it. The capital letters on the note had been cut from a local newspaper, and stuck with standard paper glue available anywhere. Footprints in the field and near the hedge and gate might have been anyone's. No knife had been found. No bloodstained boots, gloves or clothing either – though teams had been set to the unpleasant task of searching through the upper levels of the local rubbish dumps.

Jane came home on Thursday night only to make a sandwich, and to check her post and give herself a brief break. She was slapping some cold chicken and lettuce between two slices of bread when she heard the sound of the front door opening – and drew a breath of annoyance. She had calculated she would be early enough to avoid confrontation. On the other hand she did live here and could hardly avoid it forever. She refused to look round, but heard Adrian clear his throat.

'Jane? I went to see Elizabeth this afternoon. She says you—'

'Yes.' She turned to look at him, to see apology in his eyes. 'It doesn't make any difference, though, does it? I don't want to talk about it any more. I've only come in to grab a quick bite and then I'm going back to work. We're all involved in this one – and detection,' she added pointedly, 'is a busy occupation.'

'You're not going to let me say I'm sorry?'

'I'm not sure there's an awful lot of point. That was a truthful opinion you were giving.' She looked at him. 'But like I said, I'm a lot too busy to stop and discuss it. So if you wouldn't mind . . .'

'Well I do, obviously. But all right. Listen, do you know how I can get hold of Chris? Because I'd like to apologise to him too.' He frowned. 'Elizabeth seems to think he's staying somewhere else, and I must say, I'd have expected him to visit her rather more than once a day at the hospital—'

'Don't start! All right,' Jane said between her teeth, 'I'm going to tell you this, even though it's totally confidential and I shouldn't, but I'm going to just in case you start saying things . . .' She drew a quick breath. 'We think that bolt was meant for Chris. That he was meant to be killed, not the dog. This is totally on the secret list and if you're going to see Elizabeth again remember she doesn't know, and shouldn't. So *don't let it out*, not even a hint of it, clear?'

'I wouldn't. Christ—'

'I'm saying it so that you don't gossip. So you don't make snide remarks where anyone can hear you. About where Chris is or isn't, or when he visits the hospital . . . We don't know that he'll get targeted again, but we're being careful. We've got a killer out there – and I, along with everybody else, am going to be busy trying to find him. That's a warning. Don't complain about it. For preference, don't even think about it. But above all, *don't talk*!'

'Yes, I understand. And I won't. Jane . . . Are you in danger too?'

'No, I'm not.'

'You can't expect me not to worry . . .'

'I've said I'm not. I've told you too much already and I can't say any more. But I do need your absolute promise that you won't say anything to anybody.'

'I've already given it. Do you have to talk to me as if you were grilling a suspect?'

'Sorry. I just wanted to make sure you understood. You might say something to Felicity, for instance . . .' There was a sudden sour memory of hearing from Harry that Adrian had been grumbling to Felicity about Jane's obsession with work, but she left that and finished, 'Well, don't.'

'I'm not very likely to at the moment, considering she and Harry have gone off up to Nuneaton for a few days. To talk to his wife about the upcoming divorce, I gather, and arrangements for dividing up property and all that. I'm not sure Harry's entirely willing, but they've both been summoned,' he said drily, then added, 'so you're not the only one who's going to be busy. Jane, are you absolutely sure

182

you're not in danger? Because if you've got somebody who's targeting the police—'

'I've said I'm not,' she repeated. 'I've got to go back to work now.' She came past him, the sandwich still in her hand, then hesitated. 'A senior officer's arriving tomorrow to take over, and after that I don't know what the position's going to be, but – but I reckon I'll probably be thoroughly occupied for as long as it takes. So we probably won't have to trip over each other too much.'

'Please don't. I've said I'm sorry. Don't be so *bloody* inflexible!'

She looked at him, sighed, and left. She wasn't willing to think about their relationship now, anyway; there was too much else. A race against time to get Blue Betty caught and nailed before he could start his next deadly game.

Rogalleh arrived on Friday morning and went into immediate conference with Superintendent Annerley. After a while the DCI was called in as well. There seemed to be plenty to argue about, from the length of time the discussion went on. What came out of it, eventually, and not until mid-afternoon, contained some surprises.

Rogalleh was to have a free hand in running the investigation; there was nothing too startling in that. He had after all been appointed to head it. But he had particular ideas about his team.

Jane. The two WDCs from CID, Rachel Welsh and Jennie Cullen. A detective sergeant seconded from Faversham, Kate Vander. That was the primary group, and it was all female.

They would have male back-up, of course, working from the station, helping with investigations where necessary. But Rogalleh wanted only women officers in the group particularly dedicated to catching Blue Betty.

'I'm laying a bet that he'll know within a few days who I've got after him this time,' the detective superintendent said. 'He quoted names in one of his phone calls to me before; he likes to show how clever he is. And if it does make the press – if we find we can't blanket it, though another aim I've got is to starve him of publicity as far as possible – then we'll have female spokespersons quoted, and only female. I've got agreement on that. Also, that there'll be a small press release giving my name as a new appointment down here, though without saying why.'

He was in Jane's office holding a meeting with her and the two WDCs; DS Kate Vander would arrive to take up her duties tomorrow morning. It was no longer Jane's office, in fact, but Rogalleh's, for the duration. She had already moved down to a desk in the revived incident room, the other half of that large office now turned into a single-aim extension of CID. Rachel Welsh and Jennie Cullen had already been given the basic facts about Blue Betty and had been asked if they were prepared to volunteer for this particular duty. Both had instantly said yes. Jane herself had had a private interview with Rogalleh after being told he wanted her as his second-in-command.

'You've been in on this from the start, and you're a bright officer by all accounts – as well as what I've seen of you – with good CID experience,' he told her. 'I've had a look at your record. One thing comes out of it: you're a bit of a maverick, aren't you? And never mind if it's got you results in the past, you're going to watch that this time. No going out on your own, there's *always* to be back-up, someone who knows where you are. I may be counting on the fact that Blue Betty's only after male authority figures, but all the same, if you won't guarantee that, then I won't use you, understand?'

'Yes, sir, and you have my guarantee.'

'You want back in CID, don't you? Yes, I could see that.

I've a good idea why you may have left it, too, after what I heard this morning. But we won't go into that.' Morland, Jane thought: the DCI must really have let his prejudices against women detectives show. 'I'd say you're being wasted where you are,' Rogalleh had rumbled on. 'If you can't get on here, you'll need to move. Still, we've co-opted you for now, haven't we? I reckon I can work with you; I hope you'd say the same about me.'

He had also said he wanted her opinions, and Jane gave him one now, as he stopped explaining the outline of his plans to the two WDCs. 'You're setting yourself up, aren't you, sir? If he wants to go after someone in the police again, you're making sure it'll be you. Isn't that a bit of a risk?'

'Better that way,' Rogalleh said mildly, though with that same stubborn jut to his lip Jane had seen before. 'He knew I was here. I'm going to make sure he knows it again. But this time – well, let's say I'm deliberately narrowing his field. Only in case, mind.' His face was suddenly grim, but then he shook it off and looked round at the three of them. 'Well, that's all for this afternoon. We'll have a more thorough meeting tomorrow morning when Sergeant Vander gets here. Oh, and don't fire up at me if I get absent-minded and call you "ladies" – or even "girls", or anything else that comes into my head – because at my age I'm not going to remember all the time to be politically correct or whatever you want to call it. As I said to a sergeant of mine recently, you'll just have to live with the fact that old dogs don't learn new languages easily.'

'As long as you give us the work we won't mind what you call us, sir,' Rachel Welsh said with a grin. She and Jennie Cullen stood up, offered an official 'Sir' and left the room.

Formidable was one word to describe Rogalleh, Jane thought as she left the room too, after checking he didn't want her for anything else. Surprising was another. She wouldn't have predicted the tactics he had decided to use. She knew he felt responsible for his former DI's death; he had said as much. She guessed that he now had the attempt on Chris to add into the equation too. The use of his name on the note ensured that. But to insist on an all-female team to help him catch Blue Betty? That was radical. An old dog might not learn new languages, but he was no male chauvinist. And he would use any trick which came to his hand, new or old, in his pursuit of his prey.

Detective Sergeant Kate Vander turned out to be fortyish, ginger-haired, with the touch of a Kentish accent and a solidly calm manner. She had ten years' experience in CID, the last three in Faversham but previously in Dover, giving her a good knowledge of the whole area. She listened stolidly to Rogalleh's summing up of the entire situation, past and present, and asked several pertinent questions. She was clearly going to be an asset, Jane thought. She had mentioned that she had worked with Doug Phelps, who was ex-Faversham before he moved to CID here; perhaps it was he who had put forward her name.

'How far afield are you drawing your circle?' was one of the questions she asked. 'You've reckoned Blue Betty's a car driver – a car owner? – which means he can come in at his leisure and go out again to safety. What kind of area are we estimating?'

'I think he's here.' Rogalleh said it on a deep rumble. 'Last time we tried concentric circles outwards and knew he could have been moving in from any of them. But this time – no, I think he's right here. And I'll tell you why: because that's what my instincts are saying.' His dark eyes looked round at all of them. 'Yes, I did say instinct, not experience. And don't underestimate it: experience tells me not to! That prickle up the back of your neck – that's a built-in danger signal. That feeling that you know something but you don't quite know why – never ignore it. It could save your life. It's saved mine before now. You'll hear people say that real evidence is what we need, that's all that counts. I quite agree, it is. When it comes to court I want forensics, witnesses, prints, the lot. But on the way there ... and along with anything any computer can give me ... No, don't deny instinct. Mine says he's here in this city, so close in I can practically smell him.'

There was silence for a moment, but he broke it himself with an unexpected glint of humour. 'That's enough of a speech. Oh, and since I'm a man, don't start supposing I'm talking about something called "women's instinct" either! Nonexistent nonsense. Now, as to what else we know...'

He went on, listing facts, previous profiles, pieces of evidence with a concise practicality. He could quote other serial killer cases, and give comparisons; he had every facet of this type of case at his fingertips. Formidable, Jane thought again. He made it clear he was going to expect a lot from them. When he wanted them to work, they would work; if he decreed that things were to be done a certain way, that was the way they would be done.

It was quickly noticeable around the station that the men found it hard to believe in Rogalleh's choice of team. Jokes were cracked; criticisms were voiced – though not too audibly, and particularly not when Rogalleh was around. As he was, moving about the station with a cat-like quietness for all his bulk so that nobody could be sure of not finding him just behind them when an injudicious remark was being voiced. Somebody instantly coined the name 'Rogalleh's girls' but it was rapidly squashed, in public at least, after an unwisely audible scornful comment from a junior constable about 'sending women to do men's work' came to a beetroot-red halt when Rogalleh's voice rumbled directly behind his ear, 'Got something to say to me, have you, sonny?'

Jane had already told the team, during the first weekend, to ignore all comments. Kate Vander had looked up from her desk to say with amused amiability, 'I can always point out that I've been pub arm-wrestling champion for the past two years, if any of them want to know! But you're right, ma'am, it's better to let them get used to it in their own time.'

'I'd say so. *We* all know the reason for it, and maybe it'll gradually dawn on the rest of them that it isn't actually designed as a deliberate blow to macho culture,' Jane said drily. She caught a mutter from Rachel which sounded like a scornful 'If any of them has that much sense!' but let it pass without comment. 'Now then, this issue of mobile phones which we've all got to carry as well as our standard communicators. We should be getting them in the next few days, and once they arrive please do remember that the guv'nor wants us to carry them with us at all times. Oh, and just in case I have to mention it, do also remember not to be tempted to use them for private chats!'

It was another of Rogalleh's quirks, to decree that they all had this extra line of communication; though how he had got the expense past the DCI defied imagination. Jane looked towards the two WDCs.

'Right then, Jennie, Rachel, you two and I have got the thoroughly élite Sunday-morning job of going to examine that rubbish tip in case there's anything to be found from the last of this week's collections. Kate, we'll leave you catching up on the files.'

'At least it's not raining this time,' Jennie murmured wryly; she had been on one of the previous rubbish-search details.

'No, and it's just the current domestic tip. And only Friday's load. They finish collecting the shop bins on Thursday, luckily for us, so the other tip's already been checked. OK, let's be on our way!'

The sight of the scooped-out hollow in the ground, dauntingly large, was less than inviting when they reached it. The three of them climbed down in their wellingtons and overalls. This was undoubtedly one job the men were glad to have handed over with the rest of the investigation. But the place had to be searched, specifically for bloodstained shoes or boots and clothing, since nobody could have walked away from the gory scene of the dog's death unmarked.

Anything could easily have been stuffed into one of the lidded wheelie bins left out overnight on the pavement for the arrival of the dustcart in the morning. It was an all too simple method of disposal. The bins were lifted on to the cart closed, to spew out their contents invisibly inside the lorry. With such tidy mechanisation, not even the bin men would see what went into the dark interior. So they had to look, as squads of officers had been looking patiently all week. Not too far below the surface, luckily, because it had been deemed an impossible job to sift through rubbish going back for months. If Blue Betty had come out to the dump in person and buried the evidence deeper, that would be a job for mechanical diggers and would only be considered later. For the moment, it was the chance that there was something in this week's rubbish which interested the police. Anything found today would give them specific streets to look at: those covered by Friday's collections. Today's search would be the last, since they were relying on the guess that if incriminating evidence had been disposed of this way, it would have been immediate.

'At least on Sunday there isn't a dustcart the other end sending another cloud of stuff bouncing down. Ma'am— Oh no, it isn't anything, just a piece of bent pipe.' Jennie pulled out the section of curved steel whose shine had caught her eye and she dropped it in disappointment. 'I haven't found any clothing at all in this bit . . .'

'OK, try the next area . . . We may not get dustcarts but we do get the odd bag landing on top of us!' Jane glanced up as one bounced near her, to see an apologetic face peering down from the edge not far above her, and to receive an equally apologetic wave from somebody who had thrown without looking first. Until twelve, the general public could drive in to dump anything not collected from outside their homes. A couple of estate cars and vans had turned up since their arrival too to unload unwanted furniture, though those were left above ground in a designated area. 'I wonder who they think we are,' she added humorously, aware that their unmarked overalls must lend themselves to any interpretation. 'Eccentric rag-pickers? Rachel, did you say something?'

'It was only a remark. Something along the lines of, did I *really* tell the guv'nor I didn't mind what he called us as long as he gave us the work?'

Jane grinned. A few minutes later she straightened up and looked round. 'I think we've just about finished. Did somebody do that corner – yes? And we've opened any bags thrown in this morning, once their owners were gone . . .' She had noted the faces, though. 'All right, each of you do a quick circuit round the edge, keeping your eyes peeled as you go, and we'll call it a day. Meantime, I'll go and put this in the car.'

'This', inside a grey plastic sack in her hand, was a tall leather boot, the stain on which might just be blood but probably was not. Nothing else had shown up in the area, though, not even the boot's pair; some woollen gloves, also stained, also probably not with blood, had been picked up in another area and now reposed in the sack as well, but that was their sum total. Not much for an hour and a half's delving. Probably nothing relevant at all, but at least the whole week had been covered now. Jane scrambled up the least steep of the slopes, feeling grubby and dissatisfied – and then found she was being addressed by name.

'Hallo, Inspector Perry!'

Sam Connolly was regarding her with a shy and rather surprised smile. Jane saw Malcolm Jackson behind him, the white van parked just behind. She returned Sam's smile.

'Hallo. If you're rubbish-dumping you've only just squeezed in under the wire, haven't you? They lock the gates at noon.'

She was aware from the corner of her eye that Rachel and Jennie were appearing out of the dump now, though they hung back when they saw she was talking to someone. Sam said:

'Actually, we're not dumping, we're looking for dining-room chairs for the house.' He flushed and went on, 'If you come at the last minute you can find quite good things other people have thrown out, and we're a bit short of— I don't know if you know Malcolm, do you? He lives with us.'

'We did meet. Hallo,' Jane said pleasantly to the round face and glasses. He was looking in her direction, she supposed, though the sun glinting off his glasses made it difficult to know. 'Josh hasn't come with you on your furniture hunt?' she asked Sam, in the hope of alleviating his obvious embarrassment.

'Oh, he's still asleep, the rat,' Sam said with a grin, seeming relieved by the change of subject. He cast a curious glance at Rachel and Jennie. 'Do you – I mean, do the police – often come and check rubbish dumps?'

'We had a report that someone might have been dumping tins of chemicals,' Jane told him, off the top of her head, an easy and civil answer. 'It doesn't seem to be true, luckily. Well . . .'

'I saw a paragraph in the paper about somebody shooting a dog with a crossbow,' Sam offered with sudden gravity. 'I hope you catch the person who did it, it sounds horrible. There was a cop up at the uni asking if any of the colleges had an archery club. Was that why?'

'I'd imagine so. And have any of them?' Jane asked, feigning ignorance, though she remembered seeing a negative report.

'No, or I might have joined. Not to shoot dogs!' he added quickly, pulling a face. 'Only because I used to be quite good at it. Twin and I learned how to shoot with a crossbow at that awful free school I told you about – part of the loony head's commando training, until one of the governors sussed how dangerous it was and stopped it. That's why I particularly noticed the paragraph about the dog. I remember what damage those bolts can do . . . Oh sorry, I'm holding you up, aren't I? And they'll lock the gates on us if we don't hurry, too. Come on, Malcolm!'

He gave Jane another of his sweet smiles and took his silent companion away to inspect the discarded furniture. The two of them could be seen rootling through what appeared to be a stack of fridges – perhaps they wanted one of those too and knew how to put it back in order – but from the look of things they were going to be disappointed on usable chairs. Rachel and Jennie joined her at the car, and she was amused to see Jennie glancing back with definite interest.

'Students?' she asked, and then added casually, as if to mask her curiosity, 'it's usually students who come down looking to see what they can find – the ones whose parents have bought them a house to share while they're at college, but who haven't shelled out enough to furnish it properly as well.'

'Is it? You're knowledgeable.'

'Well, the other kind of poor won't look twice at other people's rejects; they want social services to divvy up instead,' Rachel said drily, as both girls got into the car. Then, as Jennie glanced back again, she added on a teasing note, 'Yes, the fair one is quite dishy, isn't he?'

'He's twenty-one, he's at the university studying politics, and as a matter of fact he lives at home with his mother,' Jane said, allowing their light-hearted interest. 'He's also the better-looking of a pair of twins, and his name's Sam Connolly. As to how I know – he's Lionel Hughes' stepson.'

'Oh.'

Jane saw in her mirror that Jennie's face had immediately sobered. She could make a guess at what the girl was thinking, too. Connected with a case, however peripherally; off limits. She almost remarked that anyone who had hoped a twenty-one-year-old was *on* limits made her feel old; but the WDC was, after all, only twenty-four. Jane said briskly, 'Once you two have got yourselves – what, fumigated? – you can go off duty. I don't believe the guv'nor's got anything else he wants you to do today. I'll get this stuff sent to Forensics, though I don't think we're going to get any joy out of it. We're going to have to hope something else comes up to give us a lead.'

She had a suspicion that Rachel at least – and maybe Jennie, too – had an inner determination that 'Rogalleh's girls' were going to succeed on this case – one in the eye for every male doubter in the station. And though that had not been the intent behind Rogalleh's choice, it could do no harm.

If only the keenness of all concerned could bring them something towards a quick result.

Chapter 16

They had a map of Birmingham and its environs pinned up on the wall of the incident room cum office now, alongside everything else – to make Rogalleh feel at home, someone had suggested humorously, though they all knew what it actually signified. A reminder of Blue Betty's earlier hunting ground; a reminder too that they were urgently looking for someone who might have had reason to be around the Midlands seven years ago, but was here now . . . In a mobile population it was possible that any number of people might have moved from one part of the country to another, but since such relocations were usually not made without cause, one thing being done was a compilation of the names of any local companies which might have a Midlands branch and might have made a staff transfer during the last six years.

'Needles and haystacks, isn't it?' Kate Vander commented dubiously. 'Bearing in mind that anybody could have changed firms, or decided to move because Auntie Bertha had died and left them a house or any number of reasons. A lot of careers aren't long-term nowadays, whether people started out in the hope they were or not.'

'Quite, but we can hardly try and trace every redundancy in Birmingham six years ago to see if any one of them came down here for a change of lifestyle,' Jane said drily, looking at the list Geoff Madox had provided for them. 'And if the guv'nor wants us to go along and see every personnel officer on this list individually, then that's— Yes, Jennie?'

'Ma'am, can I ask you something?'

'Yes, shoot?'

'I know we're looking for someone who lived in Birmingham up until six years ago, but why does it have to be somebody who was in work? Couldn't it just as easily be someone who was on the dole, or a drifter?'

'The offender profiles suggested the killer could be described as organised, intelligent and with his own transport. Of course those are only assumptions. They could be wrong. But if you grant the assumptions, then that kind of profile's usually supposed to fit somebody who's working.'

'But how do they know? All that?'

'What's the basis of offender profiling, you mean? How do forensic psychiatrists set about it? Well, they go on inference. And look for something they call a crime signature. While we're searching for evidence, they're looking for the offender's thought processes. They start out by studying the victim or victims; then they look at the means of the crime; out of that they produce a set of behaviour characteristics. Then they say, well, these behaviour characteristics fit someone with such-and-such a background, such-and-such an attitude . . . They may go as far as saying, 'This person is definitely white, over thirty, unskilled labourer' and that's what everybody starts looking for. And sometimes,' Jane added drily, 'the perpetrator turns out to be a twenty-two-year-old Asian with a law degree instead. On the other hand, profiles have been known to be remarkably accurate, so you pays your money and takes your choice, so to speak.'

'I see,' Jennie said, looking subdued.

'I'm surprised they didn't manage to get a speaker profile on Blue Betty, considering he made several phone calls,' Kate put in. 'Speaker profiles really are supposed to be accurate, aren't they? Something about the distribution of energy across sound, below conscious control, so that they can make a reasonable comparison of voices even if one's been disguised?'

'You're right, it's a pity they didn't manage to get a voiceprint. The stuff the guv'nor's given us says he always rang in to unexpected places and never stayed on the line long enough for them to set up a recording, let alone a trace. Though,' Jane added on a sharp sigh, 'we'd need to have found ourselves a suspect before we could have made a comparison anyway.' She looked at Jennie and decided she had better offer something encouraging. 'There's no need to look so down. I wasn't saying we have to throw out the profiles we've got, if that's what you thought. As I said, they're a place to start. And we do know quite a lot about Blue Betty, from both past and present actions; so with luck, and once we've put everything together, we may get a good strong lead.'

They were all aware that the killer had deliberately thrown the gauntlet down to Rogalleh, and it lent an urgency to their investigations, which of necessity seemed crawlingly slow. Kate was going out at lunchtimes and in the evenings to the pubs Lionel Hughes had been known to drink in, to make an apparently casual study of any regulars. All of them were making highly visible tours round the sports shops again, and the gun shop, and anywhere that sold knives; they could also be seen, by anyone who cared to look, examining places where incriminating evidence might have been hidden. Any burglary from a house or a garage in the past few weeks which listed 'sports equipment' among the missing items was getting a return visit from Rogalleh's team to check that no crossbow or knife was among the haul. They would all be calling on the firms on Geoff Madox's list, again highly visibly. And the appointment of Detective Superintendent Rogalleh to the city police had been reported as a brief paragraph in all this week's local papers so far.

That was a tactic of which Jane was privately uncertain, with its overtones of returning the challenge. Surely it was dangerously close to inciting... She was loath to nurse the suspicion that Rogalleh didn't care, as long as he could get his hands on Blue Betty at last. Perhaps that conclusion was unfair. The psychopath they were after had already killed again before Rogalleh put in an appearance in the district; he might have set up a second killing anyway... and Rogalleh had certainly not incited that one deliberately.

Where had Blue Betty been for six quiet years? Here, a reformed character, until the possibility that Lionel might know too much set him off again? Somewhere else? *Where?*

It was Jane who had been selected to make a television appearance on the local station's *Crimestoppers* programme, asking for the viewers' help to track down the 'mindless vandal' who had shot and slashed a family pet. She guessed that Rogalleh had only chosen her because to do it himself would lend a suspicious weight. Or, possibly, he wanted her publicly described as 'the DI in charge of the case' to take the heat off Chris. She had heard that Chris was agitating to be allowed back to work. She had never appeared in front of the camera before, and had to hide a slight apprehension as she arrived at the studios; however, the recording went well; at least the producer told her so. Driving home she felt a wry relief and a flash of amusement: had she really been so scared? She could only hope that the telephone numbers she had handed over to be flashed up for the public to ring would appear correctly when the programme went out. They were the station number, Rogalleh's mobile, and hers.

A choice for Blue Betty if, along with what might hopefully be a helpful public, he decided to make a call.

Bait.

Jane drove back into the city contemplating that – and thinking too, with a touch of guilt, that she really must get in touch with Matty. She had found a note from Adrian propped against the cornflakes packet this morning saying, 'Matty rang again last night, please ring her.' She had tried Matty's home number but had only got the answering machine. She had waited for the beep, then said, 'Hi, it's Jane, sorry I haven't been on but I'm terribly busy. I will call though!' And she must. Sometime . . .

Her thoughts were abruptly jerked away from their automatic half concentration on the road. She was within the city's limits now, joining a steady stream of cars along the ring road for the late-afternoon rush hour. And that figure ahead taking a weaving course along the pavement was instantly recognisable. Josh Connolly. She would have to do something; his erratic gait was downright dangerous, suggesting that he might stagger out unexpectedly into the road. She signalled her move to the car behind her and pulled up sharply beside him.

'Hallo! Hallo, Inspallector Perry!'

He peered at her with a giggle. 'Get in the car, please,' Jane ordered in her most official voice.

'OK . . .' He got in, unsteadily, and with another giggle. Not drink, from the lack of any smell, and it didn't look or smell like cannabis either; something, however, to tangle his tongue and give him very bright eyes and a silly manner. He said hopefully, 'Can I drive?'

'Certainly not.'

'I can. I took – took to it like a druck to water. I mean a duck. It wasn't me driving when Pete . . .' His face suddenly crumpled and he wrapped his arms round himself as if in pain. 'It was him, that's why he got killed and the rest of us didn't. They should have blamed us and locked us away, shouldn't they? We didn't even get done for borrowing the car because the master admitted he lent it to us . . .'

'What have you taken, Josh?' Jane asked sternly, letting these revelations ride over her. 'Amphetamines again? Yes, I do know you were in trouble for that before.'

'I haven't. Wouldn't know where to get them now. Wouldn't want to.' He gave a shiver. 'All I've had is calm-down pills. Honest! M-medicine. Legal. I get given them, you know. Because I'm nuts. Do you ever get dreams, Inspallector? Horrible ones where things – where you don't know if . . . I'm scared, you know. I mean, I'm scared . . .'

'I'm going to take you home.' It might be true that he was on legal medicine. Antidepressants perhaps, which could have odd effects on some people. 'Put your seat belt on,' she instructed. 'Yes, now – oh, all right, I'll fasten it then!' His movements were uncoordinated, and there was a look in his eyes which was streets away from the giggle with which he had greeted her. A deep unhappiness definitely edged with fear. Oh hell, had he taken something psychotropic? She probably ought to take him in to the station on suspicion; she did have the grounds that he had been behaving in a disorderly fashion on a public highway.

She signalled and moved out into the fast-moving traffic, but when she reached the roundabout from which a right turn would have taken her to the police station she went straight on instead. 'I'm acting on the basis that I'm off duty, that you're supposed to have been ill, and that your family's had enough to worry them lately,' she said in a voice which held a steely undertone. 'None of which means that if I find you wandering around in this state again I won't arrest you – understand? But today I've decided to believe you when you say all you've had is legal medicine. However—'

'You didn't say if you'd ever had dreams. I do. They went away after a while but now they've come back. I'm the shadow-twin, you see. Do you know about that? That there's often a good twin and a bad twin? I don't know why, it must be ge – getenics – genetics. Otherwise I wouldn't dream, would I, and do awful things . . .'

His voice had sunk to a mutter, and Jane glanced at him. He was shivering a little, and she wondered suddenly whether she really ought to be taking him to the hopsital. He seemed to be caught up in some kind of personal terror. However, Willowfield Way was coming up now. The most practical thing to do was to hand him over directly into his mother's care, with a warning. Maybe even a suggestion that Rowena should get him to hospital if she didn't know what he had taken. If Jane did that herself it would have to become official, and there *was* always the chance that he had been telling the truth; that he had been given something by a doctor and it had disagreed with him. Let Rowena decide what to do about her son.

Rowena, however, was clearly fully occupied. After Jane had decanted Josh from the car, it was all too visible that behind a brightly lit front window there was an exercise class going on; half a dozen figures were bouncing up and down in leotards. 'Ssh! We'd better go in through the kitchen,' Josh said, and began an exaggerated tiptoeing towards the back of the house.

Jane followed him. He opened a back door and immediately they were in a large and brightly lit kitchen. Chantal and Sam looked up at them from seats round a table where heaped vegetables and pans suggested they were preparing a meal, while the baby waved his arms amiably from the safety of a high chair. The sight of an unsteady Josh brought concern and alarm to their faces and the further sight of Jane added an immediate apprehension as both scrambled to their feet.

She chose to address Sam. 'I've brought your brother home because he doesn't seem to be in a fit state to be out,' she said. 'I'll tell you, as I told him, that I'm off duty. And *he* tells me that he hasn't taken anything besides legal medicine. Your mother may be wise to contact the hospital if whatever it's supposed to be is having this effect on him. Since she appears to be busy I'll hand him over to you, but you should take this as a warning – understand?'

There was little not to understand in her tone. Chantal had moved quickly to put her arms round Josh as he stood swaying, and his head went down on her shoulder. Sam managed a stammered 'Yes' and Jane decided that his face showed he was taking it seriously enough, so she could, in all conscience, go.

'Thank you . . .' Sam said, as if remembering himself, but she merely gave him a nod and began to withdraw. If she was making too much allowance for them . . . But enough else was happening at the station, she thought with exasperation as she walked back round the house, to allow her to decide that whatever Josh's problems were, they really could do without him just now.

She drove away, deciding that since she was facing this way she might as well come out the other end of Willowfield Way and take the narrow cut-through on to the nearby estate and St Martin's Hill. She was going slowly, her thoughts occupied, and had only just turned into the estate when a bicycle suddenly shot out from a back alley and swooped to a halt directly in front of her. She stamped on the brakes with a curse – but she had already seen who it was, as Sam threw the bicycle down and came urgently to her window.

'Inspector—'

'You're lucky I know how to stop!'

The words were flung scathingly at him as she wound down the window but he accepted them with no more than a breathless apology. 'Sorry . . . I had to speak to you, and coming round the back was the only way to catch you up! I know what you thought but it isn't true. And I wanted you to know. Twin isn't on drugs, honestly. Look, I know Ma tells people he had glandular fever, but actually he – he had a breakdown. He was pretty much over it until just lately, only he's suddenly gone downhill again – but it *was* only medicine he took. Stupid to give him somebody else's in my view but ... I've been persuading Ma to send him to a private counsellor, and I have now, he's starting next week. So you won't – I mean—'

Jane had to wait for the breathless speech to break off before she could get a word in. 'I told you, I'm off duty. And all right, I'll believe you—'

'You can. Truly. Twin's had a bloody awful time of it but he will get better. I – I think Lionel dying like that must have set him off again, because ... Oh, well never mind that. I just wanted you to understand!'

'OK, I do, so you can stop making suicidal gestures. With the bicycle,' she said drily, since her words seemed to have puzzled him. 'I wasn't going to report him anyway. As for him not being on drugs – no, all right, I'll accept what you say, but I was just going to add that I do know he sometimes uses cannabis, so you might watch that too. He may just have been using it to calm himself down, but it can be mildly addictive, and it may not mix with prescribed medicines – clear?'

'Yes,' Sam said meekly. She thought that he had been about to protest that pot was harmless, but her last words had apparently stopped him. She had felt obliged to deliver the warning. Josh might as well not land himself in trouble with the drugs squad. She looked at Sam's anxious face and thought of another warning to give him; not really her business but it seemed worth offering.

'I notice you often call Josh "twin". Just now – when he's in this unstable state – I think you might try and avoid it. He seemed to be in some sort of a nightmare about being a twin, from what he was burbling. Thoroughly gothic, but if he's having a bad reaction to something which is having a psychotropic effect on him ... You understand what I'm saying? Oh, and do take him to the hospital if he gets any worse; you're absolutely right that he shouldn't have taken somebody else's antidepressants or whatever they were, and you never know what they can do.'

She wound up her window to show that that was the end of the conversation, waited for him to remove the thrown-down bicycle from her path, and drove away. She had done all she could. Sam and Josh were like two sides of a coin, she thought. And for all Josh's instability there was something attractive about both of them. Perhaps it was only Sam's obvious loyalty which made him claim that his brother was the brilliant one, but if it was true, the younger twin could certainly have done with some of the elder's good sense as well, if he was going to get through the normal vagaries of life.

It must be odd to be a twin, though. Did it make you feel like half a person?

She drove into the station, since 'off duty' was actually inaccurate, and was a relative term anyway. She had no particular wish to go home, and there was always the chance that Rogalleh would be in and wanting her. However, she heard from the duty desk sergeant that he had gone home – or rather to the small hotel where he was now a permanent resident. Nobody else was in when she reached her desk either. She could always see if anything had been added to the information steadily being compiled on the computer. She went to switch it on, then paused, aware of a feeling of disquiet surfacing from the back of her brain.

Why did Josh have bad dreams and mutter about doing 'awful things'? Dreams which had gone away, but had now come back?

No, it wasn't possible. Absolutely not. He would only have been fourteen at the time of the Blue Betty killings!

A fourteen-year-old could be as tall as a man. Could hate authority figures, too.

She walked across and looked up at the map of the Birmingham area on the wall, her disquiet growing. The Connolly boys had been at boarding school up there, somewhere on the edge of the city. They had been taken away when they were fifteen and sent to a school in Scotland instead. One which was much more formal, presumably, and much stricter than the other where they could go out all night without question. And borrow a master's car freely, even when under the legal driving age. Seven years ago they had been at the Birmingham school; six years ago they had moved away.

Josh knew how to shoot with a crossbow. Sam had told her both of them had learned to do it.

Josh was brilliant but highly unstable. He had had a recent breakdown – and his instability had suddenly shown signs of getting worse since his stepfather's death.

Josh might have hated Lionel. Particularly a Lionel who had recently been hectoring his mother, shouting at her, trying to bully her.

Rowena was very, very defensive about Josh. Exaggeratedly so. She didn't want anyone from the police seeing him or speaking to him. When Josh had his breakdown and came out to live with her she even went to the extent – possibly – of employing somebody to keep watch over him. Was that because something had happened before? Surely, even Rowena would not protect... But she might, with that powerfully maternal streak in her character. Particularly if she didn't actually know, only sensed that there might be something more radically wrong with her son than she could ever admit, even to herself. And in corollary she would also never admit that there might be any connection between her ex-husband's death and her son. Yet she had fainted dead away when she heard that Lionel had died unnaturally – surely an unexpected reaction from someone of her strength and health and character . . .

A picture was forming which Jane wanted to reject, yet couldn't quite do so.

But there was no way Josh could have stolen his step-father's papers. He couldn't have taken them at night because Angelica never went out at night, so he would have had to stay over . . . There was absolutely no chance that he could have been absent from Les Beaux Vents for the length of time required for him to kill his stepfather, dump him, stay to burgle Angelica's house – all that without remark. There had been nothing to suggest Josh had been away according to the gossipy locals Hilaire had questioned. And how would he have got back, anyway? He clearly didn't have a car of his own, or that would have come to light too. He could hardly have hitched his way back, with the extra time that would have taken as well. No and no; it was all out of the question.

Jane drew breath, feeling slightly foolish. The sudden scenario she had allowed herself to build in her head was rubbish. What she had been doing was letting the nightmare of the knowledge of Blue Betty's presence get to her, so that it only took the sight of a boy wrapped up in his own nightmares to set her off.

She looked up at the map of Birmingham and its environs again. Someone from there who was here now . . . It was a discouragingly huge area. Her eyes ranged round, counting up the boroughs and the nearby towns which must have come within Rogalleh's concentric circles. Where did you draw the line? Round Edgbaston, Solihull, Sutton Cold-field? A car owner would have access from further; surely it would be easy enough to come in from Stratford, Warwick, Coventry, Nuneaton—

Why did Nuneaton give her pause?

She tried to catch hold of it, but the memory wouldn't gel. Somebody, surely, had mentioned Nuneaton the other day, and in a context which gave a connection in her mind to Lionel Hughes, too.

One of the firms on Geoff Madox's list? No, if it had been that she wouldn't be making a link with Lionel.

Oh hell, what *was* it?

Chapter 17

The annoying thing about memory was that the more you tried to delve into it, the more it offered a blank. She would just have to leave it and hope something came back to her.

Her *Crimestoppers* piece was shown the following evening. Early the next morning while Jane was having breakfast Matty rang, her voice amused.

'Ah, so I've caught you at last by ringing at what you'd claim is practically dawn! I know now why you left me a message to say you were busy, don't I? After seeing you described on television as "the detective inspector in charge of the case"! A change of role?'

'Oh, you saw it, then?' Jane leaned her shoulder against the wall and tucked the receiver under her ear so that she could reach for her mug with one hand and a half-eaten piece of toast with the other. Adrian had just left – though this morning she had come down to find he had made her a pot of real coffee, for which she had thanked him with due politeness. 'It didn't go too badly, did it?'

'No, you looked quite glam, as a matter of fact. But you didn't answer my question about the change of role. Have you suddenly got a switch? A permanent one?'

'Temporary. It was Chris's dog, you see.' Even to Matty she couldn't say more than that. 'It was pretty nasty, and he's too closely involved. So I'm standing in. Sorry I haven't been—'

'Think nothing of it. I've been out rather a lot myself,' Matty said, sounding so much like the cat which had got the cream that Jane tore her mind away from its other constant considerations and remembered where Matty had been since she saw her last. She spoke with quickly feigned lightheartedness into the deliberate pause.

'Oh yeah? The baritone was worth your consideration after all, and he's still here? Didn't I just say—'

'No, no. He sings like an angel, but he turned out to be gay. In the closet except to close friends, but definitely a mistake on Mamma's part,' Matty said sweetly and with a certain satisfaction. 'However he has a cousin, one who'd come over to watch him triumph, and *he* – well, let's say he definitely isn't. Much more interesting. Much more everything! And *he*'s still here; being rich enough to hang out wherever he wants to for as long as he wants to . . .'

'You're off, aren't you? I know that tone in your voice!'

'Instant attraction on both sides. I think he's probably a crook, but—'

'*What?*'

'Don't go all policewoman on me, dear, it's just that he'll merely smile his immensely attractive smile if I ask him how he came to make quite so much money by the age of thirty-five – and besides, most people who describe themselves as "financial advisers" probably spend their time being less than straight, don't you think? I really don't care; he's making my life extraordinarily amusing at the moment. I think I might take some of the holiday I'm owed,' Matty added contemplatively, 'so if I'm suddenly not here . . . Anyway, I've reported back as promised, and that's enough about my life and times: let's go back to you. Investigating dogs? I suppose that must soften Adrian. So can I hope in my currently sunny mood that you're getting on better?'

She sounded exceptionally daffy and most unlike herself; it must be love, Jane thought drily. There would certainly be no point in offering a blow-by-blow account of the currently rocky state of Jane's own relationship, even if she wanted to. There really wasn't anything else she could share with her, either. To have said, 'I'm actually chasing a serial killer' might bring her down to earth with a bump, but it was out of bounds. And even if it hadn't been, why spoil Matty's current sense of high-octane happiness? Jane said, into the pause which she hoped wasn't betraying, and with careful lightness, 'Oh, we're getting on fine, things are working themselves out. Look, Matty, I've got to get myself into the station in case any calls come in as a result of last night's appeal. I'm glad you're having a great time; long may it last!'

'Yes, I do hope so. All right, honey, I'll let you go, and stop burbling at you. Life has *definitely* taken an upturn, though, and one of these days when we've both got time, I may even tell you all about it!'

She rang off with a chuckle. Jane spared an amused thought for the fact that she hadn't heard Matty in quite this state for – what, donkey's years? But when her normally tranquil and discreet friend decided to run wild she did so to full effect. Well, good luck to her if she was being carried away by a mad moment!

Her words to Matty that she and Adrian were working things out had a certain degree of truth in them, though in what direction it would be hard to say ... They were speaking to each other civilly, even with occasional ease. He was voicing no open reproaches about the fact that they were still sleeping apart, offering no resentful complaints about her frequent absence, treating with patience the fact that she was more often than not deep in abstracted thought.

Jane sighed sharply, finished her abbreviated breakfast, and took herself in to work. To the constant hope which came with every new day that Rogalleh's team would suddenly come up with something concrete.

Chris was in. Jane came to a stop to see him there, in the corridor just outside the CID room. He was looking slightly gaunt, she thought, though clearly trying hard to appear normal. He acknowledged her presence with a very brief attempt at a smile.

'Hi. I'm back off leave. I'll be doing the usual stuff while you run your own area – that's the decree, so that's what we'll be doing.'

'It's good to see you—'

'It was about time they allowed me back. I'm sleeping in the section house just in case, though. Apparently Rogalleh's agreed that a second attempt isn't likely, but it's a precaution.'

'How's Elizabeth?'

'A lot better, thanks. She's gone to stay with her parents in Tunbridge Wells. Thanks for . . .'

'No need for thanks for *anything*.'

'All right, but I gather Adrian went in to see her several times while she was in hospital, and that was kind. Look, we're all involved in this even if only in the background, so you will keep me posted, won't you?'

'Of course.' Jane added quickly, 'I'm not trying to stand in your shoes, you know that, don't you? It's only that Rogalleh—'

'It's all right – they'd probably have kept me out of it anyway, but I have had the logic explained to me. And I guess it makes some sort of sense. OK, I'll – see you later, I expect.'

He disappeared into the CID room. There had been a bleak note in his voice, Jane thought, throughout the whole conversation. She wondered if she should have offered sympathy for the loss of the baby. There had been something about him, though, which had suggested he didn't want the subject raised. Certainly not here; maybe not at any time . . . He might be carrying it heavily, she guessed, that it was an intended attempt on him which had set everything else off, the killing of his wife's beloved dog, the miscarriage; a fault not really his, but he was taking responsibility for it. Poor Chris.

Still, at least they had let him come back to work to run the rest of CID.

Jane walked on to her own fief, the large office which was now home to all CID's special female team. She learned at once that a couple of phone calls had come in already in response to last night – though only from members of the public ringing to express their indignation at the wanton destruction of an innocent animal. Both calls had been on the station number; nobody had tried either Jane's or Rogalleh's so far. Later in the morning, however, a call did come in to her mobile – because the station number was currently occupied – and this one, from a woman who was prepared to identify herself clearly, was something genuinely promising. The caller had found clothing stuffed in her outside waterbutt several days ago, discovered because it had made the full butt overflow. She had fished it out with annoyance, thinking it merely an inconsiderate piece of vandalism; she did still have the wet garments piled at the bottom of her garden, though, since she had dumped them there to dry out a bit before binning them. Women's clothing, a long skirt and blouse, thoroughly dirty and stained, also what seemed to be a cloak.

'I don't know if it's any help, and I live right the other end of town from where the dog was killed, but you did say . . .'

'Yes, and thank you very much for ringing in. Could I ask you not to touch anything further? I'll be sending somebody round straight away.'

213

Kate and Rachel were rapidly dispatched, and Jane passed the information on to Rogalleh. She saw his eyes take on an immediately alert interest.

'You've told them to take the stuff straight round to Forensics?'

'Yes, sir. They should still be able to tell us if any of the stains are blood, I'd imagine – though I suppose there won't be much else to be had,' Jane added dubiously.

'Very likely not. Which is what the clever bastard will have calculated, won't he?' Rogalleh, however, didn't seem unduly cast down; it was, perhaps, no more than he had estimated. 'Where did you say the caller lives?'

'Here.' Jane pinpointed the road on the map for him. 'A good anonymous distance from the Hollings' house.'

'But as he won't have walked that far bloodstained, we can assume transport – or at least find out if anyone was seen walking with a large bundle. Have you—'

They were interrupted by a further call coming in on Jane's mobile, but it was only another of the sympathetically indignant ones with nothing else to offer. Rogalleh had tensed watchfully, but relaxed as soon as he heard the tone of Jane's answers. She looked up at him when the caller had rung öff and said with a touch of asperity, 'Another one ringing up to express their outraged feelings. I wish they wouldn't – and that we didn't have to sound grateful for their assurances of public support!'

'And you have to doubt if they'd have bothered if it was a human being rather than a dog.' It was a dry rumble. 'If you're going to ask if I've had any calls, I'll only say – not the one I want.'

'You think he'll—'

'I'm counting on it. One of these days. All your mobiles are working all right, are they? No problems with them?'

'They seem to be fine, thank you, sir. I've reminded everyone about keeping them charged.'

'They'd better be fine, at the price. But I'm told it'd take a lot of expert scanning for somebody to find the right band to listen in – whereas almost any Tom, Dick or Harry's sussed how to monitor the ordinary police communications frequency when it suits them. This time he's not going to find out easily just where we are and what we're doing.' His voice was grimly satisfied as he raised an eyebrow at Jane. 'How's the survey of firms going?'

'We've done all the banks, a couple of insurance companies, Boots, a large legal firm . . .' Jane counted them off for him. 'Nothing relevant's shown up so far. We'll do the multiple stores tomorrow, since they're open on Saturdays whereas offices may not be. And estate agents can be tomorrow or Sunday, though we've covered one or two of them already.'

'Not you, tomorrow. You worked all through last weekend, and it's time you had a day off duty. Yes, I'm well aware you've been taking care to give the others spells off, but you haven't been taking any yourself, have you? So tomorrow you will – since otherwise I'll be accused of overworking you!'

'I don't mind, sir.'

'But you'll do as you're told, just the same. Oh, don't worry, I can get hold of you if I need you.' One large finger indicated her mobile phone on the desk in front of her. 'And if I need you, I will!'

'Yes, sir,' Jane said, giving him a grin.

'When those girls come back from Forensics, all of you can get some house-to-house going to see if there was a sighting of anyone with a bundle near that waterbutt. It's all busywork we're doing at the moment,' he added, fretting round the room again and coming to rest in front of the map of Birmingham. 'And none of that got him last time . . . But he has to have made a mistake somewhere. And I'm going to find that mistake. Right, Jane, tell Sergeant Vander she can take over the stores tomorrow while you get your due time off – it'll make a change for her from pub-crawling, at any rate!'

He left, on quiet feet. Back probably to what used to be her office, now redolent with nicotine, though at least he never smoked in here.

Jane contemplated Rogalleh for a moment – his size, his way of appearing unhurried which hid a quick mind, his ability to seem to be wrapped in deep thought but with an alertness which was always there somewhere under the surface . . . Not a man to be lightly crossed, for all he often sounded soft and friendly. At his age and rank he could probably have taken an honourable early retirement if he had wanted it – but she could guess he would never want it until he had closed this particular file. There was too much there; the final killing of the last batch, his DI, not the least.

Jane shook herself and set herself back to work. As soon as Kate and Rachel came back . . . Those were the streets to be quartered.

Nothing more had come in from the public by the end of the day. The sodden clothes did offer the possibility of being the right ones, though, and were at the forensics lab now for a minute examination. And even though none of the water-butt owner's neighbours had seen anything, there was always a hope that the battery of forensic tests might come up with something useful.

With her enforced Saturday off ahead of her, Jane went home. She even agreed when Adrian suggested they go out to see a film, which was better than being in together making stilted conversation. As they arrived home afterwards, she mentioned casually that Chris was back at work. And also –

with some care, but it was a subject which couldn't be avoided – that Elizabeth had gone to stay with her parents. Adrian looked at her.

'Yes, I know, she told me she was going to. Is Chris all right?'

'Within limits, it you mean mentally. Being able to work should help.'

'Is he back because the danger's over, or— No, all right, I can see from your face that you won't tell me. And don't instruct me again not to talk to anyone. I haven't, and I won't. Elizabeth certainly mustn't know. I still wish you'd explain, though, how you can be absolutely sure that you— After all you're thoroughly visible, aren't you? On television and everything!'

'It was somebody who had something particular against Chris. We – kind of know who, though not exactly, and not where.' That seemed to be the only way round it. 'Look,' she appealed, 'I know I complained that you didn't ever want me to talk about my work any more, that you didn't like it – well, you don't, I guess, and who could blame you, it can be a thoroughly lousy job at times! But I'm not just being bloody-minded now, or trying to get back at you, when I won't answer. For this one we're all under strict instructions, and *I can't talk about it.* Don't take off at me if I put it this way, but it's – it's nothing personal.'

He took her earnestness gravely, and as the peacemaking gesture it was meant to be, but said wryly, 'Nothing personal's the way it's been between us lately anyway, isn't it? Don't you think maybe we could change that? It's – well, whatever we may have said to each other in the heat of the moment, it's not *really* necessary for you to go on skulking in the spare room, surely?'

'I'm not skulking, I come in and out to get my clothes.' She tried for a smile, but when he looked too hopeful she found she was backing off. 'Look, I – I just can't for the moment, OK? It's not you. I mean it's not you and me. It's because – just now I've got such a lot on my mind that I can't ... When all this is over I may be human again – if I ever was – but there's so much going on in my head right now that, to be blunt, I'm no company in bed or out of it. And that's just the simple truth.'

'All right,' he said, after a long look at her face which must have told him that she really was offering the truth. 'Unwillingly, but ... all right. Until the case is over, then. I've seen the way you can get wrapped up in them before, after all, and I've stuck around, haven't I? As long as you're going to give me credit for patience.'

'Credit given. I'm sorry,' she added, aware that he hadn't liked accepting her plea. She couldn't tell him that with the horror of Blue Betty on her mind there was no prospect of her being in the mood to make love – which was what sharing a bed would inevitably lead to – but she had given him as much truth as she could, and was grateful that he had taken it. She gave him a rueful look, and said with careful friendliness, 'Without trying to raise a subject we once quarrelled about – please note! – I want to pass on a message from Chris. He said it was very kind of you to visit Elizabeth in the hospital so much, and that she's feeling a lot better. Which is good, isn't it? Now, I need tea before I go to bed, and maybe a sandwich as well; do you want anything?'

He was working next day; a Saturday clinic in the morning, a visit to one of the farms to do inoculations in the afternoon. Left on her own, Jane mooched about, half wishing Rogalleh hadn't insisted on giving her time off, half aware that a break was necessary. She could shop ... the groceries probably needed renewing. If Adrian hadn't efficiently done it. She could do some cleaning and tidying as well. Both were better than sitting still, which might be a rest for the body but was none for the mind. This afternoon, she decided abruptly, she would go to the gym; it was far too long since she had done more than token exercise to keep herself properly fit. In fact she was just about ready to leave when the phone, silent all morning, gave an insistent warble; not her mobile, kept religiously within range, but the ordinary one on the wall. She thought of leaving it, but it might be anyone so she moved to lift the receiver.

'Jane? It's Felicity. Could you possibly come round?'

'What, to the practice? Adrian's not here, he's—'

'Yes, I know where he is. I'm not in the practice, I'm upstairs in the flat. Could you come?'

Her voice was always slightly husky but now there was an extra note in it. 'Is something the matter?' Jane asked – wondering, with a touch of resignation, what.

'I'll tell you when you come. Harry's out, by the way. It's me who – who wants to see you. It *is* important. If you could come now ...'

'All right, I'm on my way.' But she wouldn't stay long if she had any say in the matter, Jane thought drily, and if Felicity was hoping that she was going to act as agony aunt to personal problems ... All she wanted to tell Felicity about Harry was to get shot of him; though she couldn't, of course. Unless Felicity was actually having doubts now that he was finally getting divorced.

Running up the outside stairs to the flat above the practice held memories – of when Adrian lived there, and love was new – but Jane was well aware that the flat was different inside now, Felicity's stamp on it, a tendency to frills here and there. The door opened before she could ring, on the familiar sight of Felicity's wildly curling auburn hair and big green eyes; eyes, though, which had an odd, steely expression in them, if signs beneath that tears had been shed not long ago. Felicity said abruptly, 'Come in,' and stood back so that Jane could do so. Then she moved round to face her.

'I want to explain why I'm doing this. Not just because it's dishonest, stealing. You – you can call it revenge if you like. Because when we went up to Nuneaton last week I found out—'

'Wait a minute, what? What was that about Nuneaton?'

'It's where I used to live,' Felicity said, raising an impatient eyebrow at the interruption. 'The practice I was in before I left it and went home to Lincolnshire. And then came here. And of course it's where Harry used to live with his bloody wife. Who I *now* find out wasn't the one holding up the divorce at all; it was him, and last time he went up there they even *slept* together! Which didn't stop her deciding she still wanted the divorce after all,' Felicity added viciously. 'Oh, he made all sorts of excuses, after she'd let it out – and that was deliberate too, she was getting back at me for the past, I know *that*! But—'

'Felicity, could you just hang on a moment and tell me something?' The recollection was there now in Jane's head, belatedly; it was Adrian who had mentioned Nuneaton, who had said something about Felicity and Harry going up there. Harry, Lionel, no wonder her mind had made the link. But she had been so busy not thinking about Adrian that she hadn't... 'Had Harry always lived in Nuneaton?' she asked, trying not to let urgency colour her voice.

'They'd been there ten years. Ever since they got married. And he was probably laying the entire female population end to end before I got there – even afterwards, for all I know,' Felicity said between her teeth, though luckily rage seemed the current reaction rather than tears. 'Oh, he thinks he's got me wound round his finger again *now*, and I bet he's expecting me to be all sweet and loving and loyal when he comes back this afternoon, but – but I've had time to brew things during the last few days, haven't I? You see, when we got home, after fighting all the way back, I started going through his drawers to see if he'd got any love letters hidden away, and then I found— He admitted what they were, thought it was a huge joke. Even told me in detail how easy it was to nip in and steal them! Look, I've got them out for you, here, they're all in this bag – Lionel's files and disks. Harry even had the nerve to say they'd turned out disappointing because there wasn't really anything he could use in them – but he stole them, so I'm handing them over to you, and it'll fucking well serve him right if he gets arrested!'

Jane could only stare at her, with her heart going into a sudden trip, and then an accelerated beat.

Chapter 18

Jane took Felicity in to the station with her, along with the evidence; there was far too much risk that she might tell a returning Harry what she had done. Once there, and finding Rogalleh absent, she rang him on his mobile number. She knew as she heard the alert 'Yes, Rogalleh here?' what he was hoping the call would be – but she had something better for him.

He was quickly in. Not much later Harry Morpeth was found and brought to the station – easily found, since he had returned to the flat – and was held incommunicado while Rogalleh went on questioning Felicity, with soft patience, about the past. Blue Betty was not mentioned but how well she had known Harry and what sort of life he had led were gently drawn out of her. It came as a slight surprise to Jane to hear that Harry had worked as a sales rep for a stationery firm. That was certainly something he never admitted to nowadays. He had achieved success with his thriller-writing five years ago and had thrown in the other job at once to concentrate on it. Felicity saw herself as the one who had given him encourgement against the doubts of an unsympathetic wife, the one who had loved and nurtured him in his unhappiness. She was a great deal more inclined to go on about that, and the long years she had spent as his mistress, than anything else. Rogalleh was forming a picture of the man, though, Jane knew. A man who had lived in the right place. Who had driven around as part of his job, working irregular hours which conveniently covered his assignations with Felicity – and might cover any other assignations he wished to make. A man with a strong interest in violent crime, too . . .

But also a gregarious man with a lot of friends. A social life, with his wife, which took in parties and barbecues and trips abroad with friends made easy by the fact that it was a childless marriage. Jane could see the Harry she knew in all that – but it was a poor fit with the loner image offered in the Blue Betty profile. However, profiles could be wrong. And there *was* a callousness in Harry Morpeth; Jane had always felt that about him.

Felicity had been too busy trying to justify her vengeful shopping of the man she lived with to notice the length of the questioning, until Rogalleh wound it up with sympathy for the fact that she was wobbling back into tearfulness. When she had been allowed to go, Rogalleh looked at Jane with a distance in his eyes which indicated how thoroughly he was assessing everything. The main facts were there – along with an incredibly close fit with what they were looking for.

'He thought he was safe admitting to her he'd stolen the files because she was too much under his thumb to tell anyone. Well, well . . . I said he'd make a mistake, didn't I? So we've got him. Let's go and see how he reacts to it!'

Satisfaction was short-lived.

Harry seemed no more than irritated at having been put in a cell; he even claimed to find it mildly amusing. Faced with the evidence of Lionel's files and disks, he admitted with a slightly shamefaced charm that yes, he had nipped in while Angelica was out and taken them, on impulse. Solely because 'old Li' had always claimed there was all sorts of stuff he could have given Harry for plots if he'd been willing to, but wouldn't because he wanted to use everything for his memoirs one day. Yes, of course he would tell them when: the Sunday after Lionel's corpse had been found. The day after he had met Jane on her return from France, in fact, and he might even say it was her fault for being so snotty with him! Actually, he didn't think they'd find, when Angelica heard it had been him, that she would prosecute; she liked him, would see it had really been rather a joke . . . and he was sure he could get her to say she would have given them to him if he'd asked. Told that the police were going through the files and cuttings right now, he shrugged and said they wouldn't find anything interesting in them – he hadn't. When he heard that the police had obtained a warrant and were even now searching the flat, he raised an amused eyebrow and said that would serve Felicity right for being such a jealous little bitch.

And asked where he had been during the weekend when Lionel had been killed, he let his jaw drop, then assumed an expression of even greater amusement – and produced an alibi. He had been up in Nuneaton with his wife. For the whole weekend, Saturday to Monday. He hadn't told Felicity that was where he was going, but it was, and Nadine would certainly confirm it. They had only to ask her.

'What do you make of him?' Rogalleh growled at Jane an hour later, Harry back in his cell.

She had already given him everything she knew about Harry, such as it was, before he had interviewed Felicity. Now she thought for a moment, then said honestly, 'It's difficult for me to judge, sir, when he's a man I've always thoroughly disliked.'

'Not your type even before this, eh?' he said, accepting her difficulty. He frowned. 'He's very sure of his women. His wife will give him an alibi for the weekend Hughes was killed; his girlfriend, this Felicity, will confirm he was in bed with her on Easter morning . . . He claims to be intrigued as to why we're asking about that, too, and not bright enough to add one thing to the other! And Angelica likes him so much that she won't want to prosecute, he says . . .'

'He's always given the impression of being a womaniser.'

'And how does that fit in? Not with anything we thought we knew about Blue Betty, that's for certain. Unless all those expert assessments were wrong,' he added, his frustration suddenly showing. 'This one could be a game-player all right, I can see that, but if he's really got a couple of unbreakable alibis . . . I'll get my force up there to look into his past, and thoroughly, and I'll be on to them at once anyway for an immediate confirmation or denial from Mrs Nadine Morpeth as to whether he really spent that weekend in Nuneaton. But if she says he did . . .'

'We can still hold him for the theft. And even if Angelica does refuse to let us prosecute we can hold him on seriously wasting police time—'

'Oh yes, I haven't finished with him yet!'

He had not so much as raised anything about Blue Betty's past crimes so far. It had been shaped as a preliminary interview – but the hope that it was going to be more than that would be stymied if the alibis held up. And it would be unwise in the extreme to start questioning Harry about the old Blue Betty murders when that, if he turned out to be innocent of anything except mischievous theft, would with certainty blow all the careful silence the police had been maintaining. Harry would be gossiping about a connection between the past murders and the present one the minute the police had to release him. He would never miss the chance to give the press that kind of story.

Jane went to see if there was anything in Lionel's files and cuttings, now being meticulously examined, which referred to Blue Betty. There was not. Anything he had written about it could have been removed . . . but the stories going back over the years were all overseas assignments. The arms-dealing story was there, twelve years back, including the names of a couple of companies well known enough for Jane to raise her eyebrows; along with allegations about a then-serving politician which looked actionable but for the fact that the man was now dead. Lionel had typed in at the bottom of the computer file, 'If used, will have to omit names? Damn their eyes!' Most of his work was from a political slant and usually, except for the arms story, on fairly minor matters too.

If Harry really had stolen the files in the hope of finding something he could fictionalise, Jane could see why he might have found them disappointing. There was nothing on the kind of violent crime he had made himself a small success out of writing about.

If he was telling the truth.

Within the next few hours, his wife had confirmed his first alibi, Felicity his second, and the search carried out at the flat above the practice had come up with nothing at all to connect him with murder. And on Sunday morning Angelica – just as he had said she would – told the police that if it had been Harry she couldn't possibly press charges; he had been foolish, but he was far too good a friend, and she would forgive him.

'We have to let him go, sir?'

'No chance of doing anything else, is there?' Rogalleh's brooding gaze suggested a very sour temper. 'You can do it. On a warning that we'll be pressing charges of our own, but he'll hear about those later. And we'd better pray we're right, but he hasn't left us anything to argue with, has he? For now.'

So he hadn't quite let the idea go, Jane thought as she went to do as she had been instructed. She could understand his savage disappointment; he had thought he had his man under his hand at last, only to be balked. And it had seemed such a bright chance, everything had seemed to fit. Harry, she saw as she waited grimly in the charging area, was looking unshaven but cheerful, his light-blue eyes looking around with apparently happy curiosity. She gave him no chance to speak before she delivered the caution that he could expect to be charged in due course with wasting police time. Then she told him he could reclaim from the sergeant what had been in his pockets, and sign for it, and then he was free to go.

'An interesting chance to see everything from the inside!' he said blithely as he pocketed his cash and wallet. He had the nerve to give Jane one of his aren't-I-charming smiles. 'Do I get shown out?'

'This way.'

'Oh good, you're going to escort me off the premises. You know, I can't help admiring the way you snapped into officialdom and had me arrested,' he went on chattily as Jane walked him along the corridor to the outside door. 'No hard feelings, I promise you! It was worth it anyway to see you sitting demurely beside that boss of yours—'

'Get lost, Harry,' Jane said clearly, glad that there was nobody else about and not hiding the dislike in her voice. She pulled the door shut behind him and turned away without waiting to watch his departure. If he had known what they had really had him pegged for . . . It was just as well he didn't, or he'd be out making hay of it all over the place.

Did he know?

She walked back to the office, contemplating that his alibis seemed incontrovertible – and remembering suddenly, and bitterly, that she had allowed herself a flippant fantasy once about Harry's being Lionel's killer. Purely out of dislike. Would Rogalleh count that as a fit of instinct? As things stood it could only have been a wrong one.

In any case, if you went back to the profile, she would hardly have described Harry as intelligent. Moderately clever on the surface perhaps, but underneath she would almost have called him thick.

Or a very good actor.

Rogalleh would certainly go on bearing him in mind, she knew.

Rogalleh wasn't in the office; he had probably gone back upstairs to his own. He must be contemplating the fact that if Lionel's files had been stolen independently – if they now had to assume they had – it altered the whole basis from which they had been working. Change one assumption and the others changed too ... They might have to alter the premise, now, that Lionel had been killed because of something he knew. And *that* meant ...

Another random murder of an authoritarian type, as standard as the rest? Or that Blue Betty knew Lionel and hated him for some other reason?

Jane felt a stir of uneasiness, squashed it down, and stood uncertainly beside her desk for a moment. She was unsure whether Rogalleh wanted her to stay at the station or not. The only way to find out was to ask him, so she put a call through to his office and received a growled reply.

'It's Jane Perry, sir. I've processed Morpeth out as instructed.'

'You can go home and finish that time off you were supposed to be having, then. Until tomorrow.'

'Right, sir.'

She was outside before she realised that she was unwilling to go home for a Sunday afternoon with Adrian. Last seen, late last night, he had been waiting up for her in a tight-lipped state. He had begun, looking as if he was trying to pick his words with care, 'I've just spent the evening with

Fliss weeping on my shoulder. Surely you could have calmed her down instead of—'

'No I couldn't. Lionel Hughes is a murder case, remember? So when she comes to me with something involving that case—'

'You have to get Harry arrested and the flat searched? Bloody hell, Jane, how many times is this sort of thing going to happen?'

'As many times as it takes, I suppose. Good night,' she had said stonily, and walked past him. It *was* too much of an echo of the past, but it was no good his bringing that up against her. She had slept briefly, got up early, gone back to work. Now, with Harry released, she supposed they both might pretend to forget it. Maybe.

Jane gave a sigh, part irritation, part depression. There had been a high in believing the whole thing might be over, the man they were searching for under their hand, and it was scarcely surprising if the aftermath brought a nosedive of her spirits. She really *didn't* want to go home to disapproval after that. She decided on an alternative. She would buy a hamburger, and a Sunday newspaper, and go and sit in the Westgate Gardens. Just like anybody else who had opted for a peaceful read over a late takeaway lunch on a reasonably sunny spring Sunday.

She found, however, that the gardens – at least the nearer end of them – were thoroughly occupied with one of the demonstrations of jollity which often seemed to take place in this public space. Not, today, the East Kent Artists setting up stalls and easels to show and sell their work; this time, from the look of things it was one of the dancing schools offering a show for proud parents to observe the progress of their young and for the public to see how admirably the little darlings had been taught. Toddlers dressed as brightly coloured vegetables were being marshalled into line, while slightly larger small girls in tutus could be seen in the background waiting their turn. Jane edged her way round the throng which had gathered to watch. The further gardens would be a lot emptier anyway, even if she had to put up with the background tinkle of the music which was now starting. She could probably find a reasonably quiet spot by the river. As she made for the path which would take her through the bushes and out the other side she almost bumped into someone, and when she glanced up in quick apology found she was being looked at with recognition by a face which was vaguely familiar.

'Hallo again. Dave Leacock,' he said helpfully, smiling at her. 'Kent Ports SB?'

'Oh yes, of course, hi! Sorry, I was miles away . . .'

'And my voice is probably more familiar than my face, considering we've only actually met on a dark night in chaotic circumstances,' he said with a grin. 'I'm here to watch my daughters perform. My wife's gone off to make sure Cathy's headdress doesn't fall off and that Fiona doesn't decide to feel sick. No, I don't own a vegetable . . .' The toddlers were now weaving rather uncertainly about to the music under the tutelage of a teacher. 'Mine will appear later as a flower and a snowflake ballerina – hopefully!'

Jane made an amiable sound which could be taken as appreciation, or congratulations, or both. 'I'm just passing through,' she said with a touch of apology. 'I'm not sure if . . .'

'Oh quite, if none of them are yours you can be spared the agony. I mean pride.' He obviously was quite a proud parent, since he was hefting a camcorder in one hand. The crowd had swept away from them for the moment as people moved for a better view, so that they were temporarily isolated in a clear space. He glanced round, then added with a grimace, 'Bad business about that driver turning up dead.

231

And we'd got the French police thoroughly staking out his girlfriend's pad, too!'

'The French? But he was Dutch, wasn't he?'

'Yes, but he'd been living in Amiens. There's a Turkish quarter there and that's presumably how come he—' A scatter of appreciative clapping broke out and he looked round quickly. 'I'd better get myself into position. I think one of mine's on next. Sorry – nice to see you!'

Jane gazed after his rapidly retreating figure. Then she walked on, slowly. Why had nobody ever told them that Claus Armfeldt had been living in Amiens? That piece of information seemed to have got lost in transit. Though it was probably quite irrelevant . . .

Except that Amiens was halfway between Rowena's French address and Calais, by a slightly indirect route. Lionel could have gone that way on one of his trips; could for some reason have been introduced to Armfeldt; could . . .

No, they were following entirely different suppositions now.

It still felt like one too many coincidences. Rowena's French address a reasonably short driving distance from Claus Armfeldt's French address.

It was probably nothing.

Chapter 19

Rogalleh had apparently decided to leave it to Jane to catch the others up on the details of Harry Morpeth's arrest and release. She explained exactly what the situation was now, adding that no doubt the guv'nor would be down shortly to give them his thoughts on what difference it would make to the investigation. None from the point of view of what they had been doing; the nuts and bolts of that were still the same. But it was up to Rogalleh to decide if the change in what they had been assuming gave them other lines of approach.

Jane had already been in to see Chris to tell him personally what had happened, how it had come about, and that the burglary could be struck off CID's books. She knew he had been away for the weekend visiting Elizabeth at her parents' home, so she went to see him first thing so that he had a first-hand report rather than second-hand information. He heard her out grimly, then asked:

'Is he still a suspect?'

'Rogalleh's having his past history thoroughly checked out, but ... He's very thoroughly alibi'd, Chris. For Hughes, and for the attempt on you.'

'Is Rogalleh going to have him tailed?'

'I don't know, I haven't seen him this morning yet.'

'I would,' he said on a grim note, 'alibis or not!' She could see in his eyes that he was thinking of Hector's pathetic body and the whole snowball of effects which had come after. Then he made himself relax with a twitch of his shoulders, and asked, 'Anything more come out of your television appeal?'

'Not so far, but we should get the forensic report on the clothes soon. I'd better get back to my own department in case the guv'nor's appeared. How – how's Elizabeth now?'

'Quite a bit better, thanks. At least I suppose she is.' There was something in his expression which suggested he had had a difficult weekend. 'Her mother's talking about getting her a new pup. I think it's too soon. But then what do I know?' There was a touch of bitterness in his tone, but his face closed down quickly and she took it as a warning not to offer sympathy or ask any more questions. The fact that he switched abruptly back to work reinforced that, as he went on quickly, 'Thanks for coming in to tell me about the burglary result; I'll log it. And keep me up to date, I'd be grateful. I'd better let you go.'

Jane gave him a grave smile and went off to see if Rogalleh had put in an appearance; then, since he had not, to run through the facts for her team. After that she set them to catch up on paperwork, a necessary start to Monday morning and a useful thing to be getting on with while they waited. It was unusual for Rogalleh not to start the day with instructions and particularly now . . . When he did come in, soft-footed, there was an air about him which set Jane's nerves tingling. However he looked round at them all briskly, then said:

'Inspector Perry's told you we had a possible suspect but we had to let him go? Good. It may be a waste of time, but while we wait to see if my West Midlands force can find any scrap of evidence which connects him to the data they've got and the HOLMES stuff, I've just been arranging for a couple of WPCs to go into plain clothes and keep an eye on him. Faces he won't know – just in case.'

'You think he still could be—'

'I'm not going to take any risks,' he rumbled, allowing Rachel's interjection. 'However...' He reached absently into his pocket as if for a cigarette, then caught Jane's eye and desisted, grouchily. 'Yes, all right, ash and computers don't mix, you don't have to remind me. Now then, something else. Our man *is* here. He rang me this morning to tell me so. To identify himself, to ask why I hadn't found him yet, to— Oh, he's up to his old tricks all right, because he called me on the hotel number instead of on my mobile.'

'Sir, if he knows where you are—' Jane began urgently, but he cut her off.

'I'm careful, no need to worry. I didn't get him on this, though,' he added disgustedly, reaching into his inside pocket for his mobile phone and flicking his finger against the tiny tape recorder which was attached to it. Only his had one; the others were equipped normally. Jane knew he had assessed that Blue Betty wouldn't speak unless he knew he had reached Rogalleh personally, since that had been the pattern towards the end of the last series of killings. 'I need another recorder, one which isn't fixed on,' Rogalleh rumbled irritably. 'If this hadn't been the other side of the room I might have been able to try ... As it was, when he came through on the outside line I didn't have time. Nor long enough arms.' He brooded for a brief moment, then went on. 'I'll give you what he said. That he was sorry about the dog – by which I'd say he meant he was sorry he had to settle for that instead of a human! – but that since I'd come back he could see I must have got his message. Then he asked how I was, because it was a long time since we'd talked.'

'What did you say back to him, sir?' Rachel asked cautiously, into his pause.

'What he'd expect of me. I invited him to give himself up,' Rogalleh said drily. 'That's the advice the damned psychiatrists always used to give me; to gentle him in. Not that it

235

ever— He laughed and said, "No, it's for you to find me." Oh, I'd know that laugh, muffled though it might be! Then he said killing wasn't as much fun as it used to be, he'd got bored with it before and maybe he would again. It would depend how he felt. And then he rang off.' The heavy voice paused again, then said grimly, 'Just under one minute. As always. He times it – and nothing I've ever done has kept him on longer.'

Jane had an uncomfortable feeling between her shoulder blades; somehow, as he spoke, Blue Betty had been there in the room with them. She could see from the faces of the others that they were feeling the same. However, she spoke into the silence with quick practicality.

'It *was* the same voice, sir? Exactly? You said before that he always used to muffle it somehow; was that the same too?'

'Yes to both questions. And no, it wasn't just somebody who'd read up on old newspaper reports and remembered my name. There was enough there to be sure of that, even if he hadn't started with "This is *Blue* Betty" when that part of the name was never publicised.' He cast Jane a beetling frown for a moment, but changed it suddenly to a grudging approval. 'Careful, aren't you? Never believe anything without checking. Now then: no saying where the call was coming from but I think it was local. And I think he was using a mobile, one with a faint bleep on it. Likely it's the one Lionel Hughes is supposed to have had with him and which has never been found – so I want everything about that one checked and rechecked, in case it hasn't been reprogrammed. That's the first thing, and it may require another visit to Angelica if we haven't already got the details on file.'

'Yes, sir.'

'And next – I've already asked in the hotel, but we need a check with the neighbouring houses too. Any vehicle which has been seen a little too often in the neighbourhood – because if he's been watching me to see where I'm staying,

236

he has to have done it somehow. Following me from here to there, I reckon. That'll do for starters, and you three can get on with that while I go through everything else with Jane.'

Jane did some rapid delegation – Kate and Jennie to Rogalleh's hotel; Rachel to look in the files to see if they had a note of Lionel Hughes' mobile phone number; if not, to visit Angelica, then to check with the relevant company. Jane and Rogalleh withdrew to one end of the large room, and before he could start she began:

'Sir, did you . . .'

'Did I what?' he enquired as she paused to think of the right way to put it. A way which wouldn't sound as if she thought he had been too absorbed in the call he had been waiting for to listen thoroughly.

'I just wondered if – hearing Blue Betty's voice again, did you catch anything in it which sounded at all like Harry Morpeth? I know he's got those alibis, but as you said yourself—'

'No, and I listened for it,' he said promptly. 'Yes, I know, I might have been too caught up – but I wasn't. I'll tell you another thing. When Blue Betty said it was a long time since we'd talked, I think he meant it. I tried a couple of questions on him, but he wouldn't play; he wanted to talk this time, not hear anything I had to say. Unless it comes out that Morpeth's a far better actor than I'd give him credit for I'm ruling him out . . . though not quite, as putting a tail on him shows. I didn't want to say that to the others, not yet; I want him kept in mind. But . . .' He paused, his brow wrinkled in deep thought. 'It seems to me that if I'd just had him in and then had to let him go he'd have sounded more pleased with himself,' he said slowly. 'I don't think we've ever come face to face – yet. He's seen me, I haven't seen him. One of the things I tried to ask him was whether he was living here now or just visiting; it didn't work, though. But he has to know the area, doesn't he? To know Stelling Minnis common and that it's an empty place to dump a body. So I reckon he must have been living hereabouts. Yes, what?'

'Nothing, sir,' Jane told him, pushing the thought aside which must have made him query her expression.

'The other thing I tried was why I hadn't heard from him for six years, but he wouldn't even let me finish the sentence. That was when he came out with the one about having got bored with killing. Earlier on I had the impression he was sulking a bit because there was nothing in the papers about him. And I suppose I'd better tell you how he signed off. It was "Goodbye, Superintendent. Do try to catch me. I'll give you a bit of time, but not much!"'

Jane took in the implicit threat in the words with a sick feeling in her stomach. Which was what Blue Betty must want . . . to tighten the screw a notch, to offer the police a taunt that if they couldn't catch him he would strike again. She asked, 'Did he always do that? Try to—'

'Once or twice towards the end. Before Jimmy. After that—' Rogalleh broke off, frowning heavily. Jane could finish the sentence herself: after Jimmy, Blue Betty had simply vanished. 'And yet,' Rogalleh rumbled on, 'I've never heard him sound before as if he really wanted me to catch him. I'd swear this time . . . No, I'm damned if I'll believe all that rubbish about him wanting to be stopped. It's another of his games, isn't it? Jesus Christ and all the angels, I wish I knew why he suddenly disappeared off the face of the earth, and why the hell it's taken him six years to start again. He can't have been playing his games somewhere else, not in this country; if there'd been another series I'd have heard of it!'

There was an unusual violence in his voice. He did know only too well, Jane thought, what his deliberate challenge to Blue Betty might bring about; he wasn't indifferent to it; he had just thought – hoped – that here he would find enough leads to settle things quickly. That the man he was pursuing would make an inevitable mistake. And also – unquestionably – that he might take the bait and make an attempt on Rogalleh himself, while the Superintendent was on the watch for it, and be caught that way. But now he was worried that the killer might choose an alternative . . .

He ought to be worrying that he wouldn't. Jane tried again. 'Sir, as I said before, if he knows where you are, shouldn't you—'

'If he could track me once he could do it again,' Rogalleh retorted stubbornly. No arguing, his tone of voice said. However he shot a glance at her and added gruffly, 'If you're thinking he could take me from a distance with a rifle, there's no evidence that he's ever used guns. He likes to get close in. I know he varies his methods but there're types who use firearms and types who don't, and he's the latter. Even with the crossbow he had to come in and cut the animal's throat as well, didn't he? No, he won't use a bullet; too simple for him.'

She could only accept what he said. And acknowledge that he had probably made his own security arrangements too, perhaps in collaboration with Superintendent Annerley. He didn't tell her everything. She merely pursed her lips – and received a sudden grin from Rogalleh, a shake of the head which acknowledged her disapproval but indicated clearly that she could do nothing about it. Then he was going on, lapsing back into a grim-edged conciseness.

'Nothing more we can do that we aren't doing, I suppose. Thinking the theft of Hughes' files was connected seems to have been the wrong theory – but Hughes *could* have said something in conversation, so that's still an open question. Or he could have been chosen because he's just the type to get up Blue Betty's nose, which means they *did* meet.

Morpeth would have filled the bill, dammit! Still...
Where's that forensic report on those clothes? It's well time
they let us have it, they've had the whole weekend!'

Jane went to ring the forensic lab as he took himself out of
the room, fielding the fact from Rachel as she went that
there was nothing on the computer giving them details of
Lionel's mobile phone, so sending her off to ask Angelica
for the information. The lab, predictably, gave her the
injured response that tests took time – but did tell her that
the residual marks on the stained clothes were blood, animal
blood. And although they were trying, it would be almost
impossible to find a DNA trace as to who had worn the
garments when they had been soaked, handled and dumped
in a garden, so the confirmation of animal blood might be all
they could offer.

The right clothes, almost certainly, but still giving them
nothing concrete to go on.

Jane told Communications where she was going so that
she could be reached if wanted, and took herself off to finish
the survey of firms. They had done almost all the ones on the
list. She went out into a calm and fitfully bright morning and
realised that it was the fourth week of April already – and
Lionel had been killed in February. Too long by half. Most
murders were simpler; done in a fit of temper, or during
robbery, or as part of a street fight... But this one had
never been simple. Just over two weeks since the attempt on
Chris; did that mean they had another three before Blue
Betty would try to strike again? To fit in with a five- instead
of a six-week pattern? Was that what he had meant when he
told Rogalleh that he would give them a bit of time, but not
much?

She finished her enquiries at the last of the estate agents –
who could offer her nothing helpful; they always recruited
locally, even at managerial level – and walked down the

High Street on her way back to the car park. When she saw Harry Morpeth making a thoughtful study of the window of the Sock Shop she made an immediate decision not to go and buy some new tights after all, and made to walk rapidly past. However, he must have seen her reflection in the window because he swung round and offered her a wide and inviting smile.

'Just the advice I could do with! Do tell me, what do you think of that as a present for Felicity to show her I've forgiven her?'

He was indicating a lacy black body stocking displayed behind the glass. The mischievous look he was giving her took in her frosty expression and increased. He even laid a winning hand on her arm. 'Come on, I said there were no hard feelings. Talk to me, do, I've had my rap over the knuckles. What *do* you think of that for Felicity? Or . . . perhaps you're right and I shouldn't ask you in case you let on to her. She's always had more than a suspicion that you're my type, blonde and blue-eyed and all that!'

He really was unbelievable. Thick-skinned, or incredibly clever – which? Rogalleh had started to discount him since this morning, even with the proviso of having him watched. Jane took care not to look for the plainclothes WPC who must be somewhere about. She decided abruptly to play him at his own game and said with as much pleasantness as she could muster, 'Really? How odd, I've never felt the least attraction for anyone with the same colouring as mine.'

'Hence Adrian, all brooding dark eyes and brown hair? I've always thought he was a bit dull for you. Such a nice stable type. Mind you, I've always suspected that he and Felicity might be snuggling up a bit too much. It's always him she runs to when she gets upset, and what with you so busy all the time . . . Oh dear, I think I'd better change the subject, hadn't I? Particularly when I'm in your bad books already.'

He gave her a look of charming repentance. He was behaving exactly as usual, and looking to get a rise out of her. Since Jane had no intention of giving him that satisfaction she raised a tolerant eyebrow and gave him a dulcet answer.

'It was Felicity's bad books you were in, I'd have said. Poor girl, she really was upset, and perhaps you *ought* to give her a present to keep her sweet.'

'Plenty more fish in the sea where that one comes from, to be blunt, and a man could get tired of her throwing wobblers. Now you, with all that cool blonde efficiency . . . No? Not even with our respective partners being so cosy together? Oh dear, you're not going to turn frosty on me again, are you?'

'I don't think I'll bother,' Jane said, to his cheerfully insouciant leer. 'And I really must—'

He ignored her attempt to move away and went on chattily, 'Talking of blondes, I've just been to see Rowena again. Told you I was well in there, didn't I? And I quite fancy the little French piece, as a matter of fact . . . It certainly isn't going to last between her and that son of Rowena's. The latest is that he's been borrowing Malcolm's van when he hasn't got a driving licence. I told Rowena, it's only the sort of thing twenty-one-year-olds do, and she can't keep him tied on her apron strings forever!'

'I don't suppose that went down well,' Jane said, making it a merely conversational response. Harry, the specialist in innocent malice.

'What? Oh no, not very – though I *didn't* mention that I know why she gets into such a fret about him. Old Li told me all about it, in confidence. But since she's scared to death of anybody finding out, there's such a thing as tact.' Tact, from him? But he was going on, his light-blue eyes still watching her. 'You know, I don't believe you've heard about it, have you? I mean the spell the boy spent in a Turkish jail last year, after he was caught trying to leave the country with a bag of cocaine in his luggage.'

'Really? He seems to have got off.'

'Ah well, that's the interesting bit. Old Li did some clever stuff with the money Rowena raised for the boy's defence and found the right person to bribe to get the charge dropped. Mind you, young Josh had a bit of a bad time during the four months he was in jail, I think. You can suppose he might; he's young and not unhandsome. Still, Li murmured something about some old lag befriending him, which improved matters. But,' Harry added, with a shrug, 'on the whole you'd have to think it served him right for being stupid enough to get caught in the act. You should have heard old Li on the subject of stepsons who are bright enough to get themselves to Cambridge to read advanced science and then dumb enough to chuck it all away.'

'It all sounds most unfortunate,' Jane commented, very neutrally.

'I suppose it could be for him if it came out – would the authorities take it into their heads to play it by the book and send him back to stand trial after all? I'd guess that's what worries Rowena. Not, of course, that he hasn't always sworn he was innocent,' Harry added carelessly, 'and that since he would never touch the stuff one of the so-called friends he was on holiday with must have put it in his luggage. A bit of an unlikely story considering he wouldn't name names, I thought, even if Li and his mother pretended to believe it! Oh, help!' He offered her a sudden rueful smile, all charm and apology and with the air of having been struck by a sudden thought, 'I suppose I shouldn't really have let all that out, to you of all people. Be a pet and pretend I wasn't so indiscreet!'

Jane looked at him. She had the sudden suspicion that Rowena had been less friendly than he had claimed – had even, perhaps, put him down quite hard. And his response to the denting of his massive ego had been this piece of spite. Unless it was just that he had wanted the satisfaction of showing he knew something Jane didn't.

Before she could speak he had given her another wide smile, and came out with a suddenly brisk 'Well, can't stand here chatting all morning, delightful though it is. I think I will go in and see if they've got that garment in Felicity's size. She really would look quite fetching in it.'

He gave her a careless wave of the hand and headed off into the shop. As Jane walked on, her mind was busy with the things he had told her . . .

Josh a science student – and Matty had said that a knowledge of industrial chemistry would give someone the requisite expertise about KCN, the poison used to kill Lionel. Josh with access to transport, if he had been driving Malcolm's van. Josh with a motive to murder his stepfather – if Lionel had been threatening to get him sent back to Turkey, in response to Rowena's not making the Willowfield Way house over to him immediately. That must have been the agreement between them when he did his rescue act, surely, and it explained his anger over the house.

Josh whose earlier family home was at Lower Hardres, which was the next-but-one village to Stelling Minnis. The memory of Rowena's mentioning that had come unbidden into Jane's head when Rogalleh had talked about somebody who must know the area.

And Turkey coming up again. Josh not long out of a Turkish prison. Claus Armfeldt living in the Turkish quarter of Amiens. Were they looking at the illegal immigrant run again?

244

Her uneasiness was back, and redoubled. But – Josh as Blue Betty?

He *couldn't* be . . .

Chapter 20

She would check everything Harry had told her, every last word of it if she could – certainly before she went to Rogalleh with another theory which might fall down at the first hurdle. She needed every minor detail covered.

Particularly when it was a theory she was loath to believe in herself.

She would do it privately, for the moment. And after some thought she knew where she could start on this very personal line of enquiry. She would ring Hilaire.

It was useful that Rogalleh had had them issued with the mobiles, since that meant she could put her requests to Hilaire in privacy. She rang him from her car – and found him in, and very pleased to hear from her.

He listened carefully to what she wanted to know. 'I'll come back to you on all of them – on the number you've just given me, yes? Though I don't know if that last one will be at all easy . . . Still, I'll certainly try.'

She had given him quite a list. First, whether any of Rowena's French neighbours could tell him whether Josh had been absent for any length of time – particularly during the weekend of his stepfather's last visit and directly afterwards. Second, whether Josh was ever seen driving the white van belonging to Malcolm Jackson. Or any other vehicle. Third, whether he could find out from the Amiens police if anyone resembling Josh had been seen in the company of

Claus Armfeldt; they would have heard of Claus since they had already been asked various questions about him. And lastly, whether he could find out if Josh had in fact been in a Turkish prison before his arrival in France.

'So, you've come up with various things since we last spoke,' Hilaire said, 'and they've given you some idea about the boy, hm? On a drugs-smuggling charge in a Turkish prison rather than glandular fever, then!'

'I've been told it didn't come to trial and the charges were dropped, so that may make it harder to find out. And it *may* be only a rumour. If he arrived at his mother's in November as you told me before, he'd have been held in Turkey since about July. It's just that I need to know if it's true—'

'Because it gives you a tie-up to this Claus Armfeldt. Yes, I see. OK, I'll do the best I can!'

She hadn't been able to talk to him about Blue Betty; though if Josh really came under suspicion perhaps she would need to. But that could wait. Get everything else checked first. Then, and only then, if suspicion really pointed that way . . .

A confirmation of what subject Josh had been reading at Cambridge next. Back to the station first, though. Things were under control; Kate and Jennie were still trying to find out if anyone had been seen near the hotel, or following Rogalleh from the station to the hotel, and Rachel was checking Nokia, though the records they had come up with so far suggested that Lionel's phone – if that was the one Blue Betty was using – must have been reprogrammed to some other number. By the time Jane went out again she had the Cambridge University Registry number with her in her bag.

She elicited the information she wanted without making it a police enquiry, the registrar happy to look up the facts she was asking for when she produced the story that she was ringing from one of the schools Joshua Connolly had previously attended. She looked thoughtfully at her scribbled note. A scholar, Trinity College, reading physics and higher maths. At present on an intercalated year – a year off between the second and third years of his course; she had also been given the unsolicited information that in his second-year exams he had got a starred first.

He really was very bright then. A top college at a top university, and a scholarship to get there ... and he had been doing well. And yes, it was science, but ... physics, a subject which at that level was all abstracts, and a world away from practical chemistry.

Why was she glad to discover that?

She wondered where else she could find out about Josh, and came up with a name. Yes, she could, if she phrased her questions very carefully. She would have to think about it first, though.

When she arrived at the station the following morning she found that a mass of computer printouts had arrived by urgent delivery. For the next few days, if nothing more immediate came up, Rogalleh had decreed that they should comb through everything from the West Midlands files about Blue Betty, plus some extra stuff from HOLMES. He had been forced to do it this way because to download it all direct on to the station's computer system would not only have taken a lot of time, but also far too much of the available capacity. Let alone that the system would have had to go off line to everybody else. Technology might have its enormous advantages, but it had built-in disadvantages too. So, he said grimly, they would go back to eyes and memory as they raked through for any tiny detail which might show similarity enough to help them.

'Helluva job!'

'Yes, but if that's what we gotta do ...' Jane gave Kate

and the other two an encouraging grin. 'Yes, I know, it would be far easier to choose something to compare and press a Find key – but since we don't have that option we're just going to have to use brainpower, aren't we? Pick a section, everybody – yes, the profiles too, I see they're there. And if anything even marginally strikes you, go to the computer and check it against what we've got on our own database.'

There was more than enough to keep them busy, though at least the fact that it was raining sporadically made it more encouraging to be inside. After a while Jane stretched, allowing herself a pause. She had given Rogalleh a guarantee that she wouldn't be a maverick, would always say where she was. She said casually, 'One thing's come to me that we haven't followed up. Sam Connolly lives here and he's studying politics, which is the same as Lionel's chief interest. I know he told us he didn't see much of his stepfather because Angelica doesn't like Lionel's former family, but we might just ask him if he ever used to meet Lionel. As a personal thing. Just in case he's innocently sitting on some fact Lionel told him about someone he'd met ... or saw anyone particular in Lionel's company, for that matter. I think I'll have to deal with that. Hm – I don't really want to see him at Rowena's and get her all upset again ... The uni must have started up for the summer term by now, so if I can find out what his schedule of lectures is, perhaps I can get hold of him up there.'

'Sounds like a good idea,' Kate agreed. 'Dear God, these profiles went into detail, didn't they? "Highly intelligent, probably unfulfilled potential" – well, I suppose that makes sense, but "Upward change of class, probably lower-middle background leading to resentment and disorientation" – that's assuming a lot, isn't it? I know the voice descriptions of Blue Betty say "Educated but pretending not to be,

deliberate mistakes", but even so, how do you get to specifically *lower-middle* from there?'

'You said it used "probably" rather than "specifically",'
Jane pointed out from where she had moved to the phone.
'Oh hallo, that's the university switchboard, is it? I'm sorry to
bother you, but could you possibly tell me what the timetable
is for politics students this term? Third year, I think. You'll
transfer me? Thanks.'

The politics department could tell her what lectures and
seminars its students should be attending and even, helpfully,
where. It looked as if the best time to catch Sam would be
after the following morning's lecture when, since he would
also have a seminar in the afternoon, he would probably stay
on the campus rather than going home. Jane duly took herself
up to the university the next morning, to the sprawl of modern
buildings perched on top of the hill overlooking the city.
However, when she reached the lecture hall which had been
specified, it was deserted, and she bit her lip in annoyance. A
pair of semi-entwined students approaching along the corridor looked at her curiously, and the boy said politely, 'Are
you looking for someone? The third years who are usually in
there are on a reading week.'

'But most of them are probably reading in college,' the girl
clamped close to his side volunteered. 'Do you want someone
in particular?'

'Sam Connolly?'

'Oh, Sam – he's in Darwin Library, I saw him not ten
minutes ago. Darwin College, over the other side. You go out
of here and—'

'Yes, I know where it is – thanks!' Jane told her helpful
informant with a smile.

'You'll find him in one of the carrels,' the girl called after
her as she walked away, adding with a grin, 'If you can see him
behind the heap of books. They've got finals coming up!'

Darwin College, on the far side of the campus, was a conical-shaped building with flat wings, built in the dark-grey brick the architect seemed to favour for the whole site. Its library, reached up a curving staircase, was full of students hunched over tables in an atomosphere of absorbed silence. Sam was in one of the carrels, concentrating far too deeply to notice Jane until she touched him gently on the arm. Then he looked up with an irritated expression, which changed to one of his sweet smiles, though with a look of faint surprise.

'Sorry to disturb you, but can we talk?' she murmured softly.

'Sure ... A coffee break would be good anyway.'

He left his leather jacket on the chair to bag his place, and also scribbled a note saying PLEASE DON'T REMOVE! which he placed on top of his pile of books. Then he came to join her, speaking only after they had emerged from the library and started back down the stairs. With the very slight stammer which sometimes appeared in his voice, he said, 'We can go in the dining room, they'll be serving coffee but it won't be crowded. Is that all right?'

'Fine, as long as we can talk privately. And look, I'm sorry to disturb you. Finals, somebody told me?'

'Yes, they start in three weeks,' he said ruefully, 'and this is when I start wondering if I ever knew anything in the first place!'

'I remember the feeling. I did law. University College, London,' Jane told him, giving him a friendly smile. 'Heavy when you get to this stage, isn't it?'

'But you decided to go into the police instead of ... ?' He broke off to help them both to cups of coffee from an urn, adding quickly, 'You don't have to pay, you can have this on my student ticket. Look, over there's an empty table.'

252

The huge room, hexagonal with a high brick ceiling, was scarcely crowded, a mere scattering of students clumped here and there at its long tables. Sam led the way to the far edge near one of the narrow windows, a long way from any of the other seated figures. He gave her a curious look as they sat down, and Jane smiled at him again.

'As I said, I'm sorry to disturb you. I just wanted to ask you a few more questions about your stepfather. I know you said you didn't see much of him, but some, surely? Since you shared an interest in politics?'

'He came up here so I could show him round when I first started,' Sam told her. He wrinkled his brow. 'You're still looking for someone who knew him, aren't you? I did meet him a couple of other times, for lunch. But not lately. Because things got awkward – Angelica and all that, and then the – the argument about the house ...' He seemed to be picking his words carefully, and added, 'You k-know they were quarrelling about it, Ma said so, and since it was kind of – escalating, I tried to keep out of it. So I hadn't seen him lately. I have tried to think if there was anyone he mentioned, but he didn't, and anyway it's actually months since I saw him.'

'You were fond of him?' Jane asked, reading his face.

'Well, yes. He could be a bit of a cuss, but ... It's difficult when people split up.' He cast her a glance, his mouth going down ruefully, adding quickly and with a ready loyalty, 'Ma did have a tough time with him. But she was still fond of him too. It was only Angelica who ... Anyway, I'm sorry I can't be more help.'

'It's OK. It occurred to me it would be worth asking you, that's all, just in case he'd ever mentioned anybody. But he obviously didn't, so we can leave it there.' She stretched and looked at him amiably. 'Tell me, how's Josh, is he any better?'

He took the change of subject without a blink, though he offered her a glance as if to make sure that it was a friendly question rather than a police one. Her expression seemed to reassure him. 'He's seeing a psychotherapist – I told you I'd managed to persuade Ma, didn't I? – and he seems to like the guy all right, so that ought to help. I wish I'd been there for him more, I didn't know he'd got so snarled up. Sometimes he's fine but – but psychotherapy's bound to stir a lot of things up, isn't it? I just wish . . . I decided you were right about the twin thing, so I've been trying to be careful to – not to . . .'

'Were you always close?' Jane asked, since he had stammered to a halt. 'Some twins are but some aren't, so I've heard.'

'We were. I rather wish he hadn't got this sudden thing about it. But then I *wasn't* there for him when—' Sam broke off very abruptly and Jane could almost see the block going up; the matter of Turkey which mustn't be mentioned. It was no surprise when he finished quickly, 'When he had his breakdown. From overwork I should think. Still, with any luck he'll be able to go back to Cambridge next year.'

'You'd be bound to grow apart a bit going to different universities. He didn't come over to stay with you while he's on his time out?' Jane asked the question easily, but Sam shook his head.

'No, I suggested it, but Ma wanted to keep him under her wing in France. So I hadn't seen him since—' He broke off again and added very quickly, 'I had to stay here at Christmas because Ma didn't want the house left empty; a bit of a bummer actually. Still, I had friends in so it was OK. Our father took off not long after we were born, if you were wondering about that. Which is why Lionel was – well, our other parent, really.'

'Yes, I see. Having a stepfather didn't make the two of you jealous?'

'The three of us – there's Izzy as well, our sister,' he corrected her. 'No, we weren't. Twin and I – I mean Josh and I – had each other, and Izzy always had lots of friends. No, we just took him for granted, I think. And then when we went away to school at thirteen ... Twin had shot up and was bigger than me by then,' Sam said with a sudden grin, 'so I was lucky he was always a gentle soul, or he could have taken it out on me for when we were little and I was the solid one!'

'This is at the mad boarding school, is it?'

'That's the one. It probably wasn't as bad as I made it sound,' Sam added tolerantly. 'I suppose we did learn something there!'

'But it's where Josh got into trouble with amphetamines, isn't it? Sorry to raise it – but you can see why I had doubts when I found him in the state I did.'

'Look, that time with the speed was just one occasion,' Sam protested, gazing at her, 'and I *wish* you wouldn't hold it against him. He got bored that's all, because he always found all the work we were given to do too easy. And there was a boy in the year above us who had all the money in the world to play with and got hold of the stuff, and twin was stupid enough to try it – but that's *all*, he's never touched anything since. In fact it put him right off, and I know that, because he felt so guilty about the boy who was killed that he said he'd never ever take anything again.'

'Except pot now and again?'

'He might have started smoking the occasional joint lately, but even that's surprising, from him.'

'OK, there's no need to fire up at me. Were you involved in the amphetamines thing too?'

'No. I might have been, because we always did everything together in those days, but I was too scared to try it. And if the bloody school hadn't been so lax twin wouldn't have ended up with a black mark against him either,' Sam said angrily. 'It isn't fair, he was just about the goody-two-shoes of the school before that happened. I was the one who used to give the masters the runaround, he never did – until that one night. So—' He broke off, glowering at her; then suddenly seemed to remember himself and flushed, saying stiffly, 'I'm sorry. But if you will rake up the past as if it was relevant *now* – it isn't! It's bad enough that Josh . . .'

'Bad enough that Josh what?' Jane asked gently into his pause.

'Oh, it's just this psychotherapy thing I was telling you about. I suppose it will do him good when he gets thoroughly into it, but it seems to have stirred him up into feeling guilty again. As if he was feeling responsible all over again for Pete Gale driving that car into the side of a building. And I – I can't do much for him right now. Let alone that I've got finals, there's a kind of gap between us. It doesn't seem as if I'm any good for him at the moment.'

He was looking down at his clenched hands, his face unhappy. A nice young man, Sam. Jane reached over and touched one of his hands very lightly with her finger – which made him jump and look up at her.

'I've taken up enough of your time, and I'd better let you get back to studying. OK?'

'Yes, sure, sorry. I'm – I'm sorry I couldn't be any help over Lionel—'

'That's all right, it was only an outside chance.' They were both on their feet now. Jane added, 'Good luck with the exams.'

'Thanks. Um . . .'

'Yes?'

'I didn't mean to land you with all that. It's just on my mind a bit. And I – I don't really have anybody I can talk to.'

'No problem,' Jane said, smiling at him. 'Go on, go and bury your head in those tomes waiting for you upstairs so you've got all the right answers to whatever questions come up. I can find my own way out.'

He gave her a grin and walked away. She had got everything she could from him without asking direct and obvious questions. Josh as a schoolboy appeared to have been virtue itself, except for that one occasion. And surely – *surely* – his twin would have known if there had been absences, wanderings at night, unexplained times when he was out when he should have been in; let alone signs of disturbance which would have *had* to have been there. But Sam had shown not a flicker to suggest he was covering anything up. No worry either in talking about that time. Anger that his twin should have a black mark on his record for one lapse – but nothing to suggest that Josh had always been the erratic person he now appeared to be. And he had reason enough to be traumatised now if he had had a bad time in jail, followed by the sudden and unnatural death of the man who had got him out. No need to see it any other way.

She still had to hear from Hilaire. All the same, the idea that Josh could possibly be Blue Betty could go way down on the list of likelihoods.

She was obscurely comforted by that; perhaps because the thought of a fourteen-year-old killing cleverly and repeatedly was horrifying. But then not comforted at all, since it gave them the same old problem. Who was Blue Betty? Where was he?

How long did he plan to give them before he struck again?

The rest of Wednesday passed in intensive scrutiny of the papers. Thursday morning the same. It was on Thursday afternoon that Rachel let out a gasp; and when Jane

257

looked up she was staring white-faced at the computer VDU screen.

'Ma'am – I was just going to look something up, and then . . . Look!'

Jane moved quickly beside her, the others craning round too. The screen was lit, with just one line of writing across the middle of it.

ROGALLEH TIME IS RUNNING OUT BETTER HURRY

It sat there winking at them. Jane drew a sharp breath.

'Ring for the guv'nor, he'll want to see this!'

Jennie reached rapidly for the internal phone. As she did so Rachel spoke again on a horrified note.

'Ma'am, if he can hack in to send us a message, he'll be able to read everything on the system as well. He'll know *everything we've got*!'

'Quite. Clever little bastard, isn't he? But I don't know what the hell we can do about it. Sir, this came up on the screen just now,' Jane said as Rogalleh came swiftly into the room. 'I don't know if there's any way to trace . . .'

Even as she spoke and Rogalleh's eyes fixed on the screen, the message flicked out.

'Damn him!' Rogalleh said, quietly but explosively. 'That's one he's never tried before! Or maybe he did get into our system but without letting on about it that time.'

'I don't know how easy it is to—'

'Too easy for the ones with the right know-how nowadays. And who *hasn't* got access to computer equipment? Damn and hell!'

'He'll know everything that's in there, I suppose.'

'Probably had a good scan of it before he sent the message. All right, go on with what you were doing, and I'll go upstairs and see what everybody thinks about changing the passwords. For all the good it'll do!'

258

WITH INTENT TO KILL

He walked out savagely. The silence in the room he left behind him was almost palpable. Then Jane said briskly, 'All right, let's do as he said and get on with what we were doing. Rachel, what was it you were about to look up?'

'Nothing much – just a comparison between the clothes from one of the Birmingham sightings and the ones found here.'

'Go on with it, then. If you're being listened in to – or is it watched in to? – there's damn all we can do about it for now.'

'We could type in GET LOST YOU OAF and see if it brings a response,' Kate grunted.

'And I'd dearly like to, but not without the guv'nor's say-so. Anyway,' Jane said with exasperation, 'I'd lay a guess chummy's off line by now. Like the phone calls – less than one minute. There's one thing,' she added in a deliberately cheering manner, since both the WDCs were still looking shaken, 'he can't scan all this stuff we've got on paper, can he? So if we do find something in it he won't have any warning.'

They could only go on searching for that something. That went on all through Friday too. Instructions had come down from above that every entry code to every system in the building was to be altered – which was a bugger, Jane thought – and the message had come up on several other screens as well, to bring a feeling of tension all over the station.

ROGALLEH TIME IS RUNNING OUT BETTER HURRY – a mocking and unnerving message guaranteed to spoil anyone's night's sleep.

Rogalleh gave them all Saturday off, with the usual proviso that they could be called back at any time. When Jane came down to a late Saturday breakfast, she found a postcard from Matty. It appeared to be from the Bahamas, and

259

showed a long beach fringed with decorative palm trees. The scrawled message said, 'I did take that holiday, Kremer very annoyed with me but who cares? I'm not on this beach, I'm on a yacht. Might get married, thinking about it. Have fun, lots of love!'

'She's mad,' Jane said aloud.

'Who is, Matty? I saw it was her writing.'

'She scribbles with flabbergasting casualness that she's on a yacht and she might get married. To whoever-he-is, I suppose – I don't even know his name!'

'No doubt she'll remember to tell you it if she does marry him,' Adrian said, sounding so unsurprised that she suspected he had already read the card. 'I wish her luck, personally. Are you going in to work today?'

'No, you?' They were back to polite conversations. What else was there? It was better than being frosty with each other, anyway.

'No, I'm ...' He paused briefly and then went on, 'I'm going over to see Elizabeth at Tunbridge Wells. Chris is working this weekend, apparently. I ... don't suppose you'd like to come?'

'I can't, I've got to stay within range. But give her my love.'

He nodded and returned to his newspaper. Another little formal exchange over with. No use thinking about it anyway ... and she could hardly ask him if Felicity and Harry had made things up, far too dangerous a subject. By the time he folded his newspaper with deliberation and began to clear his half of the table they had neither of them spoken another word – though he gave her a gravely civil 'Goodbye, then' before he went out of the door.

It was just as well he left when he did, because a few moments later Hilaire rang on the mobile, before Jane had had time to do more than stare at Matty's postcard again with amused exasperation.

260

'I have those answers for you,' he said as soon as the formalities were over. 'I'll take the last one first. Yes, Joshua Connolly was arrested in Turkey last July and spent time on remand in a prison just outside Ankara. It wasn't altogether easy to discover this, and I was given the reason for his eventually being released without charge in November as "an amnesty". OK?'

'Thanks, Hilaire, you're an extremely efficient angel!'

'No problem. Now the other things. Nobody's seen Joshua driving any vehicle. Not his mother's car and not Malcolm's van either, and those are the only two available. Certainly not Malcolm's van, in fact, because Malcolm was always using it himself. The jobs he did, small building work, were all for other English people renovating barns and so on, and since the houses were usually way out in the country he would need his own transport, yes? That's what I'm told. Amiens police could give me nothing on a boy of Joshua's description being seen with Claus Armfeldt or with any of the people Claus was known to know, I'm afraid, so that's another negative. But . . .'

'But?' Jane prompted.

'The other query. Pierre Gachet told me that Madame Hughes and Chantal and even Lionel were all out looking for Joshua on the Sunday morning of his stepfather's last visit. Not Malcolm, because he was still off working – it was some weekend job laying a floor and he stayed over – but Madame was apparently in a state of alarm about her son's absence because his bed had not been slept in on Saturday night. Monsieur Gachet thought the boy was probably tired of being cooped up and went off to a disco somewhere. In fact, when Lionel left, Joshua was still not found, and Monsieur Gachet puts it down to his aquaintance being in too much of a temper to stop and exchange his usual few words with him. Any help?'

'I don't know. When was Joshua seen again?'

'Well, his mother said he came back on Sunday evening, when she apologised for having bothered everyone with her enquiries. Monsieur Gachet didn't see him again until – he thinks – Tuesday. Joshua told him then that he'd gone for a long walk, got lost, and slept under a hedge. He laughed about it. You could say that perhaps he wanted to get stoned and decided to do it out of the house to save being told off. Or,' Hilaire said acutely, 'you could say it's interesting that he wasn't there just when his stepfather was getting murdered. Is that what you're thinking?'

'I – hope not. I'm going to have to bear it in mind, though. I suppose nobody saw Joshua coming back, hitching? No, you would have said if they had.'

'I didn't hear anything to that effect. Anything else I can help you with?'

'I don't think so, thanks, but you've done wonders. And thank you. So, how's life treating you?'

'Quite well, I think. And you?'

'Not the best time I've ever spent,' Jane told him. 'We've got another case on which has appalling complications. Wish I could talk to you about it and hear your opinions – but I can't, let alone that it would take a long time and give you an outrageous phone bill! So I'll just say thanks again, and—'

'I wish you were coming over; that was a good day.'

'Yes it was. It's your turn to come over this side next – but I can't promise you anything near the same standard of food!' Jane said with a chuckle. She visualised Hilaire's handsome face on the other end of the line, until she realised she was doing it and hastily stopped. Well, it was only because he was more companionable than any other man in her life at the moment, and in the same profession so that he understood it. 'Goodbye,' she said with quick cheerfulness. 'Thanks again, see you one of these days.'

She'd had to ring off, she told herself, remembering her own warning to her team not to use the mobiles for chatting. Rogalleh might be wanting her. The phone remained stubbornly silent, however. And went on doing so.

Until Sunday morning.

He had told her to take Sunday off as well unless he summoned her back. She got up to find that Adrian hadn't come in at all – perhaps he had been invited to stay over by Elizabeth's parents, but she had no time to contemplate that. The bleep came loud and clear and she snatched up the instrument and snapped efficiently, 'Inspector Perry here.'

'Communications, ma'am. Superintendent Rogalleh wants you to meet him straight away at seventy-four Archer Street. That's off—'

'Yes, I know where it is, thanks, and I'm on my way. Did he give a reason?'

'Yes, ma'am,' the voice said – and Jane was aware this time that there was a tremor in it, of excitement or nervousness. 'There's a body. With a mark on it. But he told us not to say what mark in case this is an open line—'

'Fine. Has he sent for a scene-of-crimes team?'

'Yes, ma'am, we did that straight away. And we've just got Sergeant Vander on the other line and she's on her way too.'

'OK, I'm on the move now.'

Oh God, it had happened. That message mockingly telling them there was not much time ... There had been too little time, they hadn't managed to stop him. Oh, hell and damnation, *why* hadn't they? It felt like an unbearable failure. And it was Sunday today. Had he developed a taste for Sundays? But, dear heaven, this time it was only *three* weeks!

She was already in her car, and turning the key with urgent fingers.

Chapter 21

The body was in the bathroom on the first floor of the house in Archer Street. Not only in the bathroom; it was in the bath, naked. And the room was full of flowers.

Rogalleh was there, standing quite still studying everything. He glanced round as she came in and offered a brief, bleak instruction.

'Come here and look at his forehead.'

Jane stepped forward carefully. There were flowers floating in the bathwater, hung around the room, a ring of them on the floor – a variety of spring blooms, draped everywhere, drooping. The face of the man in the bath held a rictus, a stiff grimace under wide-open eyes. And on the forehead a neat diamond shape had been drawn, in what appeared to be blue biro.

Identical to the one Jane had seen on Lionel Hughes. The same shape and colour as the one chalked on the side of the Hollings' shed.

'His name's Michael Harvest, he's forty-five years old, and the lady he lives with came back this morning – though she was originally intending to be away the whole weekend – and found him. That circlet on the floor was on his head, like a crown. She snatched it off because she had some idea of reviving him. He's in rigor, though, so death must have been last night. He was electrocuted.'

Rogalleh's concise summing-up ceased. Jane could see,

now, an electric toaster lying in the bottom of the bath beside Michael Harvest's feet. Her eyes quickly followed its flex out of the room. 'Goes to a plug just outside in the passage,' Rogalleh told her, 'and it was already unplugged when Mrs Wright found it. Chummy did the business, then turned the electricity off and decorated the body, at a guess. And the room. I'm told they don't commonly keep flowers in here.'

'That must have taken time.'

'But since Harvest was alone in the house he had time, didn't he? Must have been aware Mrs Wright had left for the weekend. Ah, good, the SOCO team's here,' Rogalleh added as somebody in a white overall appeared in the doorway. 'Better leave them to it.'

He came stepping delicately past Jane to let the scene-of-crimes officers do their work, and she followed him with equal care. Halfway down the stairs they met Kate Vander; Rogalleh said briefly, 'Go and stand in the doorway and look, you need to have seen it.'

'Do we know anything about Michael Harvest, sir?' Jane asked as they carried on downstairs, after giving Kate a brief acknowledging glance in greeting.

'He's a psychotherapist, Mrs Wright tells us. Works from home, well thought of, specialises in teenagers mainly but has a few other clients as well. She's in shock of course, but first-on-scene got that from her. She's in the living room,' Rogalleh added – unaware of the cold feeling which had suddenly formed round Jane's heart. 'We'll go and have a word with her next.'

'Sir—'

'Later.' They had come to an open door, and inside the pleasant room ahead of them Jane could see a woman, attractive but white-faced, seated stiffly on a sofa, with a WPC in attendance. 'Mrs Wright,' Rogalleh said softly, 'this is hard for you I know, but a few questions?'

A bustle in the hall outside suggested that somebody else had arrived. Jane heard Dr Kremer's voice, sharply bad-tempered; yes, of course, it would be him as duty pathologist with Matty away. Rogalleh turned his head to her briefly to say, 'Shut the door', and Jane did so hastily. Better if Mrs Wright saw and heard as little as possible of the necessary practicalities which would be going on . . . She found she was being introduced by Rogalleh and met a pair of wide, shocked eyes as the woman tried to murmur a polite greeting. It *was* hard for her – desperately hard – and even with automatic professionalism in operation, Jane could feel for her.

Hard for those who hadn't managed to stop Blue Betty striking again, too . . .

Rogalleh was asking gently for a repeat of exactly what Mrs Wright had found and when, when she had gone away and when returned. His paternal rumble soothed, as always, and if his sympathy had grimness behind it – as it must – it was invisible. He elicited the answers. He asked softly for details of Michael Harvest's life. He had had a girl to see on Saturday morning, Mrs Wright said; she herself had been going off to a social work weekend conference but today's lecture had been cancelled at the last minute due to illness. So she had decided to come home. Yes, she had left first thing on Saturday morning. She and Michael had been living together for two years – happily, she added with a gulp, they were both divorced. She couldn't believe what she had found. It was impossible . . .

She took them into Michael's study, on request – more of another sitting room than a study, with comfortable armchairs as well as a desk – and said that that was where he saw his clients. She opened a drawer and produced his appointment diary. Rogalleh flicked through it, and Jane saw him pause. He said merely:

'I'll keep this, if I may. Now then, Mrs Wright, it'd be best if you go back into your sitting room and stay there with the door shut. We've things we have to do, you understand? I'll leave a woman police officer with you and perhaps she can make you another cup of tea.'

A jerk of his head instructed Jane to come with him. Outside – and a suitable distance from the closed door behind which the WPC would be keeping Mrs Wright company – he looked at Jane with a frown and flipped open the appointment book at the place he had been keeping with his finger.

'Eleven on Friday morning – isn't that a name I've seen recently? Connolly?'

'Yes, sir. Joshua Connolly is – is Mrs Hughes' son, and the twin of the one you met. Sir—'

She had had a sinking feeling ever since hearing that Michael Harvest was a psychotherapist; a desperate knowledge that this was a death she might have prevented. Her urgency was broken into, however, by the arrival of one of the SOCO team from upstairs carrying something in a clear plastic bag in his hand. He held it out to Rogalleh.

'A lot of wiped surfaces, sir, but this may be what was used to wipe them. The bath's an old-fashioned open one on legs and this had dropped behind it. Thought you might want to have a look before we take it away.'

The damp and crumpled dark-green material looked like a sweatshirt. It was spread out enough, however, for the white writing on its front to be visible. Jane could pick out the words 'Trinity College Chess Club'.

'Sir,' she said again on a breath, 'Joshua Connolly's an undergraduate at Trinity College, Cambridge, though he's on an intercalated year at the moment. Living with his mother.' She saw Rogalleh's dark eyes fix on her intently, gulped, and went on, 'And I know quite a lot about him. He

268

may have been missing from his mother's home in France when his stepfather was killed. He's been showing signs of disturbance lately. He and his brother were both taught how to shoot with a crossbow when they were at school. I've been following up—'

'Since when?' he asked sharply.

'Just recently. I didn't get the information about France until yesterday morning. It's only partial anyway. And it didn't seem possible that . . . I know he was at school in Birmingham at the right time, but he would only have been fourteen!'

'Ten-year-olds can kill,' he grated. He reached out and twitched the plastic bag from the scene-of-crimes officer's hand. 'I want this – you can have it back later.' As the SOCO shrugged and went back upstairs, Rogalleh looked round, then opened a nearby door and after a glance inside pushed Jane into the room revealed. It seemed to be a dining room. With the door shut behind them he turned on her. 'Right, now, everything you've been finding out!'

She could feel his anger. Knew the cause for it, too . . . It was already there like a stone inside her stomach. She ran through everything she had learned and done, as quickly and concisely as she could. He listened without interruption. When she had finished he flung the door open and bellowed, 'Sergeant Vander!'

Kate appeared promptly. 'You'll come with me,' Rogalleh instructed. 'We've got a suspect to arrest.' He swung back on Jane. 'No, not you – you can wait for me back at the station.'

The look he gave her would have withered a tree. Following up a line of her own. Not sharing her information. Or not until too late. She could feel all that in his glance, but answered merely, 'Yes, sir,' though he didn't even wait for her to say it. He swept Kate away with him.

Frances Ferguson

Well, he knew where Josh was, because she had told him;
he knew how to find the house in Willowfield Way, too,
because he had been there. Would he radio in for back-up
on his way to arrest Josh? Probably.

But surely . . .

Even now, as Jane's mind returned from the shock she
had felt, some core inside her stirred to deny the obvious-
ness of it. Would Blue Betty really leave them such a trail of
clear clues? Josh's own therapist? A sweatshirt with his
college logo on it? The latter could have been careless-
ness . . . but from a killer who had never before been
careless?

Sam had said that the psychotherapist was stirring things
up in Josh. All the same . . .

Rogalleh had said that his conversation with Blue Betty
gave him the feeling that this time, his prey wanted to be
caught . . .

She went back to the station and made a quick typed copy
of everything she knew about Joshua Connolly from the
rough notes she had been keeping for her own benefit. It
reached her at second hand – the station was buzzing with it
– that Rogalleh had brought a suspect in for questioning; but
he didn't send for her to sit in. She got somebody to take in
to him the notes she had made, even her query that there
might be a link between Josh and Claus Armfeldt due to the
Turkish connection and the position of Amiens, bringing the
immigrant run back into things again. She fielded questions
from various people who popped into the office; one of
them, after an hour or so, was Chris. He showed surprise
that she wasn't in on the questioning, but she gave him a
shrugged answer.

'Rogalleh's got his own methods. He might think I'd be –
oh, reassuring, or something, considering I've seen quite a
bit of the family.'

'I hope this one's a true bill. Pity there had to be another homicide before you could get him, but at least there's solid evidence, I heard. Maybe there'll be more after the search warrant Rogalleh's had sworn out... You haven't been sent on the search either? No, you said, you know the family too well. Rogalleh must be sure he's got his man because he's using male officers in the search,' Chris added drily, 'along with my two WDCs – sorry, *your* two WDCs.' He added moodily, 'I'm still being kept out of it though. Makes me feel like a spare wheel... Yes, do you want me or Inspector Perry?'

The constable who had come in wanted him, and he went away. Jane was left to herself. 'Pity there had to be another homicide'... Yes indeed. One she was responsible for... If Josh *was* Blue Betty, she could have prevented it. If she had voiced her suspicions earlier... Even yesterday morning, when she had heard from Hilaire that Josh might have been missing from Les Beaux Vents when Lionel was murdered, would have been time enough. But she had thought they would be given longer, that she had time to brew it.

It was a long time later when Kate came in, a cardboard cup of coffee balanced in her hand. 'We're taking a break,' she announced on a gusty sigh. She was, Jane thought, carefully showing incuriosity for the fact that she had been chosen to join Rogalleh for the questioning rather than Jane. 'The search – you've heard? They found a trunk full of women's clothes in the attic at Willowfield Way. Large enough for a tallish male to dress up in, too. Nothing more definite than that, though. And since I've emerged I've heard there's a private car park at the end of Archer Street with a closed-circuit surveillance camera overlooking it in case of theft – and, would you believe, they've been through the film and there's a shadowy figure in a long skirt and headscarf passing across it, with late Saturday night's date and time on it? Not going to a particular car, though, so if it was him and he was using transport he must have left it somewhere else.'

'He wouldn't have been bloodstained this time so he might have been walking. Identifiable photo?'

'No. Carefully back view. Looked rather deliberate, they said. Which is in character. As other things are not, are they? And the boy's . . .' Kate frowned. 'I have to say, he worries me. And Rogalleh's—'

'What?' Jane asked as she came to a halt.

'He's clever, and he's a senior officer, but – he is obsessive, isn't he? Off the record? And he seems so all-fired sure . . . Sure that he's close to coaxing a confession out of Joshua, but it doesn't seem like that to me.' Kate looked at Jane. 'You've met Joshua before and I saw that you described him as disturbed. I reckon he is – for all the FME pronounced him fit to be questioned. Yes, all right, we're looking for a disturbed psychopath, aren't we? But one who sits there looking unhappy and saying he might have committed murder but he can't remember?'

'Is that what Joshua's doing?'

'Yes. And talking about dreams and voices. He does seem to be aware of the Blue Betty murders, I have to say that. He knew that "Blue" came into it too . . . but right at the start of the Birmingham cases the name "Blue Betty" was mentioned in the press before the Blue got dropped, and if he was at school up there he'd have read all the reports – avidly, if I know teenage boys.' Kate frowned again. 'He keeps agreeing that he could have killed people, and that he expects he did if people keep telling him so. Wearily and politely and with an edge of despair. Not a joker, no way.'

'Split personality?'

'I'd say that's what Rogalleh *doesn't* want to think. He wants a straight conviction, not a plea of insanity. So he's got to tell himself that what he's being offered now is just another game. To me, it seems as if the boy really isn't sure whether he's guilty or not. Or he could be suffering from, what do they call it, *folie de grandeur*? Or is it *folie de deux*? The one where if somebody tells you a murder's been committed you take responsibility for it?'

'The evidence—'

'Yes, I know, but it only comes down to opportunity and the fact that it is his sweatshirt, doesn't it? He admits it is his but says he thinks he left it somewhere. As far as killing his stepfather's concerned, he did protest about that – but then shook his head and said, "I thought I just went for a walk, but maybe I did kill him – did I?" He admits he used to know how to shoot with a crossbow but says he doesn't think he'd shoot a dog because he likes dogs; he says he supposes he could have driven his stepfather's car back to France and then stolen another one to get home, but he doesn't remember doing it... Oh, I don't know! He's supposed to be very clever, so perhaps he is playing games with us as Rogalleh thinks. It's a first-class defence in its way, after all.'

'He hasn't been charged yet, presumably?'

'No, at the moment he's just helping us with our enquiries. He said politely that he didn't want the duty solicitor, thank you. Though I reckon,' Kate said drily, 'seeing the way his mother was when we went to pull him in, she'll be marshalling her forces right now to fetch in every solicitor in the book if necessary. And would have done it already if she hadn't been held up by its being Sunday! Oh well, I'd better get back. A ten-minute break, Rogalleh said, and I don't want him to have to come looking for me.'

She went off to the renewed questioning. What she had

said sounded like the Josh Jane knew. Was he genuinely a split personality?

Was he Blue Betty?

If he wasn't . . .

He could have left his sweatshirt at Archer Street when he went to see Michael Harvest on the Friday. The killer might have used it for his cleaning-up operations thinking it was one of his victim's own. That would make a lot more sense than Blue Betty leaving it by mistake. It was true that it could have slipped down behind the bath and gone unnoticed, but . . .

Why choose that particular therapist? Josh's therapist. Surely too coincidental for a random choice.

Unless . . . unless it wasn't random. Who knew that Josh was disturbed, and prone to guilt, and so far from his usual self that he might take responsibility for anything anyone suggested to him?

Harry Morpeth probably knew.

But he had those confident alibis. If it were not for that, she could, savagely, see it appealing to his mischievous mind to leave evidence pointing straight at Josh. To send the police in the wrong direction. Even to get Josh put away for insanity in Blue Betty's place. But that would mean that Harry *was* Blue Betty in spite of everything. Could he be? And what about the tail on him – or had that been stopped?

Jane let out a sigh, along with the bitter acknowledgement that she was casting around for something to show that she was not responsible for Michael Harvest's murder. That it wasn't a death she could have circumvented. They had been warned that time was running out; Blue Betty had taken care to tell them so. And who knew better than students about hacking into computer systems? Particularly students whose subject was higher maths as well as physics, no doubt.

She wasn't sure what she was meant to do here, aside from

sitting and letting thoughts run round and round in her head; but when the clock had ticked round to six she received a message telling her to go home. Rogalleh was still keeping her at an icy distance, then.

After the circumstances of the day it seemed supremely unimportant to find herself exchanging empty commonplaces with Adrian: how was Elizabeth? Elizabeth seeemd rather better, thank you, and glad of company. And he'd stayed over? Yes, her parents had been kind enough to invite him – since Chris was too busy to come this weekend. Jane retired to her solitary bed early; but then lay there with her eyes wide open in the dark.

If the Blue Betty case was solved, she should be glad of it.

If it hadn't taken another death on the way there, she would have been glad of it . . . But it was no use lying in the dark with that picture before her eyes: a room obscenely decked with flowers, the naked body of a man whose only job had been to help people lying in the rictus of death amid that false beauty, with his killer's signature drawn neatly on his forehead.

She went in to work in the morning to find that Rogalleh's attitude towards her seemed to have softened; at least he growled a good morning at her when she came into the room, before turning back to Rachel and Jennie, who were already there. 'We've had him for less than twenty-four hours, so we've got time yet,' he was saying to them. 'I reckon he'll be telling me the whole truth before the day's out, in any case. His brother came in early to bring him clothes and a razor; had to be told he couldn't have the razor, of course, but he left the clothes. Now, what I want from you two is a print-off of all the stuff on the Hughes murder so I can use it to refresh my memory. Get to it. Jane, a word?'

'Sir?' she said as the two WDCs moved away to do as he had asked.

'As I said to the others, I think we'll get there. Once he sees I won't stand any more nonsense about not remembering. Oh, the French girl turned up at the station last night – Chantal something? – and tried to make out that whatever time we wanted to know about, Joshua was with her. Every minute of every day and night except for Friday morning when he was seeing his therapist, according to her, and even then she walked there with him and met him again straight afterwards,' he said drily. He should have been looking tired, since he must have worked nonstop yesterday, but instead, though the lines on his face had deepened, he seemed subtly more alive. 'When she was challenged on times she claimed he was in bed with her all Saturday night, and when she was told Joshua hadn't said that, replied that he just didn't remember. He's supposed to have been in bed with her on Easter Sunday morning too, and never out of her sight the weekend Lionel Hughes was killed and for days after . . . She was lying, of course. Not a very good liar, either. His mother put her up to it, I expect.'

'She claims to be Josh's girlfriend so she may have thought of it for herself.'

'No matter which, it won't wash if he won't confirm it. She demanded to see him, of course. And was refused.' He paused, then went on, 'I want you to get the Harvest murder written up – and put on the computer after the girls have finished. See if you can get hold of the SOCO details if they've got anything for us yet; include whatever first-on-scene can tell you. We need it all logged. I . . . I'm going to keep Kate with me for the questioning; better not to have a change of personnel. You can listen to the tapes of yesterday's. I've left them on the table over there.'

'Yes, sir.' She drew a breath and added, 'I'm sorry . . .'

'Nobody could have known he was going to shorten his timespan like that. Caught us all on the hop. Maybe a dog wasn't satisfying enough,' he added grimly. 'Well, we've got enough to hold him on for now while we check everything else. I'm off to see if he's stopped pretending to be mad this morning. Kate should have had him brought out of the cells by now.'

He seemed very sure that they had the right man at last, as he went off with a spring in his soft tread. Jane found his words coming back to her as she listened to the tapes of yesterday's interviews. *Was* Josh pretending to be mad?

His voice sounded very like Sam's, only without the fraction of a stammer which came into his twin's speech now and again. He seemed unhappy, confused, half sure he must have done something if people said he had. Something terrible.

But something somebody else had told him . . .

Jane stirred uncomfortably. If she could hear that in the words, why couldn't Rogalleh, with all his experience?

Kate – even steady Kate – had called Rogalleh obsessive. He *was* obsessed with catching Blue Betty, but that was natural enough. Had it got worse since that phone call, when he had at last heard the voice again of the man he was hunting, with its proof that it genuinely was the same person and that he was here? Perhaps.

It would suit Blue Betty if the police believed they had got their man. Was making Rogalleh think that he wanted to be caught at last another subtle game? Because he was going to provide an alternative, plant evidence, set things up so that Josh would go down, because the boy was too wrapped up in his nightmares to offer a proper defence? Suppose – suppose Blue Betty actually had got bored with killing, wished he hadn't started again, wanted to stop and yet not be caught . . .

While Josh was in custody they were safe from more killings, either way. If he was Blue Betty, he'd have no chance to do them. If he wasn't, then there would be no more murders while the police had him, because it would be a giveaway.

An inconclusive answer. One she had no business thinking of, with one glaring mistake already behind her. But at least the tension they had all been living under was relieved. Already around the station there were signs of it. Blue Betty was banged up, and if Rogalleh was sure of it nobody else need doubt it. They could hold him for the legal maximum time, and if he hadn't made a full confession by then they could apply for an extension.

It wasn't as easy as that. When Kate came into the office at noon Jane could see that something had happened. And soon heard what.

'The guv'nor's seething, but there wasn't anything he could do. What with Rowena Hughes sweeping in with not only a very efficient lawyer in tow, but also a psychiatrist all prepared to say the boy wasn't fit to be questioned further. The trouble is, when we got the FME back in she agreed with him – since Joshua suddenly developed the shakes. We hadn't got anything different out of him anyway.'

'So, what? What's the situation?'

'The lawyer gave Rogalleh a very cool "charge him or let him go". So Rogalleh said he was planning to charge him – and got given Chantal Mentiment's alibis again, and the fact that everything else is circumstantial. Joshua was wearing his chess club sweatshirt, Mrs Hughes says, when he went to see his therapist on Friday, and came back without it, so that's why it was in the house. The fact that there were those clothes in the attic at Willowfield Way certainly won't stand up as evidence – and Mrs Hughes claims they were old ones of hers and her daughter's anyway, things due to go to jumble sales but stuffed in the attic in the meantime. And Joshua's had somebody with him at any time you choose to

278

mention over months... His mother wouldn't care what he's done, I'd say,' Kate added drily. 'It's pretty obvious she'd swear black was white for her kid. And that lawyer will let her. As for the way Joshua's been telling us he may have committed murder, the psychiatrist's all set to call that duress, and give any amount of fancy diagnoses.'

'And? They've got Joshua transferred to a secure hospital?'

'No such luck, though the guv'nor tried for it. He had to back off on the charges, too, with that lawyer facing him down. He was forced to let Mrs Hughes take Joshua home – though on recognisances to return to the police station for further questioning,' Kate added. 'Best he could do. And you never saw anybody so hopping mad.'

'Where is he now – the guv'nor?' Jane asked.

'He's just finished ordering a round-the-clock surveillance on nineteen Willowfield Way. Can't do more than put a car outside on the public highway, but I suppose that's something. Just as well he'd agreed to the request to take the tail off Morpeth on Friday,' Kate added drily, 'or there wouldn't be anybody left who wasn't on overtime, and *that* wouldn't go down well, would it? Anyway, then he growled that he was going to Forensics, in person, to see what the SOCOs have got from Archer Street which might help him. Yes, I know, they won't have finished their analyses yet – but would you have cared to try and stop him? Anyone who did would get ground between his teeth. I don't know exactly what he wants *us* to do. Any ideas?'

'You can help me get all the details of the Archer Street murder entered. I've got the facts sorted on paper, but then I stopped to listen to the tapes,' Jane said quickly. The task had better be done, and properly, by the time Rogalleh came back. Or woe betide, from the sound of things. 'Here, this is the first-on-scene report, I guess that had better go in first . . .'

So Josh was out. That thought sat in her head as she recited statements to Kate, easier than trying to follow what she had written and look at the computer keyboard at the same time. Josh was out, with Rogalleh still believing him guilty. He might be. Maybe those months in the Turkish jail had set him off on an old course. Why hadn't Sam shown any uneasiness about his twin in earlier years, though? Or was Sam, Josh's other half, a good actor? Better by far than she had given him credit for?

Just as they finished logging the Archer Street murder, Rachel and Jennie came back. Nothing, really, for them to do, until Rogalleh should return and provide instructions. Jane and Kate went to lunch themselves. The canteen was buzzing with the fact that the probable Blue Betty had had to be released into a psychiatrist's care. At this rate, Jane thought drily, some careless word would escape the station and get into the hands of whatever reporter managed to pick up on the Archer Street murder. Mrs Wright had seen the blue diamond mark too – so how long would it be before she let that out to some apparently sympathetic member of the press, and then somebody acutely added things up and all hell broke loose? Not long, she could bet.

She went back via the front desk, with a casual query about whether anyone from the press had shown up yet, though she found they had already had a warning to stall if that happened. She was turning away when she spotted a familiar white van parked directly outside. Slightly battered, more than a little scruffy, as befitted a jobbing workman . . . She had got no further than wondering what Malcolm Jackson's van was doing there when she realised that the man himself was in the foyer, hanging about and looking as neutral as ever. She simply hadn't noticed him. Now that she had, she walked up to him.

'Mr Jackson? Inspector Perry. We met—'

'Yes, I remember. I've come for some clothes Josh left here.'

'Have you asked at the desk?' He nodded. 'All right, then, I expect they'll be brought to you in a minute.'

'Hope so. Mrs Hughes sent me down when she found they'd been left behind.'

'Well then – oh, this looks like them.' A constable had come out through the internal security door with a large brown paper package in his hand, and was glancing round. The light flashed on Malcolm Jackson's glasses as he looked towards the constable, and then he stepped forward awkwardly. The package was handed over and signed for. Then the man was gone, sloping back towards the outside door.

She could hardly have asked him outright whether Josh had been borrowing his van. She only had that from Harry, anyway. And even if he had, Malcolm had probably been primed by Rowena Hughes to lie about it.

She went through the outside door herself, to check out a rumour she had heard in the canteen: that some graffiti artist had decorated the glass of one of the outside notice boards with a fancily curlicued signature in red paint. Not that it was her job at the moment to worry about whether a nicely designed public relations poster was visible or not ... but it was something to do. She saw the white van driving off, then forgot Malcolm Jackson as she inspected the cheerful vandalisation of police property. Chief Inspector Lowell probably knew about it already.

She went back in, her mind heavily occupied.

If Willowfield Way was being watched, surely there was no chance that there would be another killing. Anyway, there was that definition of serial killers: a cooling-off period between one crime and the next . . .

Rogalleh came back, to harry them all to find something in the old files he could specifically connect to Joshua Connolly. The area where the boys' school had been was now marked with a red ring on the Birmingham map. He wanted the distance from all the original Blue Betty murders mapped. He scarcely looked at Jane; angry with her again. Angry with himself too, and frustrated. He had been so close . . . It was plain he had got nothing helpful from the SOCO report, and when he stamped away, presumably going to his own office to lick his wounds, it was something of a relief.

It was mid-afternoon when something crystallised in Jane's mind and she decided to ring Hilaire. Only on the off chance, but . . .

She made an excuse to leave the office and went out to the station yard to call from her car. The first time, he wasn't in; the second, half an hour later, he was, and he listened attentively to her request.

'OK, I'll try. I'll get back to you as soon as I can. Jane?'

'Please don't ask me any questions, and it may be a complete dead end. I – I just need to know, that's all.'

'Done. I've got a meeting I'm supposed to be at, but I'll ring you.'

It was the best she could do. Only an idea. No use going to Rogalleh, he would merely stare at her in disbelief. And she wasn't the most popular person in his books right now in any case. It was just something her brain had suggested to her . . . some place in the distant confines of her brain, anyway, bringing a sudden question to which she felt the urgent need of an answer.

The watch on Willowfield Way was to be constant; sometimes a clearly visible patrol car, at other times an unmarked car from CID. Rogalleh didn't seem to be worrying unduly about women officers now, though he had scheduled Rachel and Jennie for a shift starting at ten p.m. Neither Kate – who had been working all day anyway – nor Jane was included in the surveillance. Jane went home feeling restless. Surely things were safe, with Josh under surveillance? And there was the time factor too . . . She answered Adrian when he spoke to her, but barely noticed when he gave up and said stiffly that he thought he would go round and see Felicity. She had said earlier that Harry was going out this evening without her, and was feeling rather down about it.

'Fine. Sorry, I've got a lot on my mind . . .'

'So I see. I may see you later, then. If you haven't gone to bed to avoid me before I get back.'

She ought to have said she wasn't trying to avoid him. He had gone, though, before she got round to it. And when her mobile phone gave its bleep fifteen minutes later she dived for it. 'Hilaire?'

'Inspector Perry, it's Communications here. A Sam Connolly's ringing you and he says it's urgent. He won't speak to anybody else. What would you like me to do about it?'

'Give him this number.'

She rang off and waited.

He came on the line so quickly she could have guessed his desperation, even if it had not been there in his voice. 'Inspector Perry? Please, could you meet me? I know you all think – *please*, it's really urgent!'

'About what?' Jane asked crisply.

She heard him hesitate. Then, 'Twin's gone out. I know he isn't meant to. No, I'm not going to tell the bloody police car parked outside, and I'm only telling you because I – because you seemed like somebody reasonable. But if you pass this on to them I won't say another word—'

'Calm down, Sam. Are you sure Josh has gone out? He'd surely have been seen if—'

'Well he wasn't or they wouldn't still be there, would they? I don't know how he got by but he has. And even Ma doesn't know, nobody does but me, she thinks he's in bed but if anyone'd know he doesn't sleep as a hump with the covers over his head, I would. Look, do I have to say all this? He's gone, and I think I know where, and if you'll just meet me we can go there. I haven't got a car, and Ma's is off the road at the moment. But you see, what I think – why it's so urgent – I think twin's in real despair, and he may do something to himself. Oh, for God's sake, won't you help?'

'Don't ring off. Yes, I will. Where do you want me to meet you?'

'I'm in a phone box on the estate. Nobody took any notice when it was only me coming out,' he said, sounding bitter. 'Pilgrim's Way, the phone box at the end of that. Please will you come *now*? And – and please, I'm trusting you – *please* don't tell anyone else!'

'Wait there for me, and remember it may be a few minutes. But I'm on my way.'

So Josh had gone out . . . and Sam wanted her to come and meet him. Without telling anyone else. And on the urgent plea that his twin might be going to commit suicide.

She needed that call from Hilaire. But he hadn't come back to her yet, and maybe events were overtaking him.

If somebody was using Josh . . . somebody clever, and subtle, and so sociopathic that he would manipulate another person without conscience and behind an innocently bland face . . . That would fit the Blue Betty profile far better than Josh did. And she knew that inside herself she had started to believe that. It was the only thing which made sense.

The question was, what did he plan to do next?

She reached out her hand for her car keys. There was only one way to find out.

Chapter 22

There was something she had to do first. She picked up her mobile phone, that inevitable companion of the last few weeks, and punched up Rachel's mobile number.

It was answered promptly. Jane said crisply, 'Rachel, it's Inspector Perry. Where are you and Jennie at the moment?'

'We're just about to go and relieve the surveillance team outside Willowfield Way, ma'am.'

She had hoped so, with her watch showing quarter to ten. 'I want you to do something else instead,' Jane said, her voice official. 'You needn't tell the other car you're not coming, they can just hang about and wait until you do get there, OK? And never mind if it makes them grumble, because first I need you to tail me. You're in plain clothes and an unmarked car, aren't you?'

'Yes, ma'am.'

'Good. Keep a discreet distance but don't lose me. You know my car, don't you? But here's the number.' She recited it. 'I'll be picking somebody up from outside the phone box in Pilgrim's Way in . . . How long will it take you to get there?'

'Less than ten minutes. We're already in the car; we were just leaving.'

'I should be about ten. If I'm there first I'll make sure to slow things down until I see you; if you're there first hang about at a reasonable distance until you see me. I can't give you any more details but it's important that you follow and don't lose me. But I don't want you seen either. Got it?'

'Yes, ma'am,' Rachel told her.

'Good,' Jane said, and rang off. Safety precautions in place. They just had to be good enough. As she went out into the dark she hoped that wherever Sam planned to take her wasn't far. But, wherever, she had to answer his urgent summons.

She saw him beside the phone box, a taut figure caught in the filtering gleam from a nearby streetlamp. She had already passed Rachel and Jennie's car and thanked God for their unquestioning obedience. And that they had been scheduled for surveillance, making them instantly available. It would have been difficult – and probably dangerous – to stall for too long . . . Sam came quickly to her as she slowed and was already pulling at the door as she reached across to unlock it. His face was a picture of worry. She said, once he was in:

'All right, Sam, where are we going?'

'It's a place which used to be our secret hideout. I'm almost sure twin will have gone there. The old school at Lower Hardres. It's been shut up for years but they've never got round to pulling it down.' His voice was jerky. 'Oh Christ, I hope I'm right – I hope he hasn't gone somewhere else . . .'

'If you think that's where he is we'd better try it. You used to live in the village, didn't you?' They were already moving and he hadn't tried to tell her the way; he must simply have faith that she knew it.

'Yes, and that's why . . . I don't know what your bloody people have been making him believe! But he's so far down . . . If he kills himself it'll be your fault, you know that, don't you?'

'And that's what you think he's gone out to do?'

'*Yes,*' Sam said on a drawn breath. 'He wouldn't just hide, so yes, I do. He was like someone who's come to the end.' He added worriedly, 'I wish I knew how long he's been gone. He told Ma he just wanted to sleep and please would nobody disturb him. If I hadn't looked in—'

'All right. We're on our way. And when we get to the village you can direct me.' She was keeping to a decorous speed, though she knew he wanted her to go faster. They had swung out along the New Dover Road and a flicking glance in her mirror showed her the following car a decent distance back. The road would soon narrow, then a couple of miles from the city's outer limits there would be a sharp turn left to the villages; Lower Hardres, Upper Hardres and Stelling Minnis. Where all this had begun – at least from her point of view. After a few minutes Sam leaned forward and said:

'You turn there, by the signpost.'

'I know.' She was already slowing for it. Then they were in narrower and more twisting lanes, a bumpier surface, her headlights reflecting against hedges instead of houses. 'We'll reach the village in a minute. Where's this school?'

'At the other end, I'll show you. It was the old primary school before they built the new one. It may be a listed building or something; anyway, they've never pulled it down even though it's all boarded up. It's got some trees round it – there!'

They had passed the houses which made up Lower Hardres and the old school could be glimpsed as a dim barnlike shape behind a batch of clustering trees. A nice deserted spot, Jane thought grimly. The nearest house was at least two hundred yards distant. The schoolhouse itself stood well back from the road, but if there had once been a yard in front of it that was gone now, the trees crowding in instead. No lights were showing. Jane doused her headlights. 'There's no electricity in there, I suppose,' she said practically, 'so we'll need a torch to look round. Luckily I've got a strong flashlight—'

'He *is* here!' Sam said abruptly. His eyes must have adjusted more quickly than hers to the moonless night. Stars gave a soft glimmer though no more than that – but as he pointed Jane caught a flash of white under the dark shadows of the trees, the square edge of a vehicle parked well back. 'I was right. Come on—'

'Wait,' Jane said firmly.

'I can't, don't you see? He might be doing anything!'

'But wait for the torch. How do you get in? A loose board on one of the windows?' She got out of the car and her peering eyes adjusted to let her see a little more clearly. There were upper windows as well as lower, but she could see dark crisscrosses of wood barring those, while below everything looked even more thoroughly sealed. 'Show me—'

She was interrupted by a sound. Her mobile phone gave its sharp summoning bleep, slightly muffled by her inside pocket but still audible, and sending a reverberation against her heart. She bit back a swift curse, thinking *Not now!* But it had to be dealt with, it could be urgent, Rachel to say they had lost her . . . She hadn't seen the following car as they came through the village. 'Sorry, I have to answer that,' she told Sam crisply. 'Go and check that that really is the van you think your brother's come here in. Because if it isn't we ought to be somewhere else, oughtn't we? But then wait for me, I won't be a moment.'

It wasn't Rachel; it was Hilaire.

'The answer's yes,' he said without preliminaries. 'You were right. These are the details.' And he gave them to her, with swift efficiency. 'Does that help? It's something nobody's taken into account before, so—'

'Thanks, Hilaire, and yes it does, more than you could

290

know. I can't talk, I'm in the middle of something, but *thank you*. I'll ring you again and explain.'

It answered everything. All her doubts and suppositions. Jane swung round quickly to look for Sam – and couldn't see him. Damn, oh damn, where was he?

He must have gone inside. Even a cautious flash of her torch didn't reveal him. Though it did show the white van, clearly now.

She hesitated for a brief second, then punched up Rachel's number on the mobile still in her hand. It was answered with the same promptness as before, and Jane said quickly, 'Where are you?'

'Parked a hundred yards behind your car, ma'am. What do you want us to do?'

'Move in closer. Right up close, in fact. The building you can see behind the trees is the old Lower Hardres primary school. There's a white van beside it which I want one of you to disable. After that I want you to keep a sharp watch and make sure nobody comes out. No—' Jane caught herself up, making herself speak slowly and clearly against her feeling of urgency. 'First, before you do any of that, send for back-up. Priority. I'm pretty sure Blue Betty's inside the building. Tell them so. And I'm going in.'

'Ma'am, you can't!'

'I've got to, because somebody else is in there with him. Which means a hostage situation, or even another death, if I don't manage to prevent it. So I must.' After Michael Harvest, she said silently. Who, if she had asked the right questions sooner, would still be alive. 'I'll go in carefully,' she said brusquely, 'and without taking any unnecessary risks. Now get that back-up, and fast, and then do the other things I've told you.'

'Jennie's already calling in while we're talking, ma'am. But—'

Jane rang off before Rachel could finish what was probably a renewed protest. She walked swiftly towards the building. If she had had time to waste she could have comforted the girls with the reminder that Blue Betty didn't kill women – though were they still sure of that? she wondered drily. She wasn't. After all, he had killed a dog, and that wasn't in his previous record either. She paused for a quick study of the building. How had Sam got in?

She would have heard him if he'd been scrabbling at one of the windows, surely, even against her intense listening to Hilaire. Besides, from close up they all looked solidly sealed still. But if he'd gone round the back . . . She needed to find a way in quickly; what looked likely? On impulse she put her hand against the wide front door, double-hinged, in its arched stone surround. And felt it give against her gentle push . . .

The place was open.

She went in softly and pulled the door closed behind her so that her eyes would adjust to the thicker dark. She wasn't going to announce her presence with her torch . . . It wasn't quite dark anyway; there was a dim glow of orange light coming round the corner at the far end of the passage in which she stood. And she could hear the murmur of a voice too. She waited for a moment, listening hard. Then she stepped forward on quiet feet and crept along the passage. She passed a door each side but they were both closed. What was happening would be ahead of her, anyway; where the voice was, which sounded increasingly like Sam's.

As she rounded the corner cautiously she could see and hear more clearly. See through a doorless arch just ahead of her, into a big room where the light was coming from. See right up the room, in fact, which looked as if it must have been the old school hall; there was a small raised platform at the far end of it. A row of candles had been set along its edge

292

with their flames standing up with barely a waver in the still air. But what was in front of the platform was what drew her eyes immediately as she took another careful step forward.

Josh – *was* it Josh? – was slumped on an upright chair, dressed in a flowing skirt and with his face garishly made up. Above him, tied to a broad crossbeam which traversed the room ten feet up, and dangling invitingly down, was a thick rope with a noose on the end of it. And yes, it had to be Josh, because Sam was kneeling beside him, shaking at his arm, talking insistently.

'You can't do this! You haven't done anything – truly you haven't, we all know it, why do you think you have? It doesn't matter what the police say, you *haven't*. Twin, can you hear me? Josh? You don't have to do this, and you can't!'

He didn't look as if he was getting through. His brother looked dazed, semiconscious. Jane stepped forward again, very quietly, bringing her into the lee of the shadowing doorway so that she could peer into almost the whole room. There was a high arch at the far end where the beam was, making it look like the inside of a barn, though the near end was different, with a much lower ceiling. A stairway ran up one side of the hall against the wall. And when she looked down to the floor of the hall she could suddenly see that what had looked at first glance like random objects scattered at Josh's feet were, in fact, carefully laid out. There was a large cut-out diamond in what was probably blue paper, though the glow from the candles leached its colour. There was a small but deadly looking crossbow, ready primed with a bolt, set to one side of it; to the other, what looked like a small, flat booklet – a passport? – and a mobile phone; in front, a – yes, a bath sponge. With a flower laid on top of it.

Souvenirs. Of murder.

Sam was still talking insistently, trying his hardest. Barely breathing, Jane tried to peer into the shadowed edges of the room – this end, where the light from the candles barely reached and darkness crept thickly back. He had to be there. Somewhere. The person who had set all this up for Josh. He had to be hiding himself in the shadows where Sam hadn't seen him; maybe round the corner which was just out of her sight ... What was he waiting for? To see if the other twin had brought anybody with him? Well, she would keep still and lull him into thinking that wasn't so, wait for him to show himself, catch him off guard.

Even as she framed the thought a figure stepped forward into her eyeline – out of the dark corner which was where she had supposed he must be.

An unnerving figure, because it could have been the boy slumped in the chair all over again. The same long, sweeping skirt. A fringed shawl. A headscarf instead of Josh's long hair. The glimpse of a garishly made-up cheek ...

The voice which spoke was high-toned, and sibilant. As Sam, who must have sensed a movement in the room or caught it out of the corner of his eye, looked up and saw what faced him with widening eyes and a startled disbelief, the voice said:

'Don't try to wake him up, he's mine. He has to die, you know. And you do too, now!'

'What the *hell*—'

'Don't argue with me, and he's too far gone to help you.'

As the words finished there was a sudden lunge forwards – a horrifyingly smooth and swift movement in Sam's direction, and with an arm coming up and a flash of steel in the hand. It happened so fast that Jane was caught in a frozen moment, only able to think, *No!* Oh God, she had left it too late! But even before she could try to move, there was a blur

294

as Sam went into a rolling dive. His hands snatched for the crossbow. He flung it up and fired all in one movement.

For an unaimed shot it was brilliant. The flying bolt caught the edge of the raised arm, and though it didn't pierce it but clattered away uselessly on to the floor, even that much had caused a startled, evasive jerk which set the figure off balance and stumbling, and the knife flying out of his suddenly loosened grip. It came skittering towards Jane to land a foot away from her. She moved so fast then that her muscles almost cracked, scooping it up, whirling to face the man whose garishly painted cheeks gave him a nightmarish unreality. It was like looking at a lethal clown . . . She brought her flashlight up, switching it on as she moved it, pinning him in the bright beam, and spoke sharply, letting her voice come out like a whip.

'Police, and this place is surrounded, so don't move!'

Even as she uttered the words she caught the sudden sound of sirens, their urgent wail piercing the night as they came closer. 'Good, even more of us!' she said coolly, staring into the face of the man who was half crouched six feet away from her. 'Malcolm Jackson, I'm arresting you for the murders of Lionel Hughes and Michael Harvest, and for the attempted murder of Joshua Connolly. You don't have to say—'

He didn't let her finish. When she saw his bunching muscles she thought he was going to fly at her – but that wasn't the direction he took. Nor did he move towards Sam, who had come to his feet breathlessly, looking belligerent. He hurled himself suddenly towards the steep slope of the staircase against the side wall, and was up it on all fours like a flying, long-skirted monkey. To vanish through a door at the top which closed behind him with a slam. The thud of feet could suddenly be heard above, across the ceilinged area of the room.

'Is there a way out up there?' Jane flung urgently at Sam.

'No, there used to be a fire escape but it fell off, and anyway they've sealed the door. And the windows are barred.'

'Good. Are you all right?'

'Yes, he didn't— Jesus, was that *Malcolm*?'

'Yes,' Jane said shortly. 'Stay still and look after Josh. I don't know what he's been given but he looks pretty ropy. Malcolm's probably been feeding him something psychotropic regularly.'

'Jesus,' Sam said again, with anger in it this time – but Jane had turned away from him. She kept her eyes on the staircase as she flicked her phone out of her jpocket. The footsteps above had stopped . . . She went on listening for them as she spoke.

'Rachel? Yes, it's me, I'm all right. Blue Betty is in here, but he's upstairs and hopefully can't get out. He hasn't got a hostage now and I don't *think* he's armed, but I can't be sure about that. But tell them to watch all the upper windows in case he does try to break out somehow. And an old fire escape door, though it's supposed to be sealed. All right, getting this?'

'Yes, ma'am. Superintendent Rogalleh's just arrived.'

Jane had thought he might have. 'Tell him they can come in safely downstairs,' she said, 'but for God's sake stress this: there are two young men with me and one of them's in drag but *he's not Blue Betty*. He was an intended victim. Blue Betty's up above us on the first floor and, I hope, trapped. Will you make sure they know all that, please?'

If her priority call for back-up had brought anyone carrying sidearms – and it might well have done – it would be just as well not to get Josh shot.

She saw that Sam was trying to get Josh out of the skirt, with a look of distaste on his face, and was using the material to wipe his brother's face; she almost told him not to because

296

it was evidence, but then changed her mind and left him to it. She could hear movement out in the passage now, and an armed response officer appeared abruptly with his gun at the ready. He was one Jane knew, and she watched him swing his weapon to cover all possible areas of the room. Once he had checked everything he gave her a quick grin and then said, 'Clear, sir,' before he stood back watchfully and let Rogalleh come into the room.

He was alone. 'Blue Betty's up there, sir,' Jane told him quickly, indicating the ceiling with a jerk of her head. 'I could hear him crossing the room but I haven't heard anything— No, listen, that must be him moving now.' It was a bump, a sliding sound, and then silence. 'He was trying to stage Joshua's suicide and we caught him in the act,' Jane went on swiftly once she was sure the sounds had stopped. 'He'd dressed Josh up to look the same. He ran off up there when I told him the place was surrounded. Sam had brought me out here because he was worried when he found his brother was missing.'

Rogalleh gave her a sharply assessing look, and she was suddenly aware that she was quivering with tension, as taut as a bowstring. With an effort, she relaxed her muscles into something nearer normality. She saw Rogalleh accept her words and give a small nod, then he asked, 'You think he's not armed?'

'I can't be sure, but he dropped his knife.' Jane was abruptly aware that she was still clutching it. 'This one. His name's Malcolm Jackson. He's listed on his passport as being a research chemist with a home address in Aston, Birmingham, but he's spent the last six years in a Turkish jail. The same one Joshua was in. He was let out in November at the same time as Joshua, and I think he must have befriended him and that's why Mrs Hughes took him in. I only found all that out tonight,' she added quickly, 'and after I'd set off for here. That's when I called for back-up.'

'Hm. I suppose you're going to tell me what he was in jail for as well?'

'Trying to smuggle out a valuable historical artefact which he'd illegally bought while on holiday. They gave him seven years but let him out early for good behaviour,' Jane told him. Hilaire had managed to be amazingly thorough.

Rogalleh gave her another very thoughtful look before his eyes went round the room, taking in the candles, the noose, the items laid out on the floor. For a long moment they rested on Josh, slumped back into semi-inertia with Sam defensively beside him. Then his hand came up to raise a communicator to his mouth. 'Two to come out, witnesses not crims. Get a few people in here with lights. A few, not many, and be careful not to disturb the layout in the room. Any movement at the upper windows?'

A crackling answer told him there was none. 'Do you know what there is upstairs?' Rogalleh asked Jane, but it was Sam who chimed in with an answer.

'It's just one room. It was a sort of loft for storing things in, I think. Unless they used it as a classroom, but the school can't ever have been very big. It's really just an empty space with barred windows.'

'Good. Can your brother walk?'

'I – I think so . . . Josh?' Sam stooped and managed to heave his twin to his feet, but though he remained there, he was swaying. Sam added worriedly, 'But I don't know how heavily he's been doped.'

Rogalleh gave the boys a comprehensive glance, then snapped, 'We'll play safe. Ambulance,' in the direction of one of the uniforms who had by now appeared in the room. There were three or four of them with large flashlights, coming in as carefully as they had been told. As the first one reached for his communicator Rogalleh added, 'Take them out first, make your call from there, and send somebody else in to take your place. You can put him in one of the cars until the ambulance gets here.'

The Connolly brothers were escorted out. 'We need this room undisturbed as far as possible,' Rogalleh instructed. 'It's evidence. Particularly some of the things he's laid out, I see . . .'

'They *were* in a pattern,' Jane told him, 'only it got disturbed when . . .' It would be time enough to tell him later that Sam had had to save his life by using the crossbow. For now, the most important thing was what they were going to do about the man upstairs.

Rogalleh's mind was on the same track. 'I'm not waiting until he gets tired of it, and he might be doing anything to himself,' he said grimly. 'We'll need some light up there. And I'll take one armed response officer, with the other one outside in case there is some way he can break out. Right, are we ready? This order: ARO, light, me, Jane. And as she and I have both got torches as well, that should do us.'

So he was taking her up there with him. The staircase was narrow, but was built of stone, so there was no need to worry about rotting treads. They went up with careful quiet, however, with somebody below instructed by a sign to listen for movement above the ceiling. There was the door . . . The armed response officer kicked it open with a sharp movement and was inside on a breath, the sergeant with a wide-beamed flashlight held high going in after him in a coordinated movement. Jane could see little but the flash of reflected white light. Then she heard the ARO call out grimly, 'Here, sir!'

Rogalleh stepped into the room and she followed. The ARO was over at the left-hand end of the dusty empty space, standing at a safe distance with his gun braced and aimed steadily in a downward direction. The huddled figure against the wall beyond him was sitting still, skirts spread out, headscarf lost, the garish make-up looking even more unreal as it was sent into black-and-white relief by the harsh glare. But the eyes – no glasses across them, and perhaps he only ever wore them as an anonymous disguise – caught the light, looking up sulkily, so that it was like watching a child who had been caught dressing up.

There were, Jane saw suddenly as she followed Rogalleh, scrawled shapes everywhere within his hand reach – on the walls, on the floorboards both sides of the seated figure ... Diamond shapes repeated over and over, in dusty, chalky blue.

Malcolm Jackson had something between his fingers – something very small – and as she watched he rubbed the rest of it away, fastidiously. He looked up at Rogalleh, seeking his face and finding it with an acknowledging stare. He said in that high voice that Jane had heard him use downstairs, 'My chalk's run out. Ironic, isn't it? But my goodness, Rogalleh, it has taken you a time!'

'But I've got you in the end, haven't I?'

A flash of sulkiness came back into the eyes. Then – with a slow movement which acknowledged the presence of the gun – Blue Betty lifted part of the full skirt and put it across his mouth. He gave a muffled laugh, then said with an air of light malice which came clearly through the distorting cloth, 'How many deaths did it take, Superintendent? Can you count? Such a pity you've spoiled my game!'

Chapter 23

'All right, before you say anything else, tell me what put you on to him.'

They were back at the station, and alone in the incident room. Blue Betty had been processed in – remarkably docile, and without resistance – but Rogalleh was allowing time for him to be settled before he did anything further. There was no shadow of a doubt this time, after all.

The words Rogalleh had just spoken were a command, though the gaze he fixed on Jane held no disapproval. It was more like respectful curiosity, with a touch of wryness in it as if to acknowledge that he had had Joshua pinned too firmly in his sights to consider an alternative. He went on, 'It can't have been the other Connolly boy letting all that out to you on the way, or you'd have left him outside with the girls.'

'I didn't want Sam to go in; I told him to wait but he slipped in while I was talking on the phone,' Jane said in mild protest. 'The call I'd been waiting for from France suddenly came in and— Yes, all right, sir, sorry. I asked my French police contact to check on Malcolm Jackson because . . .' She drew a breath, frowning. 'Because it seemed to me there had to be somebody else. His twin said that Joshua would never touch hard drugs after the amphetamines affair; well, somebody was giving him something. And maybe Josh's psychotherapist had to be the next victim for fear of what he might be finding out. But when I tried to think, who ... What it came down to in the end was something you said, sir, at the beginning. When you told us to trust instinct.'

'Trying flattery? To make up for the fact that what you really want to say is that you knew I was making a mistake, and that's why you looked elsewhere?'

'No, actually, it's a fact,' Jane assured him, risking a grin. His words had been dry but his expression was amiable. 'I started thinking about everybody Josh knew, anybody who might be able to get close to him. And then it suddenly came to me that there was one person I'd never considered, that nobody ever did consider. He was right in the middle of things and I'd met him several times, but – when I thought about it, I'd got no real impression of Malcolm Jackson at all. Every time I'd met him all I'd seen was a black hole, nobody there. A weird kind of total anonymity; you see him, then you forget him. Instantly. And that's not natural ... You usually get *some* kind of feeling off another person.'

'So you thought you'd make some enquiries about him?'

'It did occur to me that that could be a very useful quality for a serial killer. But that it could all be my imagination and I could be entirely wrong. It just seemed worth – on instinct – making one particular enquiry about him. With the knowledge that it might well come up blank. There was only one thing I actually *knew* about Malcolm Jackson: that he'd arrived at Les Beaux Vents at the same time as Josh. But somebody had mentioned in passing that Josh had been befriended in jail by "an old lag". It kind of seemed to fit together that if Malcolm had been in the same prison as Josh, and happened to have been let out at the same time, Rowena might well take him in. She would if he'd helped or protected or been good to her son. And considering we were looking for somebody who'd vanished for a few years ...' Jane looked up at Rogalleh. 'It was an off chance, no more than that. I asked my French contact to check it out, because he'd already checked for me whether Josh really had been in prison. So he'd know who to ask. That was it. He came back to me with all the details, more even than I'd asked him for . . . and then it was obvious.' She stopped, then added with a touch of bleakness, 'I wish I'd thought of it sooner.'

'We all wish that from time to time. It's no use, because it would mean turning the clock back; you just have to live with it. You prevented something tonight and got our man banged up at last, think about that.' His rumble held understanding, and she knew that he was also telling her his own load was heavier. There had been a lot of deliberate malice in 'How many deaths did it take, Superintendent? Can you count?' 'Well now,' he said, rousing himself to briskness, 'your verbal report on tonight, from the beginning. Starting with Sam Connolly trusting you enough to make that call, and going on from there.'

He already knew how it had started – and somewhere, the surveillance team which had been in the car in Willowfield Way would be having a bollocking even now for ignoring Malcolm Jackson's van when it drove out because it only appeared to have him in it. Perhaps it had, at that point, and he had fetched his passenger from the lane at the back. Whatever he had been giving Josh must have been designed to make him easily suggestible and obediently malleable. He probably trusted Malcolm, too, and – guessing – Jane thought Josh probably had in his nature that same streak of loyalty which Sam showed, and would never have mentioned Malcolm when he was being questioned. If he even knew who it was who had been putting thoughts into his head.

Jane pushed that aside and began to run through the night's events as fluently as she could, grateful for the tape recorder standing on the desk between them so that when she came to write it out there would already be a prompt. It was late, and she was twanging with the tiredness which came from release of tension.

Too late for any questioning of Blue Betty to start tonight. That would be for tomorrow.

Even if he retreated into stubborn silence, they had him for two murders and two attempted murders. The laid-out souvenirs were incontrovertible evidence of those.

Jane was in on Rogalleh's first interrogation next morning and found that silence was not what Malcolm Jackson wanted at all. Now that he was finally caught he was eager to talk about everything he had done. It spilled out of him. Whatever Rogalleh asked, he answered. They dealt with the more recent murders first. Yes, he had killed Lionel Hughes. It had come to him that he must because of the way the man behaved; like a bully, shouting at Rowena, upsetting Josh. Malcolm had already met Claus Armfeldt by then, drawn to visit the Turkish quarter in Amiens when he had discovered it existed, almost homesick for the language he had been hearing for the previous six years ... It came through with an odd unreality that he had actually been happy in prison. He passed it off with a shrug; 'it was peaceful and you didn't have to make choices'.

Lionel's killing was going to be a one-off, so he wanted to plan it all with a satisfying elaborateness. And since Claus had told him about the illegal immigrant run – even offered to see if he could get him recruited for a subsequent trip – he decided to use it.

He was supposed to be off laying a floor, a convenient excuse when the house concerned was empty. Instead he had stopped Lionel on the road to offer the lure of a good news story; though if Lionel had refused to play he would have killed him then, too simple for fun but it would have been done anyway. But Lionel took the bait. They went on in convoy to Calais, then he joined Lionel in his car to give him fuller details, and went across as his passenger to wait for the lorry's arrival the other side. There, while they waited, Lionel had munched some sandwiches, then Malcolm had offered him whisky from a hip flask. He had added water to it at the last minute, on the grounds that they had better not take it neat and risk not being thoroughly alert. Not just water, of course. He knew plenty about poisons and it wasn't that difficult to obtain the one he wanted. Lionel had lapsed into unconsciousness and died while they waited. All nicely according to plan . . .

It had been simple, then, to use Lionel's mobile phone to tip off Immigration; then, since he knew Claus was also equipped with a phone, to tip him off as well that there was a trap set up on the M20 so he must take a different route. And yes, he had told Claus, he was here; he had decided to see just how the immigrant run was done before he took up the offer of joining in another time. He gave Claus another urgent warning to turn off on to the Minnis and stop so they could talk. When Claus climbed out of the cab he had knocked him out. Dumped Lionel's body and placed Claus, unconscious, in the car. Called Immigration again. Opened up the hatch on the container lorry. Taken Claus away in Lionel's car . . .

He had planned, in fact, to bury him in the woods after giving his unconscious body its lethal injection of heroin, and it was only there that the careful scheme had gone slightly awry. The lights of a slowing car suggested that the immigration people might unexpectedly be arriving that way. So that perhaps he should get out fast . . . However, it had been fun, an added spice of risk, to drive out rapidly with the Dutchman dead in the car, and then dump the body in Dover Harbour before he took Lionel's car back to France on a ferry. A slight pity that he had had to change the method of Claus's disposal, because if he had been able to bury him the police would have gone on running round like headless chickens trying to find him. Still, it had been amusing when they turned up at Rowena's to know that they hadn't the first idea what had really happened . . .

Jane, listening with a sudden crawling feeling up her spine as the voice ran happily on, knew with disbelief how close she had been to a killer that night, as a forgotten memory came sharply back to her. A car suddenly driving across her path out of the woods . . . As long ago as that, he had been right *there*?

'How did you know the area so well, to do all that?' Rogalleh's voice asked against her chilled unreality, friendly, curious, softly factual.

'Oh, from Josh. They'd put him in a cell with me. Because we were both English. I used to get him to talk about places he'd been happy, describe them, tell me every detail – it helped him, took his mind off things. When he'd been— It helped him.' There was something in the voice – almost a protectiveness? – but then the feeling that something surprising had been there disappeared abruptly as Malcolm's face closed down and he looked at Rogalleh with an inimical expression in his eyes. Which changed almost at once to a careless slyness as he added, 'I was always good at using whatever I could find out, wasn't I, Rogalleh? We both know that. *And* how good my memory is. Now, I've told you all about that one; shall we move on?'

'In a moment. It sounds as if you were fond of Joshua – then. It hasn't looked like it since, though, has it?'

'He shouldn't have—' The words jerked out sharply; a sudden real emotion which turned into a sneer. 'Such a loving family, aren't they? And that silly little French girl as well, as if he'd look twice at *her* when he's got four times her brains—' He stopped again and that careless smoothness

306

came back into his voice. 'Besides, I get bored with people, don't I? Would you like to know why I'd got plenty of money to play with? It was all still sitting in the bank waiting for me. Useful capital. The insurance on my parents' house, which so conveniently got burned down when I was twenty-one. Such a tragedy that the smoke alarms didn't wake them, as everybody told their poor bereaved only child so sympathetically at the funeral!'

Rogalleh chose to ignore the obvious implication, merely saying calmly, 'We'll stop there, time to change the tape.' There was a tone behind the words which said that the madman sitting in front of him was going to do things *his* way, in the order he chose, not any other. And he certainly was mad, Jane thought . . . How could there ever be any doubt of it? She had to listen to him – but it was with a feeling of revulsion.

She thought Rogalleh must be aware of it when he took Kate in with him instead of Jane for the next session. Maybe he knew how hard it was for anyone to have to hear Blue Betty's triumphant spoutings for too long. A lot of senior people started turning up wanting to sit in on the questioning, too, as if the psychology of a serial killer was too interesting to miss, and that released Jane further. Rogalleh, though acceding to the requests, clearly wanted to reduce Blue Betty's audience where he could. An audience was what he liked.

'Mad as a hatter, isn't he?' Kate said, as down-to-earth as ever. 'He's been on about a voice telling him what to do – not that the guv'nor's going to accept that one!'

'It wouldn't surprise me if he was psychotic, though, would it you?' Jane asked.

'As long as they can put him away forever, it doesn't matter what he is. With so many stories up his sleeve—' Kate broke off, shaking her head. 'The guv'nor's been trying to make him stick to a strict sequence, but even he doesn't always succeed. They just want to cover the last ones down here, I gather, and then they're going to move him up to Birmingham to deal with the earlier stuff.'

'And well rid . . .'

'Quite. He went after DI Hollings as his next victim, it seems, because it was who went round to interview Rowena when she arrived back in England. And "the voice" suggested it would be an amusing reminder for Rogalleh, since he'd seen him by the time the idea came to him. Yes, *amusing* is the word he used. Christ,' Kate's voice held a grim note, 'isn't it easy to see just how much in the middle of the picture he was, once you know? And he was either supremely overconfident that he wouldn't be noticed, or he really had lost his edge during the six years he was banged up!' She added, 'It's incredible how much he fits all those profiles, too. Even the class thing. His father was a jobbing builder, apparently – with a great scorn for namby-pamby intellectual sons who go to university.'

'It figures.'

'Yes. And the loner thing, and being in work, and with a car . . . He worked in a commercial research lab, fairly isolated sort of job at his level, though it seems he'd never risen to the kind of heights he was expected to from the promise he showed at university. Rogalleh's got that bit of background from seven years ago now he knows who he's looking at – and it appears Jackson went off for his annual holiday one day and just didn't come back, to the annoyance of his bosses. Apparently they never reported him missing, though. They seemed to think it wasn't worth it, considering he hadn't taken any valuable papers away with him. Not exactly your caring work environment!'

'But he didn't have any friends they could ask.' Jane didn't bother to phrase the words as a question.

'That's what they say. So after a month they wrote him off and took on somebody else instead. Funny to think the psychologists managed to get such an accurate picture of him, and it still didn't help. Since the police never got close enough to pick him out.' Kate looked thoughtful, then shook her head. 'That's where it falls down a hole, isn't it? I must say ... I wouldn't like to be living inside Rowena Hughes' head, knowing now what I'd been giving house room to. And all because he'd been kind to Joshua in jail!'

'I think he probably was, oddly enough. Maybe he sort of identified with him. A clever but helpless little brother, needing protection. Living close together like that ... It could even have been the first time he'd ever thought of another person as a friend.' Jane was remembering the unexpected note she had heard in Malcolm's voice – and the resentful enmity which had flashed out afterwards. 'The trouble was, once they were out Josh belonged to everybody else, didn't he? And if you've been befriended by a psychopath, and become the object of the only real emotion he's ever felt—'

'Psychopath is right, real emotion I'd doubt. You know something? I'm not even sure I want to talk about the evil bastard any more. He gives me goose-bumps. So if you don't mind, I'll go off in search of some very strong coffee!'

She departed. She would undoubtedly find that everybody was talking about Blue Betty, out to glean anything they could about him; it was one of the reasons Jane was keeping out of the canteen. People kept dropping in to see her as it was – with congratulations for the successful outcome, with curiosity, even with one sidelong and slightly awkward reference to 'Rogalleh's girls' having done it after all, offered as a wary joke in case she took it the wrong way.

Chris had been in too – very briefly. He had said without elaboration, 'Thanks. I gather it was you who landed him. I

309

owe you.' Then he had turned on his heel without giving her a chance to answer, and took himself away.

The incident room had to be wound up but everything properly logged on completion first. That provided an occupation. Jane saw Rogalleh occasionally, when he looked in between sessions, but he seemed to be satisfied that he could leave her to do what was required. He was looking more like an ageing elephant than ever, she decided, and almost gave him a grin for his air of being creased and crumpled all over but plodding steadily on to get everything down here wound up.

After three days, it was – though she didn't realise he had actually summoned her to say goodbye until she was up in his room.

'You can have your office back,' he greeted her, adding with what was definitely a pretence of irascibility in the dark eyes, 'and don't wrinkle your nose and tell me you can still smell smoke in the curtains; you'll just have to indent for them to be cleaned, won't you? I'm off back to the West Midlands tonight. And chummy's being sent up under guard in a secure van later tonight too.'

'Good luck with him, sir.'

'I hope so. They'll get the psychiatrists out in force for his defence, I don't doubt. But with any luck I'll get some into court on our side, too, to swear he knew precisely what he was doing.' His voice was inflexible. Then he shook his big shoulders and rumbled softly, 'No need to brood on that yet, we won't get a court date to bring him to trial for months. And in the meantime ... Well, he's giving me more every time he opens his mouth, and there's plenty there to show he's rational. By the way, young Joshua. He's in hospital but doing all right, I've heard. They've just got to clear a lot of stuff out of his system. You were right: Malcolm was feeding him careful doses of all sorts of things.'

'I'm glad I wasn't right when I thought he was Blue Betty.'

'You mean you're glad *I* wasn't right. You can say it; I'm not so small I won't admit a mistake – even if it was a justifiable supposition at the time.'

Jane had to bite back a grin, along with the temptation to give him a solemn assurance that he wasn't small at all. He gave her a very thoughtful look. Then he said abruptly, 'All right, what about you? What are you going to do about getting back into CID? You know, and I know, that's where you ought to be. That's one of the things I called you up here to say, before I bid farewell to the whole team and give you all due praise for a job well done. You've been worth the choice, all of you.'

'Thank you, sir, and we've all found it an experience working for you, too.'

'Nicely put,' he growled, with the glimmer of a smile. 'But it doesn't answer my question. You'll need to move, I can see that – but with this as a recent plus on your record you should get a DI job somewhere, no question. And you can have my recommendation wherever you ask for it. So? Are you going to tell me there's something down here to keep you fiddling-arsing about in a job a dozen other people could do? Or are you going to start going through the *Police Review* to see if there's any area with a bit more space to manoeuvre which wants an ambitious young DI, and get back to using your talents the way you really want to?'

He had a point. Jane could run an instantaneous review in her head. Her private life had drifted away so far as to be almost out of sight; was there really anything left of it? Her best friend had taken off on a mad jaunt which might be permanent. Her live-in lover was ... Well, it was certainly true that there was little left between him and Jane except politeness and a feeling that time and patience had more or less run out. Unless she was prepared to change, and turn herself into the sort of person he thought she should be.

She had to acknowledge that yes, she did want to get back into CID, permanently. A lousy job sometimes, but the one she wanted, and where she felt alive.

She would give Rogalleh no immediate answer to his challenge, and it seemed he didn't expect one, since he began to shift himself out of his chair with the words, 'Well, time to go and make the rest of those goodbyes. I doubt if Superintendent Annerley's all that sorry to see me go, but then I wouldn't be altogether keen on somebody doing things their own way on my patch either. Still – we got him, didn't we? I've got a file to close at last . . .'

Jane, following him decorously out, wondered if he would retire once he had finally taken this one to court. Maybe. Though she couldn't imagine him contentedly digging a garden instead of padding around exercising his considerable intelligence on the criminal fraternity. Besides, where would he smoke, without an office to hide in where he couldn't be contradicted? She grinned behind his back, suddenly visualising a Mrs Rogalleh half his size but with a firm ability to keep her husband in line. It was amusing to consider that she might be just as formidable as he was.

Jane contemplated his suggestion that she should get hold of the *Police Review* and start looking for another job. There might be a DI post going somewhere in the Met, and the fact that she had worked there before would give her a good chance. Big cities were where the work was. But . . . this area of Kent was where she had begun to feel she belonged. It had grown on her: the cathedral city, the countryside all around, the nearness to the rest of Europe . . . The people, too.

312

All right, she would think about it.

She found she was smiling as she followed Rogalleh down the stairs, and knew that – actually – she had already thought. She wasn't going to give up that easily. Not on any part of her life. There might be difficulties here, but . . .

No, this was where she wanted to be. And where she would stay.